MY
HUSBAND
NEXT
DOOR

BOOKS BY K.L. SLATER

Safe With Me

Blink

Liar

The Mistake

The Visitor

The Secret

Closer

Finding Grace

The Silent Ones

Single

Little Whispers

The Girl She Wanted

The Marriage

The Evidence

The Widow

Missing

The Girlfriend

The Narrator

The Bedroom Window

Husband and Wife

The Married Man

Message Deleted

MY HUSBAND NEXT DOOR

K.L. SLATER

bookouture

Published by Bookouture in 2025

An imprint of Storyfire Ltd.
Carmelite House
50 Victoria Embankment
London EC4Y 0DZ

www.bookouture.com

The authorised representative in the EEA is Hachette Ireland
8 Castlecourt Centre
Dublin 15 D15 XTP3
Ireland
(email: info@hbgi.ie)

ISBN: 978-1-83525-275-8
eBook ISBN: 978-1-83525-274-1

PROLOGUE

He always parks in the same place. Two houses down from her house, tucked behind the contractor's van that's been sitting there since Monday. It's too big for the drive, so the owners leave it on the street, and he thanks them silently each morning for their consistency.

Consistency is a good thing, as is preparation. It's not just key. It's everything.

You can't just decide to take someone. Not someone like Ellie, anyway. People like her, she has people who will miss her. Friends and family who won't wait a minute longer than they have to when it comes to calling the coppers.

He glances at the dashboard clock. 09:59.

At exactly ten o'clock, she appears. Like clockwork. It's one of the things he admires about her. The self-discipline. The commitment. Qualities he likes to think he shares himself.

Out she comes, wheeling her bike down the short garden path. She is fresh-faced, not a trace of make-up, her skin still clinging to the softness of girlhood. Short hair, the colour of honeyed chestnuts, tucked behind one ear. She is petite like a little bird, but with a quiet, assured grace in the ways she moves –

like someone who doesn't need to make herself stand out to be noticed.

One anomaly he spots is she has no helmet. That's a big risk to take. She should really wear one. Her rucksack is light blue, with a dangling keyring in the shape of a strawberry. Something childish about that. Maybe she's kept it for sentimental reasons from when she was younger. He likes that. It shows she is still grounded. Not like some of the other young women on her course. Many of them are already too hardened, too worldly. A bit too brazen for their own good.

Not Ellie. She still lives with her parents. Still pecks her mum on the cheek before she leaves, even if she doesn't know he can sometimes see it through the front window. She still says goodbye to the family dog and she still cycles to college, even when it rains.

He watches her mount the bike and pedal off. She's steady. Confident. She turns right at the end of the street, same as always. He waits three seconds, then starts the engine and rolls out slowly, keeping at least three cars between them.

She doesn't know how closely he's been watching. How deeply he knows her. Her timetable, her route, the way she sometimes nibbles the end of her pen when she's trying to concentrate. He's seen that. It thrills him to study her from the safety of his car, parked under the sycamores outside the college. A perfect spot, unnoticed, like an old, abandoned coat draped across a fence. He's got her routine pinned down so well, he could draw her day blindfolded.

She reaches the college gates and chains the bike to the rack on the left, third one down. She's completely oblivious to all that's around her, doesn't even check. Of course not. Why would she?

He parks where he always does, in the next street over, and walks the long way round, a takeaway coffee in hand so he looks like he's waiting to pick someone up. From here, he can see the back entrance. She won't use it, but it's still good to have eyes on all exits. There's a pleasure in that – the coverage. The breadth of his knowledge.

At 15:07, she emerges. Slight delay today – maybe a question from her tutor. She has that kind of face – people stop her, ask things, expect her to be helpful. And she is helpful. He watched her guide an elderly woman to a clinic once. Another time, she stood with a crying new girl who'd missed her bus. Ellie had called the girl's dad, waited with her until he came.

Ellie is kind. She's... pure. Yes, that's the word. You don't get many of those anymore.

He starts the engine and follows as she pedals off again. He doesn't tailgate – he's not an idiot – but keeps her always just in view. The roads are quiet at this time. Most people still at work or waiting for school pickups. She cycles past the Co-op, past the cricket ground, through the housing estate with the identical red-brick homes and the new saplings staked around borders like skinny soldiers.

And then, there it is ahead of them – the stretch of woodland.

He's already chosen the spot. Walked it. Measured visibility from the road, considered possible foot traffic. He saw a dog walker there last week and monitored him for a few days, just to assess the risk. An older man with a set routine. He won't be back until after five. And currently it's 15:22.

He accelerates gently to close the gap and lowers the driver's window. This is the moment he's practised a thousand times. In his head, in his notes, in the quiet rehearsals at night when the house is still and the neighbours' windows are all dark.

Ellie's short, neat hair shines as she cycles. Her posture is relaxed. He presses the accelerator just a fraction more, gliding up beside her.

She hears the car and he sees her glance as he steers closer still. A flicker of fear before her eyes widen.

That's all it takes.

She veers, a sharp swerve off the tarmac, her wheels catching the edge of the verge. The bike judders. There's a sound like a choked sob, and then she's down, falling sideways into the long grass with a sharp cry.

He pulls over, fast. One movement to hit the hazard lights – just in case, just in case anyone sees and thinks he's doing the right thing. Good Samaritan.

But no one sees.

No cars and no dog walkers. Not today.

He leaves the engine running and pops open the rear door as he jumps out. The bike is half-tangled in the ditch and so he drags it down the rest of the way, stamps once on the wheel to buckle it.

Ellie is scrambling to her knees. Confused. Dirt on her cheek. Her bag's come loose, contents spilled.

He moves fast.

One step, two – she turns, mouth open, and he presses the prepared cloth to her face.

She writhes and that surprises him. She's stronger than he expected. Her elbow catches his ribs and he absorbs the sharp pain while he holds the cloth firm. Counts backwards in his head so he can be sure.

Thirty seconds. Twenty-five… fifteen… ten, nine, eight…

Then her limbs slow. Twitch once. Go slack.

He scoops her up and she's featherlight. Like lifting laundry. Her head lolls against his shoulder. Her breath is a soft puff against his collarbone. He doesn't look at her face but he feels himself stir.

He places her gently on the reclined passenger seat, arranges her limbs so she won't knock against the door when he drives. He closes the door carefully, checks the locks. Next, he opens the back doors and throws in the bike. Finally, he goes back for her bag, gathers the spilled items before climbing back in.

He glances at his watch. Thirty-eight seconds and still no

cars. No witnesses. He lets the engine idle for a moment. Feels the steering wheel hum beneath his fingers.

This feels powerful, but he's not drunk on glory. Nor relief. Just use of skill and clever control. Like a magician.

He drives away, slow and steady, back onto the main road.

Not a single soul in sight.

ONE

SYLVIE

THURSDAY

There are just ten more minutes until the book club members arrive. Enough time to cast one last look around my small conservatory, making sure everything is just right for this, my turn to host.

The room glows with warmth. The heating is on, sucking the late October chill out of the air, while the golden flicker of candle-light adds a touch of theatre to the scene. Fairy lights, draped along the top of the bookshelves, cast shadows over the spines of well-loved novels, some of which I've read over and over again.

Plump cushions in autumnal shades – burnt orange, deep plum, moss green – are arranged with comfort in mind on the two armchairs and the long bench seat by the window. I've draped a couple of knitted throws over the back of the sofa, oozing – I hope – the promise of cosiness.

My sense of tranquillity is fractured by the murmur of the television in the next room.

... police have urged the public to remain vigilant...

I freeze for a second, my hands hovering over a cushion.

... local woman still missing...

My stomach tightens. I should turn it off. Block it out. But the chilling words are already seeping into the warmth of the room. Some part of me knows this won't just go away. It's too close to home.

I move to tweak the refreshments I set out earlier. Adjusting the angle of the platter of biscuits, rotating the cheese straws. I position the bowls of crisps, salted nuts just so, waiting for the restless feeling that's pressing at the edges of my mind to ease off.

I've made a pot of coffee and there's gallons of tea at the ready. And, because this is book club and not a parish council meeting, there is also plenty of wine, the red already open and gently breathing in the corner. A small indulgence and a pleasant distraction from the troubles of the outside world.

This month's book choice, *The House of Shadows*, is propped up beside the glasses. The gothic thriller will be tonight's discussion point apart from anyone who might've 'forgotten' to read it... of which there's usually at least one.

The front door opens, and a familiar voice calls down the hallway. 'Hello? Mr Rent-a-Muscle here, at your service.'

I turn as my husband, Matt, appears in the doorway, grinning. Fresh-faced, fit and always willing. I still feel like I've won some cosmic jackpot.

Matt has come over to bump the furniture into a rough circle, making the most of the space. He's a gem. And maybe – just maybe – the age gap is part of the reason our unique living arrangements work so well.

There are ten years between us and the real talking point – the thing that got us written up in the *Daily Mail* two months ago – is that we're married, but we don't live together. I live at number forty-five and Matt's at number forty-one, just two doors down. Identical houses on the outside, but entirely different worlds within.

Some people think it's plain odd. For others, it's pure genius. I just know that it works. He turns and walks away just as I'm about to speak.

I walk to the hall to see Matt standing in the doorway of my small lounge, his gaze fixed on the television. The screen flickers, casting a pale glow over his face.

'Matt?'

He glances back and sees me watching him. He strides over to the TV and, a second later, the local news channel is silenced. Back in the hall, his expression is grim.

'Don't tell me there's another one missing?' I ask, my stomach tightening.

'No, no.' His reply is quick. 'But you don't want that bringing your evening down, so I turned it off.'

His voice sounds light and casual, but his shoulders are rigid. He's trying to protect me without making a thing of it, but I know he's just as worried as everyone else is around here. He has a news alert on his phone, and we often talk about what might have happened to the young woman who went missing just a stone's throw from here. A young woman who went to Jess's school. I know the subject is bound to come up at book club.

Matt leans down and kisses my cheek. His hair is still damp from the shower, a faint trace of aftershave trailing him in the air. He's wearing a navy jumper over a white t-shirt, sleeves pushed up as if he's just come from doing something rugged and capable – chopping logs, or maybe wrestling a stag to the ground.

'You do know you're not actually employed to do my manual labour?' I say, folding my arms and trying to lighten the mood again. 'This is just a favour to your wife.'

'That's what you think. Just wait until you get my invoice.'

He steps inside, surveying the conservatory. 'Looks nice and cosy in here. Very *you*.'

'Ha! Meaning what?'

'Dunno... very stylish, but a bit bossy maybe.'

'Bossy, me?'

'See that?' He gestures to the book I've propped up on the table. 'That's an instant threat to anyone who might not have read it.'

I dig him in the ribs. 'Unlike you, I take book club seriously.'

'I take books seriously, too. Just not in an organised, enforced way.' He grabs a biscuit from the perfect platter and winks. 'See, that's why we work. You're order. I'm chaos.'

'The moon to my sun.' I beam.

'More like head girl and loveable rogue.'

I roll my eyes, but I can't help smiling. It still amazes me, sometimes, how we got here. I bought this house nine years ago after Carl, my first husband – and father of my daughter, Jess – died suddenly from a heart attack while he was out running. We downsized and came here for a new start at the very time neither of us wanted one.

Then, three years ago, our sleepy little street buzzed with news that number forty-one had been left to the grandson of the late Mr Smallbone. A young man who'd apparently upset the Smallbone family applecart when solicitors had read out the will.

I remember picturing a fresh-faced graduate, pale and sleep deprived, clutching a cardboard box of possessions and a half-dead houseplant. Someone I'd probably feel duty-bound to feed.

What I didn't expect was Matthew Tyce. Early thirties, six-foot-two, broad-shouldered with a charismatic smile and the kind of dirty laugh that, quite frankly, should have come with a health warning.

And now, two years on from that, here we are. Living separately. Together.

He nudges the last chair into place just as the first knock sounds at the door.

'Here we go. Showtime,' I say, smoothing my jumper.

Matt stretches his arms behind his head, flexing a bicep. 'I could stay, you know. Add a bit of youthful energy to the proceedings.'

'Youthful energy? Cheeky devil. It's a nice thought, but you'd derail the entire evening.'

'Would I, though? I'm great at discussion.'

I stare at him. 'You haven't read the book.'

He grins. 'Not a word. Bet I'm not the only one.'

'Come on, let's have you out.' I steer him towards the hallway, but he turns just before the door, his expression softening.

'Shall I come back later?' he asks.

It's a question with an answer all in one.

I smile. 'Definitely.'

He lifts my hand to his lips and presses a quick, warm kiss to my knuckles. Then, with one of his trademark winks, he disappears out the back.

I take a breath and open the front door.

'Welcome to book club,' I say, ushering in the first two members.

And in the back of my mind, I'm already thinking about the night ahead – and the man two doors down who manages to make each of our homes – mine and his – feel utterly complete.

TWO

Penny from over the road arrives wrapped in a quilted coat, a bottle of wine in one hand and a plastic box in the other.

'Evening, Sylvie,' she calls, stepping inside and handing me the container. 'I made some flapjacks.'

No sooner has Penny settled onto the bench seat than our most senior member, Vera, appears in the doorway, gripping a tartan shopping bag like her life depends on it.

'It's cold out.' She shivers, loosening her scarf. 'I hope there's something stronger than tea in that pot.'

'There is, Vera. Don't worry, we'll soon get you warmed up.'

She sniffs and shrugs off her coat, lowering herself onto an armchair and surveying the room with the air of an octogenarian monarch taking her throne. Penny gives me a quick grin and I smile back, but I feel a bit fluttery inside. I look confident, but I always worry the conversation might dry up when it's my turn to host book club.

'Jess not here yet?' Vera asks, accepting the glass of red wine I offer.

'No, but she is coming,' I say. 'I think getting out of a flat takes a bit longer when you're the size of a small planet.'

I'd ordered my daughter, Jess, an Uber myself, insisting she's ferried door to door. The missing girl is never far from my mind. Right on cue, the front door swings open again.

'Mum, your house smells amazing!' Jess calls, her voice light and slightly breathless. A second later, she appears, cheeks flushed, hands cradling her belly. 'I need to take one of those scented candles home with me.'

I give her a one-armed hug, careful not to squish her. 'How's baby?'

'Currently treating my bladder like a trampoline.'

'Ah, the joys.' Penny chuckles. 'I remember it well.'

'I thought you were dragging Kendra here tonight?'

'I did, too,' Jess says, 'but she got a late offer to go clubbing, so we've been dumped again.'

I roll my eyes. Jess and Kendra have been friends since primary school, thick as thieves for as long as I can remember. Her parents split up at an early age and Kendra was always round ours for tea, seemed to like the stability we had back then before Jess's dad died.

They still see a lot of each other, although these days their lives couldn't be more different. While Jess has settled down with Ed and, soon, the baby, Kendra seems to float from one thing to the next – new jobs, new house-shares, new boyfriends, never staying in one place for very long. In fact, she's been known to just take off and live the commune life for a few weeks when the mood takes her. She's fun, in her own way, but hopelessly unreliable. And she's let Jess down more times than you can shake a stick at.

Not that Jess will hear a word against her. 'That's just Kendra,' she always defends her friend with a shrug, as if that excuses everything. And for Jess, I think it most probably does.

By the time seven o'clock rolls around, the conservatory is alive with the hum of conversation, the clinking of glasses, and the occasional burst of laughter. Eight women, including me, arranged in a loose circle, wrapped in the glow of wine, blankets and good company.

Half a glass of wine down, I start to relax. Everyone seems to be enjoying themselves. I think it's going to be OK.

'Right. Time to confess your sins.' I tap a spoon on the side of my wine glass to get their attention. 'Who hasn't read the book?'

Penny raises a hand, grimacing. 'I only managed to get halfway through, sorry. It's been non-stop with the house and all.'

'What house?'

Penny blinks. '*Our* house. We're renting it out and moving to Portugal. We're finally doing it.'

Penny and her husband have talked about emigrating for a long time now, but nothing's ever happened with it. A ripple of surprise moves through the group.

'Seriously?' I say. 'When?'

'Within the next few weeks, if all goes to plan. We'll rent the house out for a year and then, if we love it there, we'll sell it. We've been cleaning and painting and throwing stuff out. You know how it goes, I don't know how we've managed to clutter up the place so badly in the space of fifteen years. But we're finally there and the house goes up for rent this week.'

'Penny, that's amazing,' Jess says. 'I had no idea you were thinking of leaving so soon.'

'We always said we'd do it one day.' Penny shrugs. 'Brian's been retired nearly a year now and we've kind of run out of excuses. My hours have been reduced again at the library and it feels a bit like now or never.'

I squeeze her arm. 'Good for you. But you do realise you're going to have to host a farewell book club before you leave?'

'Absolutely.' She grins. 'I'm sure there'll be plenty of time for that. We have to find a reliable tenant first.'

We talk about *The House of Shadows* for a while. I listen

keenly, nodding as people discuss themes and character motivations – but then the conversation takes a turn.

'That part where she's abducted...' Lisa, who lives a few doors down, shakes her head. 'I struggled with it to be honest. I couldn't stop thinking about what's happening here. In real life.'

A hush settles over the group.

'The missing girl,' someone murmurs.

'Ellie Walker's parents are devastated,' Lisa continues. 'One of my regulars at the library knows them. Says they're barely functioning. They're both off work, just trying to get through each day really. Their church is holding prayer nights.'

A wave of sadness washes over me. Ellie, a student nurse and just twenty-two – that's only two years older than Jess – disappeared without a trace three weeks ago.

'It's terrifying,' Penny says. 'Brian's insisting I don't go anywhere alone after dark. Not that I needed telling.'

'It's like something out of a nightmare remembering she went to my school,' Jess murmurs, hand resting protectively over her bump. 'Only it's worse because it's real.'

The room feels colder, despite the heating. Vera picks up the bottle of red wine and pours more into her glass. Her hand is unsteady and some of it sloshes onto the white cloth covering the coffee table, leaving a vivid red stain.

In the middle of the shift in mood, I hear the front door open again.

'Sorry, forgot my phone,' Matt announces, appearing in the doorway.

A ripple of amusement moves through the women, the melancholy forgotten.

'Ah, here's the man of the moment,' Penny teases.

'What can I say? The pull of coming to book club was just too strong.' He grins, ruffling a hand through his hair. 'That, and I need my phone to prove to the lads I *did* read the group chat.'

Lisa smirks. 'Admit it, you just wanted to bask in the glory of your recent celebrity status. Put an appearance in for your fans.'

'Ah yes,' Matt says dramatically, 'fame at last. Next stop: reality TV.'

Jess rolls her eyes at the others. 'Mum and Matt get one feature in the paper and suddenly they think they're Nottingham's answer to Posh and Becks.'

Laughter lifts the group mood and I marvel at how we can all swing from worrying about a missing woman to joking about our new celebrity status. I suppose it's how we all cope and carry on.

'Alright, alright,' I say, shaking my head. 'Now, go and find your phone, Matt, before Vera starts asking whether we're planning to have any children.'

Matt snorts. 'Bit late for that.'

Vera swats at him as he ducks out of the room, still grinning.

'Matt's such a lovely guy,' Penny says as the door clicks shut. 'You're a lucky woman, Sylvie.'

'I know,' I say, feeling warmth rise in my chest. I glance over at Jess, young and blooming with my first grandchild in her belly. Lucky doesn't even cut it.

A sharp gasp cuts through the moment.

Lisa's hand flies to her mouth, her phone trembling slightly in her grip.

A silence stretches as Lisa's widening eyes dart across the screen, her face draining of colour.

'Lisa?' I prompt, my voice uncertain. 'What is it?'

Lisa exhales shakily. 'Ellie's parents have spoken to the press, pleading for any information. There's a picture and they look wretched.'

The words drop like a dead weight amid our light banter.

'It's so sad,' Penny murmurs.

The room holds its breath. No one speaks.

Around us, the candles flicker. The heating hums, low and

steady. But the warmth in the room has vanished. A cold, creeping dread inches up my spine.

I look over at the refreshments. The biscuit platter I'd spent ages arranging so artfully is messed up and the dish of olives has been knocked over.

'Has anyone got any further comments about the book?' I say quietly, but nobody answers.

'Maybe we should call it a night,' Vera says, clearing her throat. 'I think we're all a bit distracted now.'

No one argues.

One by one, the women gather their coats, their voices hushed, their movements quick. I order Jess an Uber home and hug her tightly before she leaves, whispering for her to text me when she's home. Penny squeezes my hand.

And then, suddenly, the house is deathly quiet.

I sit for a moment in the empty conservatory, staring at the abandoned glasses, the plates with half-eaten biscuits. Penny's untouched flapjacks.

Outside, beyond the glow of fairy lights, darkness presses against the window. I think about Ellie's poor parents. Still waiting and praying for her safe return.

I text Matt.

Can you come round now?

I don't want to be alone.

THREE

Matt brings me tea in bed. His bed hair is a bit flattened on one side, a mess of dark curls on the other. Somehow, he still manages to look hot. He's wearing boxer shorts and the muscles in his thighs shift as he sits down beside me. A deep crease marks his cheek where he's lain against the pillow.

Last night he offered to tidy up the conservatory. 'You're all tense, I can see it in your face. Get yourself to bed and I'll be up soon.' I didn't argue; I felt strung tight as a wire. I still do.

I take the tea gratefully, cradling the mug in both hands.

Last night's book club had been a bit of a mess. We hadn't discussed the book for very long before Lisa brought up the missing girl, and then the news notification had unnerved everyone.

Matt reads out loud from his news app about the appeal from Ellie's parents.

'I'd imagine the police have spent too much time looking in the wrong places. They say the first seventy-two hours are critical in the hunt for a missing person and after that... well, you know the rest.'

I try to push thoughts about it all down this morning, but the stuff Lisa told us about Ellie Walker's parents refuses to stop needling at me. I keep picturing her poor family, their house in limbo with the silence of waiting. Of not knowing.

Matt watches me over the rim of his mug. 'It's no good getting yourself all worked up about it,' he says gently. 'It'll just pull you down.'

I look down at my tea. A few tea leaves float on the surface and I wonder if the bag split.

'Worrying won't affect the outcome,' he goes on. 'And you know Jess is safe.'

I give a little shudder. 'I don't, though. No one's safe until he's been caught. The police don't warn people to be vigilant for no reason, Matt. And I keep thinking about Ellie's parents... what must it be like, not knowing if your child is alive or dead? All that stuff Lisa was saying about how they're suffering.'

Jess texted me when she got home last night after book club, just as she promised. But even so.

Matt exhales, rubbing a hand over his face. He walks over to the window, his broad back facing me. I sense he doesn't want to talk about it, and he doesn't want me to talk about it. People deal with stuff differently.

I shift in bed, pulling the duvet up over my legs. To be fair, it's not just Matt. Jess also tells me I need to stop obsessing about it all, that I'm going to make myself ill.

'Mum, I'm fine,' she says. 'I'm not going to take any silly risks, but equally, I'm not about to let some crazy dude decide what I can and can't do in my life. Or where I go.'

I get on her nerves, and I know I hover too much. But I think – I hope – she understands it comes from a good place. A place of love. Even Matt has shown concern, offering to pick her up and take her home on a few occasions.

'It's about time that boyfriend of hers gets himself a proper job. When the baby comes, they're going to need a car.'

Matt can get impatient with Ed and his lack of motivation as, I confess, I sometimes do.

I picture the two of them in their tiny rented flat in Sneinton, just over a five-minute drive or a half-hour walk, from where we live at Lady Bay. With its partial view of the historic Green's Windmill, Jess instantly fell in love with it. The flat is stuffed to the brim with second-hand furniture and mismatched crockery, and they're always broke but never seem to mind. 'Neither of us want to be slaves to a career we hate, Mum. We're not bothered about material things.'

That's all well and good when it's just the two of them. But now there's a new baby on the way.

Matt angles the blind slats open with a finger and light slices into the room, cutting across the bed in sharp strips.

'There's a to-let sign going up across the road,' he says. 'They're keen, I'll give them that.'

I take my tea and get out of bed. Through the slats I watch as a guy in grey overalls hammers the sign into Penny and Brian's small front lawn. The sign looks fresh and bright, not yet dulled by rain or dust.

'It's up for six-nine-five a month,' Matt says, showing me his phone screen. 'Listing's already up on Rightmove. Priced for quick rental, I'd say.'

I stare at the house. Penny and Brian's place has always looked pristine. Clean white paint. Winter pansies in the window boxes. A car that never seems to move.

Usually, I see Brian from my kitchen window cleaning his car every Sunday morning, come rain or shine. In the spring and summer months, Penny always wears a pretty floral headband and matching gardening gloves when she does the weeding.

I try to picture someone else living there. Someone new on our quiet little street.

'Wonder who'll be moving in,' I murmur.

Matt doesn't answer. I take a sip of my tea, but it's already turned cool.

More change is coming. I can feel it.

FOUR

Matt's fork scrapes across his plate, metal on ceramic, an unpleasant sound that sets my teeth on edge. He's saying something about a difficult client who wants his large garden landscaping but won't give Matt any creative licence in the planning.

My phone screen blurs in front of me. I read the text message again.

We're at the City hospital. Jess started in labour at 6 a.m. but don't worry, she's fine! Text when we know more. Ed

6 a.m.? It's past ten o'clock now!

Four hours. Four hours my daughter has been at the hospital and needed me by her side. I push back from the table so abruptly that my chair legs screech against the wooden floor. Matt stops his client rant mid-sentence and looks at me.

'I need to get to the hospital,' I say, already standing and scanning my husband's cluttered kitchen worktop for my handbag. 'Jess has been in labour since six this morning and he only texts me now!' I push my phone towards him so he can read the text message.

Matt sets down his fork carefully. He's watching me like a man assessing a brewing storm. 'Sylvie—'

'Four hours, Matt! Why didn't Ed tell me sooner? Anything could have happened!'

'But it hasn't,' he says gently. 'She's fine. Ed said so in the message.'

Usually, he'd be critical of Ed dragging his feet. I shake my head. 'I need to be there. I can't just sit here eating bloody avocado toast while—'

'Sylvie, listen.' Matt leans forward, his hands clasped on the table. 'Maybe let them have this time together. Just for a bit, eh?'

His voice is careful, his expression measured. I know exactly what he's saying. *Give them space. Don't crowd them.* But what does he know? Has he ever given birth? No. Has he ever lain there, racked with pain and terrified, wondering if he was about to die while his mother sat at home having a leisurely breakfast? Definitely not.

'I have to go.' The words come out sharper than I intend. 'Jess needs me to be there.'

Matt sighs but nods, the fight leaving him. 'Fine. I'll drive you, but I can't stay. I've got to see that power-mad client I was just telling you about.'

'That's fine. I'll get a cab back.' I snatch up my coat. My hands are trembling.

As we step out into the cold, my mind starts spinning. Jess won't have packed properly – she never thinks about practicalities like this. She'll need nightwear, toiletries, things to make her feel at home.

'Maybe we should stop by their flat,' I say, double-checking I have her flat key on my own fob as Matt unlocks the car. 'Pick up some things for her.'

He shoots me a look. 'I'd leave that to Ed.'

'But—'

'Sylvie.' His tone is firm. 'Ed will step up, I'm sure. Give him some credit.'

I clamp my mouth shut and fold my arms as he pulls out onto the road. It's not about the pyjamas and toiletries, really. It's about doing something useful.

By the time we reach the hospital, I'm jittery with nerves. The car park looks full, people moving in and out of the building, doors slamming, voices merging into one loud hum. Matt pulls up in the drop-off bay.

He reaches for my hand, squeezes it. 'Give her my love and text me, yeah? Let me know how she's doing. Try not to worry.'

I nod. He kisses my cheek, and then he's gone, merging back into the flow of traffic leaving the hospital. I stand for a moment, inhaling the cold air and trying to steady my nerves. Then I gather myself and push through the sliding doors into the chaos of the hospital.

The smell is the first thing that hits me. A mixture of coffee and cooked food from the Costa Coffee in reception, but it's not a pleasant odour. There are so many people moving around. Some hurrying, others shuffling along. Porters, nurses clutching clipboards, patients in wheelchairs with blankets over their knees... the place is a hive of activity, like a mini city.

At the reception desk, a harassed-looking woman directs me to the maternity suite. I take the lift, my stomach churning.

When I step out and walk into the waiting area, I spot Ed immediately.

He's slumped in a chair, elbows on knees, rubbing his face with both hands. He looks up as I approach him and for a second, just a fraction of a second, his expression speaks to me as clear as if he'd said it out loud: *Oh no, what's* she *doing here?*

A flicker of dread that dissolves almost instantly, replaced by a tired smile. But I know what I saw.

I force my own smile wider. 'How is she?'

'Oh hi, Sylvie. You didn't have to come.' He sits up straighter, rubbing his hands over his thighs. He nods to the door leading through to the patient rooms. 'The doctor is with her at the moment.'

'So what's happening? Is Jess OK?' My voice sounds high. Too eager.

'She's fine, I think. We kind of panicked and came in when she started getting pains this morning, but when we got here, they said it's early days still. So... it could be a long one.'

The hesitation in his voice makes my stomach twist.

He doesn't want me here.

I glance at the door, my pulse hammering. I should be in there. Not standing out here trying to prise information from Ed. I've already been through childbirth and I know what Jess needs. I can rub her back, stroke her hair, help her with her breathing. That's key once the contractions get closer together.

A nurse emerges and heads over. She's young, with dark-blonde hair tied back in a neat ponytail. 'Jess is doing really well,' she tells Ed. 'She's not fully dilated yet, but progressing nicely. You can go in now.'

I open my mouth before I can stop myself. 'I'm Sylvie, Jess's mum. Can I see her, too?'

The nurse hesitates. Looks at Ed.

'I won't stay long.' I look at the nurse and back to Ed. 'Just to give her a quick hug. Then I'll leave you to it.'

Ed's jaw tightens for a fraction of a second before he nods. 'Course you can, Sylvie.'

Something inside me flares – resentment, shame, anger... I'm not sure, but I swallow it down.

We follow the nurse down the corridor into a private room. It's bright and clean, the walls a soft pastel yellow, a window letting in weak morning light. Machines hum quietly, and the air smells of antiseptic.

The nurse pulls a curtain and there she is.

My baby girl.

Jess is propped up in bed, her face pale, her usually neat, dark bob sticking to her cheeks. When she sees me, her eyes widen.

Not with annoyance. Not with dread. Just with relieved surprise.

I go to her and take her hand. It's clammy. 'Oh, sweetheart.' I kiss her forehead, stroke wisps of hair back from her face. 'You're doing so well. You're going to be brilliant, I know it.'

Her lips curve into a tired smile. 'Mum...'

'I won't stay,' I say, swallowing the lump in my throat. 'I just wanted to see you. I'll be back the second Ed texts me, alright?'

She nods. I squeeze her hand one last time, then step back. I don't say anything to Ed. I don't trust myself.

Outside, the lift is slow. Too slow. Tears blur my vision as I step in and press the button for the ground floor.

And then I'm out.

Out of the antiseptic air, out of the too-bright corridors and out into the cold. It seems even busier now, people walking into the hospital, people walking out. I stand still, in the middle of them all, but they walk around me, don't even seem to notice I'm there. It's like I'm invisible.

I walk to the kerb and order an Uber. While I wait, I feel a single tear slide down my cheek.

My daughter is having a baby. My first grandchild.

And I feel – if I'm honest – utterly desolate.

FIVE

Scarlet Mae. Her name feels impossibly delicate and beautiful. I murmur it under my breath, cradling this tiny, swaddled bundle in my arms.

My granddaughter's face is impossibly perfect – petal-soft skin, a rosebud mouth, the faintest smudge of dark eyelashes resting against her cheeks. She sleeps, her breath warm and steady, her tiny fingers curled into loose fists.

A wave of love, so fierce it almost knocks me breathless, rises inside me. I have my daughter – I know this feeling – but this experience is different. This is *my* baby's baby. Not only a part of Jess, but a part of me, too, and of all the women in our family who came before.

I glance over at Jess, lying pale against the hospital sheets. Her eyelids look heavy and there's a drawn, waxy look about her. The doctor told us she suffered a great deal of blood loss last night. So much so, a transfusion was required. But they told us everything went well, and she should be good as new in a few days.

'You look too young to be a gran, Mum.' Jess gives me a weak smile. 'Maybe we should call you Glamma.'

'Thanks, but no thanks.' I grin. 'I'd be happy to age ten years to have the privilege of being Scarlet's granny.'

Jess lets out a little laugh, but Ed is silent. He sits beside my daughter, his fingers twitching over hers, the other hand scrubbing at his stubbled chin. He looks shell-shocked, hunched in the chair, his leg jiggling nervously. I watch him for a long moment, my arms tightening slightly around the baby.

Matt has already warned me off before I came here. 'Don't go wading in, Sylvie. If they need help, they'll ask for it.'

But aged twenty and twenty-five, they're barely past being kids themselves. They haven't got a clue know how much help they might need. Nobody has with the first baby, do they? It's a shock to the system once you get home and you realise your life, as you knew it, just blew up.

The sleepless nights that stretch into exhaustion, the gravity of the new responsibility starting to sink in. I can remember sitting, utterly exhausted from lack of sleep, and looking at baby Jessica, screaming her head off, thinking, *This is not like it looked in the mother and baby magazine.*

And now it's my daughter's turn. Jess is barely holding herself up in this hospital bed, and Ed... well.

I stroke Scarlet Mae's downy head with the tip of my finger and glance back at my daughter. 'Why don't you and the baby come to stay with me for a few days after you're discharged? Just until you feel a bit stronger and able to cope?'

I brace myself for the predictable response – 'We'll be fine, we can manage' – but instead, I see relief settle over Jess's face.

'Thanks, Mum,' she says, exhaling. 'Before you came, we were just talking about what needs to happen. Thing is, Ed's got some studio time booked in over the next few weeks, and we can't afford to lose the money.'

Her voice trails off and my focus shifts to Ed's slumped

frame. His crumpled band t-shirt, his long, straggly hair unwashed, his hands restless. When Jess met him, he was a budding musician. He's still a budding musician. His prospects, as far as I can see, haven't moved an inch. I wanted more for her, but although they've had their problems, even split up for a short time a while back and then got back together... she seems happy and they're stronger now than ever. And, as Matt is fond of reminding me on a regular basis, that's what matters despite what we think of him.

'That OK with you, Ed?' I ask.

He startles slightly, like he hadn't considered he needs to be part of this conversation. 'Yeah, that's great. I mean, if that's what Jess wants.'

'That's settled then.'

A lightness flutters in my chest. There are things to do, stuff to get organised, and now, I can do them. I can make sure Jess eats properly, make sure she rests. I can ensure Scarlet Mae is properly cared for, that she's warm and safe and not left in the hands of a man who currently seems incapable of keeping his own thoughts straight while Jess recovers.

In the car on the way home, I press my forehead against the window, watching the thick grey clouds as we drive.

'I'll need to get the spare room sorted for Jess,' I say, thinking aloud. 'I'll have to move quickly but I want to make it nice. I'll need to get a cot, obviously, and some proper bedding. Maybe one of those night lights that shine stars on the ceiling. Oh, and a changing table – I don't want her having to do it on the floor or the bed when she's feeling weak.'

I can already picture the layout, the fresh scent of crisp new sheets and the softness of new baby blankets.

Matt nods easily, his hands loose on the wheel. 'We can pick some bits up later if you like.'

'And maybe some blackout curtains, in case Scarlet Mae is a

light sleeper. Do you think I should get a little fridge in there for Jess to keep her made-up bottles in?'

'You're going all out, aren't you?' He grins, but there's no teasing in it, just amusement.

'Of course I am. They need somewhere comfortable.' I glance at him, lips twitching. 'So, when are you going to meet Scarlet Mae, Grandad Matt?'

He shoots me a look of mock horror. 'Grandad? Absolutely not. I'm far too young and handsome for that title.'

I grin. 'Alright then – what do you fancy? Cool Uncle Matt, or Too-Handsome-to-be-a-Grandad Matt?'

He snorts. 'Come on, my ego's not *that* big. I'll settle for "Matt the Magnificent", thanks very much.'

'The perfect compromise.' I give him a wry grin.

'I'll pop in with you tomorrow to see them both, unless they come home. I can't believe our little Jess is a mummy.'

I glance at him, my heart warming. Matt and Jess have always got on well, but they've been mates over the years, often jokily ganging up on me to decide what movie to watch, or voting for a Papa Johns rather than a sensible cooked dinner. Matt has never tried to be her father and has always left any disciplining or rule-making entirely to me.

But he's always been there for her parent evenings at school, ferried her back and forth countless times to school discos or sleepovers at her friends' houses. Now, there's no doubt in my mind that he'll soon be looking out for little Scarlet Mae too.

He clears his throat. 'Remember that client I told you about... the tricky one? Turns out he's recommended me to his brother, up in Newcastle. This guy has a big house, loads of land and wants it all landscaped. Could be a lucrative job.'

'That's great,' I murmur. I mean it, but who cares about landscaping? My mind is still arranging furniture and deciding on nursery colours.

'Thing is, I'll have to go up there for at least a couple of days. Get a feel for it, talk through some ideas.'

'Fine. Sounds good.' My fingers drum against my leg. I'm itching to get back and make a start.

Matt turns the car onto the home stretch, the familiar curve of our street just visible beyond the neat, clipped hedges. My hands feel warm in my lap, my head still buzzing from the fact I'm now a grandparent. It's happened! I glance at Matt, his fingers loose on the wheel, the faintest hint of a smile at the corner of his mouth. He's always so steady, so easy. Nothing ever ruffles him.

We pull up outside the house, and as Matt cuts the engine, I notice Penny over in her front garden. She catches sight of us and waves, her face lighting up.

'She looks happy,' Matt says, opening his door.

I step out, stretching my legs, and Penny is already crossing the road towards us, secateurs dangling from one hand. There's something sprightly about her today, a little burst of energy in her step.

'You're back!' she calls. 'Oh, I've been dying to hear how it went. Tell me everything!'

I pull my phone from my pocket, tapping the screen to bring up the photo I took earlier. 'Here she is, meet Scarlet Mae,' I say, turning the screen towards Penny. The image glows between us – Scarlet, bundled in a soft white blanket, her tiny fingers curled against her cheek.

Penny lets out a delighted gasp. 'Oh, Sylvie, she's absolutely gorgeous! Just look at that little face. And she has Jess's pretty eyes!' She glances up, eyes shining. 'You must be over the moon.'

I smile, my excitement momentarily nudging my other thoughts aside. 'This feeling, Penny, it's like nothing else. She's just perfect.'

Penny claps her hands together. 'How wonderful. And she's fine? Jess, I mean?'

'Tired but doing well. She's coming to stay with us for a bit, just until she finds her feet.'

Penny's eyes shine. 'I can see her before we go! It means I'll get to meet Scarlet Mae. What a gorgeous name. Oh, that's really made my day.'

I laugh. 'You look like something's already made your day.'

'Well, I have some exciting news, too. The house is already let!' She presses a hand to her chest in gratitude. 'She's a lovely woman, Brenda, in her sixties. It's just her and her cat. She seems very friendly, keen to get involved in everything. And' – Penny leans in slightly, lowering her voice – 'she's already talking about buying it, if we decide to sell once we're settled in Portugal.'

Matt lets out a low whistle. 'Blimey, that was quick. Congratulations!'

'I know, it's all happening at once. But Brian has found what looks like the most perfect cottage for rent in Tavira... it feels like everything's falling into place.'

A breeze stirs the last of the autumn leaves around our feet, and I glance at my house, its windows glinting in the weak sunlight. There's a crispness to the air and I exhale, releasing some tension I hadn't even realised I was holding on to.

'It does feel like that, doesn't it?' I say, meeting Penny's bright gaze. 'Like – for once – things are going right for us all. I'm made up for you and Brian, I really am.'

We say our goodbyes with a promise I'll let Penny know when Jess and Scarlet Mae are home so she can visit.

Matt and I step inside, the warmth of home settling around us.

I'm already thinking about dinner and about getting started on the spare room. I'm happy for Penny and Brian and relieved our new neighbour-to-be sounds nice.

It's such a relief to feel at last that life is lining up neatly for a change.

SIX

He leaves the engine running for a moment longer and sits. Listening to the soft hum of it. There's something ceremonial about endings. Even quiet ones like this. Especially quiet ones.

There again, this is not really an ending at all. It's just the beginning.

He turns off the ignition.

The silence wraps around the car like a fog. Only the faint sparkle of the fairy lights inside the building, powered by a silent generator out back. No mains electricity out here. Not anymore. No signal. No prying eyes.

Nobody in his day-to-day life knows this place exists and that's the way he intends to keep it.

He opens the rear door of the van.

Ellie's head lolls slightly with the movement, her chin dipping towards her chest. Her eyelashes look long and dark against her cheeks like a shadow. There's a faint line of dried blood near her elbow – just a graze from the fall. Nothing serious.

He lifts her carefully, one arm beneath her knees, the other braced across her shoulders. The gravel crunches beneath his boots as he carries her up the short path. The door opens with a click. He left it unlocked to assist on his return.

No one ever comes here now. Except him.

Inside, the air is warm and still. He goes through to the back and lays her down on the bed – simple, narrow and made up with clean white linen. A folded blanket at the end. A water glass on the table. Lavender oil, unopened. He's tried to think of everything.

Sitting beside her, he waits for his breath to settle.

She's beautiful like this. The stillness of her. The unguarded face. Her breath is shallow but steady, a slight puff of air every few seconds. Her hands are small and delicate, her jaw so narrow and fragile, he could crush it with one hand.

He brushes a strand of hair from her forehead.

'You're safe now,' he whispers.

Slowly, he begins to undo her jacket. One button, then the next. He's careful. This isn't about that. Not base. Nothing crude.

He just needs to see. To know what he's working with. Find out who she is underneath all the surface noise.

SEVEN

Jess and the baby have been home almost a week now, and to say I'm dog tired is an understatement.

In my enthusiasm to get my girls back home with me, I'd forgotten two things: one, I've got considerably less energy now compared to when I was a twenty-four-year-old new mum, taking baby duties in my stride.

Secondly, I'd completely forgotten just how challenging the new baby stage is – the endless feeding, changing, rocking, mopping up sick at three in the morning while murmuring nonsense like, 'It's fine, it's fine, everything's fine,' when absolutely nothing is fine because I haven't slept properly in days. And I've just found baby sick in my hair yet again.

On the plus side, Jess is doing well, all things considered, but she's still weak. The doctors issued firm instructions before she was discharged, three days after the birth. 'You need proper rest, Jessica. No overdoing it, no lifting, no unnecessary stress.' I can still see the consultant's serious expression as she listed everything Jess had to avoid.

She lost a lot of blood after the birth, more than they were comfortable with. The transfusion has left her utterly drained. The doctors think she might have postpartum anaemia, which sounds fairly minor until you see her struggling just to sit up. She gets dizzy if she moves too fast, and the first couple of days home, even standing for too long left her breathless.

She tries to hide it, of course, but I can see the exhaustion in the way her hands tremble when she buttons up Scarlet's tiny sleepsuits.

I've taken it upon myself to make sure she properly rests, which means I've essentially become a full-time nanny, house-keeper and general chaos-controller, all rolled into one.

Scarlet Mae is a dream... when she's asleep. The problem is, that's not often, and never when we'd like. She seems to have an uncanny ability to wake up the second I sit down, as if she has some kind of internal alarm set to detect when I'm about to take a break.

To date, her main hobbies seem to include: feeding, crying because she wants feeding, and filling her nappy the second I change her.

'She looks exactly like you when she does that,' I said to Jess yesterday, when she furrowed her little brow at me as if disapproving.

Jess gave a weak laugh. 'That's exactly what I was afraid of.'

My house seems to be full, all the time. Matt is constantly on the move, fetching things, carrying things, making endless cups of tea that everyone forgets to drink. Then he'll disappear for a crafty hour or two, back to his peaceful man cave, two doors down, which I don't mind admitting makes me mad with envy.

To give him his due, Ed has been around a lot as well in between being at the studio, doing his fair share of pacing up and down with the baby when she won't settle.

We've had lots of visitors. Jess's friends, Ed's mates, Penny from over the road, all cooing over Scarlet, passing her around like she's a precious artefact on loan from the British Museum.

Kendra is here now visiting Jess and Scarlet. She perches on the arm of the sofa, one slim, long leg crossed over the other, her phone glued to her hand. When she arrived, she shed her heavy coat to reveal skin-tight leggings and a skimpy top.

She's barely looked at Scarlet since she arrived, aside from a cursory, 'Oh, she's so cute,' before returning her attention to whatever's happening on her screen. I watch as she scrolls, her pointy black-painted thumbnail flicking upwards in sharp, practised movements.

I turn back to Matt. 'Would you nip to the supermarket later? Just a few bits – milk, bread, maybe more biscuits. People keep turning up, and we've only got those weird oat ones left.'

He nods, draining the last of his tea. 'Yeah, no problem.'

Before I can add anything else to the list, Kendra lets out a snort. 'God, listen to this.' She clears her throat dramatically, then starts reading from her phone. '"Women in the area are being urged to remain vigilant after the disappearance of a local young woman. Police advise against walking alone at night and recommend informing someone of your location at all times."' She rolls her eyes. 'Honestly, I can't *stand* this victim mentality. Hiding away at home just because some psychopathic pervert is on the loose? Don't they know that's probably exactly what he wants!'

Jess, curled up in the armchair with Scarlet Mae dozing on her chest, murmurs, 'Yeah, you might be right about that, Ken.'

I frown. 'That's all well and good, Kendra, but it doesn't mean you should take silly risks. Looking after yourself isn't the same as cowering away in fear.'

She waves a dismissive hand. 'Oh, *purlease*, Sylv. I'll do exactly what I want, when I want, like I always have. No loser is ever going to dictate how I live *my* life. I say it all the time on the socials.'

The problem is, I've known Kendra long enough to know she *does* take silly risks – the drunken walks back home alone, getting into cars with people she's just met, hooking up with men she barely knows. Jess might excuse her behaviour as 'just Kendra being Kendra', but it makes me uneasy, and I hate the influence she might have on Jess.

'Maybe,' Matt says suddenly, setting his mug down with a sharp clunk, 'you should be careful what you post online. Just a thought.'

Kendra raises an eyebrow at him, amused. 'Oh yeah? And why's that?'

Matt shrugs. 'This man, whoever he is... he might not be as stupid as you think. He certainly seems to be running rings around the police at the moment.'

I see just a second of hesitation on Kendra's face, as if Matt's comment has actually landed somewhere useful beneath all that bravado.

Then she scoffs. 'Oh, come on. You think he's sitting somewhere, scrolling through news articles, getting offended by my comments?' She laughs a little too loud and Scarlet stirs before mercifully settling again.

'I'm just saying, you never know,' Matt says lightly, standing up. 'He could be monitoring what people are saying online.'

Kendra rolls her eyes again, but this time, she doesn't look quite as sure of herself. She stands. 'Anyway, I've somewhere to be. Despite people encouraging me to put my life on hold.'

Later, Penny pops over, and with Jess and Scarlet both napping for once, I jump at the chance to sit and talk to someone who isn't covered in baby milk.

She presents me with a gift box the size of a small suitcase. 'I've filled it with all the practical things no one ever remembers to buy – extra muslins, baby nail scissors, gripe water, a thermometer that doesn't involve sticking anything anywhere unpleasant.'

'Oh, Penny, you're a saint,' I say, peeking at a pack of bibs, all neatly embroidered with tiny animals. 'Jess will love it.'

She beams. 'Brian keeps telling me I'll have to scale back my mothering instincts when we move to Portugal, but I think the locals will just have to get used to it.'

'So,' I say, once she's settled herself on the sofa with a cup of tea, 'tell me more about this new tenant of yours. Brenda, isn't it?'

'Yes, she's moving in tomorrow.' Penny takes a sip of tea, then leans forward slightly, lowering her voice as if imparting a secret. 'She's a retired nurse. Quite the character!'

'Really?'

'She's very chatty. Friendly. She seems excited to be here and very keen to get involved in the community, but I get the sense she hasn't got much family or support.' She pauses, as if weighing something up. 'She said something a bit odd when we were going through the tenancy agreement. She already knew the names of some of the neighbours. She asked after Brian by name before I'd even mentioned him, and she seemed to know quite a lot about things that have happened on the street.'

'Oh?' I raise an eyebrow. 'Like what?'

'Nothing major, just little things – like, who used to live at number twenty-two before the Harrisons, that business with the cat that went missing last year, even the time the bins weren't collected for three weeks and we all had to complain to the council.'

I frown. 'Maybe she's got a friend who lives around here?'

Penny shakes her head. 'I asked that. She says she doesn't know anyone who lives here. Just that she's "always taken an interest in her surroundings".'

I pull a face, but there's nothing sinister about what Penny's saying... some people are just naturally nosy.

Picking up my mug, I glance towards the window and across the road, where Penny's soon-to-be former house stands.

Quiet and waiting. Tomorrow, Brenda the ex-nurse will be moving in.

'Well,' I say, shaking off the feeling, 'I'm not quite sure how, with everything going on here, but I'll make a bit time to pop over and say hello. Make her feel welcome.'

'You always do,' Penny says, smiling. 'I told her she'd soon make friends here and she seemed pleased about that. And would you do me a favour? Any problems, anything you think I should know about in relation to the house... will you let me know?'

'Course!' Scarlet Mae starts to stir in her Moses basket, making the tiny, snuffling noise that I've learned means I have about thirty seconds before she launches into a full-blown wail. I groan, pushing myself up from the sofa.

'Wish me luck,' I say. 'Think of me when you're on your sunbed sipping a cocktail.'

Penny laughs. 'You don't need luck, Sylvie. Looks to me like you just need a good night's sleep.'

'I can but live in hope.'

'You know,' she says, almost to herself, 'it really is a lovely street, this one. No wonder Brenda feels it's exactly the right place.'

I hum in agreement, but a little thought niggles at the back of my mind.

The right place for what, exactly?

EIGHT

BRENDA

SATURDAY

Brenda lowers herself into the armchair by the picture window. She'd instructed the removals men to place it, angled just so, allowing her a clear view of the street without being too visible herself. A sliver of curtain provides cover, an unobtrusive shield. Somewhere from where she can watch without drawing attention. That's important because Brenda likes to watch.

Ivor watches too, although with far less discipline. The cat perches on the arm of the chair, his long tail flicking lazily against her sleeve, his green eyes pinned to her breakfast.

The toast on Brenda's plate is cut into two neat triangles, buttered – she's not a fan of margarine – with marmalade spread right to the edges. There's reassurance to be found in small consistencies. The china teacup that belonged to her mother sits to her right, its handle aligned perfectly with the edge of the saucer. Comforting.

The crunch of the toast is satisfying and the bitter tang of Seville oranges just right. None of that cheap unbranded supermarket stuff. Brenda is willing to pay for quality. She chews slowly and methodically. No rush. There never seems to be much rush these days.

Mornings are for control, for order. It's essential to properly set up the day. She takes pleasure in the small rituals – her tan, fleece-lined slippers positioned parallel beneath the coffee table, the butter dish returned exactly to the centre of the fridge shelf. Everything where it should be. *A place for everything, and everything in its place.* That's what her mother always used to say.

Ivor stretches, arching his back before slinking to the floor, winding himself around her ankles and leaping onto the windowsill. He presses his nose to the glass, whiskers twitching. A car door slams outside, but Brenda doesn't look up.

Another sip of tea. She picks up her tablet, waking the screen with a tap. They had to use these things at the hospital. She found it irritating at the time, having to learn something new, but now she's completely au fait with the touch-screen technology, which, it turns out, is very useful.

The glow reflects in her glasses, making her eyes appear oddly luminous. She scans the article's headline again, though she knows it by heart now. Still, there's something to be gained from repetition, from absorbing every word, every nuance.

Some people skim carelessly and miss details. Brenda is not one of those people.

12 September

Daily Mail

Together but Apart: Why This Couple Swear by LAT Love

When Matt Tyce, 35, inherited his late grandad's house, he never expected to find love just a few doors down. But that's exactly what happened when he met Sylvie, 45, his now wife and next-door-but-one neighbour.

Unlike most married couples, Sylvie and Matt don't share a home. They're part of a growing trend known as 'Living Apart Together' (LAT), where couples commit to each other but maintain separate households. And for the Tyces, it works like a dream.

'I love Matt, I really do,' says Sylvie. 'But I also love my space. My house stays neat and tidy, and I never have to pick wet towels off the floor.'

Matt, lounging comfortably in his own (decidedly less tidy) living room, grins. 'And I get to leave the loo seat up without being told off. It's a win-win situation.'

Their arrangement started out of practicality – Sylvie had already settled into her home and lived there with her daughter when Matt moved onto the street. But as their relationship grew, neither felt the need – or desire – to change it.

'We see each other every day and do all the things other married couples do,' says Matt. 'We have dinner together, go on holidays, and spend weekends at each other's places. But at the end of the day, we've each got our own space to retreat to.'

Their narrow, quiet street in Lady Bay is the kind where everyone knows everyone, and Sylvie – who helps run a popular book club – loves being at the heart of the community. 'I value my independence, but I also love that I can just walk two doors down to see Matt or spend an evening with friends discussing books over a glass of wine,' she says.

According to relationship experts, LAT relationships are on the rise in the UK, especially among people who value inde-pendence or have lived alone for a long time. And for Sylvie and Matt, it's the perfect balance.

'People always ask when we'll move in together.' Sylvie laughs. 'But why mess with something that's already perfect?'

For now, the couple are happy just as they are – close

enough to pop round for a cuppa, but far enough apart to never
argue over whose turn it is to do the dishes.

Brenda sets aside the tablet and shifts in her armchair, careful not to disturb Ivor, who has now settled in a perfect coil on her lap. From her vantage point, she can see both houses – forty-five and forty-one.

The woman's – *Sylvie's* – is neater. That much is obvious. The window frames are painted a pale sage green that Brenda guesses will complement the climbing roses trailing up the trellis in the summer months. The front step is swept clean, a ceramic planter of bright violas positioned beside the door. It's the sort of house that suggests care and attention have been applied.

Number forty-one, by contrast, looks unkempt. The curtains are mismatched – one white, one an odd shade of mustard – and neither drawn back properly. The wheelie bins are scattered and someone has left an empty beer can on the low wall by the gate, which the owner has failed to remove. No surprise, really. She'd read the article and a man like Matt, well, standards probably aren't his priority.

Brenda sips her tea, though it's already quite cool and the bitterness more pronounced. Her early impression is that the street seems friendly enough. Neighbours pausing to chat to each other, a boy cycling past and calling out a greeting to someone in a garden she can't see.

Perhaps, in time, she might also become part of the community. She likes the idea in theory – some company, conversation, a sense of place. But people can be unpredictable and judgemental. She knows that better than most.

She strokes Ivor absently, fingers running over the soft rise of his spine. Her last place had seemed promising too... at first. There had even been a book club she'd almost joined. A woman at the indoor market who'd once invited her for coffee, then had conveniently forgotten about it the next time they met. Brenda hadn't pushed. She knows better than to force these things.

It had all unravelled eventually, as it always does. And it's always her policy to leave on her own terms rather than wait to be edged out.

Brenda watches as the front door of number forty-five opens.

A movement catches her eye, and she stiffens. A young, attractive woman emerges, walking to Sylvie's front gate. Her long coat blows open revealing tight leggings, knee-high boots and a stripe of pale flesh under a cropped top. Her dark hair is twisted up in a messy knot, tendrils escaping in the breeze.

She must be a friend. She pauses at the gate, tapping out a message on her phone with both thumbs. She looks up and down the street and then saunters off in the direction of the main road.

For a brief moment, before the front door swings shut again, she catches a glimpse of a woman in her forties wearing jeans and a white t-shirt, shoulder-length brown hair tied back fashionably with a scarf. This must be Sylvie.

Brenda exhales slowly. How nice, she thinks, to have someone to chew the cud with. A bit of company. A bit of warmth to start your day.

Ivor shifts, stretching luxuriously before resettling. Brenda strokes his ears, watching the now-closed door.

Yes. It must be very nice indeed.

NINE

SYLVIE

MONDAY

Jess isn't picking up as quickly as I expected after she left the hospital. If anything, she's slowing down. She sleeps more, not less, and when she is awake, she is pale and quiet, pushing food around her plate and insisting she isn't hungry.

She's still trying to do everything with Scarlet herself, but I can see how much effort it takes. How her hands tremble slightly when she feeds the baby. How she leans against the pillows, exhausted before she's even begun.

I call the GP surgery first thing, and the receptionist promises me a doctor will call back. He does so, mid-morning. His voice is calm, reassuring.

'It might take time for her to get her strength back, especially after a transfusion. Plenty of fluids, good nutrition. Don't worry about the sleep – it'll do her good. Call back if there's no improvement by the end of the week.'

I thank him and hang up, but my discomfort doesn't loosen. A few extra naps I could understand, but this is different. Jess isn't just tired – she seems drained, as if the life is slowly trickling out of her.

Meanwhile, I'm practically running on fumes. There's no end to it: laundry, bottles, nappy changes, never-ending rounds of visitors. And Matt, although he's been supportive, isn't exactly present. Yes, he runs errands, fixes things, drops off groceries and medication when I ask him to, but there's always a reason he can't stay very long. Always somewhere else he has to be.

I glance out of the window now and see the Kawasaki Ninja parked in its usual spot outside Matt's house, indicating his best friend, Nige, is visiting yet again. The motorbike is lurid green with gleaming chrome wheels, the sort of fancy boy toy that looks faintly ridiculous for a rider in his mid-thirties. It's a lovely model – if you like that sort of thing. I don't.

Even Jess has noticed. 'I don't know why Matt lets that loser stick around so much.'

Nige is a nice enough guy even if he has a lifestyle like he's still in his early twenties. He and Matt were mates long before I met him, and I've never had a problem with their close relationship. But right now, I admit it's galling to see how little Matt's life has changed while mine has turned into an endless cycle of baby wipes and broken sleep. He still has his own space, his own routine, his mates dropping by to talk about motorbike engines and to watch footie. And me? I haven't had an uninterrupted night's sleep in ages.

Nige, unmarried and a free spirit, certainly seems to be making the most of Matt's availability.

I step away from the window, pushing the thoughts aside, but for the first time, I find myself questioning whether keeping two houses is as ideal as it first seemed.

It worked for us once, but now things are changing and perhaps it's time for our circumstances to reflect that.

· · ·

Ed arrives late afternoon, as he does most days, straight from the studio. From what I understand he works on other bands' sessions there and is also recording an album with his own band.

'He's living in cloud cuckoo land,' Matt said scathingly when I told him about the album. 'Recording a few tunes in some crummy backstreet studio isn't going to get them a record deal. They should be doing the rounds, performing in pubs and clubs. That's where the money is.'

Matt has definitely got a point, but I have to give Ed his due – he has stepped up. He's very hands-on with Scarlet Mae and is keen to learn. It's surprised me and pushed him up in my estimations.

Ed's currently watching Jess carefully, frowning. 'I don't like the look of her, Sylvie,' he murmurs while she dozes on the sofa.

'Neither do I,' I admit. 'The doctor says to give it a few more days, but if she's no better, I'm calling them again tomorrow.'

He nods. 'Good.'

It's a relief to know I'm not just imagining Jess's downward spiral.

Ed takes over with the baby for a couple of hours so I can have a rest upstairs. I have no intention of fully sleeping, but the moment my head hits the pillow, I'm out cold. When I wake, the room has grown dim. It's nearly teatime. I blink, stretch, then move to the window, pulling back the curtain.

Across the road, a small removals van is pulling away from Penny's old house. Her tenant, Brenda, must have arrived.

Downstairs, I find all three of them – Jess, Ed and Scarlet – fast asleep. To avoid disturbing them, I slip into the kitchen.

I take a bottle of Prosecco from the fridge and a small, unopened box of Celebrations from the cupboard. I fluff my hair in the hall mirror and then head across the road.

Brenda is at the door in seconds, wide-eyed, her expression

reminding me of a startled owl. She's a completely unremarkable lady in her mid-sixties with short, practical grey hair. She has soft, ordinary features: the kind of face you'd struggle to pick out of a line-up.

Behind her, packing boxes are piled in the hallway.

'Hello! I don't mean to intrude,' I say, glancing at the chaos. 'You must be up to your eyes in it, but I just wanted to pop over and say hello. I'm Sylvie and I live at number forty-five.' I turn and gesture vaguely across the road.

She looks genuinely delighted as I hand her the fizz and chocolates. 'Oh, that's very kind. Thank you so much, that's just lovely of you! I'm Brenda, by the way. Won't you come in for a moment?'

'Thanks, but I have my daughter and her new baby staying with me just now, so I must get back. But I wanted to bring you a little something to welcome you to the street,' I say. 'Once you're settled in, pop over anytime for a coffee and a chat.'

Brenda beams. 'Thank you, Sylvie, I will. I most definitely will.' She hesitates for a moment. 'You mentioned your daughter's new baby... is this your first grandchild?'

'That's right. Her name is Scarlet Mae.' I give a sheepish smile. 'I confess I'm completely smitten.'

'Goodness, you don't look old enough to be a grandma!' Brenda exclaims. 'Congratulations.'

I smile and thank her. We exchange a few more pleasantries before I take my leave, scooting back across the road noticing that Nige's bike is *still* parked outside Matt's house.

Inside, Ed and Jess are now awake. Jess looks pale and sounds weak, but her mouth quirks into a familiar teasing smile. 'I thought you'd finally had enough of us and run away, Mum.'

'Not yet.' I grin. 'Just welcoming our new neighbour across the street.'

'Brenda?'

'Yes, she seems nice enough. I've told her to pop over for a coffee once she's settled in.'

Jess nods, shifting slightly to resettle Scarlet Mae. Her movements are slow and careful, as if even that takes effort.

'I'll go and make us some tea,' I say, watching her carefully.

As I fill the kettle, I find myself thinking back to Brenda, to the way her eyes had lit up when I'd handed her the fizz and chocolates. She'd seemed genuinely overwhelmed by the small gesture, as if she wasn't used to kindness.

For some reason, it makes me feel lighter.

And Penny was spot on, too. Brenda seems like a normal, friendly lady who'll fit in well around here.

TEN

Jess is trembling by the time I help her out of the shower, her skin damp and clammy under my hands. She sags against me as I wrap the soft towelling robe around her, and Scarlet Mae stirs in the papoose strapped to my front, making a little grizzling noise of protest.

'Are you alright?' I ask, tucking the robe closer around Jess's shoulders.

She nods, but her eyelids are heavy, and she moves as if she's wading through water. My stomach tightens. She should be getting stronger, not weaker.

The doorbell rings just as we're halfway downstairs.

I sigh, shifting the baby slightly to soothe her. 'They can sod off. It's barely nine o'clock.'

Jess attempts a smile. 'What if it's important?'

'Then they'll come back.' I steer her down the last few steps and guide her towards the living room, ignoring the distorted shape of a person through the opaque glass.

The bell rings again.

'For crying out loud,' I mutter. 'If that thing rings a third time, I'm chucking a bucket of water on them. If they ring a fourth, I'll—'

A third chime cuts me off and Jess lets out a weak laugh.

Jess shakes her head and reaches for the papoose. 'Just get the door, Mum. I'll take her.'

I hesitate, but she shuffles off with the baby, and I head for the front door.

When it opens, I have to stop myself from blinking in surprise.

Brenda.

She stands on the doorstep, smiling broadly, clasping a pack of chocolate digestives with both hands like a peace offering.

'Morning, Sylvie! Thought I'd pop over for that coffee... if it's convenient?'

I stare at her, a bit thrown. I only invited her yesterday: *once she was settled in.* She must barely have had time to unpack a box. Plus, it's too early for a social call.

'Hello, Brenda,' I say, forcing warmth into my voice. 'Lovely to see you, but now's not a good time, I'm afraid.'

Brenda's smile doesn't falter. She holds up the biscuits. 'Don't worry, I won't stay long.'

I shift uncomfortably. 'It's just – Jess is unwell, and Ed's due over soon. So it's not ideal.'

Brenda beams at me. 'Oh, I've only just popped over to say a quick hello and take a peek at little Scarlet Mae.'

She steps forward slightly, putting a foot on the step, and I resist the urge to sigh.

'Thing is, Brenda, Jess really isn't well. Perhaps we can do coffee another day.'

Brenda's expression changes. She frowns, her concern immediate and genuine. 'Oh dear. What's wrong with her?'

I crane my neck as Matt's work van starts up. Behind him, Nige appears and gets astride his motorbike. Both of them pull away together.

I bite back my irritation as Brenda seizes the moment to step inside. She pushes the door shut behind her.

'She's very weak. She had a blood transfusion after the birth, so the doctor says it's normal for her to feel like this for a while.'

Brenda's eyes sharpen. 'What exactly are her symptoms?'

I hesitate, feeling as if I'm being cross-examined. 'Tiredness, no appetite... she's sleeping all the time.'

'Any fever? Skin rash? Shortness of breath?'

I blink at her. 'Penny told me you're a retired nurse, is that right?'

Brenda straightens slightly. 'I was a senior nurse, actually. Would you like me to take a quick look at Jess? Better to be safe than sorry, I always think.'

I hesitate. I don't want Brenda here. Not now. But I also don't have the energy to argue. And if letting her say a quick hello gets her back out the door faster, then so be it.

I step aside, irritated. 'Just for a few minutes then.' I wave my hand down the hallway. 'She's in there.'

Brenda strides past me, through the hall and into the living room, completely unfazed by the mess. The coffee table is littered with baby bottles, muslin cloths, a half-eaten biscuit. A basket of unfolded laundry sits beside the sofa. I cringe, but Brenda doesn't bat an eyelid.

She heads straight to Scarlet Mae's basket. 'Hello there, little one,' she coos, leaning down to gently stroke her head. 'Aren't you a beauty?'

Then, as if remembering herself, she turns to Jess. 'Hello there, Jess. I hear congratulations are in order.'

Jess musters a small smile. 'Thanks.'

Brenda sits beside her, speaking gently. 'How was the birth?'

Jess shrugs slightly. 'Long. A bit rough at the end.'

Brenda nods, eyes flicking over Jess's face. I can see her assessing, her expression unreadable.

'And how do you feel now?'

Jess hesitates. 'Tired. Just... really, really tired.'

Brenda reaches out and takes her hand, then subtly pulls up the sleeve of her bath robe. I frown. Jess's forearm is covered in a faint, blotchy rash.

'Had you noticed this?' Brenda asks me.

I shake my head, my throat tightening.

Brenda lays a flat hand against Jess's forehead, then presses two fingers to her wrist. I watch as her lips press together.

Then she stands abruptly. 'I'm very sorry, but I can't stay for coffee after all.'

I falter a little, startled at her about turn. 'Oh?'

She moves quickly into the hall, and I follow. In a low voice, she says, 'Sylvie, you need to get Jess to A&E immediately.'

My stomach drops. 'What?'

'Jess is displaying symptoms of an allergic transfusion reaction – rash, fever, tachycardia. It can be very dangerous. Don't wait for an ambulance – just take her now.'

Scarlet suddenly lets out a wail from the living room. She wants feeding. My breath catches. My brain stutters. Jess isn't even dressed...

I slip my phone out of my pocket and call Matt. No answer.

Brenda grips my arm, steadily. 'Listen to me. Get Jess to hospital. I'll stay with Scarlet until Ed arrives.'

Panic flares. 'I can't leave—'

'Yes, you *can*. I was a senior nurse, remember? Your granddaughter is in good hands.'

Scarlet's cries sharpen. Jess, still in the living room, lets out a small, wheezing cough.

I swallow hard, my mind whirling.

Ten minutes later, I am driving Jess to A&E.

And a woman called Brenda, who I barely know, is back at my house, rocking my precious granddaughter in her arms.

The office ticks over with its usual low-level hum – keyboards clicking like distant rain, the occasional trill of a desk phone and someone muttering into a headset about an arrest gone wrong in Arnold town centre. Over in the corner, an officer is fighting with the photocopier again.

DI Helena Price and DS Kane Brewster are holed up at the far end of the shared space, twin monitors glowing in the half-light of a gloomy Sunday afternoon. The blinds haven't been adjusted since the weekend, which means the overhead fluorescents are doing most of the work. Helena can feel a headache building behind her eyes. Probably tension. Or dehydration. Or Brewster.

'Right,' she says, tapping the space bar. 'Let's go through the case particulars again from the beginning and—'

She stops mid-sentence, wrinkling her nose. Brewster has just peeled the lid off a small plastic box, releasing a strong sulphurous smell.

'Is that... another egg?' she asks, risking a sideways glance. He's holding it delicately between his thumb and finger, like it might explode.

'Boiled,' he says cheerfully, cracking the shell against the corner of the desk. 'I'm on the two-day egg blitz diet, boss. Pure protein. I've lost five pounds since Friday.'

'And probably most of your friends, too,' Helena murmurs, waving a hand in front of her face. 'I've got to level with you, Brewster... it feels like I'm being slowly tear-gassed.'

He grins and shrugs, taking a bite out of the peeled egg and starting to chew.

'Let's get back to the casework.' She grimaces and turns back to the screen, scrolling down until the header appears. 'OK. So we have Ellie Walker, a twenty-two-year-old student nurse that disappears. She vanished without trace nearly two months ago.' Helena scrolls down further. 'She was seen cycling home from college. She'd taken her usual route and she was very familiar with the area. There were no signs of a struggle. No CCTV available. No usable forensics and her bicycle has not yet been found.'

'Or her handbag and its contents, including her phone,' Brewster chips in, wiping his eggy fingers on a grubby napkin.

Helena shakes her head and pulls up Superintendent Della Grey's latest internal email. To describe her writing style as abrupt is an understatement. Brewster once famously said, 'It's what you'd get if you fed a Jack Russell three espressos and then gave it a keyboard.'

'Grey's breathing down our necks. No surprise there,' Helena mutters. 'She's got the local newspaper on one side demanding an update on Ellie Walker and a Home Office liaison officer chirping on the other about where we are and why there's nothing substantial to report yet. Says here, she wants "visible progress".'

'The benefit of hindsight, eh?' Brewster sniffs. 'Maybe we should just start arresting random blokes in dark hoodies. That usually keeps the public happy for a bit.'

Helena shoots him a look.

'Let's see the map,' Helena says.

Brewster's ahead of her, already pulling up the digital version. 'We mapped out Ellie's disappearance site. Did a door-to-door campaign around the West Bridgford area and Davies Road where she lives at her parents' house. Nothing useful came up according to uniform.'

'So where do we go now?' Helena says, rubbing her temple. The headache is definitely winning now.

She watches him hesitate, the egg poised mid-air. His mouth twitches and she could swear he looks a bit peaky. Slowly, he lowers it back into the box and snaps the lid shut. *There is a God.*

'We mentioned going to see Ellie's parents again,' he reminds her.

Helena nods. 'It's time. We must have missed something. Or someone did. If there's a link to be found, it'll be there.'

Brewster sighs and leans back in his chair, the wheels squeaking a little. 'They're good people,' he says. 'Still set a place at the table for her. Got her coat hanging on the back of the kitchen door.'

Helena winces. 'Don't.'

They sit in silence for a moment while the office continues to buzz around them. It's an indifferent backdrop to lives that have been paused and cases that are unfinished. It's also the place where they work out where to go next.

'We have no choice but to start from the beginning,' Helena says, standing and grabbing her coat. 'Let's walk part of her route again. Check in with her friends. Rattle a few cages if we can.'

Brewster reaches for the box of eggs.

'Leave that here,' Helena says sternly. 'There's no way I'm getting in an enclosed space with you. It's me or the eggs.'

He groans but follows, grabbing his notebook and muttering

something about malnourishment and human rights. Helena doesn't grin, but she comes close.

Because despite the dead ends, the mounting pressure, and the grim weight of what they might eventually find, there's something solid about knowing you're not looking alone.

They've done it before and Helena is determined that, this time, they'll do it again.

TWELVE

SYLVIE

Back home from the hospital early evening, the front door clicks shut behind me and I lean against it, my breathing shallow. After diagnosing Jess and looking after Scarlet Mae while I rushed Jess into hospital, Brenda is my hero. Now she's just left and the silence feels like a shock of cold water after hours of stuffy heat, beeping machines and the low murmur of voices in the A&E department.

Jess is upstairs, finally asleep with Scarlet Mae in her arms. Matt is in the kitchen, washing baby bottles. And me? I feel like a threadbare, frail woman held together only by caffeine and paracetamol.

My stomach clenches – sharp and low, like something is twisting deep inside me – but I ignore it, as I've done for days now. There's always something more important to do than worry about what might be causing it. Jess. The baby.

I'll hold this entire bloody house up by the beams if I must.

Matt is up and off at the crack of dawn tomorrow on his big landscaping job up north, so he stays at his house tonight. I lock up after him and go upstairs slowly, gripping the banister I usually ignore when I zip up and down. Today, every step feels wrong. Off kilter, somehow. But I make it into bed, crawl under the covers and close my eyes to the sound of the wind shifting through the tree outside the window.

In the early hours, I wake with a start. I'm wet through with sweat and shaking all over. I'm almost sick before I reach the bathroom. Bile hits the sink in great heaving waves and my legs buckle. My hands grip porcelain as my vision fuzzes around the edges.

'Jess,' I croak, but the word is swallowed up by the roar in my ears.

Then the floor tips sideways.

I wake to chaos.

A stranger's voice – frantic and sharp-edged. 'Sylvie? Can you hear me?'

Feet pounding down the hallway. The cold press of something metallic and cool against my wrist. My vision clears and I blink up at a man in a green uniform.

'It hurts,' I whisper. My abdomen feels like it's on fire, molten and all wrong. My body wants to curl in on itself and I start to do so, but someone stops me.

Jess's face presses close to me, pale and scared. She's holding my hand like it's the only thing she can do, but I'm fading in and out.

There's a siren. I'm being lifted, moved. Cold air rushes over my face. I catch a glimpse of the sky – grey, bloated with storm clouds – and then I'm inside the ambulance.

I feel someone grasp my fingers with a strong, warm hand.

'Matt?' I whisper, my vision blurring.

'It's just me. Brenda,' she says and squeezes my hand a little harder. 'I'm here, now. Everything is going to be just fine.'

. . .

The emergency department lights are harsh.

Everything merges into one – curtains pulled, doctors speaking in fast, clipped tones. Someone presses gently on my abdomen and I let out a yelp. They murmur something about peritonitis, about rupture. About theatre.

Desperate and afraid, I grasp Brenda's hand. 'Don't let me die.'

'You're not dying, Sylvie,' she says calmly. 'We're going to get you sorted. I'll manage everything at home, so you don't need to worry about a thing.'

Then they wheel me away.

When I wake again, the nurse tells me it's much later in the day. My mouth feels like it's lined with sandpaper and I have a new, dull ache that runs from hip to rib and back again. There's a drain in my side and an IV in my arm. I'm foggy and sore, but I'm alive.

I say a silent prayer of thanks.

There's a small card at my bedside, written in a careful, looping hand I don't recognise.

Rest. I've got everything under control at home.

Brenda

The nurse gives me my phone and Matt calls while the ward is quiet. His voice sounds low with worry.

'Jess called and told me what happened. I'll come home. I can get someone to cover the site.'

I shift against the pillows, wincing. 'No need, Matt. Honestly. Brenda's been a dream. She's already got everything running like clockwork, and Jess is nearly back on her feet. Just focus on your work – I'm in good hands.'

I hear Matt blow out air at the end of the line and there's a short pause before he says, 'You know, Sylvie, that woman has been in our lives for five minutes and you talk about all that like it's perfectly normal. It's a bit weird to say the least.'

* * *

FRIDAY

Two days later, I come home to find the house spotless and strangely quiet.

Brenda is in the kitchen, peeling potatoes. A homemade meat pie is in the oven. Jess is on the sofa, curled around the baby with a peaceful expression on her face I haven't seen since Scarlet Mae was born.

'Hey, Mum,' Jess says. 'You look... better. Tired, but better.'

I dump my bag of medication on the floor and lower myself onto a chair, wincing as the stitches pull. 'I feel like someone's used me as a pin cushion. But I'm glad to be home. At least I know now why my stomach was so swollen and painful. I thought I'd just overdone the rich food.'

'Peritonitis can be a serious condition. You must have ignored worsening symptoms for some time, I'd say.' Brenda looks over sternly from the sink. 'I've done a bit of tidying round while you were gone. Just a few little changes. Hope you don't mind – I moved the steriliser closer to the kettle, seemed easier. And I thought the baby slept better with white noise, so I've been using my phone at nap times.'

I blink at the subtle shift. It's my kitchen. The baby routine I devised. And yet... I can't bring myself to care.

'I'll have a look through your medication as soon as I'm done with this and sort out a schedule.'

'It's fine, they've only given me a couple of—'

'Regular dosage is vital and, I'm afraid, not negotiable. I'll look at it shortly.' She turns back to the potatoes.

I roll my eyes slyly at Jess and reply, 'Whatever you say, Brenda.'

Jess nods, her voice thick. 'Brenda has been a godsend, Mum. Honestly. I don't know what we'd have done without her.'

Brenda protests, flapping the compliment away with a tea towel. But I catch the faintest flush rising in her cheeks.

The kettle clicks. The room is tidy and warm, scented with fresh coffee and toast. I close my eyes, letting it all wash over me – pain, gratitude, a quiet unease I can't yet name.

But who cares? For now, I'm just very grateful.

By Saturday afternoon, I manage to make it downstairs on my own. It feels like running a marathon, but I do it. Brenda claps her hands gently when she sees me. 'That's progress, Sylvie. You're on the mend.'

I smile, leaning on the banister. She's made chicken and vegetable soup. The laundry is folded. Scarlet Mae's nappies are stacked in tidy rows I never had time to even *think* about doing. Although I'm a fairly tidy person, the kitchen gleams in a way it hasn't in years.

But when I go to make a cup of tea, I open the wrong cupboard... twice.

'Oh!' I blink at the tin cans now on the shelf where the mugs used to live.

'Hope you don't mind, I just thought it flowed better this way,' Brenda says cheerfully. 'You always reach for the kettle first, then the mugs, then tea. So now it's all in a line, see?'

She's right. It does make sense. Still, I hesitate for half a second before I nod and say, 'Thanks. That's... helpful.'

Later, Jess mentions she's changed the baby's bottle routine slightly. 'Brenda said Scarlet Mae was taking too much milk too soon and she might sleep better if we spaced things out a bit.'

I raise an eyebrow. 'And is she sleeping better?'

Jess shrugs. 'Hard to tell. I mean, she is sleeping. And Brenda knows babies. She's really kind, Mum. I don't think I could've coped without her while you were in hospital.'

I nod because Jess is right. And neither could I cope without Brenda here now. And yet...

When Matt gets home from Newcastle, he moves to drop his keys into the wooden dish by the front door. Except the dish isn't there. It's been replaced with a floral box that matches nothing in the hallway.

'Where's the key dish?' He frowns after greeting me.

Brenda, setting the table, doesn't even look up. 'I moved it – it looked a bit big. That console table is too narrow for clutter.'

Matt glances at me, his jaw tightening. 'It's not clutter, Brenda,' he says quietly. 'We use it to keep the keys in one place, save losing them.'

She gives him a smile. 'And now you can use a nice floral box instead. You'll get used to it.'

I laugh and follow Matt into the kitchen to try and defuse the situation. 'Let it go, Matt. It's not worth arguing over. We can change everything back when I'm feeling better.'

Matt doesn't laugh or agree. He goes upstairs instead.

Later, when I'm curled on the sofa with a hot water bottle and a cup of Brenda's herbal tea, he says, 'She's helpful. I'll give her that.'

'She's been amazing,' I agree.

Matt reaches for my hand and says, 'When can I tell her we don't need her anymore?'

THIRTEEN

SYLVIE

THURSDAY

Usually, I pride myself on my stamina – juggling several things and, now, looking after my daughter and my new granddaughter. Ordinarily, I'd also have my work as a reasonably busy part-time freelance copywriter, but I'm taking a hard-earned break from that for a while. When Jess first told me she was pregnant, I knew I'd want to support her as much as possible when the baby arrived. So for six months, I took on additional jobs and saved the extra money to tide me over when I took a couple of months off. It worked perfectly and that's what I'm living on now until I start the new jobs I have booked in from January. The thought of that fills me with dread, if I'm honest. I didn't count on feeling so unsteady on my feet for so long.

Standing at the kitchen counter now to fill the kettle leaves my legs trembling, as if I've just run a five km race. My abdomen aches in a dull, persistent way, and my ribs tighten whenever I take too deep a breath.

Nearly a week after my discharge from hospital, I keep waiting to feel like my old self again. Each morning, I think today's the day I'll start to feel stronger. And each evening, I realise that even emptying the dishwasher takes too much out of me.

Brenda, with her reliable calming influence, appears early each morning like our guardian angel. She glides around the house tending to me and Jess, carrying soft fruit in a basket or a fresh bottle of homemade ginger ale. Other times it's some odd new device she claims will make caring for the baby more efficient. All that, I can cope with fine.

But Jess gave Brenda her own key for my house the night I was admitted to hospital. Now Brenda thinks it's perfectly fine to let herself in whenever she wishes. Each time I find her in the lounge, scribbling on a piece of paper or tapping away on her phone like she lives here, I tell myself it's just her conscientious nature. But there's a niggle of discomfort that it's getting a bit much.

Matt is doing his best to ignore it, but I know he hates the idea of Brenda having a key. He's tried to hide his irritation in front of me, but I catch the edge to his voice whenever her name comes up.

Part of the problem that makes it so difficult to tackle the subject of the key is the fact our arrangement is so casual. When Brenda is doing all this out of the goodness of her heart, how can I broach the subject of what is starting to feel like constant intrusion?

One morning, I look up when she brings me a cup of coffee and seize the moment.

'Brenda, you're an angel and, honestly, I don't know what we'd have done without you. But you must have things at home you have to do and—'

'There's nothing,' Brenda says firmly. 'Apart from visiting my aunt at her care home, but that's only once a week.'

'Thing is, I'd really like to give you something for the time you're putting in here. I can't afford a massive amount, but I could certainly stretch to—'

She looks horrified and interjects. 'I'm doing this as your *friend*, Sylvie, not like some kind of paid help!'

I immediately start to back-pedal, worried I've offended her. 'Of course, and you *are* a good friend. The best! It's just that... I'd hate for you to feel we're taking you for granted.'

'Never.' She folds her arms, her jaw set tight. 'I can't think of anything else I'd rather be doing. So please, not another word.'

And that was the extent of my pathetic effort to try and address Matt's concerns.

I think he's kept a bit of a distance recently because he can't stand bumping into her. That said, he's started popping in again with groceries, messages and calls me to see how I'm doing. Last night, he stayed over – first time in a while – and this morning, when he went into the kitchen in his boxers, half-asleep with his hair sticking up in every direction, he bumped into Brenda. At six-thirty, standing at the sink sterilising the baby's bottles.

The expression on his face when he comes back upstairs is priceless.

'What happened?' I grimace.

'She smiled in that odd, polite way she does. She had a derisory look at my bare chest and legs and then she said, "I'm only going to be a few minutes then I'll be out of your way," and carried on as if half-naked men in her morning routine were nothing unusual.'

I have to smile at that. It's so Brenda, but even I admit to myself it's a bit much. There's no reason for her to be over at my place so early in the morning. Apart from popping back to feed Ivor, she often doesn't go home until six or seven in the evening.

Matt emerges from the shower now, towel slung low around his hips, hair damp. I'd like him to stay the entire day, but I know he won't. He's got clients to see, and truth be told, the idea of him getting cornered by Brenda again might send him running out of here as fast as possible.

I struggle out of bed, my body complaining, and stand just in time to meet him as he's buttoning his shirt.

'I still can't believe she has a key. That's where the problem lies,' he mutters under his breath. 'You need to talk to her, Sylvie. If we don't set boundaries, she'll be moving in with you. I mean, she's already here from dawn until dusk.'

After the disastrous mention of paying her, I decided to purchase Brenda a wellness basket from The White Company by way of a small thank you. I'm not going to need her help for that much longer and a gift will mark the end of what has swiftly become a set routine.

I try a gentle tease because Matt is gruff, even though his eyes are kind with concern. 'I'm still recovering, you know. Brenda's helping with cooking, cleaning and looking after Jess and Scarlet Mae... She's doing the grunt work so I can lie around feeling sorry for myself.' I nudge him lightly in the ribs, and he rolls his eyes.

'Yes, well, you can always say you only need a day or two more, then it'll be thanks but no thanks. You can't keep her on indefinitely.'

'I know. I just feel bad, like saying now I'm feeling better, I don't want her around.'

'You can let her down gently,' Matt says. 'Just mention in passing that you're doing much better, so she can hand back the key. Because if you don't, trust me, she'll keep creeping further in. She'll be rearranging the entire house next; your life won't be your own.'

I'm not entirely sure why it bothers Matt this much. It's not as if he hasn't got his own privacy and space two doors down that Brenda never infringes on.

'Maybe you should sell up and move in with me. That would solve it.'

Where did that come from? The words are out of my mouth before I can stop them.

'What?' Matt falters. It's pretty clear he's not keen on the idea.

I laugh a little weakly. 'I just think this might be a good time for us to review our living arrangements. Is that so bad?'

He shrugs. 'This is probably not the right time to be thinking about making big changes,' he says.

'OK.' I shrug, keen to get the conversation back on track. 'Brenda's lonely, I think. Maybe she just likes being needed and making herself useful. Some people are like that.'

He narrows his eyes. 'We're not the local community centre. If she wants to be needed, there are charities and people who might appreciate her time. I'm just saying, Sylvie – I'd deal with it, or you'll regret it.'

I raise a brow, trying to look reprimanding. 'Is that my lecture done for today?'

He steps close and sets a soft kiss on my forehead. 'Yes, that's me done. I'll leave you to practise your tactful approach.'

Then he grabs his coat and phone, heading out with a final wave.

When he's gone, I look around. The house feels a bit less like mine.

Brenda's presence lingers in every corner. She's already reorganised the baby's feeding schedule to reflect her increasing appetite, introduced a new system for bottle sterilisation, and even made some adjustments to the cupboard layout in the kitchen, 'to make it safer and easier for you'.

It's flattering to see how thoroughly she wants to support me. I find it sweet that she puts sticky notes near the changing station, reminding me where fresh wipes and nappies are kept, or telling me how many scoops of formula go in which bottle. It's all so efficient.

Yet something about her note-taking raises the hair on the

back of my neck. Yesterday, when I was trudging out of the bedroom, I glimpsed her in the hallway tapping away at her phone, a slight furrow in her brow. When she saw me, she pocketed it quickly. I shrugged it off at the time – maybe she was just checking her shopping list – but it's happened a few times now. She jots things down on scraps of paper, or she makes voice notes when she thinks I'm not listening: 'Sylvie used a hand sanitiser brand she didn't like at 11:15... told her not to use that brand again... small rash on baby's neck at 14:20...' It's all rather odd.

Nevertheless, I keep telling myself Brenda is thorough, that's all. She probably wants to get everything right. She might just be the type who scribbles reminders of her day, ensuring she's not missing some detail of care or housekeeping. I mean, the baby is thriving. Scarlet Mae's bottles are always washed, dried and lined up like miniature soldiers. The fridge is never out of milk or fresh vegetables. The bins are emptied like clockwork. She has made my life easier, though part of me is uneasy that I'm becoming so reliant on her.

It suddenly occurs to me it's probably not fair on Brenda, despite her offering so much help and turning down payment. I still feel like I'm taking advantage. I resolve to google a local agency to see about getting a bit of support for a few weeks.

A week and a half into my recovery, I manage to feel strong enough to walk a full lap around the small garden. The sun is warm against my arms, and the breeze lifts my hair, reminding me that life is more than the cramped rooms in which I've been lying listlessly.

Matt comes by later in the afternoon, in a stressed mood, complaining that Brenda gave him a funny look when he arrived.

'She practically asked me for ID before letting me step inside,' he says, exasperated. 'It's like she's decided *I'm* the intruder in your home, not her. Doesn't that strike you as a bit odd?'

I promise him I'll speak to her when she returns from the shops. 'Let me handle this. I'll be tactful, but firm,' I say. 'I'm going to tell her I'm back on my feet now and don't need round-the-clock care.'

He nods but doesn't look entirely convinced. We have a light meal together, but I can tell he's uneasy, glancing around as though expecting Brenda to pop up from behind the sofa.

He hasn't mentioned my comment about moving in here again and Nige's motorbike is getting to be a daily sight parked outside his house. I'm going to tackle him about that soon. If I stop Brenda coming here as much, maybe he needs to speak to Nige about his too-frequent visits. Seems to me Matt's friend is also taking advantage and yet he can't seem to see it.

After Matt leaves, I brace myself. I wait in the lounge, the baby dozing in my lap, Brenda's hand-crocheted blanket half-slipping to the floor.

When Brenda reappears, it's with a flourish – bag rustling, eyes alight. 'I've got something marvellous to show you,' she announces. Her voice is so enthusiastic that I hardly know how to reply. I stand, placing the baby in her basket.

My body still aches in small twinges, but I stretch out my spine, trying to summon some confidence. I reach for the gift basket. 'Before you begin, Brenda, I need to—'

She talks over me in a cheerful rush: 'You know how you were complaining about having to rummage around for condiments in the fridge when you have your hands full? Well, I've labelled everything, grouped them by type and frequency of use. I've also reorganised the cupboard above the sink – thought it might be easier to keep all the breakfast things in one place. I've started a container system, so the cereal and tea are easier to access without spillage. Look, I took pictures on my phone before and after – so satisfying.'

She's brandishing her phone, scrolling through images. I see a photograph of my fridge in its normal state: a tangle of jars, half-empty containers, the odd wilted vegetable. Then the next shot: neat rows of labelled boxes and small baskets. An entire section devoted to baby bits. It's alarmingly efficient. It dawns on me that, in my entire adult life, I've never had such a perfectly organised kitchen. All I can manage is a quiet, 'Wow.'

Brenda beams. 'You see? Now, you won't waste any precious energy searching for that half jar of pesto or a stray pot of yoghurt. Everything's got its place. It's like a miniature library for your food.'

As she says that, I glance over at my granddaughter, who stirs in her cot, letting out a squeak. A wave of gratitude mingles with a prickling sense of unease. My own house is becoming unfamiliar, reshaped by Brenda and her relentless helpfulness.

The conversation I'd planned to have, a diplomatic, 'I'm fine now, I don't need quite so much help, and by the way, can I have my key back?', suddenly seems churlish, even cruel.

I hand over the basket. 'This is just a small gift to say how grateful I am for your help,' I say.

Brenda's face drops and she doesn't take it from me. 'That makes it sound like you don't need my help anymore! We both know that's not true.'

'I didn't mean to—'

Jess steps into the kitchen, all bright smiles, and sees the fridge rearrangement. 'Oh!' she says, eyes flicking over the neatly labelled sections. 'Brenda, this is fantastic. You're an angel. I need you to come and sort out my flat! You've done wonders here.'

Brenda almost bursts with pleasure but instantly dampens it down and gives a modest shrug. 'I'm just doing what I can to lighten the load for your mum, Jess.'

I watch them chatting. Jess effusive with praise, Brenda

standing gracefully, putting her phone down to show Jess the intricacies of her new fridge system.

My moment to intervene is lost. I can't bring myself to say, 'Listen, perhaps it's time you went back to your own life.' It would be like hurling an insult at a saint. I set the basket aside.

But a small flicker draws my eye: Brenda's phone screen is still lit up on the countertop. I notice a set of notes, or perhaps a to-do list. I inch closer and see my own name alongside Jess's and Scarlet Mae's. It's something about me, the baby's name, an exact time for a feed, next weigh-in date, and then my eyes rest on Matt's name and something titled 'Observations'. My heart does a little wobble, but then she turns to pick up the device and locks the screen.

I can't be sure of what I saw. Part of me wants to snatch the phone from her hand and read the rest. Another part of me thinks I'm imagining things. Why would Brenda be observing Matt?

I swallow my unease. The baby begins to fuss, so I scoop her up, nuzzling her close. My breath grows shallow and tight again, the ache in my chest resuming. Jess and Brenda keep talking about containers, about how I might want to rearrange my bedroom next.

The baby calms in my arms, but my own mind doesn't. In that moment, I see Brenda's pleasant smile for what it is: polished on the outside, but concealing something that doesn't sit right with me.

I try to focus on the present, on how she has genuinely helped me. Every day is easier now because of her devotion, and I can't ignore her good intentions. But I also can't ignore Matt's warning. He's right that she's insinuating herself ever deeper into my daily life. And from the glimpses I keep catching, she's capturing everything – my routines, my preferences, the baby's little habits – like a meticulous – and obsessive – collector of data.

Jess throws her arms around me, oblivious to my tension. 'I'm so glad you're feeling a bit better, Mum. Brenda's done wonders, hasn't she? You'll never want to go back to chaos again.' She winks at me, stepping away to help Brenda admire a row of neatly labelled plastic tubs.

I force a smile. 'Yes. Life's been easier, that's for sure.' The words taste hollow, but I try to keep the uneasiness out of my voice.

In the back of my mind, I imagine what Matt will say if I ring him now: 'This is your chance to tell her or regret it.' But my tongue is tied by the sense that Brenda will see me as ungrateful, and Jess will see me as petty.

So, I do what I've done for days. I keep quiet. I watch them both admiring Brenda's transformations. And I think, maybe tomorrow, after a good sleep, I'll find the right words to ease Brenda out of her caretaker role. Perhaps I'll practise in the mirror. Smile sweetly and say, 'Thank you for everything, but I can manage on my own now,' and that'll be enough.

But as I watch Brenda flick to her notes again, a curious glint in her eye, I suspect it won't be quite that simple. My stomach twists and a new thought creeps into my mind, so unexpected it makes me shiver: what if she doesn't want to go? Because from the way she's logging my life, it's as though she's settling in for the long haul. And for the first time since returning home, I realise I might not be able to fix this with a friendly smile and an apologetic wave of the hand.

I silently promise myself I'll deal with this, one way or another, before it spirals out of my control. I just need to wait for the right moment.

FOURTEEN

BRENDA

The sparrows are back, flitting haphazardly in the hedge by the bins. With the window cracked open for air, she can hear them, too. Reckless and loud for things so small.

Brenda watches them scatter, their tiny wings slapping the air when a car door slams on the street. She's standing in the kitchen, a small piece of crust from her sausage roll balanced on her palm. A reward for Ivor if he takes his joint care pill without fuss.

'Come on, petal, open up,' she tells him, tapping his small jaw. 'No drama today.'

Ivor blinks, his tongue stubborn behind his teeth. Brenda sighs and crouches, gently prising his mouth open. He allows it, grudging but trusting, and the pill goes in, down with the bribe. She ruffles the thick fur on his head, feels the damp warmth of him. 'Good boy.'

She sits in her armchair, enjoying a clear view of Sylvie's house and front garden. Brenda's shoulders ache – too many hours tidying, folding, helping prevent Sylvie's life from falling apart. But she likes being needed. Thrives on it, if she's honest. It's a sensation she hasn't had since... well, since before the Inquiry. Since before the patient in room four and the family with the obstinate solicitor and the front-page headline in the *Daily Mail*.

She shuts that door fast and turns her eyes again to the street.

A slim figure in tight jeans and high-heeled ankle boots is striding up Sylvie's short front path, tapping at her phone screen. *Kendra*. Brenda feels her stomach clench. That young woman has the energy of a wasp in a jar. She's all edge, all performance. Brenda knows the type: the first to crumble when there's a problem.

She watches as Kendra knocks. Rings the bell. She's twitchy and impatient while she waits. Her wide grin appears too quickly when Jess opens the door and they hug.

Brenda murmurs to herself, 'She'll drag Jess into something messy, mark my words.' Her breath clouds the glass.

Movement catches her attention a few doors up. Matt's house. His friend – *Nige*, isn't it? – is on the doorstep, clapping Matt on the shoulder. Nige wears his red and black motorbike leathers like a second skin. They are scuffed and shiny in places, the smell of engine oil and cigarette smoke practically visible. He's too old for all that with his hair already thinning on top, his eyes too pale. Brenda doesn't trust pale eyes.

Nige saunters over to the bike, his helmet under one arm. Brenda narrows her eyes. He's been around there too often lately. Sometimes until very late. Once, she's sure, he went in and didn't come out again until morning. She remembers because she got up to get a glass of water and saw his bike, its iridescent sheen glinting under the streetlamp like a beetle's shell.

Matt stays at the door, one hand still on the frame, watching Nige go. Then he does something odd – small, but it causes her skin to prickle. He leans down and lifts the pot that's full of weeds beside the steps.

Brenda stares.

He's not watering it. Not moving it out the way. Just checking underneath it.

He tilts it. Puts it back in its original spot.

She murmurs, 'What are you hiding under there?'

The pot looks ordinary enough – green ceramic, nothing special. But Brenda's spine tingles because she's seen that kind of motion before. In the hospital. Patients hiding contraband, nurses with secrets. You learn to read the small quirks of human behaviour.

Matt steps back inside, closing the door behind him. Brenda stays at the window. Thinking.

She should be resting, but her mind refuses to quieten. It's always noisy in her head these days. 'Residual hypervigilance', that's what the therapist called it. A fancy term for not knowing how to relax. For seeing danger where maybe there isn't any. Or sometimes when there is.

And in Brenda's book, it's not paranoia if you happen to be right.

FIFTEEN

SYLVIE

SATURDAY

I pause halfway down the hallway, hearing soft voices in the kitchen. Brenda's tone is cheerful in that practised way of hers, and I know Matt is in there too, although he's oddly quiet.

I brace myself, because every time they cross paths these days, it feels like I'm caught between two opposing fronts. Edging closer to the door, I see Brenda at the sink, filling a glass jug with water. Scarlet Mae seems content in her padded floor pod and Matt stands by the fridge, arms folded and a faint scowl behind his polite smile.

He's brought a bag of groceries, I notice – a sure sign he's come over intending to help out. But the bag sits unopened on the counter, because Brenda has only just finished labelling neatly arranged tubs of fruit, vegetables and leftover casserole.

Instead of leaving her to it, Matt has decided to stand and wait. Rather passive-aggressively, it has to be said.

'I've made sure lunch is sorted for you, Sylvie,' she announces when I walk in. 'There's chicken and some rice that's still fresh.'

Matt is careful not to glare outright at Brenda, but he can't mask his irritation as easily from me. I can almost feel the waves of annoyance rolling off him. He probably came here expecting to roll up his sleeves, to make Jess and me some lunch, or even tidy the lounge. Instead, Brenda has everything 'under control' again. She even used that very phrase ten minutes ago, when I was apologising for not taking a call from Kendra.

'Don't worry, I'll deal with it, Sylvie. I've got everything under control.'

Matt hands me the groceries, a forced casualness in his expression. 'I got these for you, in case you were running low,' he says. Then he glances sideways at Brenda, as if daring her to interrupt.

I check inside the bag. He got the nice seeded loaf I like and some coffee beans. Bananas – not too ripe, just how I prefer them.

'Thank you,' I say. His eyes warm for a moment, but he still looks tense. Then he sets his phone and keys on the table. A statement that says he intends to stay for a while.

Brenda's calm presence and her tidy domain seem to shrink the space. She carries the jug of water to the table, placing it next to a pair of clean, long glasses. 'I didn't know you'd be dropping by, Matt. I could have made enough lunch for four of us.'

I sense a mild reproach in her words, or perhaps I'm imagining it. Matt picks up on it too; I can tell by the tightening in his jaw. He shrugs. 'I just wanted to see how Sylvie was doing, if she needed anything. After all, she's meant to be taking it easy since—'

'I'm so glad you came over,' I cut in, trying not to let friction build. 'I'm still quite sore, if I'm honest. I don't know what I'd do without both of you.'

But Matt isn't fooled by my attempt to smooth things over. He steps close to me and lays a hand lightly on my shoulder. He glances at my face, searching for signs of how I really feel. I see concern there, but also a question.

Why are you still letting Brenda run the show?

A slight wobble in my knees reminds me how physically fragile I still am, how my body isn't bouncing back as fast as I'd hoped. Some days I feel almost back to normal, then the next, I'm too tired to pick up the baby without my arms trembling.

Brenda has kept the house going, which is a relief. I try not to think about how I've noticed Matt coming around less and less. Or how, last night, I lay awake wondering why he hasn't stayed over in days.

Brenda takes the grocery bag from my hands in one swift movement. She's so practical, always tidying and fixing.

'Let me put these away for you,' she says. She gives Matt a smile. 'You look tired yourself. Working too hard? That friend of yours, the one on the motorbike, doesn't seem to have a job to go to.'

He shrugs, ignoring the question as Brenda heads for the cupboards.

'Maybe we can have a talk in the living room, Sylvie?' He casts a glance over his shoulder, looking for some privacy. I nod, and together we move out of the kitchen, leaving Brenda behind.

She hums quietly as we leave, unpacking the groceries with her back to us. Scarlet Mae gazes up at the ceiling, her tiny fists pumping the air.

'Brenda, did you want me to take the baby?'

'No, no,' she says without looking at me. 'She's fine in here with me. You go and have your little talk.'

In the living room, Matt lowers his voice. 'When the hell is she leaving?'

I blink, too exhausted to pretend ignorance. 'She usually heads off after lunch or before Jess and Ed get back from their appointments or—'

'I don't mean today. I mean permanently. When are you going to tell her you don't need her round here twenty-four-seven?'

I swallow. 'I'm going to tell her; I just need a little time. Honestly, she's a godsend in so many ways, Matt. Without her, I'd struggle.'

The truth is, the last thing I want to do is to offend Brenda after all the help she's given us. Is *still* giving us. She's just a nice lady, albeit a bit too bossy at times.

Matt rubs the back of his neck. 'She's everywhere all at once, Sylvie. Sometimes I feel like an intruder, or a child who's not allowed to do anything. You've let her set up camp here, and now she's overshadowing everyone else, including me. It's not on.'

I'm not sure what to say. I feel a bit attacked, but I want Matt to understand that although I'd like him around here more, it's not that simple. I still feel drained, and with Jess and Scarlet Mae still here, Brenda's willing efficiency means I can rest. It also means I'm not in danger of looking like a frail, older woman next to my energised, younger husband. I don't think Matt would ever view me like that, but it pays not to get complacent.

'I find her help useful just at the moment,' I say quietly. 'You've no idea how weak I still feel – my arms ache, my stomach feels swollen and bruised. Brenda sees to the baby, keeps me and Jess fed. Nige is always round at yours and your work seems so busy, so you only pop in now and again. Brenda is here day in, day out and besides, it's only for a short time.'

Matt flinches as if I've slapped him. 'So you'd rather have Brenda play nanny than ask me for help? I'd be here every day if you wanted me to be. But it feels like I'm not needed now. It's a good job Nige is around for me to hang out with.' There's a rawness to his voice that tugs at my guilt.

Before I can respond, I hear the baby start to fuss in the kitchen. Then Brenda's swift footsteps.

Matt exhales and stands up. 'We'll talk later, yeah?'

I nod, though there's a lump in my throat. We're suddenly out of sync, he and I. It's like we're dancing to two different beats, and at this rate, we'll end up stepping on each other's toes.

He goes back to the kitchen to get his phone, and a few minutes later, he's gone.

I feel the echo of his absence as the door slams shut.

While I rest on the sofa, Brenda glides about – quiet, efficient, infuriating. When I get up later to make some tea, I find the herbs are back in alphabetical order. The armchair has been moved a foot to the left. A sticky note has appeared on the fridge: 'Check milk date – opened yesterday!'

I wonder how she thinks we managed before she assumed control.

Matt's voice echoes in my head and I say carefully, 'I'd like to keep things where they are, Brenda. We're settling again now Jess is moving back home and she'll need her key back, by the way. I'm hoping to get everything back to normal.'

'I only meant to help,' she says quietly. 'You've had a lot on and I think the changes I made are for the better.'

'Yes, but... I like the kitchen the way it was before, Brenda.'

She gives a small, regretful smile. 'You know, some well-worn routines aren't always the most efficient and should be reviewed. I suppose it's just habit now, for me at least. I can leave it, if it really bothers you.'

It *does* bother me. But suddenly I feel like I've just told a charity worker to stop being so generous. She leaves the room and when she comes back in, she has Jess's door key in her hand. She places it on the table without another word.

She's so calm, so unfailingly helpful, I almost wonder if I'm the one being unreasonable.

That night, guilt creeps in and I stew over it. Her insistence. Her soft, polite pushbacks. The way she always seems to know best and gets what she wants.

It's almost as if she's done this before.

SIXTEEN

NOTTINGHAMSHIRE POLICE

MONDAY

Rain needles the windscreen as Brewster guides the car into the quiet road in West Bridgford. The houses around here are mostly substantial, 1950s red-brick detached with neat driveways set in tree-lined enclaves. Outside number 182, an orange porch light glows against the grey afternoon, a silent beacon of someone still waiting.

Brewster turns off the engine. Neither of them moves at first.

'I can't say I'm looking forward to this,' Helena murmurs.

'They offered us tea last time,' Brewster says eventually, his voice low. 'Neither of us drank it.'

Helena nods. She remembers the silence between them – the way Ellie's mother had stared out of the window like she might will her missing daughter to appear at the end of the road.

'We'll not stay too long,' she says. 'I've already explained over the phone that sadly there's no new news. That we're just revisiting the facts after your own appeal.'

They get out of the car and are met at the door by Ellie's

father, a man who looks like he's lived a lot longer than the fifty-three years listed on his file. Helena's seen it before. The way grief can take someone by the collar and shake the life out of them. His face is grey, his cardigan is buttoned wrong, and his eyes – red-rimmed but dry – flick between the detectives as if, despite her courtesy call, he's still hoping they might come with answers.

'Come in,' he says, voice resigned. 'Thanks for coming to see us again.'

Inside, the house smells of pungent lemon floor cleaner and burned toast. Helena steps around a pair of pink furry slippers abandoned in the hallway.

Ellie's mum is on the sofa, her knees drawn up like she's trying to disappear into herself. She stands when she sees them, tucking a tissue into the sleeve of her cardigan.

'Hello, Mrs Walker,' Helena says, holding out her hand. 'I'm sorry we're not here in better circumstances.'

'Has there been nothing... since our appeal?'

The woman takes her hand, managing a polite smile that crumples almost immediately. 'We were hoping you might have something new... after our appeal.'

'Mr and Mrs Walker,' Brewster says gently, 'thank you for seeing us. We're here to go back over a few things. You'd be surprised, but sometimes looking again with fresh eyes helps something new to surface.'

Mrs Walker nods, but it's clear she's not holding out much hope.

Mr Walker offers tea, which they decline. They all sit. The television is on but muted – a quiz show with a laughing host whose comical gestures feel obscene given the reason they're here.

'How are you both bearing up?' Helena says. A silly question, some might say. But she is genuinely concerned and hopes that comes through.

'We're both still off work,' Mr Walker says. 'Neither of us can think straight and we don't want to go out in case we miss a call from you.'

'Or in case Ellie comes home,' his wife adds softly. 'You sometimes hear of that, don't you? When all hope is lost, the missing person suddenly appears back at the door.'

There's a long silence then. The room is warm to the point of being stifling, but Helena resists the urge to pull at her collar. Brewster sits beside her, unusually still, his hands clasped around a notebook he hasn't opened yet.

'Ellie was doing well at nursing college,' Helena begins. 'One of her lecturers said she was an incredibly focused student.'

Mr Walker's expression lifts a little. 'She was very diligent. All she's ever wanted to be is a nurse, you see. Almost from the time she could say the word.'

His wife adds, 'She used to dress her teddy bears in makeshift bandages and perform surgeries with plastic cutlery.' A ghost of a smile tugs at her mouth, then vanishes. 'I always wanted to be a nurse. I've loved being on the journey with her.'

'Her gran was very ill when Ellie was young. Cancer,' Mr Walker says. 'We looked after her here for her last year. Ellie used to sit by the bed and hold her hand for hours. I think... it had a big effect on her. Gave her this sense of duty. A purpose.'

Helena nods slowly. There is something quietly gutting about a child absorbing pain and translating it into compassion that can help make the world a better place.

'And did she have anyone close outside her family? A boyfriend, perhaps?'

'Oh no,' Mrs Walker says immediately. 'She didn't have the time. Ellie's studies came first. Always. She never liked school, but she had a close group of friends at college. They had a group chat where they'd send each other cat memes. But boys? No.' Her expression darkens. 'Of course, her phone is still missing.'

'We used to tease her,' Mr Walker adds. 'Said she was married to the NHS before she'd even graduated. No room for boys. Not for Ellie.'

'Would it be possible to see her bedroom again?' Helena asks.

They're led upstairs. Ellie's bedroom is just the same as the day she left it. Neat, unfussy, nothing out of place. The duvet is pulled taut and smooth, textbooks lined up by subject, colour-coded sticky notes in a little acrylic organiser as if Ellie had just stepped out of the door. On the dresser, a framed photo of her and two other girls, all in nursing uniforms, beaming with ID badges round their necks.

'She's been known to sleep with her planner under her pillow,' Mrs Walker says, trying to smile. 'Said it helped her remember things. Revision by osmosis, she reckoned.'

An electronic keyboard on foldable legs stands at the end of the bed. Helena nods to it. 'She enjoyed playing?'

'Just a hobby.' Mr Walker sniffs. 'She hadn't played it for ages as far as I know.'

Helena moves closer to the desk and peers at a neat stack of notebooks, each labelled in crisp block capitals. A page marked with a pink ribbon sits open on the latest – patient care notes, written in careful handwriting. Beside it, a pen. Uncapped. As though she'd just stepped out of the room for a second. All this stuff, including Ellie's laptop, had been inspected by the team.

A peeling, coloured sticker on the lid of the laptop catches Helena's eye. She steps closer and sees it features a picture of a cartoon girl with the fading words:

When you say yes, make sure you're not saying no to yourself.

Helena frowns and repeats the words silently in her head. She takes out her phone and takes a quick snap of it before they leave the room.

Back downstairs, the mood feels heavier still. Mrs Walker

gets out the photo albums like she did last time and shows them pictures of Ellie graduating from toddler to student nurse.

Helena's heart is heavy. There's nothing new here that's going to further the case. After another ten minutes of stilted conversation and awkward silences, she exchanges a glance with Brewster and he stands.

'Well, we must get off. Thank you for seeing us again.'

'I've said this before, I know, but if anything at all comes to mind, please let us know,' Helena says, handing over her card. 'No matter how small or insignificant it may seem.'

Mrs Walker nods, but her eyes are empty with disappointment. Her husband walks them to the door. He doesn't shake hands this time, just gives a small nod as they leave. Like he's trying to be brave for someone else's benefit.

Back in the car, they drive in silence for a few minutes. The rain has eased to a misty drizzle, turning the windscreen into soft-focus glass.

'Still nothing,' Brewster says eventually. 'Feels like hitting the same wall again and again.'

Helena exhales. 'There are no threads for us to pull at. No boyfriend. No signs of struggle at the scene. No bloody motive and nothing to appease the super.'

Brewster grumbles, 'I'm starving.'

Helena glances at him.

'What?' he says. 'Since I've come off the boiled eggs diet, I'm hungry as a horse. I deserve a hearty lunch after all that suffering... or at least a sandwich.'

'Fine. Seeing as it's nearly lunchtime, pull in somewhere. I'll call the office and see if anything's come in while you stuff your face.'

They stop at a grim little petrol station just off the ring road and about a mile from the Walkers' house. Helena waits in the car while Brewster ducks inside.

She calls the office, but there are no messages.

Brewster is longer in there than expected. When he finally returns, he doesn't have a sandwich, and his expression is oddly alert.

'You're not going to believe this,' he says, climbing in, his expression serious. 'The cashier – an older woman – she saw my warrant card when I took out my wallet and decides to mention how she saw the missing girl here. Ellie Walker. The day before she vanished. Says she's certain it was her.'

Helena sits up straighter. 'Here?'

'Right here. This exact place. She recognised her from the posters. But get this: she says she came in with a man in his mid to late twenties. Brown hair, tall, solid build. They bought snacks and soft drinks.'

'But... why on earth hasn't she mentioned this before?'

'She said she rang it in!' Brewster blows out air in frustration.

'Grey's going to pummel us for this...'

Brewster nods. 'The woman said Ellie looked comfortable with him although, oddly, she thought he seemed slightly awkward as if he didn't want to be there. Cashier assumed it was her boyfriend. The guy paid. Ellie laughed at something he said and he gave her a funny look and then they left together.'

Helena's mind kicks into gear. 'Do they have CCTV?'

Brewster frowns. 'Old system. Overwritten every forty-eight hours. She didn't realise she should've told the manager to save it just in case.'

Helena swears under her breath. 'Did she say what day this was?'

'She's almost certain it was the Thursday. The twenty-first. That's the day before the last known sighting of Ellie leaving college on her bicycle.'

Helena stares out at the blurred trees across the road. 'She wouldn't be the first young woman to hide the fact she had a boyfriend from her parents.'

'Too right,' Brewster says grimly. 'She might well have been secretly seeing this guy.'

For the first time in weeks, something shifts inside Helena. It's not much. A ripple of hope, not a wave. But it's enough.

'OK, let's ring it in and get her statement,' Helena says. 'And see if she remembers anything else – accent, car, clothing, anything. Then call digital forensics. Ask them to check mast connections for Ellie's phone again. Just in case.'

Brewster nods, already scribbling in his notebook.

As Helena pulls back onto the road, her mind buzzes. They might not know who the man is. But the point is, he exists. He's real and he was with Ellie the day before she vanished and he hasn't come forward voluntarily.

'Someone else, somewhere, must have seen them together,' Helena says, thinking aloud.

Finally, this case doesn't feel like it's disappearing into fog. Instead, it feels like something just slipped out of the mist – a beacon they can follow.

SEVENTEEN

He peels the jacket away and sets it aside. Then there's her cardigan. A pale-green thing, bobbled on the sleeves. It smells faintly of her – coconut shampoo, maybe. Or soap.

Nothing too perfumed. Practical. He likes that.

Her top is short-sleeved. He runs a hand down her forearm, tracing the pale skin with the back of his fingers. Her warmth. The softness. There's a freckle on her wrist... a small one, like a dot made with a biro. A secret thing. A detail others might not know about.

He doesn't go further. Not tonight. There's no need. These things take time and trust must be built. Strong foundations are what makes it last.

He rises, opens the small cabinet by the window and pulls out the first aid tin. A flannel, dampened in the sink, cleans the nasty graze on her elbow. She doesn't flinch. Doesn't even stir.

He wraps a loose bandage round it. Not because it needs it, but he wants to and because the act matters somehow.

Caring. That's what sets him apart.

He changes her shoes for a pair of thick socks – grey, woollen and warm. She'll be grateful when she wakes. Then he tucks the blanket up to her waist, leaves her arms free. She won't like feeling trapped, he thinks, and there's no need for it, either. Not yet.

He moves to the corner of the room, retrieves the black notebook from the drawer.

It's well-thumbed, the pages dog-eared. Names written in a neat hand:

Zara – too loud. Too difficult to contain.

Jodie – no fixed pattern. Risky.

Holly – strong-willed. Too much damage already done.

Then, at the bottom of the page, in red ink:

Ellie – steady. Kind. Ideal.

He flips to the next page. Notes in tidy bullet points:

· Lives at home with both parents

· Student nurse – final year

· Works Saturdays at vet surgery – on her feet all day

· Cycles everywhere. Routine rarely changes

· Gentle temperament. Lovely smile.

He closes the book and places it beside the lamp. He wrote her just like one of the others, as if he didn't know her at all. It helped with his focus and it's all part of the thrill. Just like they agreed.

For now, it's her. Just her.

It's always been about her.

He pulls the chair closer to the bed and sits. Watches the slow rise and fall of her chest. Her short, clean hair gives her an elfin look.

He doesn't need his music now. The room hums with quiet.

Tomorrow, they'll begin properly. They'll talk and he'll explain everything. Answer her questions.

Oh, there'll be tears. And she might try to leave. He'll say all the usual things to try and calm her down.

But in time, Ellie will come to see that this is where she belongs.

He's waited a long time.

Now he must help her to understand.

EIGHTEEN

SYLVIE

Mid-afternoon, Jess wanders out of the spare bedroom. Her hair is tied in a loose bun and she's wearing her faded, brushed-cotton M&S pyjamas. She looks physically healthier now – her eyes have lost that deep shadowed look, and she's not moving like every step is a painful effort.

But there is a hollowness in her expression that worries me more than any physical ailment.

Brenda hovers close, offering a blanket for Jess's lap on the sofa, a cup of chamomile tea. Jess sips it, half-lost in thought. I try to catch her eye. We used to share everything, my daughter and I: jokes about terrible reality TV, confessions about junk food binges. The list goes on. Now, I see her turning to Brenda for even the simplest conversation. Only last night, I overheard them quietly discussing baby sleep routines, something Jess and I used to pore over together when she was still pregnant. That stung a bit more than I care to admit.

'You feeling OK?' I ask Jess, sliding down next to her on the sofa. She shrugs, her gaze drifting to a spot on the wall. A day ago, I mentioned Kendra wanting to drop by again, and Brenda made a point of telling me how Jess needs calm, how an extra visitor – particularly someone unpredictable like Kendra – might tire her out.

Jess didn't object. She just agreed, as if Brenda's word was final.

'I'm just tired, Mum,' Jess murmurs, setting the tea aside but still not looking at me. 'Actually, Ed and I were talking... we're thinking it might be time for me to head back home to the flat.'

'Already?' I try not to sound alarmed, but I can't hide it completely. 'Ed's sessions at the studio are done?'

She nods. 'He's finished his current project. And he's taking a bit of time off so we can sort ourselves out, have some real family time at home. Don't get me wrong, I'm grateful for your support, Mum, but I miss my own space. And Scarlet Mae needs to learn to settle in her own nursery.'

I want to point out how worn out she still looks, how that light in her eyes is missing, but I hold my tongue. I glance at Brenda, who's tidying cushions as if her life depends on it.

'If you're sure,' I say carefully. 'But I hope you know you can stay as long as you like.'

'I do know.' Jess glances at Brenda, then back to me. 'Thanks to you and Brenda, I'm better now. Physically at least. I just need to get back home to some normality, I think.' She leans forward, picking at the edge of a cushion. 'I do appreciate every-thing. Sorry if I've shocked you by saying it.'

I rest a hand on Jess's knee. She doesn't look up. Brenda's phone pings in her apron pocket, and she steps away, murmuring something about checking on the baby. Jess and I sit in silence for a moment. I reach for my phone too, clicking it on out of habit.

It's been weeks since they found any concrete lead on the young woman who vanished. The local news app updates: there's talk of a vigil, volunteer search teams forming again.

Jess notices my frown. 'What is it?'

I pass the phone for her to read the details. She scans the article, her eyes sliding fast across the screen. When she hands it back, her lips tighten. 'What's happening around here?'

I shake my head, flick off the phone screen and place it face down on the coffee table.

People are spooked, obviously. Neighbours are on edge, double-locking their doors. There's talk of curfews and the police continue to urge vigilance.

Jess stares at the wall, biting her lip. She looks as though she can't imagine stepping outside with these rumours swirling.

Brenda returns, carrying Scarlet Mae. She has her nestled in one arm, patting her back in a gentle rhythmic motion.

'She's being a bit fussy this afternoon,' she says, her voice calm and controlled. She eyes the phone on the table. 'Doesn't like her feed.'

'No news on Ellie Walker,' I say faintly, setting aside my phone. 'There's so much speculation online. People ought to give some thought to her poor parents.'

Brenda looks startled. 'Such dreadful business. Best to stay indoors, Jess, whenever possible. You need rest anyway.'

Jess nods obediently. I imagine Matt would say that her suggestion – staying inside, letting Brenda manage visitors – plays into the pattern we're already caught in. The sense that the outside world is dangerous, and inside we have Brenda, the unstoppable caregiver, so no one else is needed.

I feel a pang of sympathy for my daughter, seeing her eyes drop to the floor. She thinks she's making the right call, returning home to Ed, but I can't help imagining how lonely she'll be if she's still feeling low. At least here, I can keep watch over her and Scarlet Mae. Offer a shoulder to cry on if she needs it.

'We'll start packing up my stuff tomorrow, I think,' Jess says softly as if she's read my mind. 'Ed says we can load the car with essentials and then come back for bigger things later, once I feel up to it.'

The room feels stifling. Brenda stands by the window, outlined by the afternoon light. She murmurs gently to the baby. Everyone else is fracturing a little: Matt, me, Jess. But Brenda is rock steady. And that means we all bend around her almost without thinking.

Outside, on the street, a neighbour passes, walking a dog. It's just about as ordinary a sight as they come, but it makes me think about the missing woman. Our usually peaceful suburb has become a place of caution and half-locked doors.

I glance over at Brenda, carefully draping the blanket over Jess. Then I stare down at my own hands. My left ring finger trembles slightly, and I clench it, feeling my smooth, gold wedding ring and forcing myself to breathe steadily.

Everything feels slightly off – Matt's frustration, Jess's gloom, the creeping fear in the community. Brenda might have everything under control in this household, but outside these walls, the world is unravelling in ways none of us understand.

And I'm not entirely sure which is more unsettling: the thought of that unknown danger lurking beyond the safety of our home, or the growing certainty that I no longer have the final say over what happens inside it.

NINETEEN

The front door rattles. I know it's Matt before I even hear the key. He enters quietly, like he's entering someone else's house. Like it's not his. Not ours.

Even though we live apart, we've always felt at home in each other's property.

'Morning,' he says, holding up a brown paper bag. He's wearing that navy jumper I like, sleeves pushed up, fresh-faced. He looks... well. Like he's had a good sleep, eaten a proper breakfast. *Rested.* Not something I can say for myself.

I try a smile. 'You're out bright and early.'

'I heard Brenda mention yesterday she'd be out a couple of hours taking her cat to the vet. I thought I'd seize the moment.'

He kisses my cheek – not as warm and lingering as usual – and brushes past me, moving towards the kitchen. I follow slowly, my hips stiff, legs still sore from yesterday's short walk. I shouldn't be this tired. I'm meant to be recovering, not wasting away.

He's already unpacking eggs, mushrooms, a sourdough loaf, a packet of bacon. 'I know you've not been living on toast and scraps. Brenda's good. But she's more about labelling systems and sensible nutrition than sorting you out with a proper fry-up.'

I grin. 'That sounds about right.'

He flashes a quick smile over his shoulder, and something eases slightly between us.

I sit at the table, the small, trendy one I bought last year that Brenda tried to replace with one from her garage – 'Traditional and solid,' she'd said. 'Not like this flimsy rubbish.'

Matt streams his favourite Coldplay playlist while he cooks. The kitchen feels alive again, like before. We always used to take turns to cook breakfast in each other's kitchens at the weekends. Music, chat and laughter. Planning what we were going to do in the upcoming week.

He hums along to the tunes, focused completely on the task in hand. Not like me, usually faffing around with one eye on the baby monitor, the other on Jess. Watching him is calming. He sautés the mushrooms in butter, turns the bacon under the grill, cracks eggs cleanly into the pan. The smell makes my stomach growl.

'Coffee?'

'Gosh, yes.'

He brings it over just the way I like it – made with warm whole milk, no sugar. I sip and feel, for the first time in days, like there's a chance I might not burst into tears before noon.

Breakfast is delicious. Not extravagant but thoughtful in the care he's taken. He's grated a little lemon zest over the mushrooms, sprinkled sea salt on the eggs.

'You didn't have to go to all this trouble,' I say.

'I did, actually.' He's not joking. 'You're exhausting yourself, Sylvie. I should've been around more, supported you more. I just... I don't know, it felt like you didn't need me.'

I hesitate. 'Of course I did! I *do* need you. But you seemed distracted, and Nige's been here too many—'

'I've allowed myself to be pushed out,' he says flatly. 'By Brenda. But that's going to change.'

We sit quietly for a few moments, our cutlery clinking. He's right. She filled the space here too quickly and too completely. And I let her.

I think about Jess and Scarlet Mae heading home. 'Things are going to get back to normal in the next couple of days,' I say.

Matt raises an eyebrow. 'Really?'

'Yep. Jess is feeling stronger, and Ed's taking some time off to be home with her. They're ready for their own space as a family now.'

'And what about you... how do you feel about that?'

I look around. The fridge is still lined with labelled tubs. Brenda's apron hangs neatly by the door. There's a whiteboard with colour-coded meal plans I didn't approve.

'I need to feel like it's my house again.' I put down my fork and reach for his hand. 'Like we're us again. I've got the key back from Brenda, so that should help.'

He nods and gives my fingers a squeeze. 'That's like music to my ears. It's what I want, too.'

I feel my eyes prickle. I didn't realise how much I needed to hear him say that.

We finish breakfast in near silence, but it's not a strained one. It's the kind of quiet pause that tells me that maybe we're finding our way back to each other again.

Jess comes back just after lunch, carrying in Scarlet Mae, who's still snoozing in her car seat. My daughter looks tired, yes, but not frail like before. Her skin has colour again, and she's been eating without any prompting from me. There's still a stiffness to her movements, though, and a distance between us that wasn't there before.

'I thought I'd make a cottage pie later,' I tell her. 'Your favourite.'

She smiles weakly. 'You don't have to go to that trouble, Mum.'

'I want to.' And I do. I want to remember what it felt like before all this – before the hospital and our tiny, adorable Scarlet Mae. Before Brenda moved onto the street and before my home became a clinic crossed with a playgroup.

I restock the cupboards slowly, moving things back to where they belong. Tea above the kettle. Pasta in the deep drawer, not on the shelf. Most-used herbs within easy reach, not arranged alphabetically like some odd spice library. I'm reclaiming my kitchen, one tin at a time.

Matt helps with the furniture, shifting the armchair back to the reading corner, returning the coffee table to its rightful place. Brenda had moved it 'for a better flow', but it always felt like we were hosting a house viewing or something.

'There,' he says. 'Better?'

'So much better.' I beam.

He squeezes my hand and there's warmth there again. It's not perfect yet, but we definitely feels more like 'us'.

Then the doorbell rings.

Brenda stands there, holding two shopping bags. 'Sorry to drag you to the door, but I've little choice with no key.' She gives me a cheery grin, regardless. 'I stopped off a few bits we were low on. I'll bring them through, if that alright?'

We. I can't let this go.

'There's no need for you to keep doing this now, Brenda,' I say gently but firmly. 'I'm quite capable of keeping an eye on the grocery situation.'

Her face drops. 'Oh! I...' She looks down at the bags and back at me. 'You might as well have this stuff now. I've got no use for it.'

I should probably say I don't want the bloody food. I should probably ignore that slightly pleading look on her face.

Instead, fool that I am, I step aside.

Next morning, I wake feeling a little sharper. Outside, it's overcast and cold. My joints ache, but I manage the stairs easy enough.

I find Brenda already in the kitchen labelling up yet more food containers. She turns round and beams as I walk in and pre-empts my question of how she managed it with no key. 'Jess let me in.'

I take a breath. 'Brenda... this can't go on. We've had a discussion, and it's settled.'

'I'm just... trying to get the house—'

'You're not listening to me. I want the house to stay as it is now. No more rearranging. No more changing things round, OK?'

She stares blankly at me. Says nothing.

'I really, really appreciate what you've done for us, Brenda. But I think it's time you had a break too. Maybe it's time to enjoy a bit of quiet time with Ivor, hmm?'

Something flashes in her eyes – too quick to pin down. Her mouth tightens. 'Of course, if that's what you want.' Then, 'I thought I might make us a stew later. Easy on your stomach, good for energy.'

Before I can respond, Scarlet Mae begins to cry in the other room. Brenda steps out quickly and snatches a muslin from the banister just as Jess, coming down the stairs, says something about it being time for the baby's feed.

And then, Brenda snaps. 'Oh, for heaven's sake, you're fussing over her too much!'

Jess stops, mid-step. I hold my breath. The house falls silent.

'Sorry,' Brenda mutters, twisting the cloth in her hands.

'I think it's time for you to leave, Brenda,' I say quietly.

'But—'

'Right now, please.'

Later that day, two uniformed police officers knock on the door.

'Sorry to bother you, madam,' one says, his badge visible. 'We're carrying out a door-to-door, asking about any suspicious activity in the area.'

My stomach tightens. 'Is this about the missing woman?'

'That's right. We've had a report concerning a man seen loitering a few streets away. Several nights ago now, but we're speaking to every household nearby.'

They ask if we've noticed anything – odd visitors, unfamiliar vehicles, people out late. I shake my head, try to think. Jess holds Scarlet Mae protectively, watching from the hallway. Matt comes around, drawn by the sight of police on the street, and they ask him too.

No one's seen anything.

After they leave, the dread lingers. A suspicious man... around here? It feels too close. Too specific.

'They're probably clutching at straws,' Matt says. 'They've drawn a blank up until now. Anyway, I'm off out to do a couple of quotes.'

And a few moments later, he's gone.

Brenda returns not long after, cheerful as ever at the door despite my latest attempt to get her to back off.

'I'm sorry, I was out of order, Sylvie,' she says quietly, brushing cat hair from her sleeve.

'OK,' I say with a nod. 'Apology accepted.'

'I've come back because... would it be alright if I ask Jess if I can do anything to help her, before she goes? I'd like to apologise to her too, for my outburst,' she says, with a sheepish smile.

I hesitate. 'I don't know, Brenda. It might be best if—'

She bites her lip. 'It's just... she's leaving here soon, and I'll miss her and the baby so much.'

I sigh and against my better judgement, I tell her to go ahead and disappear into the kitchen before I say something I regret.

When I pop back into the living room a few minutes later, Brenda is standing next to the coffee table looking down at my laptop with an odd expression on her face.

'Oh, I thought you'd gone upstairs,' I say as she jumps a little and moves away.

'Yes, I was just... lost in thought for a moment.' She tucks her notebook and pen under her arm. The one I've seen her scribbling in from time to time.

She goes upstairs and I hear her asking Jess if she needs any help packing her final bits and pieces. I glance at her handbag left in the hallway. It's unzipped, gaping open a little and I can see she's slipped the notebook in there, the corner of it peeking out.

I don't touch it. But the image stays with me, even after I close the door behind her later.

Later, when Jess and Scarlet Mae have gone back home, I sit in the living room, lights low and Matt beside me. The unplugged baby monitor is on the table; the house seems so quiet with just the two of us here.

Outside, the street looks ordinary. I can see the faint flicker of the television over at Brenda's. I'm glad she seems to have finally got the message. I'm relieved.

But I can't shake the feeling that something around me is starting to unravel.

TWENTY

Since Jess left yesterday afternoon, I've been mooching around quite a bit. I feel a bit lost if I'm honest. Since telling Brenda I don't need her help, I've been trying to get back into a bit of a routine in the house.

I'm in the middle of loading the washing machine when I hear the doorbell. When I answer, I'm confronted with Brenda holding up yet another bag of groceries like nothing ever happened.

'Brenda.' I frown. 'What's this?'

'I thought you might be low on fruit,' she murmurs. 'Oh, and the organic porridge Jess likes but you couldn't get hold of? Well, Co-op have it back in stock again now. I got one so if she stays over, we'll have some in.'

'Jess has gone home now, Brenda,' I say carefully. 'We agreed you didn't need to keep coming round and buying groceries.'

'I found some of those nice cloths too, the microfibre ones.

Yours have had it, Sylvie, so I threw them out. We can start from scratch with these.'

That word 'we' again.

I hear footsteps behind me as Matt appears, holding his mug of coffee.

'You heard Sylvie, Brenda,' he says. 'You've been a big help but now this needs to stop.'

I die a little inside. I don't need him to fight my battles like I'm a child.

Brenda scowls. 'The last time I looked, this was Sylvie's house, not yours.'

My mouth falls open. 'We're married, Brenda. It's just as much—'

'Yes, yes, I know all about your strange "arrangement".' She glares at Matt. 'Makes me wonder who it suits, though. Who benefits from it, and why.'

'Right. Time for you to leave.' I've never seen Matt's expression as thunderous. He walks towards us. 'And don't turn up on the doorstep again without an invite.'

Brenda looks at me as if she's waiting for me to pull him up, but I avert my eyes.

She puts down the grocery bag and then turns on her heel and walks away without uttering another word.

I make a mild noise of exasperation as I close the door, but inside I'm screaming. I've done my best to draw a friendly line with her. Got the key back and asked her nicely to ease off.

'I don't know how it's come to this,' I murmur sadly.

When Matt doesn't answer, I glance up and he catches my eye with a look that says: *Seriously?*

Later, Matt corners me in the hall. We've kind of avoided each other since Brenda left. His voice is low and measured when he speaks.

'Sylvie, I know you've been trying your best to be diplomatic with her, but it wasn't working.'

'I know.' I wipe my hands on my jeans. 'I just felt like you were taking the situation over and undermining me a bit. At the end of the day, she means well.'

'So do charity collectors, but we don't give them the run of the house.'

I sigh. 'Don't be ridiculous.'

He steps closer, not touching, but close enough for me to feel the heat off him. 'It's not ridiculous. Something had to be said even if it meant offending her. She's constantly overstepping the mark and you've always downplayed it. She doesn't respect anyone's boundaries. I can even get the locks changed, if you think—'

'No,' I say quickly. 'There's no need for that. Let's just leave it for now.'

I swallow a flare of resentment. I'm tired and I don't want to carry this on. My body still aches in strange, unpredictable ways. I'm missing Jess and Scarlet Mae's cries at night even though when they were here, I craved a decent night's sleep. And somewhere under it all is the guilt that Brenda saw what was wrong with Jess when none of us – including her own GP – did. There's every possibility Brenda might have saved her life and this is how I repay her...

'She was there to help Jess and the baby when I wasn't,' I say. 'When I couldn't be. That counts for something even if she's become a bit of a nuisance.'

Matt leans back slightly, folds his arms. 'So that gives her permanent residence, does it?'

'You're not being fair.'

'And you're not seeing straight.'

We don't say anything else. He leaves the house soon after, muttering something about a late meeting. I don't stop him.

Instead, I sit on the stairs for a long time after the door clicks shut, my heart pounding like I've just run uphill.

Kendra turns up unannounced in the afternoon, bright-red lipstick, oversized sunglasses and a clutch of jangly silver bracelets that clash together and chime when she hugs me.

She wasn't aware Jess has fully moved out now and is here to drop off a parcel and 'to say hi before Jess disappears off into mummy-land, never to be seen again'.

'Tea?' I offer. 'There are still a few of Brenda's cookies left in the tin, I think.'

Kendra grins. 'Sounds perfect... bugger the diet, eh?'

We sit in the kitchen and I pour tea. Kendra inspects the choc chip cookies, pulls a face, then scoffs two.

'So?' I nudge her, smiling. 'You're glowing. Happier than usual.'

'Am I?'

'I've known you since primary school, Kendra. You can't fool me.'

She pretends not to understand, then relents. 'Well... maybe I'm just feeling happy in my life for once.'

'Maybe?'

'OK then, I *am* feeling happy. But I'm not saying anything else yet. I'm just enjoying it for now.' She's slightly awkward about it and I can sense she's trying to draw the conversation to a close.

I grin, leaning in. 'Come on then... what does he do? Is he local? Age-appropriate?' Kendra has previous with older guys, sometimes married ones.

She waves my words away. 'Stop it, Sylvie. You're putting words in my mouth.'

'Just be careful,' I say. 'You know, with everything that's going on.'

'You mean Ellie Walker disappearing?'

I nod, suddenly uncomfortable. 'She didn't disappear, they're saying it's an abduction, and yet no one seems to know anything. It's horrible.'

'Do the coppers ever know anything?' She shrugs. 'Still, you're right. I've started letting my housemates know when I go out, sharing my location, that sort of thing. Can't be too careful.'

Then, casually, she feeds me a bit of information as light as a stray feather. 'Oh, I saw Matt out the other night. Out with Nige walking into a club. Looked like they were both having a good time... reliving their youth maybe.'

My stomach clenches. 'Where was this?'

'Town centre. Late. Monday, I think. I was coming out of that new Thai place with some mates. Nearly didn't recognise him, to be honest. He looked – different.'

I smile, hoping I'm covering up my shock. 'He didn't mention it.'

She raises a brow. 'Maybe he didn't think it was worth mentioning.'

We shift to other topics after that. I'm embarrassed, don't want her to think Matt has failed to tell me. But her words are stuck under my skin now. Why didn't Matt tell me he went out? He's entitled to go out, although I'd have thought nightclubs were behind him now. But why did he make it sound like he was working? And why did Kendra use that word – *different*?

Early evening, Jess returns to pick up a bag of clothes and some nappies they'd left behind. Ed is at home with Scarlet Mae, for 'some daddy bonding time'. Jess still looks pale and her coat hangs too loose.

'I'll only be five minutes,' she says, disappearing upstairs.

In the end, she stays for over an hour.

It starts when I hand her the bag. She sets it down, and then the floodgates open. Not literally at first – just a sigh and a quiet, 'I feel like I'm doing it all wrong, Mum.'

Then she sinks onto the arm of the sofa and her face crumples. Her whole body folds in on itself, like she's trying to disappear. I go to her instinctively.

'It's alright, sweetheart.' I kneel beside her. 'You're just tired. New mums often think they're failing. Happened all the time to me.'

Jess sobs harder as I stroke her hair and offer tissues. I wanted to talk to her about what happened with Brenda, but I can't burden her with that now.

So I hover, uselessly. Watching my daughter break apart and trying to say the right thing and gather up the pieces.

When Jess finally quiets, she thanks me and we hug tightly. I offer her a lift home, but she says she'll get an Uber.

I linger in the hallway, staring at the closed door. My hands shake a little.

I to and fro a bit about what to do but, in the end, I message Matt:

You never mentioned you'd been out with Nige on Monday night.

It's a few minutes before he replies.

Yeah. Sorry, I meant to say. Just needed to blow off some steam.

I don't reply. Nige's influence worries me a bit as, far as I know, Matt hasn't been clubbing for years. But what really bothers me is not that he didn't mention it, but that he lied when there was no need.

. . .

I pop out to the car to get a favourite cardigan I left in there. I lean into the back seat to reach it and when I slam the door shut, Brenda is standing there.

We regard each other for a moment before she says softly, 'I seem to be making a habit of this just lately, but I want to apologise, Sylvie. For the way I spoke to you and Matt earlier.'

'Yes, well... it's a shame it's had to come to this, Brenda.'

She hangs her head. 'I know. I can't tell you how sorry I am. I don't suppose...' She sniffs, shakes her head.

She looks so wretched, I can't just turn my back on her and walk away. 'What is it?'

'I feel so alone, Sylvie. Without you and Jess and the baby.'

My heart squeezes. I know that feeling. I'm missing Jess and Scarlet Mae too and right now, I feel alone inside my marriage.

'Could we have a chat over a cuppa?' she says, glancing at my door. 'I won't overstay, I promise. I just need to know we're good before I go to sleep tonight.'

I glance over at Matt's house. His car has gone. He's off out somewhere, probably on the town with Nige again. So why not?

Inside, I make a drink and Brenda glances at me over her teacup, her eyes softer than usual.

'Are you feeling alright, Sylvie? If you don't mind me saying, you seem... not quite yourself.'

I start to brush off her concern, but I can't deny her words hit home. It's the way she's looking at me, open and honest, as though she's concerned and only wants what's best for me. And I'm tired. So bloody tired of the things I'm keeping knotted inside.

I set my cup down and fiddle with the handle. 'I'm fine,' I say and even I can hear how unconvincing that sounds. Brenda just waits, doesn't fill the space with chatter like she usually does.

She has her faults, but right now, for one reason or another, she also feels like the only person I can offload to.

A sigh escapes me before I can stop it. 'Actually... I'm not fine at all. Not really.'

Her eyebrows lift, the faintest hint of curiosity, but she says nothing.

'I've just been wondering if...' My throat tightens. I don't know why I'm telling *her* this, of all people. Particularly as I'm supposed to be trying to introduce some appropriate distance between us. There again, it should be possible for us to remain friends and have the odd coffee and chat. 'I've started to worry that Matt might be seeing someone else. I don't know, it seems stupid but...'

The words emerge barely above a whisper, but there they are now. Hanging between us and I can't take them back. It probably seems a bit paranoid to Brenda, me worrying after he's simply had a night out, but it's a bit more than that when I pair it with the other stuff. Little things, like him seeing more of Nige than he's done for some time and a drop in affection from his side in terms of cuddles and touching. It sounds nothing when I catalogue it, but these small things add up and amount to something more than the sum of their parts. Something that lies like a dull ache in my stomach, refusing to budge.

Brenda's expression doesn't change. She leans back, setting her cup down with care, folding her hands in her lap.

'You know, Sylvie,' she says softly. 'I can't imagine that's the case for a moment. Matt loves you. Anyone can see that.' She shakes her head, as though the very idea of what I've said is absurd.

I blink, surprised by how quickly she's dismissed it. I'd expected... what? Glee? A flash of satisfaction? I'm not sure. But this – this warmth – is disarming and unexpected.

'It's just... it feels like we've drifted apart quite a bit,' I say, twisting the corner of a cushion between my fingers. 'With Jess and the baby staying, and me being laid up after the surgery.

And then—' I almost say *you*, but stop myself, biting down on the words. 'Things feel a bit off. Like we've lost our closeness.'

Brenda nods, her expression thoughtful. 'Men don't always know how to handle things when life shifts around them,' she says sagely. 'Sometimes they retreat. Get busier with work, or say they do, because they don't know what else to do with themselves.'

I feel the knot in my chest loosen, just a fraction. Brenda has never spoken about any past relationships, but what she says makes me think she has experience somewhere along the line.

'Maybe his workload has picked up,' she continues, 'and with everything you've been through, it's easy to imagine the worst. But I've seen the way he looks at you, Sylvie. He cares about you very much.'

I let out a breath. 'You might be right. I'm just feeling... anxious. I suppose.'

She reaches across, gives my hand a brief squeeze. Her palm is cool and dry. Reassuring.

I manage a smile. 'Thanks, Brenda.'

'Anytime, love.' She smiles back. 'That's what friends are for.'

And yet, despite her kindness and wise words, beneath the surface, something rankles – like a pebble in my shoe that I just can't seem to shake out.

TWENTY-ONE

BRENDA

SUNDAY

Brenda stands in her hallway and looks at the fairy lights she's trailed over the mirror by the front door. She got the idea from Sylvie and the bulbs twinkle softly, throwing stars across the wallpaper. Fairy lights have never really been her thing. Too fussy. But looking at them now, she could get used to seeing them here and there. She knows Sylvie loves them and that's the most important thing.

Brenda smiles faintly at her reflection, pursing her lips to inspect the touch of pale-pink lipstick she's applied.

Carefully tucking a stray wisp of grey hair behind one ear, she sees her usually pale cheeks are flushed pink with anticipation. She straightens the lace collar of her blouse and marvels how she looks so much like her mother in a certain light. Where do the years go?

From the lounge, muted laughter rises and falls, interspersed with the clinking of glasses and plates. From the doorway, Brenda glances at the small buffet table. Dainty sandwiches sit neatly arranged in crustless triangles while colourful plates of canapés gleam under gentle candlelight.

Everything looks perfect and so it should. She checked the arrangements half a dozen times before the guests got here, anxious to avoid any mistakes.

But it's essential tonight goes without a hitch and is a resounding success.

Sylvie's book club ladies are gathered around Brenda's table. They chat quietly, sipping Prosecco, smiling softly when they catch sight of her in a way that makes her bristle.

They're here for Sylvie, not her. But hopefully, after tonight, she will be one of them, too. Welcomed into the community fold.

The gathering she's organised here will show Sylvie exactly how much Brenda thinks of her, and she feels certain it will repair the unfortunate misunderstanding caused by Matt.

The thought of him makes her guts twist. She'd overheard him whispering that evening about a week ago now, his voice low, authoritative. 'Time for her to move on,' he'd said, as if Brenda were disposable. As if she hadn't spent countless hours helping Sylvie through those difficult early days with Jess and the baby and then with her own illness and recovery.

How dare he just dismiss her like that? Sylvie, of course, had tried, weakly, to defend Brenda. Her voice had wavered a little under the pressure of Matt's persistence. She should have put her foot down more firmly, but Brenda understands that Sylvie is trapped in her marriage and, until now, she's had nobody to fight her corner.

This little party is Brenda's gesture of resistance. She had seized the opportunity earlier in the week when she'd seen Sylvie had left her laptop open in the living room. When Sylvie had left the room, she'd quietly copied down the book club's short email list. A bit naughty, but all in the spirit of friendship, Brenda had reassured herself. Nothing more than that.

She'd sent invitations out quickly, warmly worded with just enough charm. Sylvie needed her friends around her now – real friends, not backstabbers who manipulated and controlled her. Brenda knows how it feels to have people like that in your midst.

At precisely seven o'clock, the front door knocker taps sharply. Brenda waves her hands at the guests for silence, her eyes wide and urgent. The ladies pause mid-conversation, eyebrows raised, amused perhaps, but Brenda sees only compliance. Heart quickening, she smooths her plaid skirt, takes a deep breath and opens the door with her most welcoming smile.

Sylvie stands illuminated by the porch light, her expression tired beneath a polite smile. She clutches Brenda's empty cake plate in her hands, cleanly washed and shining in the evening air. 'Hello, Brenda. Here you go – thank you again for the cake,' Sylvie murmurs gently, her eyes flickering briefly with uncertainty.

Brenda takes the plate and ushers her friend into the hallway. She can sense Sylvie's hesitation, but no matter. 'Come through, won't you? I have something to show you.'

Sylvie follows silently, her steps careful on the polished wooden floor. Brenda leads her into the softly lit lounge. As Sylvie steps through the doorway, she reaches behind her to flick the lights brighter, and immediately the room erupts with cheerful cries of 'Surprise!'

Sylvie jumps visibly, eyes wide and startled, her hand pressed to her chest. Brenda beams, delighted by her reaction, mistaking Sylvie's initial confusion for joy.

'Goodness!' Sylvie's eyes dart around the room as she tries to catch her breath, pressing a tentative hand to her flushed cheek.

'Happy early birthday, Sylvie!' Brenda announces proudly, glancing around the room for confirmation. The book club ladies raise their glasses dutifully, polite smiles firmly in place. 'I wanted to arrange something special for you.'

Sylvie nods slowly, a fragile smile trembling on her lips as she takes in the gathered faces. Brenda feels a rush of satisfaction, a deep, nurturing pride.

'How thoughtful,' Sylvie says quietly, her voice a little strained. A normal reaction, Brenda feels sure, in the flush of a surprise. 'Thank you, everyone.'

Brenda, determined to amplify the cheer, places a glass of Prosecco into Sylvie's hand. 'It's important you realise just how loved you are.' Her words linger oddly in the air, but Brenda hardly notices.

'Indeed,' says Vera, lifting her own glass again. 'Here's to friendship, and surprises!' A murmur of assent circles the room, glasses clinking softly.

Brenda watches Sylvie closely, a careful observer of every flicker of emotion across her face. Sylvie sips her drink quickly, eyes darting repeatedly toward the clock above Brenda's fireplace. Brenda frowns inwardly; it's rude, she thinks briefly, to look impatient at your own party. But Sylvie's nerves must surely be due to Matt's influence. Brenda forgives her immediately, deciding instead to take control.

'A little music, I think,' she declares brightly, stepping quickly toward her ancient stereo stack, switching it on. Strains of an old ballad drift into the room, slightly too loud, its melancholy tone oddly incongruous with the forced cheer of the occasion.

Several women exchange glances, but Brenda remains oblivious, swaying lightly to the rhythm.

Sylvie's eyes catch Brenda's, briefly haunted, and for a moment Brenda considers if she's miscalculated. The air thickens slightly with unspoken unease.

'I hope you like your birthday surprise,' she says, a little haltingly.

'It's lovely,' Sylvie finally says, offering Brenda a tentative, hesitant smile. 'Thank you, Brenda, truly. It's very kind of you, but I can't help but wonder how you managed to invite everyone.' She is still smiling. 'I mean, you don't have their details...'

Brenda frowns for a moment, then grins. 'Yes, I was going to mention that. I might have had a little peek at your contact list and jotted down a handful of emails. Just for the book club, of course.'

'You *what*?' The way she says it forms a knot deep in Brenda's gut. 'You hacked into my laptop?'

'Goodness me, of course not! It was open on the coffee table, and it was open on your book club spreadsheet. That's what gave me the idea for a gathering,' she says brightly. 'I wouldn't ordinarily snoop, of course, but I had good reason to this time. It was for your benefit, after all. I wanted it to be a surprise.'

Sylvie opens her mouth, then closes it again. She's making Brenda feel unreasonable, as though she's done something terrible... but then she blinks and gives a little nod. Brenda feels warmth flooding through her, relief dissolving the brief discomfort. Of course she's done the right thing. Sylvie just needs time to adjust, to understand.

She's suspicious of her husband and Brenda had played a clever hand, appearing to defend the awful Matt and reassure Sylvie she can see he cares about her. The last thing Brenda wants is for Sylvie to think Brenda is waiting for his downfall.

After tonight, Brenda feels sure things will change. Sylvie will see exactly who cares most, exactly who she needs in her life.

Then, despite Matt's obvious jealousy of Brenda, the two friends can carry on from where they left off.

TWENTY-TWO

SYLVIE

'She did *what?*' Jess's shocked voice bounces out of the phone like she's been electrocuted.

I sigh and close the kitchen cupboard a little too hard. A jar of paprika topples off the shelf and clatters to the floor, spewing red dust like an open wound.

I switch the call to loudspeaker and kneel to clean up the mess.

'She accessed my laptop to get the book club contact list,' I say, 'and invited everyone round to hers for an early birthday surprise. In my honour, apparently. Like I'm seven, or something, and worse still, I don't turn forty-six until the new year!'

'She didn't invite me!' There's a short silence, the weight of it pressing into my ear. Then, 'It's... I dunno. Kind of weird she'd do that, Mum. Totally out of order with the laptop, too.'

I sigh. 'Yes, Jess, I am very aware. I feel as if I should have said something but... when she's gone to the effort and everyone's there smiling at me, I just...'

'I know,' Jess admits. 'I get it.'

I dump the crumpled paper towel in the bin and stand. The kitchen feels stuffy so I pull open the back door and cold air knifes in from the damp, still garden.

'What does Matt say about it?'

'I haven't told him yet.'

'Mum—'

'He's warned me more than once about Brenda overstepping the mark.' I wrap my cardigan tighter and lean against the doorframe watching my breath puffing away in soft clouds. The fence panels tremble in a sudden gust of wind. 'We're not getting on great as it is and he'll just give me that look. You know the one.'

'The disappointed-married-man special.'

I don't laugh, and neither does she.

Jess sighs. 'I mean, honestly, we *owe* Brenda for helping out after all this time and for spotting my condition. But I'm starting to wonder where all this will end.'

'Me too.'

'So what are you going to do?' she asks.

'I don't know,' I say, swallowing the dryness in my throat. 'I was thinking I might speak to Penny. See what she thinks.'

'Isn't she in Spain now?'

'Portugal. Tavira. But she did ask me to keep her informed of any concerns with the house and suchlike.'

I send Jess off with a promise to keep her posted and a half-hearted joke about vetting all future helpers. As soon as the call ends, I pull up Penny's last message thread and tap out a quick text.

Hope Portugal is treating you both well! Wondered if I could give you a quick ring about something? Nothing urgent but would love your advice!

The reply comes back within two minutes.

Lovely to hear from you! We're just back from a beach walk –
call anytime you like.

I hit the call button before I have time to chicken out. Penny answers on the third ring, her voice breezy and warm. 'Sylvie! Oh, it's so good to hear your voice!'

I smile despite my concerns. 'You too. How's the sun?'

'Relentless! You should see poor Brian's face – like a wizened tomato. And we're renting this gorgeous little white-washed house, just a stone's throw from the sea. It's like something on a postcard. I don't think we'll be coming back to the UK, put it that way.'

'Honestly, I don't blame you,' I say, and mean it.

We do the usual back and forth holiday-speak, covering tapas, sand in the bed, someone local who sells sardines out of a cool box and looks like a pirate to boot. It calms me a little. Penny has that effect and I miss it.

When there's a pause, I seize my chance.

'I wanted to ask you something. It's about your tenant, Brenda. It's... it's slightly awkward actually, but you did ask me to let you know of any problems.'

'Oh?' Penny says, instantly concerned.

'Don't get me wrong, she's been amazing. So helpful since I was laid up after my op. But just lately... things have started to feel decidedly off.'

Penny takes in a sharp breath. 'How so?'

'Brenda has sort of... permanently inserted herself into our lives. Into everything. Dropping in with casseroles and groceries I never asked for. Borrowing my boots and letting herself in and out of the house. Oh – and then yesterday—' I hear my voice climb a notch. 'She invited all the book club members to her place for *my* surprise party. But that's not the worst thing.'

'Go on,' Penny murmurs fearfully.

'She admitted when she'd had a couple of drinks that she'd accessed my laptop documents to get the book club contact list.'

There's a gasp down the line. Then, silence.

'I don't mean to drag you into it, Penny, it's just that I don't know what to do,' I say. 'I don't want to upset her, but it's beginning to feel a bit—'

'Invasive?' Penny offers.

'Exactly that.'

Penny is quiet for a moment. I can hear seagulls calling in the background, faint and scratchy. 'When we first met her, Brenda seemed really lovely. As I told you, she's a retired nurse, keen to settle in and she made a point of saying that she really wanted to feel part of the community. She was friendly but respectful. Honest, reliable... she seemed like a godsend, frankly.'

'So you didn't notice anything... unsettling?'

There's a pause. A little too long. My skin prickles.

'Not really,' she says finally. 'Except perhaps...'

I freeze. 'Except perhaps what?'

'I'm sure it's nothing to worry about,' she says quickly. 'I mean, I wasn't concerned enough to do anything at the time. It's just something the letting agent mentioned when she received Brenda's tenancy application.'

'What was it?' I'm pacing the hall now, phone tight to my ear. My pulse is ticking at the base of my throat.

'It was something to do with a reference. One of the people she put down from her old hospital.' Penny exhales. 'The agent said something didn't add up. Or maybe that it couldn't be properly verified. Yes, that was it, I think. They'd tried to reach someone – her old manager, maybe? Or someone she'd worked under – and the contact details she gave weren't valid. Number disconnected. Or didn't match the name.'

I stop pacing. 'Didn't that strike you as odd?'

'It did, yes. But then Brian and I met her, and she had all the right stories – ward names, training anecdotes, the way she spoke about people and how her work had been such a big part of her life... it just felt genuine. Like she was exactly who she said she was.' Penny sighs. 'It didn't seem worth following up on after that.'

I rest my forehead against the cool glass of the front door. Outside, dusk has begun its quiet creep. The street has a moody, strange light about it, and I feel none of the peace the evening usually brings.

'Do you know if the agent followed up?'

'I don't think so. Brenda paid the deposit in full, had spotless credit, and she was charming. Honestly, Sylvie, she won us all over.'

I say nothing.

'You're probably just feeling overwhelmed,' Penny adds. 'It's a lot, recovering from surgery, the new baby and Jess being so ill.'

'I don't think I'm imagining it,' I say.

'No, no. Of course not. I just mean... well, maybe don't jump to conclusions. The tenancy application hiccup is probably something completely innocent. You know what admin can be like in the NHS.' She pauses. 'I think Brenda has probably got carried away and sees herself as one of the family. She did strike me as being a lonely sort. If I were you I'd just gradually loosen ties. But if this continues, or you have any further problems please do shout. After all, Brian and I have to be sure what kind of person we have living in our home.'

I thank her, say we'll speak soon, and end the call. In the mirror by the stairs, I blink at my pale reflection and turn away.

Back in the kitchen, I pour myself a glass of water with trembling hands.

I think about Brenda, the woman who brought us home-made soup in a Thermos shaped like a cartoon penguin. The one who spotted my daughter had a serious allergic reaction and fed and changed Scarlet Mae when she couldn't.

I think about the way she looked at my laptop when I left it open. That time she offered to help me 'tidy up' my address book. The way her face changed – just slightly – when Jess mentioned her graduation last year and Brenda said, 'Oh yes, I remember seeing the photos!'

Even though I'd never shown them to her.

TWENTY-THREE

NOTTINGHAMSHIRE POLICE

The shop where the sighting of Ellie Walker took place is a Spar.

Helena has one of the popular general stores close to her flat and is familiar with the bright strip lighting, the shelves stacked with the kind of everyday essentials people are likely to run out of.

When they walk in, she recognises the same faint scent of coffee beans, sausage rolls and ham from the deli counter. A clutter of newspapers, supermarket flowers, and the multipack crisps and confectionery near the till give it that organised, lived-in feel of somewhere you pop into for a carton of milk and a loaf of bread and you'll probably leave with two or three other items you didn't intend to buy.

Outside, the petrol forecourt gleams wetly in the drizzle. Inside, everything seems drab and over-lit. Irene Humphreys, the cashier who initially spoke to Brewster, stands behind the counter like a tired lighthouse keeper, watching the rain snake in ribbons down the window.

Helena approaches her first, flashing her warrant card out of habit. Brewster and the forensic imaging specialist, Lena

Cavanagh, follow behind. Lena carries a padded laptop case and has the unfazed look of someone who's done this before on a damp Tuesday in Nottinghamshire.

'Mrs Humphreys?' Helena offers her best approachable smile. 'Thanks for agreeing to talk to us again. Are we OK to head into the staff room like you said... if that's alright?'

'Course, love. It's a bit scruffy, but it's warm in there and the kettle works at least.' Irene calls out and a tall, pale young man with light-brown hair and a scattering of acne steps out from an aisle and heads towards the till.

'I shouldn't be too long, Andrew,' she says. 'Give us a shout if you get stuck with anything.'

Andrew eyes the detectives, but nods and turns his back to tidy the stock display.

With a stiffness in her gait, Irene leads them through a short corridor, past stacked pallets of cheap energy drinks and a large bin that smells faintly of bleach.

The staff room is little more than a large cupboard with a table, four mismatched chairs, a microwave, and a fading poster about hand hygiene that has peeled away at the corners. A worn fleece hangs from a hook beside the fire exit.

'Tea?' Irene offers, already reaching for the kettle.

They accept and Helena exchanges a look with Brewster and settles opposite where Irene will sit while Lena sets up her laptop, checking the software boots correctly before glancing up.

When Irene has made the tea, Brewster introduces them again and takes a bit more time to signpost Lena's involvement. He takes Irene through what will happen and points out they will record the interview.

'We'll talk about what you remember about the man you saw with Ellie Walker,' Helena begins gently. 'Lena here is going to help you put together a visual of him – a sort of digital sketch, but more interactive. We'll start by talking you through what you saw the day before Ellie disappeared. You ready, Irene?'

Irene nods, folding her hands in her lap, her fingers pale and a couple gnarled with arthritis. She nods. Her eyes – small and sharp – dart to the image of Ellie printed on the incident file on the table.

'So, first of all, you're sure it was her?' Helena asks. 'We need to be certain.'

'Certain as anything. I might sometimes forget what I go into the stock room for these days, but I don't forget faces. Besides, I've seen her in here a few times and it was definitely her. Brown backpack, that little flicky fringe. Same pretty dimples when she smiled – though she didn't look too cheerful that day.'

Helena leans in. 'She didn't?'

'No. She was quiet and looked a bit down in the dumps. The man she was with said something – made a bit of a joke, I think – and she laughed but then he gave her this look.'

'What kind of look?'

'Hard to say. A strange sort of look, that's the only way I can describe it.'

'Did they seem like a couple?'

Irene hesitates. 'I wouldn't say so, not exactly. See, it was him who didn't look comfortable. Not aggressive, nothing like that, but it felt to me like he wanted to get out of the place. Maybe he knew what he was about to do to her and felt nervous I'd seen them together.'

Helena feels a subtle thread of unease start to unravel in her chest. 'Let's keep it to what we know to be factual if we can.'

'OK, so let's try and build an initial picture of him,' Lena says gently. Helena had watched as she'd booted up the EFIT-V software and pulled her chair around beside Irene's so she has a good view of the screen. 'We'll do this in stages and there's no rush at all. You can direct the pace. I'm going to ask you a few questions about his face. Don't worry if you can't remember everything. Sometimes details come back when you're least expecting them to.'

Irene gives a nervous laugh. 'Hope you're not in a rush, love.'

Helena watches as Lena begins the cognitive interview, a specialised technique designed to enhance the accuracy of eyewitness accounts by gently prompting with carefully shaped questions.

Lena begins. 'When you first noticed the man, what struck you about him?'

'His jaw,' Irene says right away. 'It was sharp and lean and looked like he hadn't shaved in a few days.'

'What colour was his hair?'

'Mid-brown. Not dark, not gingery. It looked a bit messy. Like he'd run a hand through it instead of using a comb. Brown eyes, I reckon.'

'Good, good.' Lena nods, tapping the keyboard as Irene speaks. She starts running the EFIT software, showing Irene grids of slightly different male faces.

'Start with picking the one that's closest to him. Don't worry about it being exact at this stage.'

They go through five rounds, each one narrowing the likeness as Lena tweaks skin tone, eye depth, the angle of the jaw. Helena watches the screen as a stranger slowly materialises – one who may have the answers they've been chasing for weeks.

'Can you tell us anything else about his face?' Lena asks. 'Any marks, scars or moles you can recall?'

'No marks,' Irene says. 'But he squinted a bit when he looked at her. Like he was trying too hard to understand her. And he had this funny little smile – like only one side of his mouth was grinning.'

Lena clicks a box and adjusts the mouth accordingly.

'This is very helpful, Irene,' Helena says. 'I know it can feel like a lot to go through, but you shouldn't feel pressured.'

'It's alright, love,' Irene replies. 'It's just... that young woman... it's hard knowing he might have done something to her after that. And I could've stopped it, if I'd have noticed something.'

The image now shows a man in his late twenties or early thirties, average build, five o'clock shadow, brown eyes, slightly tousled hair. Not unattractive. Not memorable either. The sort of face that wouldn't turn heads but might watch you a beat too long in a crowd before you noticed.

'How close would you say this is?' Lena asks, tilting the monitor.

Irene peers at it, then tilts her head. 'That's him. Or as close as I'll probably get, I reckon.'

'We'll make a note that you're fairly confident,' Lena says, saving the image and following procedure by exporting a copy with the relevant accompanying data.

Helena feels her pulse flicker as she looks at the face. For the first time, they're not just chasing shadows. This man exists somewhere. And just under over two months ago, he stood beside Ellie Walker in this very shop, paid for her Lucozade, and walked out with her into the cold evening.

Now they have a face and there's something about the features that almost looks familiar. She peers closer. Maybe. Or maybe not.

'It would really help the case if we use this image in an appeal,' Helena says. 'Would you be willing to give a formal statement?'

Irene nods. 'Course. Anything I can do to help that poor girl and her family.'

While Brewster sits down with her to take the official statement, Lena quietly packs away her kit. Helena steps into the corridor and dials the office.

'Can you run an internal check on an EFIT we've just generated?' she asks the duty sergeant. 'We've got a decent image of a male seen with Ellie Walker a day before she vanished. We'll send it through within the next fifteen minutes.'

Back in the staff room, Brewster finishes typing, then closes the laptop with a soft click.

'You've been incredibly helpful, Irene,' he says. 'Thank you.'

Irene waves them off, already returning to the sales counter to relieve her colleague.

Outside, the rain has begun to ease, leaving streaks on the car roof and tiny rock pools in the potholes.

'So, what do we think?' Brewster asks, sliding into the driver's seat.

Helena doesn't answer straight away. She's still picturing Ellie – standing in that shop, shoulders tight, eyes tired. Not afraid. Not exactly. But something about this seems not quite right, either.

'It doesn't feel to me like she was abducted given the circumstances,' she says at last. 'It feels like she went with him. Willingly. Perhaps ignoring her own feelings.'

'Hmm. Was it someone she knew? Or thought she knew?'

Helena stares ahead, the windscreen wipers ticking a slow metronome. 'Maybe. But if he meant no harm then where is she?' Helena nods. 'And more to the point, why didn't he come forward when she went missing to say he'd seen her?'

'My thoughts exactly, boss.' Brewster glances down at the EFIT image on his phone. 'Let's hope he sees his face and panics.'

Helena exhales. Whoever he is, according to this witness's statement, he was one of the last few people to see Ellie Walker. And she has the feeling that once they find him, they'll be closer to finally understand what happened on that quiet, ordinary afternoon that ended with a young woman going missing, leaving her family lost and devastated.

TWENTY-FOUR

Ellie wakes slowly. She feels a bit like she's trying to swim up through treacle.

The first thing she notices is the light. Soft, golden and flickering at the edges. It takes her a moment to register fairy lights, strung along the walls in loose loops. The room is small but clean. Pale walls, wooden floor. An old dresser with chipped paint and twinkling lights around the cracked mirror. A folded blanket at the foot of the bed.

The second thing she notices is him.

He is sitting in a chair in the corner. Not looming above her, just quietly there. Watching from a distance. His posture is relaxed with one hand resting loosely against his chin.

She stays silent.

Her heart beats hard, but it is not with fear. Not exactly.

'Hello there,' he says, his voice low and steady.

Ellie swallows. Her throat feels so dry, but she forces herself to sit up. Her clothes are still on, though her shoes are gone. She flexes her toes inside thick woollen socks that aren't hers. Grey and soft.

She's brought this on herself, she knows that. But... sometimes you think you want something and when you get it, it doesn't feel at all like you expected.

'There's no need to be alarmed,' he says softly. 'You're safe here with me. You must know that.'

She studies him like she might a stranger. In one sense, he's about as ordinary as a man could be. Nondescript. Brown hair, neither long nor short. He's not what you could call handsome, but certainly not ugly. He's just... a man. The sort most people might pass by in the street without a second glance.

It's been a while since they talked for all those hours. Since they discussed this. It had all seemed so exciting at the time but truthfully, she never really thought anything would come of it.

Her mind moves on. Tries to remember how she got here. She remembers cycling down the road, past the woodland. The flash of movement beside her... then nothing. Darkness. The chemical bite of something sharp in her nose, her throat.

'You drugged me.'

He inclines his head, as if that's a reasonable observation.

'I didn't hurt you,' he says. 'I said I wouldn't, didn't I? You must remember that.'

She glances down at her arm. The small graze on her elbow, cleaned and antiseptic cream smeared. Absently, she brushes her fingers over it.

'I could scream the place down. Nobody would believe you,' she says, looking around. Testing him.

'You could, but there's nobody around to hear you for miles.'

He doesn't look concerned. Doesn't flinch.

She tries again. 'I could scratch your eyes out when you come close.'

He smiles at that. 'You could try.'

A pause hangs between them, long enough for her to feel the weight of it bearing down on her.

She does not scream, and she doesn't lunge for him. Instead, *she leans back against the headboard and lets her gaze drift again to the fairy lights.*

'You've gone to a lot of trouble to make me feel comfortable here,' she says. 'The lights, the blanket. The socks.'

'Yes,' he says. 'I'm the kind of person that likes to be fully prepared.'

She takes a breath. 'And what happens now?'

He exhales slowly, as though he's relieved that she's finally asked.

'I want to keep you safe.'

A laugh catches in her throat. 'From what?'

'From being unhappy. But if you want to enjoy it like you said, it's time to play your part.'

He looks at her then, as though he doesn't feel the need to give any further explanation.

Outside, she hears the wind moving through the trees, soft and constant. Whispering secrets.

Despite everything, she doesn't know what this is. But it's not the prison she feared. Not as bad as the one she just left.

Let them worry. Let them panic.

For once, she's free of their chains.

Deep down, she can feel the thrill of it all. Why not just surrender and enjoy it?

TWENTY-FIVE

SYLVIE

The sky seems low this morning, a solid, grey slab hanging above the houses that feels like it's never going to break up. The kind of wintry weather that feels heavy and claustrophobic without ever quite breaking into rain.

I button my padded jacket up to the chin and glance up the street. Someone a bit further down has decorated their porch with Christmas lights and has tethered a large inflatable Santa Claus on top that moves with the wind.

'Too early,' I mutter under my breath. It's barely December but people seem to decorate earlier now.

I pause at the kerb, looking across the road at Brenda's house. It still looks as pristine as the day Penny and Brian left. The paintwork is sparkling white, the front path brushed free of leaves. Only the car has changed – a small pistachio-green Fiat Uno now squats on the drive, its bumper sporting a faint scuff near one wheel arch.

I stare at it. I hate confrontation but I have to go through with this. For my sake and Penny's, too.

I spy Ivor in the front window, perched on the sill. His yellow eyes catch mine, unblinking. He looks faintly disapproving, as if he knows exactly why I'm here. I straighten my shoulders. It's not going to be easy, keeping Brenda sweet while trying to find a chink in the armour she's constructed around herself. I want to stay on the right side of her – but not this close.

Arm's-length is the order of the day, as Matt tried to advise me.

The doorbell chimes twice before I hear movement inside. Through the frosted glass, a shadow appears, hovering and then, the door opens and there she is.

Brenda's face flickers with something guarded – even sullen – for a moment, but then her mouth stretches into that wide, toothy smile.

'Sylvie!' she exclaims, throwing the door open like she's been dying to see me. 'How lovely... Come on in!'

I smile, trying to mask the tightness in my chest. 'I hope I'm not interrupting anything.'

'Not at all, not at all!' She waves me inside, and I follow her into the hall, the space neat and orderly. A soft waft of lavender comes from somewhere and, when I glance into the kitchen as we pass, I can see it's spotless. Every surface looks wiped clean, not a mug or plate out of place.

In the living room, Brenda directs me to the sofa and I perch on the edge of a fat seat cushion while she disappears to get us coffee. The room is traditional, verging on old-fashioned. Cream walls and rose-patterned cushions scattered. A mantelpiece that's crowded with ornaments: a pair of porcelain dogs, a brass carriage clock, framed prints of bucolic landscapes. Everything is arranged just so, which doesn't surprise me given the way she's organised my own house.

Ivor jumps down from his post at the window and slinks across the room, tail flicking as he stops directly in front of me to stare. Brenda comes in and sets down a tray on the low table.

'Play nice, Ivor.' She chuckles, handing me a mug. 'He's not used to visitors.'

She offers me the plate of shortbread biscuits, which I decline.

'I popped over because I just wanted to thank you again,' I say, putting down my mug and folding my hands in my lap. 'For organising the gathering the other night, I mean. It was such a thoughtful thing to do.'

Brenda beams, leaning further back into the armchair opposite. 'Oh, it was a pleasure, Sylvie. I met so many wonderful people – the book club ladies are just delightful.' She leans forward, clasping her hands together like she's preparing for a long natter. 'I do feel so lucky to have landed somewhere so welcoming. It's a real community full of nice, warm people.'

I nod, trying not to feel sour. I let her talk a little longer about who she met, which cake went down best, how someone has already invited her to join a local walking group. I can feel the discomfort pressing at me, but I wait for a pause before I speak.

'I do think it was out of order to open a private document on my laptop, though. You shouldn't have done that, Brenda.'

She frowns. 'How else could I have thrown you a surprise party?'

'Well... you could have asked Matt, or Jess, although neither of them was invited,' I say carefully.

I feel Ivor's gaze still fixed on me. Waiting. Judging.

'Oh! I'm sorry you feel that way.' She visibly bristles. 'The laptop was open and I saw a tab marked "book club". It's not as if I rifled through your personal documents.'

'Yes, I know you did it for the right reasons. It's just...'

Brenda scowls and inspects her fingernails.

Time to cut to the chase before I lose my nerve.

'I've been meaning to ask.' I pick up my drink and settle back. 'Which hospital did you work at?'

Brenda falters, surprise flitting across her face, just for a moment or two. The colour rises in her cheeks, and she smooths her skirt, eyes flicking toward the window.

'I started my career at King's Mill Hospital in Sutton-in-Ashfield,' she says, her voice a little less strident. 'Then later, I was successful in getting a promotion and started working at the Queen's Medical Centre in Nottingham.'

I'm watching her carefully. She's picking at a loose thread on her sleeve, the only sign she's not quite as at ease as she pretends.

'And you became a senior nurse. That's impressive.'

Her chin lifts, a little of the old confidence creeping back. 'Senior nurse, yes. Twelve years at the QMC and I had a lot of responsibility. I ran the ward some days when the ward manager was off. People respected me and I like to think I made a real difference to the patients.'

She launches into a story about a time she spotted a misdiagnosed stroke on a night shift, how her quick thinking saved the patient. She tells it well, her voice swelling with the memory, as though she's painting herself back into the role of the hero. The way she frames it, she's the only thing that stood between the unfortunate patient and certain death.

I nod, let her talk. It's easy to see how people might fall under her spell.

'So if you were senior nurse, who did you report to there?' I ask lightly, swirling the coffee, but not drinking it. 'Must've been a big team.'

'Oh... well...' She hesitates again, just a beat too long. 'Several people, depending on the shift. But mostly to the ward manager. Margaret Ellis. She was wonderful. Firm but fair.' She looks at her hands again. 'I think she had a soft spot for me.'

I file that name away and set my cup down, leaning forward just enough to make my next question feel conspiratorial.

'After all those years, it must have been hard to retire, step away from a place where you made such an impact. Did you miss it?'

The silence stretches a beat or two longer than feels comfortable. Brenda's eyes drift to the window again, watching the world outside as though it might offer an answer.

'I was tired,' she says at last, her voice softer. 'Long shifts took their toll... and I worried I might make a mistake. I couldn't live with that. Better to leave while I still had my reputation intact.'

I offer a small smile. 'I imagine they were devastated. You must have left quite a hole in that place.'

Brenda seems to brighten at that, her voice lifting again. 'Oh, Margaret begged me to stay. Said I was indispensable. Even offered me a part-time role. But I knew it was time. I was ready.'

I let the words settle between us, watching the way she twists the signet ring on her finger.

'Did you consider it? The part-time option?'

Her smile freezes. A small crack in the glaze.

'I... not really. I was ready to go in the end. It wasn't the same there anymore.' She swallows. 'Things change, don't they? New management came in, and... well. It became apparent some people weren't as appreciative of experience as they should be.'

Her tone sharpens on the last sentence, making her sound defensive.

I nod again but my mind is turning over the details. *Margaret Ellis. New management.* I'm definitely sensing some unspoken friction in the final stretch of her career.

'That's a shame,' I say. 'All that experience. You must miss it sometimes.'

Brenda shrugs. 'I keep in touch with one or two old colleagues. Well, let's say I *did*. Some people prefer to move on.'

My heart beats a little faster. Maybe I have the thread. The colleague: someone who knew her and worked alongside her at the QMC. Someone who knows why she left.

I smile as I stand. 'Well, I should let you get on. Thanks for the tea, Brenda. And again – for the party. It really was lovely.'

She sees me to the door, all warmth again. Ivor watches from the hall, his glare cool and suspicious.

Back on my side of the street, I pause by the gate and glance back. Brenda is still there, watching me through the glass, the smile sliding from her face as soon as she thinks I'm not looking.

Two doors down, Matt's car is gone so there's no good me popping round for a chat with him.

As soon as I step inside the hallway, I steel myself.

It's time to find out who Brenda really is.

TWENTY-SIX

As Matt is not yet home to talk to, I go straight to the laptop and open it up. The screen lights my face in the late-morning gloom. My fingers hover, uncertain for a second. Then I type:

Queen's Medical Centre. Ward manager, Margaret Ellis.

I click through the first page of results. Staff directories, some medical conference notes from years back. A photograph turns up – a bit of a grainy image of a woman in her mid-fifties, round face, steel-grey hair swept back into a low ponytail. Smiling but formal with cool eyes. There's a LinkedIn profile, just the bare bones with no recent updates. Retired.

I hesitate, the cursor blinking back at me. Brenda's words echo faintly: *Some people aren't as appreciative of experience as they should be.*

What had she meant? New management? A falling-out?

A ping jolts me. Messenger. I flip over to a new tab.

Hi Sylvie, are you going to Brenda's next book club meet? Sounds like it'll be a fun one!

I blink at the message, read it twice. Brenda's *what?*

There's an email notification too. Another book club friend, the subject line chirpy: *Looking forward to Brenda's event!*

The message inside is worse.

Thanks for organising the last one – it was lovely. Brenda mentioned you've agreed she'll host the next one and has suggested we make a few changes to our format. All sounds good to me... any thoughts on the list she sent through?

Lisa

I slam the laptop shut. I didn't agree to this. I never even suggested Brenda should host.

I pace over to the window and stare out at her house across the street. The curtains are partially drawn and Ivor is back on his windowsill perch, tail twitching.

My phone buzzes.

Your new neighbour, Brenda, is such a gem!

The text is from our oldest book club member, Vera, who is a notoriously hard woman to please.

Loved the surprise get-together. She's such a natural organiser.

I lean against the wall, press my knuckles into my mouth. There's a pressure behind my eyes, like something's building that I can't hold back.

She's wormed her way in just like Matt told me she would. Not just into my life, but into my circle. My people. And the worst of it? They all love her. Brenda's charm offensive is in full swing and I can feel the ground shifting under me, too fast to stop.

I need to talk to Matt. I'm happy to eat my words and tell him he was right.

I scroll to his name and hit call. It rings twice, three times, then I get his voicemail.

I hang up before the beep and try again. Same thing, so I text instead.

Need to talk. You were right about Brenda.

I add a kiss at the end, an olive branch.

Ten minutes later and I've still got nothing back.

I sit down on the edge of the sofa, my phone in hand, staring at the screen like I'll will him to respond.

I check the time. Whatever job he's on he should be at least glancing at his messages. By now, anyway. He's always got his phone with him. I've often complained that just lately, he and I can barely have a conversation without him checking if he has any notifications.

I open my laptop again, needing a distraction. I click back to the search window, flicking through more pages on Queen's Medical Centre. News articles, a retirement piece about the hospital's expansion. Nothing on Brenda. No staff newsletters, no incident reports, no smoking gun.

I pull up Margaret Ellis's LinkedIn again, hesitate, and then click Connect with a message.

Hi Margaret, hope this isn't too forward. I'm a new neighbour of Brenda Howard, who worked with you at the QMC. Just wondering if we might have a quick, confidential chat?

It feels intrusive, but my fingers hit 'send' before my common sense can catch up. The ache in my jaw returns – I've been clenching my teeth. I stand, shake out my hands.

I call Matt again.

Voicemail.

The sick feeling curls tighter in my stomach. Even though he's working, he always gets back to me if I text or call him. He's the boss, after all.

I rattle off another text message.

Where ARE you? Can you just let me know you're OK?

I try to tell myself I'm being ridiculous. It's just Matt. He gets caught up sometimes. Meetings run over. He's got his head down for ten minutes... that's not unheard of if he's been doing a lot of manual work on this big, new job.

But I can't shake the thought, sharp and sour at the edges: *What if it's not just that?* Somehow, the past few weeks, we've grown apart with everything that's been happening. Finding out he's having nights out he hasn't told me about. And what with Jess and the baby and my own recovery...

To give Matt his due, he's tried several times to speak to me about his concerns Brenda's involvement has been instrumental in interfering in our lives. But I refused to listen. Until now.

I open the back door for a bit of air and stare out at the garden. The shed stands dark and austere against the fence, the patio slick with old rain. We sat right there last summer, our wine glasses in hand, an upbeat playlist on low and Matt grilling sausages too long. His smile was relaxed, the crinkle at the corners of his eyes softening when he caught me watching him.

I check my phone again.

Nothing.

The ache in my chest sharpens. How long has it been like this, really? Him distracted, distant. I've been so tangled up in Brenda, in what she's doing for us, that I haven't really taken a good, hard look at what's happening right in front of me.

I scroll back through my recent WhatsApp messages with

Matt. They've thinned out. No more little check-ins, or silly memes. No real-time photos from his often long days out landscaping. Just logistics. Times. Brief plans.

When did that start?

I close the door and sit down again, suddenly too tired to stand. The living room feels cold, so I crank up the heating. I've suggested we review our living arrangements a few times now and he finds a way of not really replying.

Is my husband...? The words stick. I can't even finish the thought. But the question crouches there like a big black spider in a dark corner of my mind, biding its time.

I call him again. My hand shakes when I get his voicemail.

I leave one this time. 'Matt, can you just call me back? Please? I... I need to talk to you.'

My voice sounds thin and desperate, but perhaps that's what it needs to get him to call me back.

The minutes crawl by. Turn into another hour.

I grab my phone and type:

Is there someone else?

The blood rushes in my ears the moment I hit send, but it's gone now. The question needs asking.

I pace the room, back and forth, watching the shadows stretch outside. The streetlights blink on at four o'clock, throwing Brenda's Fiat into stark relief across the road.

A new message pings on my laptop and I rush over.

Margaret Ellis.

Happy to chat. What's this about?

I hesitate, my fingers poised.

Then a ping from my phone. Matt.

In a meeting. Can't talk now. What's going on? What are you on about?

The relief rushes in, quick and foolish. I text back.

Just call me when you can.

No reply.
I scroll to Margaret, heart racing again.

I just wanted a confidential chat about Brenda. Could we meet for coffee?

The typing dots appear, pause.

Got my grandkids here today and then I'm on holiday for two weeks. Could meet up when I get back?

I agree and thank her. It's not the sort of thing I want to discuss on the phone; I'll get far more detail from her if we meet up face to face.

Even as I close the laptop and settle into the silence again, there's no comfort. Just that gnawing sense that everything I've built – my friends, my marriage – is shifting beneath me.

TWENTY-SEVEN

SYLVIE

The rattle of a key in the lock startles me. I sit up straighter, my heart lifting and sinking at the same time, the way it seems to do lately.

A few moments later, Matt appears in the doorway, his grin easy and warm. This is the version of him I've missed being around. He holds his arms wide like he's trying to catch me mid-fall.

'Hey, gorgeous. I've come to whisk you down the road for breakfast at mine. How does a chat over poached eggs and wholemeal toast sound?'

One of my favourites. The voice with that playful note in it... takes me back. For a moment, it feels like the way it used to be. He's not mentioned my frantic text messages yet.

I feel my shoulders drop a little, warmth spreading into my chest. I'm not really that hungry, but I find myself saying, 'Sounds perfect. Give me five minutes.'

He waits on the sofa while I grab my bag and brush my hair, catching my reflection in the mirror. The lines around my eyes seem deeper today. Too much watching the window, waiting for calls that don't come. But I push all that aside, stand a little taller, and follow him outside.

The street is draped in that dull, damp grey again, soft-edged but heavy. Brenda's house across the road sits neat and silent, her squat little Fiat unmoved on the drive. I keep my gaze forward as we walk. The air is damp enough to stick to my skin, but there's no wind today.

Inside Matt's house, the warmth hits me straight away. It feels familiar and relaxed. His coat is slung over the back of a chair, the faint scent of coffee and aftershave lingering. The kitchen looks tidy enough, but there's a dustiness in the air, like it hasn't been disturbed properly in days.

A few empty wine bottles line the counter, waiting to go out to the glass box at the side of the house. One's missing a label, peeled halfway off. It's not one of our usual brands.

I sit at the kitchen table while he fusses with the toaster, the hiss of the kettle filling the silence. He moves easily, his sleeves rolled up and his hair tousled. He looks sexy and undone. I let my eyes trace the curve of his neck as he leans over the hob, the faint scrape of the knife against the plate as he butters toast.

'Anything I can do?' I offer.

'Nah,' he says without turning. 'You sit. Let me look after you for once. It's the least I can do after neglecting you last night. Work was crazy and... I just fell asleep when I got in.'

I rest my chin on my hand, watch him plate up the eggs. He ambles over and slides the plate in front of me, pours the coffee, then joins me at the table. For a few minutes, we just eat. The toast is warm, the egg yolks perfectly runny.

He catches me looking at the wine bottles and gives a sheepish smile.

'I should've taken those out last week,' he says. 'Too many nights sat here on my own, but I've kind of felt you didn't want me around at yours. What with everything that's been happening, I mean.'

I nod, unsure what to say. The coffee tastes a little bitter, but I swallow it down.

Halfway through his breakfast, he leans back, stretches.

'I got a big job in, last-minute. That's where I've been – Barnsley. I know you've got enough on with Jess and the baby, so I didn't want to bother you with it until I knew what was happening. I've been back and forth, trying to sort supplies.'

Barnsley. So Brenda was right. He's been distracted by work.

'I'm waiting on deliveries, so I've been able to come home today,' he says, catching my expression. 'But I'll need to head back up tomorrow, maybe the day after. A night or two, that's all. Depending.'

My shoulders drop before I even realise. 'Sounds like you've got a lot on. I wish you'd told me before; I've been...'

'You've been what?' He frowns.

'I don't know. Worried, I suppose. You've been rubbish at keeping in touch lately. Ignoring me and seeing a lot of Nige.'

'Sorry, babe. I should've paid you more attention.' He reaches across the table, brushing his thumb over the back of my hand. 'It's good, though, right? Solid work. Just bad timing, with everything that's going on. Nige is at a bit of a loose end, that's all.' He shifts in his seat. 'He's been having a few problems at work and... well, I want to be there for him. It won't last forever.'

I squeeze his fingers, let my hand settle there. 'I'm glad you've got the work.'

We finish breakfast quietly, the scrape of cutlery filling the gaps between us. When the plates are cleared, he pulls me away from the table and into the living room towards the sofa.

'Come here,' he says softly, settling beside me.

I fold into him, the shape of his body familiar against my

own. His arm loops around my shoulders, and I rest my head beneath his chin, breathing in the clean scent of his hair.

He kisses the top of my head, murmuring against my hairline. 'Once this job's done, I promise I'll take a proper break. We'll go away somewhere. Just us. Somewhere warm. You can drink cheap wine and I'll take advantage of you.'

I laugh, delighted. 'You always did have a talent for romantic gestures.'

He smiles into my hair. 'Seriously, though. We'll go away. Maybe Spain? You love Barcelona.'

'Sounds amazing.'

'Or Italy. You remember that little house we stayed at near Sorrento?'

'I remember the mosquito bites.' I frown, but my heart softens.

'We'll go back there soon,' he says, his voice low. 'We'll sit in the sun, drink too much limoncello, and you can read thrillers and bore me with the plots.'

I close my eyes, let myself believe in it for a moment. The warmth of him, the weight of his arm. It's so easy to fall back into this.

My phone vibrates in my pocket.

I shift, pulling it free, still half-draped against Matt.

Jess.

I answer, pressing the phone to my ear. Her voice sounds higher-pitched than usual. A bit panicky.

'Mum, can you come over? Just for an hour or so? Ed's at the studio and I need to pop out.'

I sit up a little. 'Of course, love. Everything OK with you? How's Scarlet Mae?'

She hesitates. I hear the restlessness of the baby in the background, a faint squeal.

'She's fine, but... thing is, I haven't heard from Kendra since yesterday morning. I know she hangs around that commune place sometimes – you know the one: no phones allowed, living off-grid and all that crap – but it's not like her to go quiet this long. I just want to check in with her.'

'You want me to sit with Scarlet Mae while you go and find her?'

'Would you? I just need to know she's alright.' She hesitates. 'You know how she can get a bit crazy at times.'

Kendra likes to live on the edge. She's always been the same.

I glance at Matt, who's already watching me, eyebrow raised.

'I'll be right there,' I tell Jess. 'Give me half an hour.'

When I hang up, Matt squeezes my knee. 'Everything OK?'

I nod. 'Just Jess being Jess. Kendra's gone AWOL. She's worrying, wants to check on her.'

Matt rolls his eyes. 'Jess isn't her mother.' He stands up and stretches. 'I can run you over there if you like?'

'Thanks but I'm fine. I'm best to have my car if I'm longer than expected there.'

He cups my face, kisses my forehead. 'I'll call you later then, yeah? Before I head back.'

I manage a smile, but as I step back outside into the grey, the warmth I felt earlier starts to thin again. Jess's concern about Kendra needles me, a new thread of worry to add to the others.

TWENTY-EIGHT

BRENDA

Brenda stands in the doorway of her small office, a converted box room, pausing before she steps inside. She inhales deeply, her nostrils filling with the scent of new stationery and printer ink, comforting aromas mingled with the undercurrent of urgency she always feels when she has a current project. She adjusts the thick woollen cardigan around her shoulders and crosses the threshold, closing the door softly behind her.

The room is dim. The blind is pulled and that's the way she likes it. The stark overhead light is too much. Brenda moves towards the desk lamp, flicking the switch and bathing the small office in a warm pool of amber. She looks around slowly, her eyes drifting across the meticulously organised space. She has spent hours curating this room, arranging and rearranging every detail. It serves as the nerve centre of all her efforts, and the only place where she truly feels in control.

On one wall, multiple cork boards hang neatly, covered in photographs pinned in orderly rows. Scarlet Mae dominates the first board – smiling, laughing, sleeping peacefully – innocent and unaware of Brenda's watchful eyes. Beside these, images of Sylvie and Jess fill another board. Shots she's taken on her phone camera and then printed off when she's back home.

Sylvie, her head tilted back and caught mid-laugh, the sunlight catching her hair. Jess, cradling a newborn Scarlet Mae, a faint, tired smile on her lips. Brenda's heart aches gently as she touches the photographs, her fingertip lingering.

These are *her* new people. Her found family.

A smaller cluster of images – proper photographs – are pinned discreetly along the bottom edge of one of the boards. Brenda's breath quickens when her eyes settle on these images.

These pictures were not hers to take, borrowed quietly one afternoon while Sylvie recuperated upstairs after her operation. Brenda recalls the quiet thrill of flipping through Sylvie's photo albums, heart fluttering at each tender moment captured. Sylvie's wedding photos are currently in the bottom of her chest of drawers. A deliberate gesture Brenda hopes might hasten its fading from Sylvie's own memory when she thinks she's mislaid them.

Brenda pivots slowly, facing the opposite wall. This is her information wall. She takes a step closer, eyes sharpening. Here, pinned neatly in chronological order, lies the story of Matthew Tyce's lies and gaslighting.

Photographs, handwritten notes and printed maps cluster together, taut strings of coloured wool connecting each piece of evidence. Brenda's hand brushes over a photo of Matt, snapped surreptitiously from across the street. His expression unreadable, eyes shadowed, posture tense. She'd watched him closely, learning the language of his movements, the subtle shift in his stance that betrayed the secrets that lurked beneath his surface charm.

'You're hiding something, you dirty rat,' Brenda whispers, her voice barely audible but rich with satisfaction. 'They're all dirty rats.'

Matthew Tyce has no time for her. These past few years, people have always dismissed her easily and Brenda is aware of this. A quiet, older woman, uncoloured hair and plain features offering easy invisibility. She's never minded – rather, she has learned to use it to her advantage. Underestimated can often equate to being unseen... invisible, even. Sometimes, that serves a purpose.

Her gaze drops to the top drawer of her desk and her fingers tingle slightly at what lies inside. She pulls it open carefully, revealing a neatly arranged assortment of compact devices. Her pulse quickens. She has quite the collection now.

Most ordinary people would be stunned at the quality and effectiveness at what you can buy online these days for a reasonable sum. There's the miniature camera disguised cleverly as a button, capturing HD video with startling clarity. Beside it, a sleek black recorder no larger than a thumb, sensitive enough to pick up whispered conversations practically through walls. And her favourite – the magnetic tracking device, small, powerful and discreet. It's this remarkable tool she had quietly slipped beneath the wheel arch of Matt Tyce's car on a moonless night a couple of weeks ago.

The houses on the street had been cloaked in darkness and no one had noticed her drifting down the driveway, a shadowy figure clad in dark clothing. Brenda had felt a surge of quiet triumph, returning unnoticed back home. Mission accomplished.

For the last fortnight, she's been tracking him, recording every move he makes. Patterns had quickly emerged, irregular but revealing. Twice she'd driven out, following the coordinates to check the equipment was working accurately and to see with her own eyes what Matt Tyce was doing.

Interesting. Very interesting.

Each time, she'd parked at a careful distance from his location, watching from behind oversized sunglasses and a nondescript scarf. Her heart had raced, palms damp, as she glimpsed his furtive exchanges – a car idling in an empty car park, lowered windows. A slight figure slipping into his car, almost unseen.

'Got you now,' Brenda murmurs, allowing herself a brief, satisfied smile.

And then, the plant pot. Brenda recalls the chill of excitement as she'd discovered the item beneath Matt's favourite terracotta planter. She'd waited until darkness, gloves on, flashlight clenched between her teeth as she uncovered the secret beneath it. Honest men had no need of going to these lengths, so what, then, was he up to?

That night, Brenda lay awake, replaying the moment over and over. She could almost feel Sylvie's relief when Brenda revealed this betrayal. Sylvie would finally understand. Brenda has the power to help her see clearly. To free her from Matt's manipulative grasp.

TWENTY-NINE

NOTTINGHAMSHIRE POLICE

The EFIT image glows on Helena's monitor, paling under the glare of the office's artificial lighting.

Lena stretches a hand over to fine-tune the jawline and the depth of shadow under the man's eyes. Brewster sits beside Helena, arms folded, his gaze flicking between the screen and the clock. The face they've built is ordinary enough – brown hair, unshaven – but thanks to Irene at the Spar shop, it has weight now. It's something. *It's someone.*

Helena's eyes feel gritty from staring at screens all morning, but still she stares at the EFIT image. The feeling of slight familiarity hasn't left her since she first saw it but she has to move past it as a potential distraction. After all, they only have Irene's word that this is an accurate representation of the man Ellie Walker came into the shop with.

The plan today is to finalise the image and circulate it to internal teams by lunchtime. Release to the media is scheduled for late afternoon. Stirring the waters to see who bites.

The shrill ring of her desk phone slices through their quiet focus.

Helena answers it, her eyes still on the image. 'DI Price.'

The control room operator speaks and Helena feels the colour drain from her face. The hum of the office fades beneath the words being uttered in her ear. *Body. Young woman.*

'You've secured the scene?' she says, aware Brewster's attention has shifted from the screen to her.

'Yes. Uniforms are containing the area. CID requested on site.'

Helena puts the receiver down slowly. Brewster and Lena are both now watching her, their expressions hovering somewhere between curiosity and dread.

'A body has been found,' Helena says, her voice level though her chest feels hollowed out. 'A dog walker stumbled across a body in the woods near Wollaton Park. A young woman. Uniformed responders are on scene, but they're requesting CID.'

Brewster exhales. 'We'll need to delay the EFIT release until we know what we're dealing with.'

Lena nods. 'I'll save our progress. I think we're almost there, anyway.'

'Come on, Brewster.' Helena stands, grabbing her coat from the back of the chair. 'We'll need to leave right away.'

They take one of the older pool cars, its diesel engine grumbling as the wipers clear away the drizzle clinging to the windscreen. Brewster drives, his knuckles pale on the steering wheel. He occasionally glances at Helena but says nothing until they're on the A52 heading west.

'You think it might be Ellie Walker?' Brewster asks finally, his voice quieter than usual.

Helena stares straight ahead. The rain has thickened to a sullen mist and the trees seem to fold into one another with the grey sky sagging so low.

'There's a distinct possibility it's her.' Helena rubs her hands together, tries to summon warmth that isn't there. 'Control didn't give me any descriptions or information but... seems the most likely scenario.'

She leans her head back against the seat, the hum of the engine vibrating against her skull. 'We've had no progress at all until the cashier spotted Ellie with the unknown man. If we've found Ellie Walker then everything shifts.'

Brewster chews his lip, eyes fixed on the road, and Helena gets it. They've seen enough bodies, enough broken shapes in lonely places, but each one brings its own weight. Its own mess.

'You know what's sticking with me?' Brewster says after a moment. 'What Irene said. That Ellie didn't look scared. That it was the guy she was with who looked uncomfortable.'

'Agreed,' Helena says. 'She said it was a strange look, but not aggressive.'

Brewster grimaces. 'I can't shake the feeling there's something we're not seeing. It feels like we're chasing the shadow of something that's not what it appears, if you get me?'

Helena nods. Doesn't make sense, but she knows what he's getting at.

The car dips into the edge of Wollaton. The streets narrow and old stone walls lining the parkland. They pass a row of dog walkers gathered beneath dripping trees, hoods up, glancing toward the flicker of blue lights in the distance.

Helena's ribs start to ache.

They pull up near the cordon, where a thin stretch of woodland squats densely between the park's edge and the outer paths. Blue-and-white tape flutters in the damp breeze, flanked by uniformed officers standing guard. Beyond them, a huddle of shapes – paramedics, SOCOs, a forensic tent half-raised like a reluctant flag. A few members of the public linger behind the tape, some drawn by concern, others by a morbid curiosity she's witnessed a lot at crimes scenes like this one.

Helena steps out of the car, the wet grass engulfing her shoes. The rain has eased to a fine mist and settles on her coat like a second skin. She nods to the officer at the cordon, who lifts the tape for her and Brewster.

The woodland is quiet and still, muffled by damp earth and the soft drizzle of rain that drips sadly from bare branches. The body lies half-covered by fallen leaves, maybe fifteen metres from the main footpath, where the ground dips slightly toward a shallow hollow. The beady-eyed pathologist, Rolly McAfee, stands nearby, his arms folded, expression set.

Helena crouches beside the body. Young woman. Early twenties, maybe. Short dark hair slicked with rain. Her clothing is intact – jeans, a pale jumper, a thin jacket. Nothing torn. Nothing out of place except the unnatural tilt of her head, the line of livid purplish bruising around her neck.

'Not Ellie Walker,' Brewster murmurs beside her.

Helena studies the girl's face. Wrong hair, wrong frame. Someone else entirely. As yet unknown.

'I'd say she's been here a few days,' McAfee says quietly. 'No obvious signs of a struggle. Ligature marks consistent with strangulation, though I'll confirm at post-mortem. No ID on her. We'll check fingerprints.'

Strangled.

Helena feels the chill seep deeper into her bones.

'Her clothing looks too clean for someone who walked here,' Brewster remarks, pointing to the body. 'No mud on the soles, no snagged threads. She didn't come through these woods on foot.'

'Killed elsewhere and dumped here?' Helena asks, though the answer feels obvious.

McAfee nods. 'Could well be the case.'

Helena stands slowly. A young life discarded so callously.

'There's no CCTV in the park,' Brewster mutters, glancing through the trees. 'Closest cameras would be on the main road. If someone drove her in, they were careful. There are no visible tyre tracks this close.'

Helena breathes out through her nose, scanning the clearing and the white-clad SOCOs painstakingly searching the vicinity. There's always the hope for something to be discovered – a scrap of fabric, a footprint, a mistake. But in Helena's opinion, whoever left this girl here knew the lie of the land. Knew how to walk away from their vile act, clean and unnoticed.

She turns back to McAfee.

'Can you prioritise her post-mortem?'

He nods. 'Already booked her in for first light tomorrow.'

Helena watches the precise activity around the body. Photographing, measuring, logging every inch of ground with the expectation it might offer answers. Her head feels heavy. Awash with the weight of unanswered questions.

As she and Brewster step back toward the path, he openly shudders.

'You know, I swear I got a strong whiff of formaldehyde back there.'

Helena rolls her eyes, grinning. 'Just your over-active imagination getting the better of you again, Brewster.'

He's had the heebie-jeebies ever since he heard the unsubstantiated rumours at the station. Essentially that McAfee practises taxidermy in his spare time, sometimes using roadkill.

Helena glances beyond the cordon. The onlookers are still there – phones raised, eyes curious. The face of the woman they've found will soon be everywhere, another headline. Another reminder that their case isn't closed. It's only yawning wider open.

Brewster sighs beside her, rivulets of rain streaming down his face.

'We've got one woman missing and another just turned up dead,' he says. 'If they're connected, we've lost the thread.'

'Or,' Helena says quietly, 'we might have found the thread. We just don't know yet what it's pulling us toward.'

They walk back to the car, the ground sucking at their

boots. The rain starts again – thin, persistent, enough to blur the edges of everything.

And it occurs to Helena that somewhere out there, the man in the EFIT might be watching their every move. Confident he's still well ahead.

THIRTY

BRENDA

Brenda sits stiffly by the front window, one hand rhythmically stroking Ivor's silky fur. Her fingertips move automatically, the smoothness of her movement disconnected from the tight knot forming in her chest.

The street outside is quiet, dead leaves fluttering like rotten confetti in the biting early December wind. Shadows drift across the pavement as storm clouds gather overhead.

Matt's car appears and pulls up outside the house. Brenda's fingers pause mid-stroke, her spine lengthening. She watches him step out, noting the casual indifference of his glance towards Sylvie's house. Just a glance, nothing more. He doesn't even feign interest in his wife. He lifts his head slightly, as though debating whether to approach, then shrugs lightly to himself and heads towards his own front door.

A heat curls inside Brenda's chest, spreading slowly outward like an unchecked fever. She recognises the signs in herself immediately, knows she ought to dampen the flames before they leap higher. The therapist's soothing voice whispers somewhere in the back of her mind, encouraging calmness, caution. But today, Brenda has no patience with all that well-being nonsense. Today, she only feels righteous indignation, the protective fury burning inside her at Sylvie's pain.

She felt this before, the last time. A memory flickers briefly, the edges a little blurred now. Brenda pushes it back down. Today, she will be strong.

Ivor yowls indignantly as she stands abruptly, surprising him on her lap. She mutters distractedly, already pulling her cardigan tightly around her shoulders. She slips on her sturdy loafers and shrugs on her jacket as she strides towards the front door, pushing her phone and keys into her pockets.

The front door swings closed behind her with a heavy, decisive sound. Brenda crosses the road quickly, her breath steaming slightly in the crisp air. She rings Matt's doorbell sharply, twice. Impatient. The chime echoes faintly inside.

She hears Matt cough and his slow, unhurried footsteps approaching. He opens the door, looking vaguely irritated, a half-eaten biscuit clutched in one hand and a mug in the other. He eyes her warily. 'Brenda,' he says flatly.

'Can I come in for a moment?' Brenda doesn't wait for permission, stepping boldly forward, invading his space.

Matt looks startled and instinctively moves aside, clearly unused to confrontation.

'What is it?' he says sharply. He pushes the door nearly shut but leaves a small gap, as though preparing for her to leave as quickly as she arrived.

Brenda takes a deep breath, her voice loud and unwavering in the small, dim space. 'Sylvie's worried sick about you. You haven't answered her messages, haven't bothered letting her know where you've been. What on earth do you think you're playing at?'

Matt's mouth drops open briefly, his eyes narrowing.

She watches as he shifts on his feet, clearly thrown off balance by Brenda's direct manner. 'Now just hold on a minute—'

'No, *you* hold on a minute, Matt.' Brenda cuts across him forcefully, stepping closer until he has no choice but to lean back slightly. 'Do you have any idea how distraught your wife has been? Any idea at all how worried she is, wondering what you're up to?'

Matt's jaw clenches tightly, his irritation now palpable. He puts the mug down sharply on the hall table, droplets of tea splashing onto the polished wood. 'Brenda, you can't just stroll into my house and start—'

'I can when I see my friend is in pain,' Brenda snaps, standing firm, her frame rigid with tension.

Matt stares at her, his face flushing, his eyes brightening with anger. For a heartbeat, silence stretches taut between them, thick and charged. Then he pushes his shoulders back, squaring up to her assertively. 'You need to leave. Now,' he says quietly.

Brenda lifts her chin defiantly. 'I know what you're up to, Matt.' She lets her words hang deliberately in the air, a subtle but unmistakable threat. 'I haven't told Sylvie yet, but when I leave here, that's exactly what I intend to do.'

She watches Matt falter, his indignation momentarily eclipsed by something else. Fear, perhaps, or guilt. Brenda feels a surge of satisfaction, confidence flooding through her veins. She has him exactly where she wants him.

Matt seems to assess her anew, his eyes narrowing with wariness. He reaches slowly behind Brenda and closes the door, cutting off the last trace of outside light. The hallway darkens immediately, but if he's trying to intimidate her, he's going to be disappointed.

'You'd better come in,' he says quietly, his voice low, carefully devoid of emotion. She's acutely aware of how vulnerable she is now, alone in his territory, but she holds her nerve. If anything, she feels more powerful than ever.

Matt gestures awkwardly to the small lounge, hastily clearing scattered magazines from the sofa with quick, irritated movements. Brenda doesn't sit. Instead, she stands stoically, her hands folded tightly in front of her.

'You have no right to interfere,' Matt says, his voice strained.

She watches carefully as he runs fingers distractedly through his hair, as if he's working out how to regain control of the situation.

'I have every right when Sylvie is involved,' Brenda replies calmly, meeting his eyes without flinching. 'She trusts me. She confides in me. She's unhappy and frightened because of *you*. And I won't stand by while you destroy her happiness.'

'This is ridiculous. *You're* ridiculous.' Matt spits the words out aggressively, but Brenda sees the way his hand trembles slightly as he grips the back of the chair. 'I don't know what you think you've got on me, but you've got it all wrong.'

'Have I?' she challenges quietly, lifting an eyebrow slightly, enjoying the subtle shift in power between them. 'Then explain to me why you've been lying to her. I know what you've been up to. I've got the evidence.'

He stares at her for a long moment before looking away sharply, his jaw muscle clenching.

'There's more going on here than you realise,' he finally says, voice lowered almost to a whisper. His eyes flick towards the door, as though he's nervous someone might overhear.

'Then why not tell me? Share the load?' she says softly, leaning forward just enough to draw him in, offering a false promise of understanding and confidentiality.

Matt hesitates, visibly torn, his breathing slightly ragged.

Then, almost too fast for her mind to catch up, he grabs her upper arm hard.

Brenda cries out. 'You're hurting me!'

His face presses close to hers as he flattens her up against the wall of the hallway. His skin is red, his teeth bared. As he raises his fist and it flies towards her, he doesn't look like Matt Tyce at all.

He looks like a monster.

THIRTY-ONE

SYLVIE

When I arrive at Jess's, I almost bump into Ed. He's just leaving the flat and looking at his phone. His eyes dart up, startled to see me.

'Oh, it's you, Sylvie!'

I step back to give him room. 'Hi, Ed.'

His hair is sticking up at odd angles, and there's a suspicious-looking patch of something – baby sick? Or maybe cereal, on his t-shirt. He glances back inside, then down at his watch.

'Jess is in, but I was just going out... got errands to run.' He trails off, gesturing vaguely to the stairwell.

'How are you?' I look towards the door and lower my voice. 'How's Jess doing? I know she's been a bit worried.'

I'd sat with the baby on Wednesday when she went looking for Kendra. She'd called in at her favourite drinking holes in town and the community art place she helped out at. But there had been no sign of her so Jess had dropped by the shared house she rented a room in. Jess had calmed down on her return. 'Her housemates aren't worried at all. Just laughed it off and said she'll turn up.' Jess had shrugged her shoulders, tired, and seemed at a loss why she'd panicked so much.

Ed nods. 'She's still worried sick about Kendra even though she's not saying much about it. She wasn't sleeping great before, but now, it's worse... she's never in bed when I wake in the night. She gets up and sits on the sofa with a cup of tea.'

'Well, let's hope Kendra turns up. It's two days she's been missing now, but not the first time she's gone AWOL.'

Ed nods. 'So glad you said that, it's what I've been trying to tell Jess! This will be another one of her disappearing acts.'

'I'll try and talk to her,' I say. 'You get off.'

He looks relieved. 'Thanks, Sylvie. She'll listen to you. Nice to see you.'

'You too.'

Ed disappears down the stairwell and I find myself thinking how, when they first met, I worried they weren't a good match. I didn't think Ed was motivated enough in his work or drive to do better. But since Scarlet Mae's birth, he's really shaped up to be a support to Jess and their new baby and I now realise that's the most I can ask for, for my daughter and new grandchild.

I step inside the flat and immediately smell warm milk and something slightly burnt. The hallway is cluttered with bags and coats; a wheel of Scarlet Mae's pram is wedged in a pile of shoes and a rolled-up yoga mat is balanced precariously on top. A single, forgotten sock hangs from the radiator.

'Hello?' I call.

'We're in here!' Jess's voice calls from the living room.

I navigate the chaos, pushing aside a blanket draped over a solitary dining chair. The room looks like it's been ransacked. Baby clothes spill from every surface, used wipes littering the coffee table. A dirty muslin cloth dangles from the arm of the sofa alongside a cold mug of tea resting on a stack of what looks like junk mail.

Jess sits cross-legged on the floor, her laptop open beside her, a half-eaten slice of toast balanced on the keyboard. She looks up and smiles.

'You made it! Sorry about the mess. I haven't had time to tidy round this morning.'

I glance around the room and grin. 'The past few weeks of mornings, you mean?'

Her greasy hair is scraped up into a messy bun and she's wearing one of Ed's jumpers with her leggings. She snorts. 'OK, you rumbled me.'

A flutter of guilt catches me in the throat. I've been so wrapped up in Brenda, in Matt, in the whole strange unravelling of things my end, I haven't seen Jess as much as I should have done. We've done mainly snatched phone calls, texts and the odd picture of Scarlet Mae asleep, drooling down the front of her Babygro. Have I inadvertently let my beloved daughter and granddaughter fall to the bottom of the pile?

'I've been scouring Kendra's social media and she's not been active for days.'

'How's Scarlet doing?' I ask, lowering myself onto the edge of the sofa. The cushions are scattered and crushed and something crinkles beneath me.

Jess nods toward the crib. Scarlet Mae sleeps peacefully, arms thrown above her head, the rise and fall of her chest barely visible. Her cheeks are pink with warmth and my heart fills.

'Out for the count,' Jess says. 'We had a restless night.'

'Is she feeding OK?'

Jess sighs. 'Mostly, but then sometimes I worry she's getting fussy and... maybe I'm overthinking everything.'

I smile, gently. 'Everyone overthinks everything. Try one side until she comes off by herself. Then offer the second. If she's not interested, that usually means she's had enough for now.'

'Right. OK. That makes sense.' She rubs at her eyes with the heel of her hand.

I watch her for a moment. Her colour's better, and the patchiness from the allergic reaction has gone, but there's something else now. Her eyes look troubled, as if she's carrying a new weight.

'Jess?' I say carefully. 'Are you feeling OK?'

She nods. Then her mouth wobbles, and she presses her lips together, blinking too fast.

I reach for her hand. 'You're worried sick about Kendra. Ed told me before he just left.'

'It's true. It's just... I know Ed thinks I'm worrying about nothing and, as you've both said, she's got history in disappearing now and again. But... there's something I haven't told Ed. I don't know why.'

I lean forward, keen to help her feel better if I can. 'Talk to me.'

'Me and Kendra, we had a disagreement.' She folds herself tighter, pulling Ed's jumper over her knees like a comfort blanket. 'We haven't exactly fallen out, but... as you know, she came round after Scarlet Mae was born, to your house a few times. She was all excited and cooing, and then she stopped replying to my messages. Said she was bored of baby chat. That she needed a break from "mum energy". Can you believe that? I mean, what an insult.' Her voice cracks, and tears spill over. 'And to think I wanted her as Scarlet Mae's godmother.'

I reach for her hand. 'Oh, love. That was a bit mean of her.'

'I thought maybe she'd come round after her housemates didn't seem overly concerned. They seemed certain she'd have gone off for a day or two like she sometimes does. So I gave her space and I've heard nothing. I've been texting, calling her but her phone is always off. So yesterday, I decided to just go. Turn up at her shared house in Lenton. Ed watched the baby, and I got the bus to her house again. But she still wasn't there. One of her other housemates answered the door and said he thought she might've done a bunk.' Jess frowns. 'But he told me her room is still full of all her stuff. I know it wouldn't be the first time, but her laptop, toothbrush, everything is still there.'

The tears come properly now and she wipes them away roughly with her sleeve.

'I kind of feel like it might be my fault. Like maybe I bored her away. Or made her feel trapped in some way.'

I shake my head. 'Jess, no. Kendra's always been unpredictable. You know that. Remember that time she decided she was moving to Berlin? She packed everything she owned into bin bags, then changed her mind halfway through the EasyJet flight booking?'

Jess lets out a weak laugh. 'Oh gosh, yes. And then she made us throw a goodbye party anyway.'

'Complete with sauerkraut and bratwurst. Which she bought from a petrol station.'

We're both laughing now, although Jess's is laced with sadness.

'Whatever's happened, it's not your fault,' I say again. 'And like Matt says, you're not Kendra's mother.'

Jess's face hardens. 'Why would he say that? It's got nothing at all to do with him.'

'Hey, what's brought this on?' I'm taken aback by her snappy retort. 'He's allowed an opinion too.'

Jess frowns and looks away.

'Look,' I say, trying to appease her a little. 'Kendra does what Kendra wants. She always has, you know that.'

Jess sighs. 'I know, I know. That's what Ed says, it's just... I hoped she'd... I don't know. Grown up a bit, I suppose.'

I give her hand a squeeze. 'You're the grown-up now. It's hard when friends are in different stages of their lives. You see people differently and sometimes that means they fall away.' I hesitate. 'But it's probably just a temporary blip. She'll come round, I'm sure.'

'I hope so.' Jess sniffs and touches my arm. 'Thanks, Mum. I do feel a bit better now.'

Scarlet Mae stirs, a twitch in her foot first, then a snuffling sound. Jess cranes her neck to check her, but I'm already up and beside her basket, lifting her out gently. She blinks up at me, her mouth working in sleepy confusion.

'Hello, little one.'

She yawns, her whole body stretching and then curling in on itself before she settles on my shoulder. Jess watches us, her face soft.

'You make it look so easy,' Jess murmurs.

'I didn't find it easy at all when I first had you, but I learned. And so will you.'

I sway gently, patting Scarlet Mae's back. Yes, her flat is a big mess, the kind of mess that would have once made me clench inside, but today, I honestly don't care. The love and feeling in this room outweigh it all.

Jess comes to stand beside me. She rests her head briefly on my other shoulder and I feel the old closeness settle between us. No need to perform, no need to fix. Just my two girls with me.

'Thank you,' she whispers.

We stand that way for a while, the baby between us, small and warm and real.

Later, when I leave the flat, I pause outside on the landing, the cool air hitting my cheeks, and reach for my phone. Matt's name hovers on the screen.

I don't press call. Not yet. But I know I will. Jess is right; people change. Life gets messy. But some things, and some people, are still worth fighting for.

THIRTY-TWO

The image of her parents' faces flickers behind Ellie's eyes. Their tight, expectant smiles, the endless questions, the curfews and check-ins. Her life has been mapped out and it has pushed her onto a pathway she never chose.

Adult nursing. Staying close to home. Making sensible choices. A secure career.

That's what they *wanted, not her.*

After Sophie died, nothing was ever going to be the same.

Sophie – her older sister and the golden child. The one they couldn't save from blood cancer. And so they caged Ellie instead.

'I didn't think you'd go through with it, you know. Not really.'

'I'm a man of my word. You must have realised that.'

'Yes, but after all those hours chatting together online and then you just disappeared. I thought you'd got cold feet. Thought it was too risky.'

He shakes his head. 'No way. That last conversation we had, when I asked you to trust me, I said it would be a surprise, didn't I? I said it would happen when you least expected it.'

'I know that, but... it's been a few weeks now and I'd made up my mind you were just bluffing.'

'And now here we are.' He looks around the room. 'I watched you, you know. You never suspected a thing. It was... exhilarating.'

She shifts on the bed and tucks her knees up beneath her chin.

'Tell me.'

'I mapped out your routines, even considered a few other girls. I watched you for hours, took photographs. I enjoyed reminding myself I could take you at any time but I wanted to make the feeling last a bit. Really throw myself into it.'

She scowls. 'You didn't have to use the chloroform.'

'Authenticity is important. I wanted you properly scared especially after seeing you with that sap at the Spar shop. Were you... scared?' He stands up and walks over to the bed.

'I was,' she says softly, flattening her legs and reclining against the soft pillows. 'I still am. A bit.'

He takes off his t-shirt and climbs onto the bed. She can smell him. He's hot and slightly sweaty like an animal. Unfamiliar. She holds her breath and closes her eyes, feeling the weight of him when he climbs on top of her.

Afterwards, she says, 'I'm not going back there ever again. I hope you know that.'

His eyebrows lift, just slightly.

'You might change your mind and then we'll be in trouble.'

'I won't,' she adds, firmer now. 'I'd rather stay here, even if I never leave this room. Even if you never leave her.'

He doesn't argue. He listens to her with a kind of odd fascination. Something about him makes her think he knows exactly how she feels, although he's never said as much.

They sit in silence for a while. The hum of the generator outside is faint but steady. Like a heartbeat.

'This is our new reality,' he says simply. 'We did it.'

'You *did* it.'

'Like *you* wanted. Like *we* planned.'

She nods, but he's the one on the line here in terms of the law. She could so easily twist it to her favour, if she wants to. 'I thought you'd ghosted me.'

She studies his face, how he looks so different in the flesh. He'd disappeared *offline* so suddenly. Sent her a message to say he felt too guilty to carry on their 'relationship'. When she tried to reply, his user handle – and all their conversation threads – had been erased as if he'd never existed at all.

So what had changed?

'It was all part of the plan, don't you see now?' he says. 'I wanted to surprise you. To make it all feel as real as possible.'

'You said you had everything you wanted now at home,' she says.

'It was a lie.' A muscle tightens at the corner of his jaw. It's the first flicker of emotion she's seen in him. 'There's nothing there for me. Nothing at all.'

Her heart stirs and she feels it then – the danger. Something's changed in him; something has warped and broken somehow. But it doesn't send her running. It coils inside her like a secret. The fear of it all going wrong here is better than a lifetime stuck with her parents and their stifling expectations.

'So, what happens now?' she asks.

'I'm going to take care of you.'

'Until what?'

'Until you're ready.'

She huffs out a breath and then shakes her head when she thinks about the other stuff they'd discussed at length.

'You think I'm just going to settle in here? Live the rest of my life in this room?'

'I think you're smarter than you let on. Remember our other plan?'

That makes her smile. No one's ever accused her of being

smart, not in the way he means, anyway. She's been called sweet, soft-hearted and hard-working. A good girl. Always obedient.

And the next part of the plan is wild. It fills her with dread and thrills. She never fully believed any of this would actually happen. She does now.

Ellie swings her legs over the side of the bed and lets her feet touch the cool wooden floor. He tenses, just a flicker in the shoulders, but he doesn't move or tell her to stay where she is.

'I want some water,' she says.

He gestures to the glass on the bedside table.

'Have you drugged it?'

'Try it.'

She does. Drinks it in one long gulp, wiping her mouth with the back of her hand.

He watches her, silent and brooding.

When she's finished, she sets the glass down with a deliberate clink.

'I feel like I know you really well, but you're not what I expected,' she says.

'Neither are you.'

That makes her smile again, though this time there's something genuine beneath it.

He reaches down and produces something that looks like a photo album. Moving over to her, he perches on the edge of the bed.

'What's this?' she says.

He opens the album and she gives a short gasp. 'What have you... how did you get this?'

He smiles. Hands her the album.

'I know what happened,' he says softly. 'I know what they did to you.'

THIRTY-THREE

BRENDA

Standing in her office surrounded by the various rewards of her covert monitoring, Brenda straightens, pulling her cardigan closer around her. She rubs the angry red marks on her upper arm. It will be bruised tomorrow. She'll make sure Matt Tyce won't get away with this, despite his threats.

It's time to put her plan into action.

She reaches for her mobile phone, scrolling to Sylvie's number. Silently, Brenda rehearses what she wants to say, her heart racing. She presses the call button before she loses her nerve.

Sylvie picks up quickly. 'Hello?' Her voice is quiet and slightly rushed, as if she was just in the middle of doing something.

'Sylvie, it's Brenda. I really need to speak with you, dear.' Brenda's voice is calm, but rings with gentle urgency. There's a pause at the other end. 'Are you able to talk?'

'Yes, it's just... I'm just leaving Jess's house. Is everything alright, Brenda?' She can hear the concern edging into Sylvie's tone.

'There's something I think you should know,' Brenda says

quietly, letting her voice tremble slightly. 'It's about Matt and it's difficult for me to talk about. But I do think you'll want to know, sooner rather than later.'

There's silence on the line, heavy and strained. 'Brenda, what do you mean? Give me a clue what this is about, at least.' Sylvie's voice is low with concern.

'Not on the phone,' Brenda insists softly, her tone confidential. 'We need privacy to talk properly; I don't want to risk him walking in on us. I can come over in the morning, if that suits?'

'I suppose so...' Sylvie hesitates briefly.

'I wouldn't ask unless I was absolutely certain you need to know,' Brenda says gravely. 'You deserve the truth. But... please don't mention this call to Matt. That's important.'

'But—'

'Can you do that? Otherwise, I'm best not to speak to you at all.'

'Yes, OK.' Sylvie sighs as if Brenda is being overly dramatic. 'I won't mention you called.'

They agree a time to meet, Brenda ending the call with soft reassurances about how everything is going to be alright. When the call ends, Brenda exhales slowly, leaning against her desk, knees suddenly weak with exhilaration. It's begun. The first steps toward reclaiming her rightful place in Sylvie's life.

Matt will be exposed, Sylvie freed from a loveless marriage, and Brenda will stand at her side, loyal and cherished once more.

She reaches up, carefully detaching a photo of Matt from her office wall and studying it thoughtfully. Brenda's finger presses firmly against the image, creasing it deliberately.

'You've underestimated me, Mr Matthew,' Brenda murmurs coldly. 'That was your mistake.'

Outside, shadows lengthen across the street. Brenda moves towards the window, drawing the blinds tight, shutting out the gathering darkness. She'd intended visiting her aunt today, but she can't afford the distraction. Tomorrow will bring revelation, confrontation and justice. She allows herself a rare smile, confident now in her purpose, in her power.

Brenda switches off the lamp, leaving the office in darkness. Her footsteps echo gently on the staircase, descending back into the quiet normalcy of her house. For tonight, at least, Brenda allows herself peace, secure in the certainty of her plan. She hums quietly, a tuneless lullaby drifting softly through the empty, cold rooms of the house.

THIRTY-FOUR

SYLVIE

When I get back home from Jess's house, the silence rushes at me like fog. There's nobody here. No Jess, no Scarlet Mae and no Matt. No radio or TV on, no distant clatter from upstairs, no sound of the boiler humming. Just the click of the front door behind me and my own shallow breath.

For a moment, I stand there in the hallway, coat still on and my bag slipping from my shoulder. I wonder whether I ought to just go over to Brenda's house right now, demand to know what all the fuss is about. But then... she'd been adamant it had to be in the morning.

I shrug off my coat and shoes, the silence thickening.

Jess's house had been loud and chaotic with baby squeals, background television and traffic passing on the busy road outside. *Life*. Being back home feels like someone pressed pause and not in a good way. I look around and everything is as it was, and yet nothing here feels the same as it used to. The contentment is gone.

Matt's slippers are by the radiator. Slightly skewed from the last time he kicked them off... days ago, now. One of his favoured brushed-cotton checked shirts is hooked over the banister rail.

What is it that Brenda feels she has to tell me about my husband? This could just be another of her dramatic episodes, of course.

I head upstairs and my legs feel leaden, like they can't carry me around much longer.

I change into jeans and one of Matt's old jumpers, partly because it smells of him, partly because it's so big and I can cuddle myself up in it. I sit in front of the mirror and brush my hair, rehearsing what I'll say when I call him.

I think we need to talk properly, Matt. We need to reset.

No… that sounds a bit too formal.

Let's stop pretending things are fine when they're not, shall we?

Too accusing. A bit aggressive.

I miss you.

Better, but too passive?

In the kitchen, I perform my usual distraction and wipe down the already clean surfaces. I turn on the radio then click it off again. I check my phone half a dozen times, but there's never anything from Matt. He's supposed to be in County Durham working on a big patio and pergola job at a country house, but he hadn't said he'd be staying away several nights.

I open our message thread.

Yesterday: *Will be home late. Don't wait up.*

That was it.

I call him. It rings three times before going to voicemail.

'It's me. Just wondering when you'll be home. Give me a bell when you can.'

I hang up, then immediately text:

All OK? When will you be home? Miss you.

I try not to think too much about the 'Seen' status that doesn't appear. Maybe he's in a meeting. Maybe his phone died. If his Find Friends was working, I'd be able to see exactly where he is. So frustrating.

On Instagram, I see a photo of a couple walking dogs on the beach – arms linked, big grins. The caption reads: *Still laughing after twenty years. Married my best friend.*

I flick past it too quickly and nearly drop the phone when Matt calls back.

'Matt?'

'Hey,' he says. The background's noisy – muffled voices, a faint echo, like he's in a pub or a hotel lobby.

'Where are you?'

'Just wrapping up here. Sorry I missed your call.'

'No worries, but when will you be home? I need to talk to you. It's important.'

There's a pause. 'What about?'

'About us, Matt. I want us to have a proper chat about stuff.'

'OK, but it's a bit full-on here. I've got a site meeting at eight tomorrow morning, so I'm going to have to crash up here again tonight.'

'Where exactly are you?'

'County Durham. The client's place is sort of... off the beaten path.'

'Your location's been turned off on Find Friends.'

Another short pause.

'Yeah, probably signal. It's patchy up here.'

'OK,' I say, trying to sound reasonable. 'So you'll be back tomorrow?'

'Should be. Unless something changes. Look, I should go – I have to call a supplier before they close. I'll text you later, yeah?'

'Love you,' I say, but he's already hung up.

I lower the phone and stare at the blank screen until it dims and reflects my face back – shadowy and blurred. I look older, somehow.

Something flutters low in my stomach. Not panic, exactly. More like the moment just before a storm breaks when the birds go quiet. He's not himself. I can just feel it.

I sit down at the kitchen table and stare at the opposite chair. His chair. I remember the time he... I shake the thought away. No time for sentimentality when everything's going wrong.

Anyway, it was months ago. Before we stopped laughing as easily.

I open the wine. I'll have just the one glass. I pour it too full and sip too fast in front of the TV. There's some game show host on spouting nonsense in the background.

I keep thinking about Matt's tone on the call. Polite. Cool. Just plain *off*.

Not really him at all.

I remember one time, he said he was working late and being evasive just like he is now. It turned out work was sparse and he'd taken out a short-term loan to give me the impression he was still doing well. It seemed a needless thing to do; he should have just told me so I could support him. But he said he didn't want to worry me.

I found out from coming across an envelope stuffed with cash in his t-shirt drawer. He'd said it was to pay a supplier who was hassling him. Might have been true; I'll never know.

But it planted something in me. A worrying sense that Matt doesn't always tell me things – not lies through his teeth, exactly. But stretches the truth to avoid me questioning him.

I check our joint calendar app on my phone. There's a note in for the job's start date, but nothing about the rest of his travel or meetings this week. Usually he logs everything in, gives specific details, even when it's just a reminder to order cement.

I open the wardrobe. We always tend to leave from here if we go walking on a weekend, but his hiking boots are gone. So is the waterproof jacket he keeps for surprise showers. Maybe he's telling me the truth after all, and I'm just getting paranoid.

I make a cheese and tomato sandwich, eat three bites and bin the rest.

I pour another glass of wine, put on a film but turn it off before the opening credits have finished rolling.

I look around. I used to love this house, but right now it feels like a museum. Every room is pristine but lifeless. Even the ticking clock seems too loud, like it's counting down to something.

A sudden sound makes me jerk, but it's just the heating clunking on.

For a split second, I think I hear Matt's key in the door. Of course, it isn't. I have to accept he's not home, and if he's really busy, he might not come back tomorrow either.

I look at my empty wine glass from earlier. Then I look at the clock.

I walk over to the fridge to top up my glass. On the counter, the screen of my phone lights up and distracts me. It's a new message from Matt.

Relieved, I smile and open it.

Hey, why aren't you picking up? Missing you already.

I stare at the message.

I re-read it three times. Check my notifications... no missed calls.

Why aren't you picking up? Missing you already.

I don't know how to reply. I don't know if I should reply.

Why would he say I'm not picking up, if he hasn't called me in the first place?

I don't think my husband meant to send this message to me.

I think it was meant for someone else.

THIRTY-FIVE

The next morning, the doorbell rings before I've had my second cup of tea. I check the time and it's early – 8.42 a.m. My stomach tightens.

When I open the door, Brenda is standing there, holding a large plant in a pot, one of those spiky dragon trees with long green fingers. She smiles, wide and warm.

'I saw this and I thought of you,' she says, stepping inside without waiting for an answer.

'Oh, that's kind of you, thank you. It's lovely,' I say, taking the pot. It's heavier than it looks and damp soil clings to the ceramic base. 'I won't ask why the word "dragon" reminds you of me.'

She grins. 'They're very hardy, apparently. You can neglect them for weeks and they'll still cling on. Sound familiar?'

I'm not quite sure how to react to that. But I take it from her and carry it a little way into the hallway, setting it close to the door and the light from the glass panel.

Brenda follows me in, already taking off her coat. Already at home.

Back in the living room, she takes the chair opposite mine like it's always been hers. 'Sorry it's so early,' she says. 'I just couldn't stop thinking about everything, and well... I thought our chat was better done earlier rather than later.'

Brenda watches me closely, her eyes sharp behind the softness.

'What's all this about?' I say. 'What do you want to tell me about Matt?'

'I think you've been holding stuff in for too long.' She looks at the window and then back again. 'You need someone on your side, even if Matt doesn't like it.'

'It's not really like that,' I say quickly, pushing away thoughts of the strange text he sent me last night. 'Matt and I – we've been distant, yes, but I'm sure there's a reasonable explanation.'

Brenda nods. The kind of reluctant nod people give when they don't entirely agree but want to appear gracious. 'Well, that's sort of what I want to talk to you about.'

'OK.' I take a breath. 'I'm listening.'

She leans forward, voice low. 'It occurred to me that sometimes when men start to pull away, it's not always work that's causing the problem.'

I look away. 'Are you saying you don't think Matt is working away?'

'I don't know if you've noticed, but I have a very good view of this side of the street from my front room window.'

'And?' I sigh. 'Just say what it is you've come here to tell me, Brenda. It feels like we're going round in circles.'

'OK, if that's the way you want it. Yesterday, I went round to confront Matt about the stuff I've been witnessing. He was very unfriendly to say the least. He did this when I wouldn't back down.' In a quick movement, she slips off her cardigan sleeve and I gasp at the red finger marks there. 'That's your husband's handiwork.'

'I don't believe it.' I've said the words without even thinking about it. 'I mean to say that Matt isn't a violent man. He's never laid a finger on me, or Jess. I've never seen him lose his temper at anyone.'

'Secrecy breeds suspicion and resentment. You've always been the type of person who sees the best in people, Sylvie, and that can leave you vulnerable.' She slips her arm back into the sleeve. 'A rat trapped in a cage will go for the jugular every time. Isn't that what they say?'

Her words sting my skin like nettles. Brenda's only known me a short time but she's talking about my marriage in such casual terms, as if we've been lifelong friends.

'What did you accuse him of? How do you know he's not working?'

Brenda doesn't answer. Instead, she pulls something from her pocket – a folded scrap of paper. My name is scribbled on the outside in her loopy handwriting.

'I don't want to appear a snoop,' she says, passing it over. 'But I was looking up that landscaping job Matt mentioned. You know, out of curiosity. But I couldn't find anything in County Durham. The firm you said he's working with has a website, but it doesn't list a current project there. Their last post was tagged in Whitby, not Durham. Look.'

I unfold the paper. She's printed a screenshot from social media. There are a group of people standing next to a van, captioned: *Sunrise before the slog begins*. The location tag says 'Whitby Harbour'.

'Could be an old photo,' I say, though I already know it isn't.

Brenda shrugs. 'Maybe. Or maybe he doesn't want you to know where he really is. Now, you have to ask yourself why that might be.'

I should tell her to mind her own business. Say she's stepping way out of line, but she's tapped into my deepest fears.

Something lies heavy on my chest when I think of Matt's vague tone, the way he brushed off my questions. The late text message he sent that didn't make any sense. As if it was meant for someone else.

'Of course, I'm not saying he's definitely cheating,' Brenda continues blithely, 'but something's clearly not right. Anyone can see that.'

'I can't confront him over a tagged post.'

'No, but there are other ways to find out what he's up to. Quiet ways he needn't know about and that's why I wanted to talk to you without him knowing.' She hesitates. 'You have a key to his house, I presume?'

I look up.

'Brenda—'

She holds up a hand. 'I'm not saying break in and rifle through his drawers. Just... what's the harm in popping by while he's away? You're just making sure everything is as it should be. You're his wife, and you have every right to do so.'

She's right, but just the thought of it makes me uncomfortable. 'It's not the sort of thing we'd do in each other's homes.'

Brenda sniffs. 'Maybe it's time you did. If he's innocent, there's no harm done and you'll feel better. If he's not... well, I reckon it's better to know than to let it rot you from the inside out.'

Her voice is low and urgent. Persuasive. I hear myself saying, 'I don't know...' but I'm already picturing it – standing in his kitchen, checking around for clues like some desperate character in a thriller. It's absurd.

And yet.

'You know what I'd do, if I were you?' she says.

'Go on.'

'I'd start by checking his emails. Just a little peek. Sometimes men keep things hidden in plain sight. Or perhaps you could speak to someone who's worked with him lately. Just casually.'

'You make it sound like he's plotting something criminal.' She claims to know rather a lot about what men do and think for someone who's never been married.

She smiles. 'I'm just saying – protect yourself. That's all. He's so very keen in keeping two houses on; you said so yourself. Why might that be, I wonder?'

I rub the side of my face. My skin feels sore and tight.

'Let me help you,' she says softly. 'Let me take some of the burden.'

'I don't want to start... spying.'

Brenda doesn't speak. Just sips her tea and lets the silence stretch. And I feel myself falling into it.

'Maybe just a quick visit round to his place,' I say eventually. 'To reassure myself.'

'Good,' she says, setting down her mug. 'That's sensible. It's what I'd do.'

After she's gone, I feel restless and troubled. I move through the rooms slowly, unsure what it is I'm looking for.

Upstairs, my bed is rumpled, unmade from getting up this morning. I sit on the edge of it and close my eyes. I can still hear Brenda's voice, marshalling my thoughts.

Sometimes men keep things hidden in plain sight...

What did she mean by that?

The phrase repeats itself again and again in my head. It becomes sinister and dreadful.

I shake my head. I'm not this person. I don't snoop, I don't track people, I don't go through my husband's things.

But then lately, I don't seem to be myself at all.

When I check my phone there are no new messages from Matt.

The last text message I opened wasn't meant for me. The more I read it, the less it sounds like him. Or maybe the less I remember who he really is.

His door keys sit in the little wooden dish on the hall table.

I stare at them for what feels like a long time and then I realise I've already decided.

Maybe I should go around there. Just to look, to reassure myself. That's all.

I glance toward the kitchen.

The dragon tree's shadow stretches long across the laminate floor, like creepy fingers reaching into the house.

THIRTY-SIX

SYLVIE

SUNDAY

Something jerks me out of sleep. I sit bolt upright, my heart pounding as I try to work out what just dragged me awake in the early hours. Darkness presses against the windows. The bedside clock glows. Just before midnight. I blink, trying to separate dream from reality, but there it is again – a noise downstairs.

A thump. Then another. Sharp. Not footsteps. Not the door opening.

I freeze.

Maybe Matt has come home super-early, forgetting I've deadbolted the door. Maybe fumbling with his keys, frustrated.

Hope catches in my throat before reason crushes it again. Matt would probably come around the back to knock. And anyway, this isn't knocking. It's hammering. Someone is banging hard on the front door.

I slide my legs out of bed and reach for my dressing gown, all the time listening. The house is still around me until the next three heavy strikes. A fist banging frantically on the door.

I stand and the carpet beneath my feet feels cool, like something's seeping up from beneath the floorboards. I steel myself and move quickly into the dim light of the shadowed landing.

I snap on the landing light and the shadows disappear.

When I reach the top of the stairs, I look down. The porch light slices across the inner welcome mat through the frosted glass panel. Beyond it I can see movement. A figure... someone standing close to the front door.

'Mum!' It's Jess, her voice hoarse with terror and panic. 'Mum, open the door! Please!'

I stumble the rest of the way down, my heart lurching. She's crying. Yelling. She's going to wake the street.

'I'm coming!' I yell, reaching the door and snapping on the hall light. I tug clumsily at the bolt, my fingers trembling. It sticks but I manage to fumble it loose, yank the chain, throw the door open.

Jess almost falls inside, her face blotched and wet with tears. She makes a noise – half-sob, half-gasp – and collapses into me.

'Jess... what is it?' I hold her, trying to steady us both while pushing the door hard enough that it closes. She's shaking and can hardly catch her breath.

'It's Kendra,' she whimpers. 'I didn't know who else – Mum, I don't know what I'm going to do...'

'Sit down,' I say, trying to guide her to the stairs. She tries to resist at first and then her legs buckle beneath her. We sit together on the bottom step, side by side, my arm around her. 'Jess, take a breath. Tell me, what's happened?'

'They found a body,' she says again. 'In the park. It's—' She breaks off, a sob ripping through her. 'It's Kendra.'

My mind goes blank. For a moment, what she's saying doesn't make any sense. It sits there like a ghoul at the front of my mind. Then the pieces start to join. *The body of a young woman the police found in Wollaton Park.*

'It's *Kendra*?'

Jess nods, unable to speak.

I grip the banister to steady myself. The wall tilts.

'She's dead,' Jess says finally, and the words land like a slap. 'Kendra's dead. They found her body.'

I blink at her. 'No.'

'It's true. They just – the police just rang. One of the officers went to her house and they told her we were—' Her voice breaks. 'Her housemates told them we were best friends. They said they wanted to let me to know before it... gets out. She's been missing for days. I should've done more and now—'

Her words collapse again into crying.

I pull her into my arms, the way I did when she was seven years old and found the neighbour's missing cat dead in our garden. But this is different. This is... vast and impossible.

Kendra. Not just missing. Not just on one of her crazy benders. *Dead*.

I think of her as a schoolgirl. Her nervous smile, the way she perched on the edge of our sofa, looking awkward, like she didn't quite belong despite her always being made so welcome.

And now her body has been found, dumped in the park.

'I thought she was just laying low,' Jess whispers. 'I thought she was angry. I thought... we would sort it out, Mum.'

'You couldn't have known,' I say. 'Did the police say... what happened?'

Jess shakes her head. 'I feel sick. I can't stop imagining her lying there in that wood, all alone.'

I know what she means. My brain is already filling in blanks with awful images. First Ellie Walker goes missing and now Kendra has been found... two girls who attended the same school, lived in roughly the same area.

I get us to the sofa somehow and my daughter curls against me, her knees tucked up, making herself small and invisible.

She's a mother herself now, but in this moment she's my frightened little girl again.

Outside, the wind picks up and I hear the broken fence panel rattle.

'They haven't said how she died,' Jess says eventually. 'Just that she's dead. And that it's definitely her. They said that, too.'

My arms are around her but my thoughts are skating off in a hundred different directions. Matt. The woods. Brenda. The timing of it all.

'Did they say who found her?' I ask.

'A dog walker, early in the morning, I think. But the officer said she's probably been there a couple of days.'

I close my eyes against the horror of it. Kendra, in this house, alive and vibrant, visiting Jess and Scarlet Mae. Scrolling through her phone, voicing her strong opinions whether people want to hear them or not. And now... silenced forever.

'I should have done more, Mum. I can't get it out of my head. What was I thinking?' Jess sobs.

'You've just had a baby, Jess! Stop kicking yourself when you're down.'

'But I knew she was acting weird, and I just kept brushing it off. Telling myself she was bored of me having the baby tying me down. I even thought part of her might be jealous because we're the same age and she's nowhere near having a child of her own.'

'You had no way of knowing it would come to this.'

She hesitates before saying softly, 'But I did know she was scared.'

I look at her. 'Scared of what?'

She swipes at her wet face. 'She thought someone was watching her.'

My pulse jumps. 'What?'

She sniffs, nodding. 'She didn't say who. It was just... little things that were freaking her out a bit. Her post disappearing at the house. And she told me she was getting weird messages from an unknown number.'

'Had she told anyone about it? The police?'

Jess shakes her head. 'She found her bedroom window open when she got in one night and she said she was certain she'd shut it before going out.' Jess looks at her hands. 'I told her she was being paranoid. Told her to stop partying and to get some sleep. How could I have been so callous?'

'Don't be hard on yourself, Jess,' I say gently. 'Like we said before, Kendra has previous. Remember when she used that fitness tracker app to prove her neighbour was stalking her, and it turned out he was just training for a marathon and happened to run past her house every night about seven o'clock?'

Jess laughs through her tears. Or tries to. But it peters out to nothing.

'I did think she was spiralling, Mum, when she told me all that stuff. You know Kendra, she could get a bit paranoid. Thought people knew things about her they shouldn't.'

'What sort of things?'

She shrugs. 'She wouldn't tell me everything but I guessed she'd met someone and she kind of admitted it. That's what she said. But when I pushed her for details, she just... stopped saying anything at all. And soon after that, she made excuses why she couldn't come round to see Scarlet Mae.' She looks at her hands. 'I shouldn't have pushed her so hard.'

Maybe I'm just feeling happy in my life for once. I'd wondered if she had a new boyfriend but I didn't push her either. Now I wish I had.

I feel numb. 'Why didn't you tell me, if you were so worried?'

Jess shrugs. 'I didn't think it was anything important at the time. Just Kendra being Kendra. And then coming back home and coping on my own with Scarlet Mae... I've been all over the place.'

I hold her tighter and the guilty feeling creeps through my veins like poison.

'I can't go home,' Jess says suddenly. 'Not yet. Ed said maybe I should stay here with you tonight and he'll look after the baby.'

'Of course you can,' I say. 'Stay as long as you need.'

She nods and rests her head back into the sofa cushion, closing her eyes.

I glance at my phone on the armrest. I had no more text messages from Matt last night despite me sending him one before bed.

Was that last text meant for me? I've had no missed calls.

Somewhere, in the back of my mind, I can feel something cold taking root. Not fear. Not grief, but something else. Like a pattern of disaster is forming. It's one thing after another lately. Where did my calm, ordered life go?

I think of the way Kendra cold-shouldered Jess. Brenda advising me to snoop on my husband. The way Matt and I have drifted apart without me really noticing until now.

And then I think: *Maybe none of this is separate.*

Maybe it's all connected somehow.

Jess drifts into a sort of sleep, half-conscious, the occasional sob escaping in between her breaths.

I drape a blanket over her and stand, a bit unsteady on my feet. The living room feels claustrophobic, packed with too many shadows. Too much left unsaid.

In the hallway, I brush past Brenda's dragon tree and slide the locks back into place on the front door.

And then I see them again. Matt's house keys in the wooden dish.

I check back on Jess in the living room. She's sleeping soundly now, little soft snores escaping her pale lips.

I return to the hallway and slip my coat over my nightwear, pulling on my flat boots. Then I scoop up mine and Matt's keys and let myself out of the back door, locking it behind me.

THIRTY-SEVEN

NOTTINGHAMSHIRE POLICE

MONDAY

The briefing room smells of instant coffee and damp jackets. Rain lashes at the windows behind Helena, grey ribbons of water slicing down the glass. Across the table, Brewster has commandeered half the surface with takeaway cups and various discarded snack wrappers.

Helena scans the walls. Whiteboards displaying maps, time-lines, Post-its peeling at the corners. There's a photo of Ellie Walker pinned up high, her smiling face trapped in a freeze-frame at a recent fundraiser at Nottingham Trent University. Beneath it, a fresh addition: Kendra Marsh. The crime scene photo has been cropped for the sake of the room, but it's enough to show her energy and spirit. Twenty years old with bold, attractive features and short dark hair.

Helena thinks of the body of this young woman. She crouched beside it at the crime scene. Saw at first hand the violet bruising around her slender, pale throat. Someone had dumped her body in the woods and she'd been dead for a few days.

Helena looks away.

Brewster gets to his feet, tapping at the whiteboard with a pen.

'So – Kendra Marsh. Twenty. Last seen six or seven days ago, housemate thinks. Kendra was found early on Thursday morning in woodland at Wollaton by a dog walker. Clothing intact, one earring missing. Her handbag and phone had been dumped nearby.' He presses a button and, on the large plasma flatscreen suspended from the ceiling, a blurred image appears. A phone with a locked screen, cracked at the corner. 'The phone provided us with initial ID – a fingerprint match and SIM registration.'

Helena stands and joins her colleague at the front of the room. 'No outgoing calls had been recently made and the call logs have been wiped. Her last texts are three weeks old. The phone metadata is weird – big activity gaps, then nothing. It could have been disabled remotely or wiped manually.'

'Fingerprints match her minor record,' Brewster adds. 'A student protest three years ago – drunk and disorderly, nothing heavy. But it got her into the system. That's how we've confirmed her ID before post-mortem.'

Helena swallows. The dead girl had been passionate and organised once. Angry about something she cared enough about to march in protest. Now she's lying on a slab in the path lab, relying on strangers to find her some justice.

DC Leary flicks through his file. 'Both parents deceased and no other family on record. Her landlord confirms she was renting a bedroom in a three-bed house on Larch Road.'

Helena has already read this statement, but hearing the sad facts read aloud has more impact.

Brewster crosses to another whiteboard, pre-prepared with a list of bullet points. The marker squeaks as he adds a new one.

'When uniforms spoke to a current housemate of the late Miss Marsh, the officer's report notes he found her, and I quote:

"evasive" and "visibly rattled". But she did give us the name and number of one Jessica Langley – Kendra's best friend. She said Jess had had a baby recently and they were close, but the friend had been round looking for Kendra.'

Helena walks to the window and looks down at the car park. Rain patters down on the stark black asphalt leaving silvery streaks. At least it looks fresh out there; inside the room, the air seems to grow ever more stagnant.

Brewster answers a few questions from a couple of officers and then Helena moves to the front.

Later, when the team meeting breaks up, Helena and Brewster sit with the case file up on screen and a coffee.

'You remember that charity event Ellie attended? Two weeks before she disappeared?'

'The hospice fundraiser.' Brewster nods.

'Well, Kendra's name came up in a raft of interviews uniform carried out. She was on the door checking tickets. No formal link established at the time. But now – two young women, both local, both early twenties who were at the same event...'

'And now one is still missing and the other is dead.' Brewster frowns. 'Thanks to Ellie's service provider, we know that the phones in both cases show unexplained gaps. Activity flat-lines, then cuts out to nothing.'

Brewster pulls a carrot stick from a plastic tub and plunges it into a tub of houmous. 'Both last seen near their homes. Similar age. What do we think?'

'We think,' Helena says slowly, 'that it's very possible the same perpetrator is involved. But there are few leads. Jess Langley is our logical best shot at getting context on Kendra's life.'

Brewster lifts an eyebrow. 'Want me to bring her in?'

Helena shakes her head. 'No. We go to her. Today. I don't want to risk the press getting to the only person who might be

able to shed some light on Kendra's state of mind and movements before her death.'

Brewster chews and swallows. 'We could take a liaison
officer with us – trauma-trained, one who's good with
witnesses.'

Helena glances at him. 'I think we can do this ourselves and
she's just had a baby, so we'll want to keep it low key and not
apply too much pressure. At the same time, we need to establish
if there's something she's not saying, so it's a fine balance.'

There's a pause while Brewster's gaze flicks to the
photographs on the board and then to the rain-streaked
windows.

'You know, this is starting to feel like one of those Scandi-
noir dramas where everyone ends up completely traumatised
and it never stops raining,' Brewster murmurs.

Helena almost allows herself a smile.

Instead, she says quietly, 'I don't think I've ever told you,
but I once had this case in Leeds. Years ago, now. I was a young
DC. An eighteen-year-old woman disappeared, full of life,
everything to live for.' She glances at Kendra's photo. 'She
looked like her.'

'What happened?'

'We worked the case hard, put in every hour God sends. No
leads, no clues. Nothing. But every single member of our team
was determined to crack it. Two years later, they found her
body ten miles away in a drain shaft. To this day, they never
caught whoever did it.'

Brewster's chewing slows and Helena clears her throat. 'I
won't let that happen again, Brewster. Not on my watch.'

He nods. Pushes away his snacks. 'OK, boss. Let's make
sure of that.' He peers at the computer screen. 'Jessica Langley
is twenty years old. Lives with her partner and new baby in a
small first-floor flat in Sneinton. She has no criminal history
and, prior to having the baby, worked part-time at a small café

on Trent Bridge. Unclear whether she plans to return to work.'

Helena nods. 'We've pulled Kendra's bank records again. No big withdrawals, no weird transactions. No holiday plans. Not even a night out logged recently. No Uber trips, nothing with cabs. Appears she wasn't going far or doing much at all.'

Helena exhales. It's like shuffling puzzle pieces with no corners or edge pieces to keep it all together.

She turns back to the window. The rain has thickened to a proper downpour now, streaking the cars and the bricks and the sky into one miserable palette of greys.

She turns around. 'Grab your coat,' she says to Brewster. 'Let's go and make some in-roads.'

THIRTY-EIGHT

SYLVIE

The morning feels too bright and too ordinary for what's happened as I drive Jess back home. We don't talk much. She's subdued and I'm distracted.

She stayed the night but woke up early, understandably wanting to return to Ed and Scarlet Mae. We had coffee together and then set off. She's barely said a word this morning, but I'm glad she came to me with her grief about Kendra. My daughter is a mother herself now, but our bond is still strong.

Outside her flat, the street is full of bins that have been dragged out for upcoming collection this morning and a dog is furiously barking somewhere close by. A woman in a bright-pink fleece jogs past, oblivious. Life goes on, as if Kendra Marsh hasn't just been pulled from the woods like a piece of dumped rubbish.

We get out of the car. Jess stands beside me, pale as milk, clutching her bag with both arms like it might anchor her. She hasn't spoken for the last ten minutes. When she finally does, her voice sounds weak.

'It just doesn't feel real, Mum. Like... how can shops be opening as usual, and people going off to work?'

I nod, my own thoughts tangled, too. Kendra, sprawled and silent, found in soil. The awful image is vivid and persistent in my mind. Jess, all hollowed-out and uncharacteristically quiet beside me. And somewhere behind all that, Matt. Absent when I need him the most.

Not now, I tell myself. *One worry at a time.*

Jess uses her key fob to get into the foyer of the building and I follow her up one flight of stairs. Ed opens the door before we knock. The baby looks comfy on his hip, his hair sticking up in tufts and his shirt buttoned unevenly. His eyes widen when he sees Jess.

'Hey,' he says, gently. 'You OK, babe?'

Jess nods but doesn't answer. Ed doesn't press. He holds Scarlet Mae out slightly, like a little peace offering, and I feel something inside me shift. The baby is in clean clothes, wearing a pink Babygro with a giraffe on the front. The smell of coffee floats through from the kitchen.

I step inside, noting the clutter of dishes has gone, the floor tidied, the legion of soft toys stacked into a neat pile. It's not pristine, but it's a big improvement. Like Ed has tried to make a difference.

'I need a shower.' Jess disappears without another word. I hover in the hall, unsure.

'You'll stay a bit, Sylvie?' Ed asks, bouncing Scarlet gently.

I glance at the doorway. 'Of course.'

He passes the baby to me and Scarlet Mae nuzzles into my neck, one chubby hand curling around my finger with a surprisingly firm grip. I close my eyes for a moment, letting the weight of her settle in my arms. She smells of talcum powder and sleep, her little chest rising and falling steadily.

I walk slowly into the living room, rocking her gently, shushing out of habit. The curtains are half-drawn still and the morning light filters hazily through them.

Outside, life continues. Someone is trimming a hedge. A car stereo thrums low.

The baby looks up at me and blinks with long, dark lashes. I press my lips to her soft scalp and breathe her in.

Someone this small and innocent should be immune to the awful parts of the world, I think. She should never even know what it means to find someone in the woods.

I stroke her back, thinking of Kendra again. Of her vitality and energy the last time I saw her. Jess's little friend from primary school...

I tighten my grip on my brand-new granddaughter. She'll never be alone, I promise myself silently. Not this one. I'll make sure of it.

I lower myself onto the sofa with a small groan. Scarlet Mae's head rests against my collarbone. It takes me a moment to realise Ed is standing in the doorway, watching us.

'Not many people can quieten her like that,' he says softly. 'She knows you're her family.'

I smile. 'She's perfect.'

Ed walks in and sits awkwardly in the armchair opposite. He's not his usual clumsy self today. There's a tightness about him, like he's holding something in.

'I'm worried about Jess,' he says at last.

'Me too. But she'll get through this, Ed. With our help.'

'She hasn't been sleeping. Barely eating, even. Even before this – before Kendra – it's like she's fading away. And now...' he runs a hand through his hair '... she's even worse. I don't know how to help her, Sylvie.'

'You're already helping her. Just being here for her.'

He doesn't say anything. Rubs his eyes. I can see all his tired concern coming to the surface now.

'I'll help keep an eye on her too,' I say.

He hesitates. 'She said Kendra had gone quiet. That she was dealing with stuff. But it was vague.'

'Vague how?'

He shrugs. 'It felt like Jess knew more than she was saying. I don't know, maybe it's just me. I don't know what's normal anymore.'

The baby stirs and shifts in my arms. I rub her back, gently.

Jess returns ten minutes later, hair towel-dried and damp around the edges, a clean jumper pulled over her pyjama bottoms. Her hands twist a small towel, wringing it into a thick rope.

'Mum, Ed?' she says fearfully.

Alarmed, we both look up.

'I just had a call. Two detectives from Nottinghamshire Police are coming to speak to me. This afternoon.'

The towel drops to the floor.

Ed stands. 'Shit. That's quick.'

Jess looks dazed. She moves to the arm of the sofa and lowers herself down carefully, like she's afraid something in her might snap if she moves too quickly.

'They said it's "in connection with an ongoing inquiry". I asked if they had any news about Kendra and they said they'd explain when they arrived.'

She looks at me, then at Ed, and then away.

'I'm scared,' she says, so quietly it barely registers.

'You've no need to be scared,' I say.

Ed moves over to her, crouches beside her knee. 'You know I've got work this afternoon, babe? I'll try and swap, but—'

'Don't do that,' I say. 'I'll come back and look after the baby so Jess can talk to them properly.'

Ed touches my shoulder, relieved. 'Cheers, Sylvie. What would we do without you?'

Jess nods, slowly. 'Thanks, Mum.'

I stay another half hour. When I leave, the sky is brighter, but it feels even colder out somehow.

In the car with nothing to distract me, dread starts to pool. Now, my thoughts circle elsewhere. To last night.

I shouldn't have gone round there. I tell myself that again. But it was too tempting. Too quiet. Jess was asleep, the house still. Matt's keys were on the hall table like they were giving me permission.

I remember the creak of his gate in the dark, silent street. The sound of my own breath as I opened the door.

The house smelled of nothing. Clean. Too clean for his place.

I took a cursory look around the downstairs rooms. Everywhere tidy, which was unusual. In his office – papers stacked, files labelled, quotations ready to be sent out. Nothing personal. No scrawled notes or mystery telephone numbers. No receipts for flowers or lingerie or expensive hotel rooms. Nothing that felt remotely worrying.

I moved slowly through the rooms, my heart galloping. Upstairs, I headed for his bedroom at the front of the house. The drawers were tidy, his socks paired. The bed made with clean bedding, which was a surprise.

I'd just turned to leave the room when I saw it.

A silver hoop. Small and dainty and lying on the carpet by the bedside table. The butterfly back was missing. At the base: a distinctive but delicate knot.

It wasn't *my* earring. I picked it up with shaking fingers, turned it in the light. It glimmered prettily.

My stomach roiled and Brenda's voice played in my mind: *Men get away with things because women are too polite to ask.*

I didn't call Matt there and then. I couldn't. I knew I needed to see his face. To talk to him one-to-one.

Now, driving through the familiar streets, I imagine the woman who owns that earring. Young. Younger than me. Long glossy hair and full of confidence. The kind of young woman who throws her head back when she laughs and doesn't apologise for anything. The kind of woman who leaves her earring in someone's bedroom and never comes back to collect it.

I feel sick.

I pull into my driveway and sit there for a moment, gripping the steering wheel.

Then I go inside, drop my bag on the floor and walk straight to the kitchen.

This morning before we left, I placed the earring on the kitchen windowsill.

It glints there still in the morning light. A sliver of mockery to highlight my gullibility.

My phone buzzes – a news alert.

I pick it up and read the headline.

Police appeal for sightings of murdered woman's final movements

There's a grainy still pulled from CCTV footage. Two figures, and one is Kendra. The other – taller, broad-shouldered, his hoodie pulled low.

The caption reads: *CCTV footage from an industrial estate close to the woods where the body was found.*

The shape of the man beside her. His gait. The jacket.

My breath catches. The man looks just like Matt.

I zoom in and the pixels stretch further, blurring his shape. Now, I'm uncertain. Am I so traumatised I'm hallucinating?

But I can't unsee it. My gaze shifts from the screen to the earring on the counter and suddenly I'm not sure what scares me more – what the police might find, or what Jess might know and hasn't said.

THIRTY-NINE

BRENDA

The grass crunches under Brenda's wellies, sharp with frost. Each step she takes leaves a white imprint across the lawn.

It's freezing out here. Beneath her old trench coat, she's still wearing her dressing gown. No gloves. Her hands are mottled, red and raw, the skin cracked where her knuckles split scrubbing the kitchen floor last week.

But she doesn't feel the cold inside. Not this morning.

She jabs the trowel into the soil. The earth resists her, hardpacked and difficult. Still, she pushes on and succeeds. Ripping out a hardy geranium, roots and all, and flinging it onto the compost heap. Next in line is an evergreen hebe. Its leaves look perfect, but Brenda works on like something's buried beneath it. Something she must reach.

It was almost midnight when the camera's motion alert had lit her phone, set it off flashing like a distress beacon. She'd thought it might be a cat like last time, or perhaps the wind stirring leaves across Sylvie's porch. But the footage had shown something quite different happening.

Jess, climbing out of a taxi in the middle of the night. Barefaced and wild-eyed. Sylvie opening the door like some tragic figure, arms outstretched in her pyjamas with frightful hair. Brenda had watched from the cover of her bedroom curtain as Jess had flung herself at Sylvie. Always a drama to be had with that one.

She'd watched as Jess stumbled inside, and the front door closed. It had been almost impossible to stop herself rushing over there, but she would have had to reveal she was monitoring the house if she had done so.

An hour or so later, though, and her vigilance was rewarded.

A light appeared in Matt's bedroom at the front of his house. Not a flicker. Not a hallway spill. A deliberate light. Switched on for a purpose.

At first, she suspected it might be an intruder. But then she'd spotted a silhouette moving behind the curtain. A slim, deliberate silhouette she recognised.

Sylvie.

Her Sylvie.

Brenda grasps a clump of ornamental grass now and yanks it clean out of the ground. Soil flies.

Sylvie, right there in his bedroom. *Without telling Brenda.* Without even a whisper of intent despite it being Brenda's idea in the first place!

Sylvie had gone there alone. She must have snuck around the back of the house and along the narrow path that runs across the bottom of the gardens. It is the only way Sylvie could have left the house without alerting Brenda's surveillance system.

Her skin prickles with a thousand tiny needles. She drives the trowel down again and a tulip bulb splits in two.

Someone, a colleague, once called Brenda obsessive. But she isn't that. Not anymore. She prefers the word *methodical*. She has a strategy and that was what made her so good in her ward. Always calm under pressure.

When others flapped and panicked, she waited. That's what they never understood. Then, when it all unravelled, they blamed *her* for being calm. As though restraint were a sin.

It wasn't her fault the boy wasn't moved and given the correct treatment. They accused her of neglect, said she didn't report his deteriorating condition, but she remembers writing it down in the notes. Despite what they said in the inquiry, she knows she did. *She did.*

She hears Ivor yowling faintly from the back door. He hates her doing anything without him. She sighs and wipes her hands on the front of her dressing gown. Straightens up, grimacing as her knees protest.

She looks down regretfully at the mess she's made, the damage she's caused. She didn't mean to wreck the planting. But she'll go back in the house now. She feels a little better.

Inside, Ivor flicks his tail in protest and stalks off to sit sullenly in front of the radiator.

By seven-thirty, Brenda has showered, changed and scrubbed the soil from under her nails. Clean trousers, thermal vest and blouse under a knitted jumper, her mother's brooch clipped just beneath the collar.

Still surly, Ivor curls on the armchair cushion as Brenda moves to the front window. She twitches the curtain half an inch.

Sylvie emerges at seven-forty-five on the dot. Her coat is unbuttoned, scarf untied. Jess walks beside her, clutching a changing bag. But the baby isn't with them.

They get into Sylvie's car. Brenda narrows her eyes and watches until the car turns the corner.

Inside, she keeps busy by doing the dishes with her usual surgical precision. Her teacup from last night, the bowl with the crust of porridge she didn't finish. She arranges the biscuits on the tin's plastic tray, repositioning them so all the custard creams sit to the left and the bourbons to the right.

Ivor watches her accusingly when she leaves.

Sylvie answers the door. She looks haunted, her hair flattened down at least, her jeans and top creased and dishevelled.

'Good morning,' Brenda says, stepping inside without waiting to be asked. 'You look dreadful.'

Sylvie manages a small smile. 'Morning.'

Brenda hangs her coat over the stair newel post and follows Sylvie into the kitchen. She sets the kettle going, ignores the toaster and pops two slices of toast under the grill.

'Sit down, dear,' she says to Sylvie, already pulling out a chair. 'Let's get some heat and food into you.'

Sylvie sits and Brenda hums. It feels just like before when Jess and the baby were here and she was such an integral part of the household. When she was *needed*.

She makes the tea and then spreads butter on the perfectly browned toast with slow, careful movements, hands steady despite the raw patches on her knuckles.

Sylvie's eyes are rimmed red. She watches Brenda work but stays quiet.

Brenda puts a mug of tea and a slice of buttered toast in front of her and says, 'You want to tell me what's happened now?'

'It's Kendra,' Sylvie says, her voice low. 'She's... she's dead. Jess found out last night. The police came to the door at midnight, told her Kendra's body had been found in Wollaton Park. She's been—' A sob escapes her. 'She's been murdered.'

Brenda pauses, her toast suspended in mid-air. 'Oh no. Oh dear God, no... our poor, poor Jess.'

'The police couldn't tell her much, but... they're coming to the flat to interview her this afternoon. I've offered to go over there.'

'Of course, you must,' Brenda says, putting down her food.

She frowns. 'Kendra was a wild spirit, wasn't she? Always flitting from place to place, Jess told me that once.'

Sylvie nodded. 'She could never seem to settle.'

'Living like that, it catches up with you eventually.'

Sylvie flinches and Brenda sees it.

'I'm sorry,' she adds. 'I didn't mean for it to sound like it's the poor girl's fault in any way. Of course not. It's just... well. Jess doesn't need people like that in her life, not now she's a mother.'

Sylvie's eyes flick to the floor.

'Well, she's not in her life anymore now,' Brenda says quietly and folds her hands on top of the table. 'No, sadly that's true.'

The two women sit in silence for a short time with only the sound of Brenda munching her toast.

'How's Jess? Bearing up?' Brenda reaches for Sylvie's hand. 'Are *you* bearing up? I notice Matt isn't back home yet.'

Sylvie blinks. She reaches into her cardigan pocket and draws out a handkerchief. She unfolds it to reveal a silver hoop earring. An intricate knot design decorates the bottom arc of it.

Sylvie places it between them on the table. It catches the light.

'I found this on the floor in Matt's bedroom.'

Brenda leans in, her lips parting as she studies it.

'I knew it,' she says softly, looking up at Sylvie. 'Didn't I say as much?'

Sylvie looks away, her bottom lip trembling.

'I've kept a lot of things to myself,' Brenda says. 'Because I'm loyal to you, Sylvie. You know that. But I've seen Nige come round there late at night. They go out like two single lads out on the town. Come back in a cab, drunk. Matt thinks you're taken up with Jess and the baby, you see. He thinks nobody's watching him. Thinks he's safe in this convenient living-apart arrangement you two have.'

She waits, lets the words settle.

Sylvie picks at the edge of her toast.

'I expect Matt's told you I'm a busybody,' Brenda says. 'I know he doesn't like me being involved with you and the family.'

Sylvie hesitates then stays quiet.

'I thought so. That's what men like him do. They isolate you from the ones who can see through them. It's a form of control, you see.' She leans in closer, her voice lowering. 'You've got a big heart, Sylvie. But big hearts bruise easier. That's why I've stayed close, to protect you and Jess. And that sweet little baby girl of ours.'

Sylvie swallows, nods once. Brenda sees it – how close she is to folding. To giving in.

'You said you talked to him about moving in together... to one property?'

'I did,' Sylvie murmurs. 'But Matt didn't seem keen.'

Brenda sits back. 'I wonder why that might be.'

Silence stretches.

'I know it's hard,' Brenda says softly. 'But it might be time to start thinking about what you'll do. When the truth comes out.' She looks at the earring. 'You'll have to confront him about this, Sylvie.'

Sylvie's lip trembles. She nods again.

'I'll leave you to rest now. You've had two terrible shocks. But you'll see what I mean soon enough.' Brenda stands, brushing crumbs from her lap. On her way out, she pauses at the doorway, touches the frame lightly with her fingers. 'If you play your cards right,' she says over her shoulder, 'he won't be able to wriggle out of this one.'

Outside, the frost has begun to thaw, the air wet and heavy.

Brenda walks back over the road slowly and purposefully. When she reaches the other side, she glances down the street towards Matt's house.

The curtains are still partly drawn and there's still no sign of his car.

She narrows her eyes.

'Come home, my friend,' she murmurs. 'Let's see how well you can tell your lies now. With your back against the wall.'

She walks up the path to her front door. Her steps are light, her breath steady. Ivor watches from the window as she approaches and Brenda smiles.

Everything's unfolding even better than she'd hoped.

Brewster parks the car in the designated visitor area. The block of flats squats beneath a grey sky, its concrete exterior weathered with years of neglect. Graffiti surrounds the door buzzer, a broken swing creaking in the wind beside a patchy square of grass that is strewn with discarded crisp packets and cigarette butts.

The door to the foyer is unlocked and Brewster curses when he sees the lift is out of order.

'Only the first floor to climb.' Helena grins. 'Help you work off some of those hard-boiled eggs still in your system before you start clucking.'

'I've lost a total of eight pounds thanks to those eggs,' Brewster replies curtly as she tries not to laugh.

They climb the stairs to the first floor and follow the narrow landing humming with low-level dance music from one of the other flats. Brewster checks numbers until they reach a peeling front door complete with a cracked doorbell and a handwritten label: *Langley & Daunt*.

Brewster raises his hand to ring the bell but doesn't get the chance. The door swings open and a woman in her mid-forties stands there. She is dressed in jeans and a loose jumper, her hair bundled into a loose topknot. She smiles at them both as Brewster holds up his warrant card.

'I'm Sylvie Tyce,' she says, before either detective can speak. 'Jess's mum. Come in.'

They step into a hallway barely wide enough to turn around in. A wire drying rack is covered in tiny Babygros and leans against the radiator. It occurs to Helena how quiet the flat is to say there's a newborn baby somewhere in the vicinity.

'The baby is down for her nap in the next room,' Sylvie says quietly when they reach the small living room. 'I'm here to watch her while Jess talks to you. I'll just let her know you've arrived.'

Helena nods, already clocking every detail. A muslin cloth and a bottle steriliser tossed aside. Congratulations cards crowd the coffee table and numerous soft, pastel-coloured baby toys are scattered around. All the usual signs of early motherhood are here.

'Would you mind if we had a brief word with you afterwards?' Helena asks, gentle but direct. 'Just for a few background details. Nothing heavy.'

'Course,' Sylvie says. 'Anything I can do to help catch whoever did this.'

Sylvie leaves the room and returns a moment later with a woman in her early twenties.

Jess Langley is slim with her hair scraped back in a messy, short plait. She's in joggers and a sweatshirt and her face looks tired and drawn. Helena thinks she looks like someone who hasn't slept for more than three hours at a time in weeks.

'Hi, I'm Jess,' she says, stretching out a hand.

'Hello, Jessica; may I call you Jess?' Brewster says as she nods. 'We're very sorry for your loss. We know you and Kendra Marsh were close.'

'Thank you, we were.'

'It's fine for your mum to stay here while we talk, if you'd prefer.'

'It's best if we talk in the kitchen,' Jess says quickly. 'If that's OK.'

Helena catches the flash of surprise on Sylvie's face as she settles on the sofa. Just for a beat, there's a twitch of something – hurt, maybe, or confusion.

'Of course, if that's what you'd prefer,' Helena replies.

The kitchen is small – a modern foldable table, lime-green toaster, fridge peppered with magnets and a peeling calendar. Clean baby bottles are lined up next to the sink.

Jess shuts the door behind them. Helena watches as she checks it. Then checks it again.

She stays standing as Brewster introduces the voice recorder.

'Just a quick chat, nothing formal. You're not under caution and we'll keep it relaxed. You happy for us to record? It's just for convenience so we can avoid the need to take notes.'

'No problem,' Jess says. Her voice is flat with fatigue.

She lowers herself into a chair and folds her arms tightly across her chest. Helena notices the slight tremble in her hands, the way her eyes dart to the door every few seconds as if she's afraid her mother might appear there.

Brewster begins, keeping his voice low and neutral.

'When was the last time you saw Kendra Marsh in person?'

'A couple of weeks ago,' Jess replies. 'She came over here. Brought some nappies and a cute little onesie with bunny ears for Scarlet. We didn't talk much. She seemed... on edge and didn't stay long.'

'And when did you last hear from her?'

'I texted her a few times after that. Called her twice. She didn't answer any of my messages or calls. I thought she was just going through one of her phases.'

'Phases?' Helena repeats gently.

Jess nods. 'Kendra's been known to take off before. Usually when some new guy is involved.' She gives a sad smile. 'She lived in a commune in Devon for two weeks once, completely off-grid. I thought I'd never see her again but she came back smelling of incense and goat's cheese like nothing had happened. We joked that she needed a reality check, not a detox.'

'But she didn't let you know she was leaving this time, she just didn't get in touch?'

'That's right. This time it was different,' Jess continues, frowning. 'She was twitchy. She'd stopped asking me over to hers, which I put down to me having the baby, so I wasn't too worried.'

'Did she ever say she felt unsafe?'

Jess hesitates. Her fingers grip the sleeve of her sweatshirt, twisting it.

'Not in as many words, but she was acting a bit uptight. Paranoid, almost. I wish I'd asked more questions. Pressed harder. But she had this way of shutting you down and that's what she did to me. I just stopped hearing from her.'

Helena nods slowly. She can almost see the guilt folding itself into Jess's posture. She is still so raw from the terrible news.

'Was Kendra seeing anyone?' Brewster asks. 'Romantically, I mean?'

Jess stills. Her gaze flicks to the door and she doesn't answer straight away.

Helena leans forward, her voice gentle. 'You were so close. If you know something... anything that could help—'

'She was,' Jess cuts in. 'Seeing someone. But she wouldn't tell me who it was.'

'Why not?' Helena asks. 'If you were best friends?'

Jess's mouth tightens. 'My thoughts exactly. I could only imagine it was because she thought I wouldn't approve.'

'Why would you not approve?' Brewster frowns.

'Because I think... I had my suspicions he was married.'

Helena blinks. 'You're sure about that?'

'Not completely certain, but I know the signs. She's done it before, you see. She's always had this thing for men who are already taken. She liked the drama. Liked winning.'

'Liked the fact they were already spoken for?'

Jess nods. 'Yeah, she used to say hook-ups were far more fun when it was forbidden.'

Helena's pulse quickens. 'Did she talk to you about him at all?'

'No. But when I pressed her for details, she said if anyone found out, it would ruin everything. I assumed she meant his life.' Jess swallows. 'But maybe she meant hers.'

The silence in the room thickens and Helena lets it sit a while before asking her next question.

'Did you get any kind of impression of this person at all?'

Jess blows out air. 'I think he was controlling. She started second-guessing herself all the time. Kept saying her phone was acting weird. Worried that someone might be reading her messages. I thought it was just more drama, that she was imagining it. But now...'

She trails off, her eyes glassy.

Helena watches her carefully. Jess has shared just enough to relieve the pressure of their interview – but Helena senses there's more that she isn't saying.

When it's obvious the interview has come to a natural end, Brewster clicks off the recorder.

'Thanks for being honest about your friend's personal life,' he says. 'We'll review everything and be in touch soon.'

Helena slides a business card across the table. 'If anything else occurs to you, no matter how small or insignificant it might seem, please call me on my direct line.'

Jess nods, already rising. Her hands shake slightly as she reaches for the door handle.

As she opens it, her eyes flick to the living room door. Sylvie appears in the hallway, holding a mug.

'Baby still asleep?' Jess asks, without really waiting for the answer.

Sylvie nods and Jess retreats, disappearing down the hallway.

Helena steps into the living room, casting a final glance down the hall.

'Thanks for the tea,' Helena says to Sylvie. 'Would you mind if we asked you a few questions too?'

Sylvie sets the mug down. Her face is open, but tired and lined with concern.

'Course. I'll help however I can.'

They all sit. Brewster keeps a light tone. Helena watches closely.

'Did Kendra have a boyfriend, do you know?'

Sylvie frowns. 'She had this glow about her and said she was happy with her life. I teased her that maybe she'd got a new boyfriend, but she wouldn't elaborate. She was a private person, but I think Jess would've known if there was someone new on the scene. Did you ask her?'

Helena doesn't reply. She's almost certain Jess knows more than she said, but at the moment it's just a feeling.

The theory about the married man feels right – but it's also dangerously vague.

And the most unsettling thing of all? She didn't want her mother to hear any of it. It could just be a coincidence.

It could also be critical.

FORTY-ONE

SYLVIE

Driving home from Jess's house, my mind is all over the place. The car hums gently beneath me, a noise I usually find soothing. Today, my thoughts are louder and push at me from all directions. I find myself replaying the expression on Jess's face, the way she turned away slightly when the police offered to let me stay to support her during the interview.

It had been a shock when Jess declined. Said she'd prefer to speak to them alone in the kitchen.

I thought she'd want me there. I was certain of it because she always leans on me. Always has. But today, it felt like she didn't just want privacy, she wanted me gone. Out of the way.

That stung. And I'm not proud of how much. In that moment, I felt like I didn't know her at all.

But what came next was worse. The detectives – cool and professional – mentioned that Jess believed Kendra had been seeing a married man.

A married man.

I nearly dropped the mug I was holding. Jess never mentioned that to me. Not even hinted about it once, and we talk about everything – especially when it comes to Kendra and her, let's say, often adventurous choices. This would've been prime gossip. The kind we'd usually dissect over toast and a second cup of tea.

Even more weirdly, she'd stayed at mine last night where we'd discussed Kendra ghosting her recently and why that could be. And yet... she'd omitted this piece of vital information. Why?

After the detectives left, I'd tried to ask her about it. Gently, I broached their falling-out again, asked why she thought Kendra had stopped speaking to her. If it had anything to do with this man she was seeing. But Jess said she was too tired to rake it all up again. She couldn't even meet my eye.

I felt it then, as if she'd spoken the actual words: she wanted me to leave the flat.

The street ahead flickers with brake lights and drizzle. That's when I catch a glimpse of a familiar sign – Lenton.

My hands move the steering wheel before I've fully thought it through. I swipe the indicator and make the left turn.

Kendra moved here to a house-share a couple of years ago. Jess and I went to help her settle in. She had little more than two battered suitcases and a green-tasselled velvet lamp she insisted on taking with her everywhere.

I remember her laughing, dragging the cases up the scruffy path, talking about ordering a Chinese takeaway and cheap wine from Deliveroo. She'd been full of life. Full of herself. But then that was Kendra. She never did anything half-heartedly.

Five minutes later, I reach her road and feel my stomach dip. It's worse around here than I remember. Lenton itself is a lively area of the city with a big student population. It has a historic art deco cinema and was home to Raleigh, once the world's largest manufacturer of bicycles.

But Kendra's street is grey and tired. Overflowing rubbish sacks lean against cracked and broken walls. There's a trolley on its side abandoned in a takeaway shop doorway, one wheel spinning lazily in the wind. Further along, outside Kendra's house, the tiny patch of garden is wild with dandelions and nettles. Empty cans and a broken solar light lie face down on the path.

You wouldn't know anyone who lived here had just died. There's no sign of mourning or loss. No flowers. No press. Nothing out of the ordinary.

Sadness bulges in my throat. It's like the world didn't even notice she died.

I sit in the car for a few seconds, the engine still running. Then I cut the ignition and step out.

I press the cracked doorbell and next door, I hear a dog bark. Then someone yells for it to shut up.

The door opens and a young woman stares out at me, barefoot in grey tracky bottoms and an oversized hoodie. Her hair is scraped up, dyed a coppery brown, and her eyes look wary.

'Hi,' I say. 'I'm Sylvie, Jess Langley's mum.' I swallow, feeling unexpectedly emotional. 'I knew Kendra – known her since she was a little girl.'

The woman frowns then nods with understanding and steps aside. 'Come in for a bit if you like. I'll stick the kettle on.'

Inside, the place smells fusty, a mix of damp, stale air and incense burning somewhere. I follow her to a cramped kitchen where mismatched mugs hang from hooks next to a corkboard littered with takeaway menus and passive-aggressive notes about not leaving the washing-up.

'Chamomile OK?' she asks.

'Perfect, thanks.'

'I'm Maz, by the way. I moved in here about ten months ago.' She drops two teabags into mugs and boils the kettle. 'I really liked Kendra. Can't believe she's gone.'

When she's made the tea, we sit across from each other at a small wobbly table, steam rising between us.

'Kendra could be pretty wild.' Maz gives a regretful grin. 'In a good way, though. Funny as anything, too. You never knew what mood she'd be in, but she had this knack of making the house feel brighter. Cheering everyone up, you know?'

I nod. I know exactly what she means.

Maz sips her tea. 'She loved her crap telly, too. Knew every word of the second *Mamma Mia!* Used to blast it out when she cleaned. We had to ban it eventually, but she'd sneak it on when she thought no one was home.'

Maz laughs, then shakes her head. 'Weird, isn't it? One minute you're arguing about who left hair in the shower drain, next minute...'

I wait a beat before asking. 'Could I see her room?'

Maz's face falls a little. 'What? No, sorry. Nobody's allowed to go in there. The coppers have cordoned it off with tape, and stuff. Upstairs stinks of some weird spray they used.'

'Course,' I say, pinching the top of my nose. What was I thinking?

We sip our tea in silence for a moment. I'm about to make my excuses when I hear myself ask, 'Did she mention having a boyfriend to you?'

Maz shrugs. 'Not to me. But Jess knows all about it, right? That's what they were arguing about.'

I blink. 'What argument?'

Maz looks genuinely confused. 'The big one, a couple of weeks back. Jess came over, full of hell about something. They went upstairs, then about ten minutes later... boom. Full-on row explodes.'

I stare at her. 'Jess never mentioned an argument.'

Maz tilts her head. 'Oh yeah, we all heard it. Kendra shouting that it wasn't what it looked like. Jess yelling back, demanding to know who *he* was. Proper drama.'

I stay quiet, trying to figure out yet again why Jess would keep this to herself.

Maz chuckles. 'We crept up the stairs to listen on the landing. Terrible, really. Classic shared-house behaviour.'

I feel like I've swallowed something sharp.

Jess told me she had no idea why Kendra ghosted her. She said it had come out of nowhere. But if this happened – if there was a fight – then she's lied to me. Question is, did she share it with the police?

'Do you know if anyone else saw this man?' I ask.

Maz shrugs again, her interest already fading. 'Not that I know of. No one saw him here, anyway. But Kendra was cagey. Not like she was hiding something, more like... she was protecting it. If anyone knows who he was, it's Jess. You should ask her about it.'

Back in the car, the rain has started. Light and steady. I flick the wipers on and sit with my hands on the wheel, not starting the engine just yet.

The pieces don't fit. Why would my daughter lie to me? Was Jess protecting someone – or protecting herself?

I drive slowly, my thoughts racing ahead then looping back on themselves. Jess didn't just keep things back; she lied. And that's not like her at all. Not with me, anyway.

Seems something's changed between us when I was looking the other way.

The traffic isn't too bad and soon, I'm turning into our street where I slam the brakes harder than I mean to and jerk forward.

Matt's car is parked outside his house.

It sits there like it never left, streaked with rain. The bonnet still carries the faint outline of where someone scrawled WASH ME with their finger.

Finally, he's home.

My heart jumps, but it isn't relief I feel. It's something more daunting.

I pull up outside my place and sit for a moment. My hand slips into my coat pocket and closes around the silver earring.

It's smooth and warm from my body heat. A small but devastating truth I haven't shared with anyone but Brenda.

When I get out of the car, the smell of wet tarmac and rotting leaves fills my nostrils. I stand at my gate, looking down towards Matt's house. There's a light on in the front room, but he hasn't texted or called me yet.

I walk slowly up the path, clutching the handkerchief containing the earring tightly in my palm. It's time to face the music and get to the truth.

I'm not sure what I'm about to uncover.

But one thing is for certain; I don't think I'm ready for it.

FORTY-TWO

I let myself into the house and close the door quietly behind me. There are no windows in the hallway and, despite the long slim panel of opaque glass in the door, it's gloomy in here without the lamps throwing their familiar, warm glow across the floor.

I stand there for a long time, staring at the wall, the dragon tree and the framed print of a coastal scene that I've never especially liked. My arms hang uselessly at my sides.

The earring sits in my coat pocket like a stone in my shoe. Its presence irritates me all the time. I can't stop thinking about its delicate shape, the way the metal catches the light when I hold it in the palm of my hand.

Perhaps I should have gone straight to Matt's house. Pulled up outside and marched down there before I had the chance to overthink it. Now, my stomach is churning with nerves as I decide what to do next.

My legs finally move of their own accord, taking me into the kitchen, where I flick on the kettle and empty the dishwasher with slow, mechanical precision. Next, I wipe down surfaces that I already attended to this morning before leaving for Jess's flat.

Anything to avoid what I know I must do because there's a question I haven't answered. After all this time and all this thinking, I still don't know what I'm prepared to do if it turns out my husband has been unfaithful.

Am I prepared to walk away from him? From us? Because that's what it comes down to. It's no good me demanding answers *or else*, only to crumble if he calls my bluff. I have to decide my limitations before I confront him.

I stop wiping and place the cloth down gently. No more delays, it's time to seize the moment.

I fish my phone from my bag and call Matt. He answers on the second ring.

'Hey,' he says, upbeat. 'You read my mind. I was just about to call you. I've missed you.'

My voice is flat. 'Can you come round?'

A pause. 'Uh... yeah, OK. I've just got to catch up on a few—'

'Now, Matt.' I cut across him. 'I need you to come over now. It's important.'

Another pause, longer this time. Then: 'OK. Five minutes, tops.'

I hang up before he can say anything else. My hands are shaking.

In the hallway mirror, I fluff up my hair a bit and dab some colour onto my lips, but not too much. I don't want to look like I've made an effort. I want to look... composed and in control. Even though it feels like I might just fall apart when I see him.

When the front door opens, I feel it like a shift in the air. I hear him walk inside. Easy strides. Confident. Comfortable.

He stands in the kitchen door and leans against the frame. He looks tired and, with it, rugged and desirable. A day or two's stubble darkens his jaw, his hair mussed from the wind. There's something about the way he carries himself – so relaxed and familiar – it makes my chest ache.

He's my man. My lover and my best friend, and I love him with all my heart. I want to throw my arms around him and beg him to tell me it's all a stupid misunderstanding.

But I don't.

I can't.

He steps into the kitchen and grins. 'This all feels a bit cloak and dagger,' he says, hanging his denim jacket on the back of a chair. 'What's up? Can't bear to be away from me a moment longer?'

He walks over to me, wraps his strong, firm arms around me. I lay my cheek against his chest and squeeze my eyes shut. Just for a second.

We break apart and I place two glasses of water on the table and nod for him to sit. He does so, frowning slightly, still half in flirt-mode.

'You look serious,' he says. 'Have I done something wrong?'

I pull the handkerchief from my pocket and place it on the table between us.

He stares at it. Then looks at me. 'What's this?'

I open the folds and expose the earring. 'You tell me.'

He picks it up, turns it between his fingers like it might change shape. 'I've never seen it before. Is it yours?'

'No, it isn't mine. I found it on your bedroom floor, Matt.'

A flicker of surprise crosses his face. 'No way.'

'Yes, way. It was next to the bedside table.'

'Sylvie, I've never seen it before.'

'So what does that mean, then? Some woman drops an earring in your bedroom and you don't even notice?'

'Hang on. Are you seriously saying—'

'You tell me what I'm saying, Matt.' I stare at him. 'Because I'd love to hear it from your mouth.'

He pushes a hand through his hair and sits back. 'I honestly have no idea where that came from. I swear. But what I do know for certain is that nobody has been in my bedroom, if that's what you're getting at.'

'You're lying.'

'No. I'm not,' he says, his voice measured.

'Then why have you been acting so strange? You've been distant... distracted. And now this—'

'I'm not cheating on you, Sylvie.'

'What about that text message you sent on Friday, saying I hadn't picked up? You never called me, so who was it meant for?'

'I checked my call list and I'd rung Nige by mistake like an idiot!' He looks affronted, reaches into his pocket for his phone. 'Look, I can show you.'

I shake my head. 'Well, something's going on! Earrings don't just appear out of thin air, and if it's not an affair...' I swallow hard. 'Then what the hell is it?'

He exhales sharply. Then again, slower this time, like air leaving a balloon. His shoulders collapse inward, and he looks down at his hands.

'I didn't want to tell you this,' he says. 'I didn't ever want to see you look at me like this.'

I don't speak. My pulse thumps in my ears. I think I'm going to throw up.

This is it. The moment my world implodes.

Matt glances at the floor, at the wall. He doesn't look at me. When he speaks again, it sounds like he's dragging something out of himself.

'Nige got himself in trouble, Sylvie. And I'm talking big trouble.'

His voice is low, ragged. It hardly sounds like Matt at all. I feel the first ripple of panic and sit very still.

'He came to me a few months ago. Said he owed money. A lot. He was panicking, saying he was being threatened. He looked—' Matt breaks off, rubs his hands down his thighs. 'I've never seen him like that before and... I felt I had no choice but to help him out. I lent him some money.'

I blink. 'How much money?'

He doesn't answer.

'Matt. How much?'

'Twenty-five grand. I remortgaged the house.'

The air leaves the room. I cover my face with my hands.

'No.'

'It gets worse,' he mutters. 'Much worse.'

He pushes back in the chair, hands grabbing at his hair, eyes fixed on the ceiling.

'Nige told me he'd lost a lot of money with some fraudulent crypto-currency company he'd seen on X. I put a bit in at the start. Got a small profit and took it but then I got cold feet.'

I look at him. 'You never said.' *Do I even know this man?*

'I knew you wouldn't approve and you'd be right.' He shrugs. 'I advised Nige to do the same but he made a few more investments and got great returns. Then the stakes increased. He sank more in and there was always some reason he couldn't draw the funds out. You know the story.'

I shake my head. 'The last I heard Nige was working in a bar! Where did he get all this money to invest?'

'He borrowed from people he couldn't afford to pay back. Said he was getting messages, visits and threats. These weren't banks or high-street loan companies – we're talking proper old-school loan sharks. People with baseball bats who know exactly how to make a point.'

A pause where neither of us speaks. I wait.

'They said they knew about me. That bloody *Daily Mail* article – the photo of our houses, our names – it was enough. They told Nige to approach me for cash and if I didn't help out, I'd be in for it too and...' His voice peters out.

'Go on?'

'They knew about the baby. And Jess. They said... well, let's just say they made the threats clear enough.'

I touch my throat, trying to pull in a bigger breath.

'So you paid them off? With the equity in the house?'

He nods. 'I started off helping him, little by little. But it wasn't enough. That's where I've been, those times I said I was in Leeds or Newcastle. I was with Nige. Handing over cash. Trying to stall them. Trying to stop them coming here, to the house.'

He finally looks up, and I'm startled by the wet gleam in his eyes. I don't think I've ever seen Matt cry.

'I didn't know how to tell you, Sylvie. The last thing I wanted was to drag you into it all.'

'But you already did,' I whisper. My voice catches. 'I thought... I was certain you were having an affair.'

A sob escapes me before I can catch it. I clamp my hand over my mouth.

'Never! It hasn't and will never happen.' He leans forward, staring at me intently. 'I love you, Sylvie. Every second. Every breath. This – this was about loyalty to our family. Stupid, blind loyalty to Nige, too.'

'Because you felt like you owed him something?'

He drops his gaze, his voice low. 'Years ago – before you and I met – Nige took the fall for something stupid I did. Nothing criminal, just a work mess that could've ruined my job, my livelihood. He kept quiet, and when I thanked him, he just waved it off. Said I'd worked too hard to have it all taken away like that.'

I stare at him. 'You told me something about that when we first got together. Said he'd once "saved your skin". I thought you meant a bar scuffle or a bad night out.'

'Yeah, I know.' He gives a weak laugh. 'I let you think that. It was easier.'

His hands tremble as he rubs his face. He looks wrecked. Hollow. Pale with wide, glassy eyes.

'I'm sorry,' he says, his voice thick with regret. 'I thought I could handle it, help Nige fix things before you ever had to know there was an issue. But they kept coming back. And Nige... well, he's not the same guy he used to be. He's been suffering panic attacks, reckons they've been following him.' He sniffs. 'I've let him stay over at mine a few times but he says he can't sleep. He begged me not to go to the police because it would make things worse.'

I think about Brenda saying she'd seen the two of them going out late. Doesn't really fit, but... he looks so wretched.

I reach out before I can think better of it. My fingers brush the back of his hand. He flinches at the contact and then latches on like I'm a life raft in a raging sea.

We sit in silence for a few moments. The earring sits unresolved between us on the table. 'So who does this belong to, Matt?' I push it a couple of inches his way, but he doesn't touch it again.

'As God is my witness, Sylvie, I have never seen that earring before. You have to believe me.' His voice breaks. 'Please, you have to...'

I don't know what to say because I don't have to believe him at all. I want to believe him, but I'm not sure I can... not sure I do. He's done something reckless, stupid, dangerous. But swears he hasn't betrayed me with another woman.

Debt, poor judgement, unbelievable stupidity... Can I live with those mistakes? If so, we can sort this out.

Maybe this is why he was evasive about us moving into one house. Not because he didn't want to be with me, but because of what he'd done. Squandered away a good portion of equity his grandad left him on that idiot friend of his. Bloody Nige.

I look at him now – shoulders bowed, his face drawn tight

with shame – and I see a man unravelled. Not slick, or defensive and calculating, but haunted.

No one could fake that. Least of all, Matt.

The earring still sits there, gleaming shamelessly on the table between us. But I decide, in that exact moment, to let it go.

I believe him. I have to, for now at least.

I feel... relieved. Stupidly, horribly relieved.

'You should've told me the truth,' I say softly.

'I didn't want to scare you off. It got so... out of hand.'

I shake my head. 'You're a bloody idiot, Matt.'

'Yeah, don't I know it.'

I try to smile but it doesn't quite land. He looks so broken. So ashamed.

A long silence stretches between us before he eventually speaks.

'I'm going to fix it, Sylvie,' he says. 'I give you my word on that.'

'I know,' I say. 'I believe you.'

He nods, slowly, like he's convincing himself.

'So that's it?' I ask carefully. 'That's everything?'

He nods. 'Absolutely.'

I want to believe him. I *do* believe him.

I rest my elbows on the table, rest my head in my hands and let my breath settle. A plan is already forming. We'll go through the finances and find a way forward. We can talk to someone. There are solutions. Practical, manageable, grown-up steps we can take together.

Everything's going to be alright.

But then Matt lifts the glass of water to his lips and stares into it like it might hold a different kind of truth. His brow furrows. His fingers tighten around it.

There's something in his face. Just for a fraction of a second. A flicker of... fear? Guilt? Something I can't name for certain.

It passes before I can catch it and pick it apart. Before I can decide if I've imagined it.

I've decided to believe Matt is telling me the truth. About the earring, about the mess Nige has dragged him into. But there's still a cold whisper in the back of my mind:

He's telling you what happened, but maybe he's not telling you the whole story. That earring got in his bedroom somehow, so if Matt didn't put it there... who did?

FORTY-THREE

BRENDA

The tea has gone cold now, but Brenda doesn't care. The china cup that belonged to her mother sits delicately in her hand, shaking slightly as her fingers *twitch, twitch, twitch* against the handle.

Across the road, the downstairs window at number forty-five glows with soft light. Matt has been in there for thirty-one minutes. Brenda knows this because she's been timing his visit. She watched him stroll up the path like he owns the place. Like everything is fine.

And everything is most definitely *not* fine.

Her mouth tightens as she pictures them in there together. In Sylvie's kitchen with its garlicky warmth and pretty, matching crockery. The place where, not long ago, Brenda presided, cooking meals for Sylvie and Jess and helping with Scarlet Mae's feeds.

She imagines Matt with that lean, casual posture of his, trying his best to look innocent. Sylvie – far too soft and trusting for her own good – listening to his excuses. Ready to forgive him... until she remembers the earring and Brenda's warnings.

She closes her eyes and lets the image unfold. Sylvie's eyes wide with betrayal. Her voice rising. The moment she pulls the earring from her pocket and drops it on the table between them. Tells him to *get out*.

Brenda knows every corner of that house. Every angle of light, every shadow. She can visualise them moving through it, Sylvie storming off and Matt following, uttering one lame excuse after the other.

They must be arguing by now. They *must* be.

Brenda's fingers twitch again and the china cup rattles in protest. She puts it down and presses her palm flat against her lap to still it.

Earlier, Sylvie had gone off to Jess's house to watch the baby while Jess answered police questions about Kendra. Brenda had offered to go with her, 'Just for moral support,' she'd stressed.

But Sylvie had smiled in that careful, distancing way of hers and said no, she'd be fine. Brenda didn't believe her.

She'd waited in the armchair for Sylvie's return, her eyes fixed on the front path. She planned to be at Sylvie's side the moment she got back to support her. Her face would be the first face Sylvie saw. The only one she'd need.

But then Matt had returned home. Parked the car and gone straight inside his house. Brenda had watched him from behind the curtain, her hands clenching into fists.

A flicker of hatred burns low in her stomach. Just like it had done back then at the hospital when her colleagues had said those terrible things about her. When they had all lied.

They deserved everything they got.

She pushes the thought away and stands up, stretches her legs. The living room is in disarray. Rigid, half-eaten toast still rests on a plate from this morning. Her knitting is a tangled mess, slack loops of burgundy yarn snaking across the arm of the chair like veins. Books lean clumsily on the shelves. Somehow, things have quickly gone to pot. Brenda can't remember the last time she hoovered or dusted.

Those things used to anchor her, but none of it seems to matter these days.

There is still no movement over the road. Brenda rehearses what she'll say when Matt leaves. How she'll comfort Sylvie and soothe her. Be there in her hour of need.

Then finally, there's movement. The front door of number forty-five opens and Matt steps out into the late afternoon light, pulling his coat tighter. Brenda's heart rate spikes.

He's leaving. She did it... she kicked him out!

But then Sylvie appears behind him, laughing softly at something he just said.

She places her hand on his arm and they kiss.

It's not just a peck. It's familiar. Intimate.

Brenda lets out a roar of frustration. The sound is guttural and the cat bolts from under the radiator and dashes into the hallway.

She slaps a hand over her mouth, her whole body rigid.

No. No. NO.

How could Sylvie be so gullible? How could she not see what he is?

Brenda watches as he walks away, back to his house just two doors down. Sylvie waves one last time and then closes her own door gently.

Brenda's limbs move before her thoughts catch up. No tidying of hair, no hastily grabbed coat, not even proper shoes – just her old slippers thudding across the lino.

She flings the front door open and crosses the road.

The air smells of earth and woodsmoke. A few streets away, kids let off the odd stray firework. Brenda's jaw clenches, her breathing shallow and quick.

Sylvie opens the door. Her face glows, although her eyes are slightly puffy. But her expression is bright and she looks lighter somehow. As though a weight has been lifted.

Brenda's stomach flips.

'He's not cheating.' Sylvie is buoyant when Brenda steps inside. 'It's not what we thought.'

Sylvie closes the door behind her. In the hallway, Matt's overpowering aftershave still clings to the air.

Brenda frowns. 'You're telling me he explained the earring?'

Sylvie hesitates. 'He doesn't know where it came from. But I believe him, Brenda. You should've seen the way he—'

'So what *has* he been up to then? Because I assume you haven't imagined his absences and general evasiveness. '

Sylvie blinks. 'It's something else. It's personal. I can't go into it now, but he's told me everything.'

Brenda stares at her, incredulous. 'And you believe him?'

'Yes.'

'Sylvie, come on. That's not—'

'I know him, Brenda.' Sylvie's voice rises, sharper now. 'I know when he's lying.'

Brenda narrows her eyes, noticing how Sylvie rubs at her hands, her throat.

'You're holding something back.' She narrows her eyes. 'What aren't you telling me?'

Sylvie folds her arms across her chest. 'I'm not holding anything back.'

'You are. I can tell.'

'Brenda,' she says, wearily. 'This is starting to feel like... like maybe you *want* him to be guilty.'

Brenda takes a step back. 'Now hang on a minute. That's not—'

'You've been very involved in our lives,' Sylvie says, forcing a smile. 'And I know you care. But honestly, I'm fine. Matt and I, we're going to need to spend some quality time together. To work through any tangles in our relationship.'

'*Tangles*? Another woman's earring in his bedroom, you mean?'

Sylvie closes her eyes briefly like she's trying not to lose her temper.

'I'm tired, Brenda. And I'd really like some time alone right now, if that's OK with you.'

Brenda stands there, frozen, the air suddenly thick and stifling.

Sylvie's eyes have changed. They're still kind, but cooler now. Assessing her and finding Brenda is left wanting.

This realisation settles over her like a sudden frost. She needs to get out of here.

'Fine,' she says. 'I'll be off then.'

'I'll see you tomorrow, maybe,' Sylvie calls after her, already turning away.

The front door closes behind Brenda with a soft, final click and she stands on the path for a moment, blinking into the gloom. Then she crosses the road, her slippered feet slow and deliberate.

When she gets back inside, Ivor eyes her warily from the sofa. Brenda leans against the door frame.

Sylvie is making a big mistake.

She doesn't know who Matt is. Not really. He's very good at putting on a show and being who she wants him to be. But that's a different kettle of fish to telling the truth.

Brenda knows his type. She knows how they work. *Men.* She's seen it all before.

Sylvie needs someone to open her eyes. To help her realise she's being taken for a fool.

Brenda paces the living room. Picks up her knitting needles. Puts them down again. She crosses to the window and parts the curtains.

She can see the lamp is on in Sylvie's living room, her figure moving about inside. The shapes are soft and cosy, blurred by the double glazing.

Brenda watches, her expression calmer now. In her mind, the next steps in her plan are already forming.

The earring wasn't enough. One way or another, she needs to show Sylvie the truth.

And she's prepared to take the necessary risks to do it.

FORTY-FOUR

The photo album rests in her lap, heavier than it looks. Ellie flips another page. The photographs – some blurry and distant – all feature her at the old studio when she was into her keyboard playing.

The one they met at a couple of years ago.

She'd believed they'd met online... he'd sent her a message on Instagram and they'd moved to a musicians forum before switching again to WhatsApp.

'I noticed you back then, but you never noticed me,' he said. 'I overheard you telling a girl there you wanted to develop your music, but your parents weren't having it.'

'You were watching me all that time?' she says. 'Why didn't you just speak to me?'

He shrugs. 'I like to watch.'

She glances down again. There's one of her sitting alone on the wall behind the studio with a couple of smokers, her arms crossed, chin tucked down. She remembers that day. Her dad had stormed through the studio, demanding she come home with him. She'd nearly died with embarrassment.

He leans in slightly. 'I know, I was there. I felt your pain.'

'Then a girl, one of the smokers I'd sat with, told everyone in the neighbourhood and it got around my college.' The story morphed, worsened and it just happened – the note in her locker, the sniggers in the corridor. An online smear campaign was in full swing at that point.

'There were suddenly rumours I slept around. I didn't even have a boyfriend. I was terrified my parents would find out and so I just ditched the music aspirations and did what they wanted. They were delighted.'

He says nothing.

She turns to look at him, her eyes narrowing. 'If you were there, why didn't you try and help me instead of just taking pictures?'

He gives a faint smile but says nothing.

She snaps the album shut and stares at him, eyes scanning his face, like she's trying to trace him onto an old memory. Something about the shape of his jaw. The lashes. The way he keeps his voice low, like it might spill over otherwise.

He'd led her to believe their meeting online was just an accident. Why should she trust him now?

'I had to wait until I was in a position to help you,' he says quietly. 'We're here now and that's what matters. Tell me about your parents and sister.'

'My parents got angry at the world after Sophie died. I thought that was normal because they were grieving. I mean, I was grieving, too. But now I think they just needed something to blame. And I was the only thing left.'

He doesn't interrupt.

'When I turned eighteen, my dad said, "We can't take chances with you." Like I was a risk assessment instead of a daughter. They slapped a nine o'clock curfew on me that made it impossible for me to go to parties or out for drinks at college.'

'You were eighteen.'

'They controlled me. It might seem crazy to you and other people, but where was I going to go? I had little confidence and... I thought they'd chill out after a while but they just got worse. Played the guilt card, told me Sophie would never defy them.'

Ellie flips the photo album open at a random page. At her college prom she's standing stiffly in a peach dress that did nothing for her shape. She remembers smiling so hard it made her face hurt. Her parents had chosen it for her. She'd wanted the clingy red dress with the low back.

'I look like I was trying not to cry there.'

He says, 'Your parents made you feel small, so they could feel safe.'

That pulls at something sharp in her chest.

She shuts the album.

The silence stretches between them, filled only by the faint thrum of the generator outside.

She studies him again. Her legs are curled beneath her now, her shoulders hunched, but her breathing is slow and measured. She doesn't feel afraid.

'You know this is crazy, right?'

'Yes.'

'You've... what, built a room for me? Hidden me away?'

He smiles. 'It might feel like that. This place used to be a studio I worked at and it fell into neglect. I wanted to get you away from your suffocating parents without you being blamed. I wanted to give you the chance to feel properly better.'

She opens her mouth and tries to say no. But she can't do it.

'I don't miss them,' she says, after a while. 'That's the worst part. I'm sitting here in some freaky hidden cabin in the middle of nowhere, and I don't miss them at all. I just miss having the right to make my own choices. Do my own thing.'

'You'll have that soon enough,' he says.

'When?'

He hesitates. 'When you stop being scared.'

'Of what?'

He looks at her in that way again – like he's reading a book only he understands.

'Of yourself.'

FORTY-FIVE

SYLVIE

WEDNESDAY

I reach for my wine glass and clink it gently against Matt's.

'To us,' he says.

'To us.'

The candle between us flickers, catching the edge of his square jaw, throwing warmth across the white linen tablecloth. This place is special. And expensive. Matt surprised me with the reservation... it's a long time since he's done anything as romantic.

I watch him from across the table. He looks full of energy, almost boyish. His fingers are loosely curled around the stem of his wine glass and his impressive shoulders fill out his paisley Paul Smith shirt. He looks strong yet relaxed in the chair. This is the Matt I remember from our first months together – attractive, confident, entirely focused on me.

I smile, trying to ignore the tiny ripples of anxiety that still move in my chest like something trapped under ice. But tonight isn't for questions. Not serious ones, anyway.

The restaurant is quiet, all soft music and murmured

conversations. Outside, the sky has folded itself into blackness, the streetlamps glowing against it. It feels like we're tucked inside a pocket of something safe and sealed in the middle of the city.

'That dessert was ridiculous,' I say, gesturing at the empty plate between us. 'I swear I'm going to dream about that chocolate mousse for days to come.'

'And I'll dream about that sauce on my fish,' Matt says, mock serious. 'What was that? Italian something-or-other?'

'Sicilian lemon *beurre blanc*,' I say, proud I remembered. 'You've always struggled with the detail, haven't you?'

He pretends to look offended. 'You've wounded me now.'

I laugh, and it feels wonderful. Teasing and flirting, just like we used to act together. It's been a while since it came that easily.

We fall quiet, but it doesn't feel awkward. I let it stretch a few more moments, then say, carefully, 'So... you and Nige. Is everything sorted now?'

Matt nods, makes a cut-off gesture with his hand. 'It's done. The debt's covered and Nige has left town for a short time to let things cool off a little.'

'And you?'

'Well, the house is remortgaged as you know, but Nige has promised that once he gets another job he'll start paying me back.'

'Do you believe him? I mean, it's an easy thing to say now the heat is off him but—'

'I've no choice but to believe him,' he says shortly. Something in his expression pulls me up short.

'He hasn't... he's got nothing on you, has he? Made you feel like you had to do this for him?'

He doesn't answer straight away. Instead, he folds his napkin and rests it beside his plate. 'I'll answer all of your questions, Sylvie, I promise. Just not tonight. Please? Tonight's for us.'

I look at him. His eyes are clear, his expression open. I think I'd be able to tell if he was keeping something from me after our heart-to-heart.

'OK,' I say. 'Let's leave it there for now.'

Matt pays the bill and then we walk to the taxi rank through streets that smell of takeout food and exhaust fumes. Matt takes my hand, and I let him. We talk nonsense – the latest from one of his gardeners' colourful divorce, and how he might replace the dodgy seal on my conservatory door this week. It all feels normal and comforting.

Back in the hallway at my house, we kick off my shoes and I glance pointedly up the stairs. We both know there's no decision to be made; he's staying over tonight. Simple as that.

He catches my hand again and kisses the inside of my wrist. The gesture is unexpected and tender. My heart knocks against my ribs.

Later, when he's asleep beside me, I slip out of bed and pad downstairs in search of water.

The kitchen is dimly lit by the glow from the streetlight outside. I don't turn the under-cupboard lights on – I like feeling incognito, the way no one can see I'm here.

I reach for a glass, and that's when I notice that the worktop is clear.

I frown. I didn't come in here when we got in. Matt insisted I go upstairs to get ready for bed while he made us a cup of tea and brought it up.

I'm sure I left a few dirty dishes out earlier, beside the sink. The chopping board too – I left it near the hob. I was in a rush before we went out, so I left the kitchen as it was. Now everything is spotless. The wrung-out dishcloth hangs neatly over the tap. The surfaces are gleaming.

I jump at a grinding, whooshing sound... the dishwasher is

halfway through its cycle. I didn't load it, nor turn it on. And Matt *never* does the honours when he stays over.

I turn slowly, eyes scanning the room. The back door is locked and bolted as usual. Nothing seems out of place.

But still. My skin prickles.

I pour myself a glass of water and take it into the living room, glancing at the neatly folded blanket I cast off carelessly yesterday afternoon. I take a sip, glancing towards the window. Matt didn't close the curtains before he came up.

Brenda's house is in darkness over the road.

As I turn away, a shadowed movement catches my eye. The curtain shifted. Just for a moment. It fluttered, as if a light breeze just moved past it.

I step closer to the window and peer out, but there's nothing now. No light, no silhouette. Everything still and silent.

I stand there for another full minute, glass cold in my hand.

Eventually I pull myself away. Back upstairs. I climb into bed without waking Matt.

When he leaves in the morning, I'll go over there and sort this out with her, once and for all.

FORTY-SIX

SYLVIE

THURSDAY

I wake to a quiet house and the soft weight of Matt's arm still around my waist. His chest presses against my back, steady and warm. I'm still half-dreaming, folded into the mattress in the foetal position.

I feel his warm breath against the nape of my neck and he plants a kiss there, just below my hairline. The way he knows I like. The way that sends shivers down my spine and beyond.

The duvet slides away as he draws me in closer. Our legs are tangled, his hand splayed over my stomach. My entire body aches in a good way and I close my eyes again.

Sink back into the feeling.

For the first time in weeks, I feel safe again. Grounded in my husband's arms.

Things aren't yet perfect between us. How could they be? There are still things we've not talked about in detail, things that don't make sense. That damn earring I found at his house – so much pain and doubt wrapped up within that simple silver hoop with the twisted knot. I've told myself a hundred ways it doesn't matter, that I have to trust he's telling me the truth. But there's still a persistent niggle. There's bound to be... it got there *somehow*.

But then there's the remortgaging issue, too. All that money he just handed over to Nige. Strange, yes. Secretive, yes. But then Matt has always been generous to a fault, especially with the useless mate of his he's known since nursery school.

Nobody seems that keen on Nige. Jess was irritated by his presence on the street when she and the baby stayed and I confess, I find him immature and irritating. But Matt? He can't see any wrong in him at all. Don't people – good people – sometimes do silly things when they think they're protecting someone they care about?

Still, it doesn't stop the constant niggle that there's some other reason he helped Nige out. A reason he's not saying.

But in this moment with Matt's body pressed to mine, I choose to believe in the best of him. I choose love. And trust. Might seem naïve to some, but it's my life. My choice to do so.

Besides, it's not him or Nige I'm struggling with right now.

It's Brenda.

The crumpled throw now folded neatly on the sofa. The impossibly clean kitchen counter and loaded dishwasher. I've not said anything to Matt. I don't want to sound paranoid for one thing, plus he's warned me so many times about Brenda interfering and I've ignored him. I can do without the unavoidable: 'I told you so.'

But now, things are different. I think she's been inside the house without permission. Matt had suggested we change the locks but when she returned the key, I thought that was the end of it. Naïve, seeing as it's the easiest thing in the world to get a spare key cut.

We get up late. Matt makes his signature avocado toast, though neither of us is that hungry. He butters mine before I can say anything, slides the plate across the table. He makes the tea with one hand and answers a work message with the other.

I watch him and feel the old ache come back, the one that used to scare me – when I realised how much I loved this man. When I remembered the heartache of my first marriage.

When he kisses me goodbye, he smells fresh and clean from the shower.

'I've got to quote on a garden in Gamston,' he says. 'I'll call you after lunch and we can decide what we're doing tonight. I thought maybe a movie and takeout food round at mine?'

I nod. 'Sounds good. Drive safe.'

'I always do.' He winks, then he's gone.

I clear the plates, boil the kettle again, settle on the sofa with a book I've been meaning to read for weeks. I get through two pages before my phone rings.

Jess.

I answer quickly. 'Everything alright?'

'Yes... Mum, can you meet me? In an hour. The park near my old school. I need to talk to you.'

She doesn't *sound* alright. Her voice is brittle and she's a bit breathless.

'Is everything OK, love?'

'I just— Please, Mum. I can't do this over the phone. Ed's watching Scarlet Mae while I see you.'

I glance at the clock. 'Why the park? You can just come over here and—'

But she's already hung up.

The cold hits me the second I step outside. My coat is thick, navy wool, belted at the waist. I've got thermal tights under my jeans, boots and gloves buried deep in my pockets, but the icy air still cuts through it. My breath blooms white in front of me.

The park is almost empty. Two dog walkers cross in opposite directions, heads down, hats on, collars up. The trees are bare and rattling like old bones in the wind. The bench by the path is slick with frost, but I keep moving, pacing in slow loops like I'm on an invisible lead myself.

I feel nervy, as if something bad is about to happen. What could be worse than Kendra being found dead? I'm just over-wrought. Stretched a bit thin with everything that's been happening. It's all been too much, too fast.

Jess will want to talk about Kendra, of course she will. She'll barely have slept, and Ed will have suggested she pop over to talk her feelings through with me. But why she's chosen the freezing park instead of coming to my house and chatting over coffee, I can't begin to fathom.

I sit on a bench, stare at the lacklustre plants, the sparse, shrivelled leaves still clinging to the bushes. Roll on spring. New life, new beginnings. That's what we all need.

Jess arrives five minutes later. She's wearing a puffer jacket and beanie hat. She keeps her head down as she walks, but when she looks up, her face is pale and gaunt. Her eyes are wild with panic or fear... or both.

I'm unnerved and stand, holding out my arms. 'Jess?'

She shakes her head and looks down at the floor. Walks past me and sits at the other end of the bench, her gloved fingers trembling in her lap.

'You're scaring me now,' I say softly. 'You look shattered and stressed. What is it you need to talk to me about?'

She keeps her eyes on the ground. 'Ed said I should come and see you. I didn't sleep again last night, and he said I can't keep carrying it around. I know he's right, but—'

'Carrying what around?'

She shakes her head.

I know my daughter well enough to let her work through it. There'll be no forcing her. I bite my lip and wait, my nerves shredding.

'Jess, come on,' I say after more long, drawn-out seconds.

'Please. Whatever it is, it's only me... haven't we always told each other everything?'

She turns to look at me then. Her lips are dry and chapped like something sucked the moisture clean out. And I can see it behind her eyes. The thing she can't face, that I can't put my finger on. A sort of fear or dread I've never seen there before.

'Mum, I'm so sorry to have to tell you this,' she says, voice barely above a whisper. 'I didn't want to believe it... so I've tried to ignore it. Made excuses instead of... The married man Kendra was seeing? I think it might have been Matt.'

The world pulls away from me.

For a second or two, I can't make sense of her words. They land without meaning, no context.

My brain starts catching up, begins assembling fragments of evidence I didn't realise I'd noticed. Kendra's face the last time she came over. The way she watched Matt when he fetched our drinks. Jess saying Kendra had become evasive and cagey and wanted to stop coming around my house. *The earring.*

'No,' I say. But it's not even a full word when I utter it. It breaks in half immediately.

Jess's mouth twists and we stare at each other. It feels like my breath has stopped in my chest.

I realise I can't feel the cold anymore.

I can't feel anything at all.

FRIDAY

Brewster sits at his desk, hunched over the case file like it might offer up something new if he only stares at it for long enough. The overhead lights bleach out the page but don't do anything to brighten the room. A low mood hangs over the office, not helped by the gloomy canopy of low grey clouds that seem to press against the windows.

The desk phone rings with an internal call.

'Brewster,' he says, snatching it up. Then: 'Downstairs right now? Two of them?' He frowns at Helena. 'We're on our way down.'

He puts down the phone. 'Two lads downstairs want to speak to us about the EFIT we put together at the Spar shop.'

'The one we haven't released yet, you mean?' She stands up. 'Come on then. This case gets stranger by the day.'

In reception, two young men stand side by side like they've been glued together. Helena immediately recognises the younger one as Andrew, Irene Humphrey's colleague at the

Spar who covered the shop while they interviewed her. He keeps unknotting his fingers and knotting them again.

The other guy is taller and a bit older, but they look alike.

Brewster leads them to a vacant interview room.

'This is Simon,' Andrew says nervously. 'My brother.'

When they're sitting around a table, Brewster clears his throat. 'So, how can we help?'

Simon clears his throat. 'I haven't slept since Andrew told me that... you'd been to the shop and spoke to... The mystery man Ellie Walker was seen with in the shop? That's me.'

Now Helena sees it. EFITs are notoriously vague, but Irene had managed to capture some similarity around his eyes and hair.

'So, that was you?' Brewster says grimly.

Simon shifts in his chair. 'Yeah. See, I knew Ellie from college. I liked her, asked her if she fancied going for a coffee. We called in at the shop when Andrew wasn't on shift.'

'And what happened when you left the shop?'

'We didn't bother with a coffee; we agreed to go to the cinema at some point, but we didn't arrange anything there and then.'

Brewster frowns. 'And why has it taken you this long to come forward, Simon?'

He pinches the top of his nose. 'When I heard she'd gone missing I told Andrew I'd been in the shop with her.'

'I said he should contact you,' Andrew adds. 'But he was scared. And then you guys came to interview Irene and I knew we had to come.'

Simon nods. 'I thought I'd get blamed for her disappearance. And Ellie was seen leaving college on her bike after that, wasn't she? It wasn't like I was the last to see her. I told myself it'd only make things worse for myself if I came forward and I hadn't got any information that could help, anyway. But Andrew made me see sense.'

He manages a faint, ashamed smile that Brewster does not return.

'The fact that someone saw you together prompted us to investigate and to spend valuable police time chasing up this detail,' Brewster says. 'Time we could have put towards other leads in the case. Did you consider that?'

Simon's face pales. 'No. I never thought of that. Sorry.'

Helena keeps her voice even. 'When we spoke to Mrs Humphreys at the Spar, she told us you seemed a bit nervous, as if you were keen to get away that day. She recalled you had a strange look on your face. Why was that?'

Simon shifts, stares at his hands laced in front of him on the table. 'Ellie was... a bit off. She asked me if I'd ever fancied robbing a place like the Spar.' He glances up quickly, checking their faces. 'I thought she was having a laugh, but I got this feeling she meant it. Like she wanted to do something just to see what would happen. Not for money, just for the hell of it.' He shakes his head. 'I decided she was a bit weird, and I didn't want to see her again.'

Brewster and Helena trade a brief look.

'And what happened when you left the shop that day?' she asks.

'We were planning on going for a coffee, but I made an excuse I'd remembered somewhere I needed to be. She laughed, as if she knew I'd changed my mind. I thought she was shy, but she wasn't like that at all really. I was the one who ended up feeling nervous around her.'

'So you didn't go for a coffee?' Brewster remarks.

'No. I got the bus back to college, and she walked off, calling me a loser.' He brightens slightly. 'I went to see my tutor, Dave Cantrell, about an assignment, so you can check that's the truth.'

Helena nods. 'Well, thank you for coming in. It's well overdue, but you did the right thing.'

Brewster slips him a card. 'We may need to contact you again if more questions come up. Keep your phone on. And Simon? If you remember anything else, however small, don't wait to lose sleep before you get in touch.'

Simon nods, relief washing over his face, and the brothers retreat together, shoulders almost touching.

Back upstairs, Brewster scratches his cheek with the end of his pen. 'This is going precisely nowhere at the moment, boss. We've gone over everything we have. Twice. And now the EFIT lead is probably out of the window. I was hoping for something stronger by now, something solid we could start to pin this case on.'

'Well, we're not done yet,' Helena says, stacking her notes into a folder. 'We'll check out Simon's alibi with his tutor just to tick that box. But I feel strongly we need to push Jess Langley again. That first conversation was just a nudge. This time, I want her here at the station. Let her feel the walls closing in on her slightly.'

Brewster sighs, nods. 'You still think she knows more?'

'I'm convinced of it. And I think we also need to speak to her mum.'

'Sylvie Tyce?' he says, brows rising. 'You reckon she knows something, too?'

'Maybe nothing she'd necessarily think of as useful. But she and Jess are close and something has come between them. I saw Sylvie's face when Jess shut that kitchen door. She wasn't expecting to be left out. Didn't understand it and definitely didn't like it.'

Brewster leans back and folds his arms. 'She's unlikely to drop her daughter in it.'

'Probably not, but she might let something slip that gives us a new direction to explore,' Helena says, collating some paperwork. 'She might also know more than she realises. I think it's worth a try, Brewster.'

He nods slowly, eyes drifting to the whiteboard across the office. Kendra's face is still up there, printed and pinned beside Ellie's. Beside both of their timelines. Every time Helena looks at it, she gets the same tight pull in her chest.

They're close to getting a break. She can feel it. Close enough to get a sense of who knows something – even if the detail is still evading them.

Helena reaches for her lanyard. 'Anyway, I'm going upstairs to see the super shortly.'

Brewster blinks, surprised. 'You're going to ask her if we can do the press conference?'

Helena nods. 'I'm done waiting for the phone metadata to drop a miracle into our laps. We need public engagement. We've held back one key detail about Kendra's body – and I think now's the time to use it.'

He straightens slightly, suddenly more alert. 'Time to talk about the earring?'

'Exactly. It's distinctive – silver, twisted into an infinity knot. Not the kind of thing you see mass produced or misplace without remembering. Her left ear was missing it. Whoever has that earring – whoever took it – has some serious questions to answer.'

'Assuming they didn't just throw it in a hedge or it fell from the body.'

'If it fell in the vicinity of where the body was found, chances are we'd have found it by now. I believe someone may have kept it as a trophy.' Helena closes her folder with a quiet thud.

'Whoever has that earring is part of this. Whether they know it or not.' Brewster frowns. 'By the way, good luck with the super. I heard someone at the vending machine moaning she's got it on her today.'

'What's new?' Helena mumbles, gathering her stuff together.

. . .

Superintendent Grey's office is tidy to the point of her displaying signs of OCD. Today, Helena has already spotted her hair is slicked back so severely, it might indeed be a worrying reflection of her mood this morning.

Grey waves her in without looking up. 'Price.'

'Afternoon, ma'am.'

'Got an update for me on the Kendra Marsh case?'

'Sort of. I'm here to ask to go public with the missing earring,' Helena says without preamble. No sugar-coating. Helena has discovered, when the super is in one of her moods, dithering only serves to irritate her further.

The ploy gets Grey's attention. She looks up, straightens a fraction in her seat. 'You're serious. This soon?'

'I am. It's a detail we've kept quiet up until now. It's specific. It could jog a memory – or rattle someone who's sitting on it. And there's something else. I want to bring Jess Langley in for formal questioning.'

Grey refers to her notes. 'Jess is... Kendra's best friend?'

Helena nods. 'We went easy on her in our initial chat after Kendra's body was discovered. But this time, there'll be no tea and sympathy. I'm almost certain she knows something, and I want to formally explore that.'

Grey taps her pen in a staccato rhythm on the desk. 'I thought you also had suspicions about Jess Langley's mother.'

'I do, and Sylvie Tyce is next on our list. But Brewster and I both feel Jess is the priority. I think she could be hiding something behind all that new-mum exhaustion. I don't think she's necessarily involved per se, but I think she's scared. And, as we know, fear can make people shut down and withhold vital information.'

'What's the latest on the EFIT?'

Helena blinks. 'Funny you should bring that up, ma'am.' She tells her about their conversation downstairs.

'Another red herring.' She frowns. 'This case seems full of them.'

'It does, but I feel like we're on the right track now with the missing earring. We just need to do the appeal.'

'Fair enough, Helena, you've made your point well. I only wish everyone was as direct instead of wasting my time.' Grey look to the window and back again before exhaling. 'You've got forty-eight hours to bring me something that looks like progress. And I don't want to see your face in that press room unless you've got the full media pack approved by Comms and a clear pitch approved. And I want that earring photograph cropped so it doesn't show the background context – understood?'

'Yes, ma'am. Goes without saying.'

She studies Helena a moment longer, then nods. 'And Price – keep your head. If this goes sideways, I'll be the one getting dragged across the coals.' Her eyes narrow. 'And if that happens, I'll come looking for you.'

'Understood. Thanks for your time, ma'am.'

Back in the incident room, Brewster looks up as Helena returns.

'How did that go?'

'She was brutal, but we've got the go-ahead. Press conference tomorrow if we can get organised for then. Get Comms on standby, Brewster. I want the photo file stripped down, no extras. Just the earring.'

He nods, already moving, his phone in hand. Then he turns back.

'You still want me to get Jess Langley in here later today, boss?' he asks.

'Yep. Call her and offer transport if needed seeing as she's just had a baby and been ill. And get someone to ask Sylvie

Tyce if she'd be willing to pop in too at some point – casual tone, nothing formal. Just a quiet word should serve our purpose.'

He raises an eyebrow. 'You think she'll go for it?'

'I think she'll do it for her daughter's sake. And for Kendra. She's known her from being a kid.'

There's a moment of stillness as Brewster presses the number.

Outside, the wind picks up. Helena glances out of the window to watch a clutch of leaves whip across the car park like they're trying to escape from something.

Helena stares at the image of the missing earring on the screen.

'This is our leverage,' she says. 'This tiny, twisted piece of silver. Whoever is hiding it has no idea how loud it's about to become.'

He nods slowly, relaying the message to Comms.

The pressure is rising. Helena can feel it in her gut. One girl dead, another still missing. The longer they leave this, the further she could drift.

If Jess Langley does know the man Kendra was seeing – if she's hiding that from them out of fear or shame or some kind of misguided loyalty – then it's only a matter of time before she cracks.

Because if there's one thing she's learned in this job, it's that hidden guilt has a remarkable tendency to leak out when you least expect it.

And when it does, Helena will be there to grab it with both hands.

FORTY-EIGHT

SYLVIE

I watch the press conference on my iPad. Local social media groups are alive with what can only be described as barely concealed excitement over the forthcoming Nottinghamshire Police appeal. Jess texted to remind me too.

I sit at the edge of the sofa, elbows digging into my knees while I wait for it to start. The volume's up too loud. It's just me in the house, but I want the noise – need it to fill the silence. I wish Matt was here but he called earlier to say he's still out on his quotation rounds.

On screen, the Nottinghamshire Police logo flickers at last, then sharpens. A plain room, a lectern, a row of microphones. DI Helena Price steps up, smart in a navy trouser suit. Her neat bob is tucked behind her ears, her face unreadable.

The press murmurs grow louder then quieten down. Price doesn't speak straight away, lets the hush really settle. Then she begins.

'Good afternoon. I'm Detective Inspector Helena Price. I'm

here to update you on the ongoing investigation into the death of local woman twenty-year-old Kendra Marsh.'

Her voice is clear and controlled with no softness.

A photo of Kendra flashes up on the projector screen behind her – a familiar one now. Smiling, unaware of the horror about to befall her. Kendra, who used to come round for tea at least twice a week when she and Jess were at school together.

'We've decided to reveal a previously undisclosed piece of information in the hope the public can assist us. It concerns a missing item of the victim's jewellery.' The picture on the projector screen changes. 'A silver earring is being displayed behind me. This one was found intact on Kendra Marsh but, if we assume it's one of a matching pair, the other one is missing.'

I stiffen, peering closer at the image. Silver. Hoop-style. And there it is – the knot. Ornamental and delicate. Not expensive, but distinct. I know that earring.

I've held it in my hand. It's sitting in my kitchen drawer right now. My breathing quickens.

DI Price continues, 'We are appealing to the public. If anyone has seen this earring or knows of someone who came into possession of it recently, please contact the incident room immediately. You can remain anonymous if you wish.'

Contact details start to scroll across the bottom of the screen.

My hand goes numb. The laptop slips from my knees and clatters to the floor.

I hear Helena's voice continue. 'We believe the earring may have been lost – or removed – close to the time Kendra died. It may even have been lost during the attack. Any information, no matter how small, could be crucial to the investigation.'

The screen swims. I'm suddenly upright, stumbling into the kitchen. The drawer is stiff. I yank it and start to rifle through it, cut my finger on a rogue tin opener, blood welling instantly – but I barely register it. Beneath the old takeaway menus and crumpled receipts, my fingers find the edge of the handkerchief. I unfold it.

And there it is.

The knot glints, catching the light just as it did when I spotted it on Matt's bedroom floor. The earring he claims to know nothing about...

I grip the drawer edge. The room tilts. My knees give way, and I sink to the floor, back against the cupboards, the cold lino pressing through my skirt.

He lied. Matt looked me in the eye and lied through his teeth.

There's only one way that earring could have found its way into his bedroom and that's if he's got something to do with Kendra's death.

This is evidence. The police are looking for the earring I have in my hand this very second. This is real. It's really happening.

I clamp my hand over my mouth. I'm going to be sick. I can feel the saliva gathering in my mouth.

A banging starts up on the front door and I make a noise of pure terror. Is it Matt? Will he try to silence me?

'Sylvie?' Brenda's concerned voice floats through the closed door. 'Sylvie, it's only me. Are you OK?'

The press conference is still playing on my iPad, the press asking questions and DI Price's considered responses.

I try to respond to Brenda, but nothing comes. The earring is still in my palm, imprinting itself into my skin.

I flick the latch open and she appears in the doorway. She's dressed as if she's going to a lunch – a beige twinset and pearls. Her eyes flick over me, taking in the scene. She doesn't ask what's wrong. Doesn't gasp or falter. Just steps carefully inside and stands beside me.

'I came over because I knew it would be hard for you. I was watching it at home and just had the strongest feeling I should come over.' She glances down. Sees the earring lying in my open palm. Her expression sharpens, just for a moment.

I close my fist around it. 'I – I didn't know what it was.'

'Of course you didn't,' she says softly. 'But now you do. And you're right to be shaken. It's awful, isn't it? To realise something so dark has been right under your nose all this time.'

Her words are soft, but I get the feeling they're lined with something else. A quiet satisfaction?

'It was in Matt's room,' I say. My voice sounds strange in my throat. 'But he swears he doesn't know how it got there.'

She exhales, long and slow. 'Oh, Sylvie.'

'I believed him. I didn't think for a minute he'd—'

'Killed that poor girl,' she offers in a forlorn tone.

I let out a small noise of despair. 'I've been such a fool.'

'No, no, no. You mustn't blame yourself.' Her hand squeezes mine just a tad too hard. 'It's him that's done something terrible. Not you.'

I look at her. Her face is sympathetic, but there's not a flicker of shock. She doesn't ask any questions and it feels like she's known for a while. Seen another side to my husband I've been completely oblivious to.

'How could he?' I whisper, tears prickling in my eyes. 'She was Jess's friend.'

Brenda doesn't answer. She just strokes my hand again, then gently pries open my fingers. Looks at the earring, then folds my hand closed around it again.

'You'll have to go to the police, of course. I can come with you, too,' she says. 'If you'd like?'

I stay quiet. I can't seem to get my thoughts in order.

'Do you want me to stay while you call them?' Brenda says. 'I can't stay too long; I have to go and visit my aunt at her care home in Chesterfield. But I can stay with you a little while.'

'No, it's fine thanks,' I say. 'I just need a bit of time to... get my head around it all.'

'Of course. It must be a terrible shock.' A pause. Then, 'My advice is not to wait too long. This evidence you have in your hand is vital. You don't want the police to question why you waited to contact them or you could find yourself in trouble, too.'

I shake my head. The last thing I need is her making me feel even worse. 'You don't need to stay, Brenda. I have to think about this. Think about what I'm going to do.'

'I wouldn't think for too long.' Brenda hesitates before rising to her feet. 'You know where I am. I'll lock the door on my way out.' She smooths her tweed skirt. 'I'd bolt it this side if I were you. Just in case he comes back. You never know what he might do.'

And then she's gone.

I stay on the floor for a long time, the silver earring burning. As if it's branding my palm.

FORTY-NINE

It's very dark in here, but Ellie hears the door open softly followed by the hushed movement of someone stepping softly across the floorboards. She's sitting on the edge of the high bed in the dark, legs over the side and her feet firmly planted on the floor.

He snaps on a temporary light in the hallway and stands there for a few moments. Watching her.

'You didn't lock the door when you left,' she says.

'I didn't think you'd run, and I needed time to think about something.'

She shrugs. She's not sure where she would go, if she did run. Not back to her suffocating parents, that is for sure.

He comes closer with careful, measured steps.

'Are you hungry?'

'No.'

She doesn't look at him until he sits in the chair opposite her. Then, slowly, she lifts her chin.

'You said you've been thinking about something,' she says.

'Yes.'

A beat of silence.

'Is it bad?'

'Yes.'

She waits. The silence stretches long enough to make her think he's not going to say anything else.

Then, 'I killed her.'

Ellie doesn't blink.

'Kendra,' he says.

He pauses, as if he's expecting something from her. Shock, maybe. Outrage. But she doesn't feel either of those things.

Ellie just watches him, face unreadable.

'She knew me, of course she did. But when I told her about us, she laughed.'

Ellie frowns.

'She said, "Oh, that sad cow." That's what she called you. No remorse. No shame for what she did.'

'Did she fight?'

'She cried. And then she begged. She wasn't laughing at the end.'

'Thank you,' Ellie says. 'For doing that for me.'

A silence settles between them. It should feel bigger than it does. But here, in this strange little room with its closed-in air and muffled electricity, it lands like a long-overdue truth.

Ellie looks down at her hands. At her fingers pressing together. A small scar on her thumb when she fell off her bicycle the day he took her.

He leans forward, elbows on his knees.

'Jess is still out there.'

'And?'

'She was the worst of them, you said. Kendra did what Jess told her to do. Jess started it all.'

Ellie nods. 'Yeah. I know.'

He watches her for a moment longer. Then he says, 'I want to bring her here. I want her to face you. I want her to know what she did to you, how it felt.'

She lets out a long breath. 'And then?'

'I'll leave that to you.'

'Do you think she'll remember me?' she asks.

'She'll pretend she doesn't. But we'll remind her. Don't worry about that.'

'What will you do if I say no?'

'I'll let her go.'

'Would you?'

'I'll do what you tell me.'

Her heart twitches. She walks to the tiny square window and looks out. Black trees against a black sky. No stars out tonight.

'I used to fantasise about this,' she says. 'Those two being trapped just like I was. I used to think about what I'd say if I ever saw them again. What I'd do to them if I had the power.'

He doesn't answer, just watches her.

Ellie walks back across the room, but she doesn't sit this time. Instead, she stands over him.

She feels seen.

She feels ready.

'Do it,' she says.

FIFTY

SYLVIE

When Brenda has gone, I spend a long time staring at the wall, my heart thudding. For the first time in weeks, I'm not sure who I'm most afraid of losing – Matt, Jess, or my own sense of what the hell is going on in my house, with my family. But I have this powerful hunch I can't shake: Brenda is hiding something.

I check the time and look out of the window. Brenda's car has gone, so she must have now left to see her aunt in Chesterfield.

I use the spare key she left on the hook by the utility room in case I needed to get in to feed the cat for her. I tell myself what I'm doing is just a precaution. I'm just taking a look to try and understand what the hell is going on with her and it gives me a little time to think what to do about the police.

In the hallway, a framed photo sits on the console table. I pick it up and peer closer. It's two people: a grinning young woman in blue scrubs with one arm around an older nurse with a name badge blurred by glare. The younger woman looks a bit like Brenda.

I open the slim drawer underneath.

Inside is a file. Neatly labelled. I pull out a letter bearing a letterhead from an NHS Trust that doesn't exist. I know, because I quickly google it on my phone. Twice.

The reference is typed, but there's no signature.

The next page is a photocopy of a hospital ID badge. The photo is recent, but the badge says 2004.

At the bottom of the slim pile of paperwork is another letter addressed to Brenda at home. It's from a disciplinary panel and it states she has been dismissed from her post due to gross misconduct. I take a couple of snaps of it on my phone and put everything back exactly where I found it.

I go back into the house, lock my own door again, and sit down with my phone.

If Penny won't tell me exactly what the agent flagged up on Brenda's tenancy application, I'll ask them myself.

But first, I need a glass of wine. And I need Matt not to come home for at least an hour. Because I've got a feeling this is going to get a lot worse before it gets better.

FIFTY-ONE

SYLVIE

I punch the key code in on the entrance door to Jess's block of flats and climb the stairs as quickly as I can manage, ignoring the lift. When I reach the first floor, I'm struggling a bit and my heart sinks. It's going to take forever for me to fully get my strength and fitness levels back.

I don't ring the bell, just a short, sharp knock in case Scarlet Mae is sleeping. Jess answers quickly, the baby snuggled against her skinny body. For a moment, I'm mesmerised by my grand-daughter's pink cheeks, flushed with sleepy warmth.

'Mum?' Jess looks alarmed. 'You didn't say you were coming... is everything OK?'

'Yes, but...' I try to steel myself against the tears I can feel building behind my eyes. 'I need to talk to you. Are you on your own?'

She nods, gently pulling a damp bib from under Scarlet Mae's chin. 'Ed's at the studio, if that's what you mean.'

I step inside and close the door behind me. It smells unpleasantly sour in here like milk has been spilt and just left to dry. I walk down the short hallway, past the open kitchen door and see a pile of crusty, unwashed dishes in the sink. In the living room, the coffee table has almost disappeared under a pile of bottles, half-drunk glasses of orange squash and a few beer cans.

'Sorry about the mess,' Jess mutters, shushing the baby when she starts to grizzle.

I'm distracted for a moment by a painting hanging on the wall behind the sofa. I've never seen anything like it before and it's certainly new in here.

'Ed did it,' Jess says, jiggling the baby. 'He says painting helps him with his creativity when he's writing songs. Not bad, is it?'

I don't consider myself an art buff by any means, but the jagged red and black splodges and random spattering of paint isn't my idea of what I'd want to look at in my living room when I'm trying to relax. Unless I wanted to feel like I was in the middle of a nightmare, that is. Which brings my attention back to why I'm here.

'Jess, I... I had to come. There's nobody else I can really speak to.'

She moves to lay Scarlet Mae down in her basket. 'What's happened?'

'Did you watch the press conference? About Kendra's case?'

She rubs her eyes. 'Scarlet Mae was restless so I got distracted, but Ed told me they're appealing for information.' She frowns at my expression. 'Why are you looking like that?'

'I don't know where to start,' I say. 'The police mentioned Kendra had an earring missing and they're appealing to the public to try and find it.'

'OK,' she says cautiously, clearly unsure where I'm going with this.

My mouth is suddenly bone dry, so I stop talking and open

my handbag. I push my thumb and forefinger down into a small inside pocket and pull out the earring.

Her eyes lower in sadness. 'That looks like Kendra's earring, yes. She often wore them.' Then, the realisation comes. 'How come you've got it?'

'Jess, I don't want you to panic but... I found this on Matt's bedroom floor.'

'What? Are you serious?'

'Yes, but... he swears he's never seen it before. And he also swears to God he wasn't having an affair.' I find myself constantly switching between believing he's guilty to the hope he's innocent.

'Mum, what are you going to do?'

'I... I don't know yet.'

'You have to go to the police with this.' Her voice drops low and urgent. 'You *have* to.'

'I can't. I mean, not yet. Not until I know for definite that—'

'Mum, are you actually crazy? Kendra's dead and the earring the police are trying to trace was in his bedroom? Now you're carrying around crucial evidence in your bloody handbag!'

'But... I know Matt well enough to decipher when he's telling the truth. And he is, Jess. He *is* telling the truth. I'd know if he was lying.'

Jess covers her face with her hands. 'This is a nightmare. You can't seriously believe he's innocent after finding Kendra's earring on his bedroom floor. What planet are you on?'

Scarlet Mae whimpers and Jess lifts her out of her basket, her hands trembling.

'I'll take her,' I say, holding out my hands. I'm suddenly desperate to feel the baby's warm innocence close to me.

'She's fine,' Jess says coldly. 'Let's just focus on sorting this mess you're in.'

'I'm not in a mess. I'm... just trying to get my thoughts straight.'

'You found a dead girl's earring in your husband's bedroom and you're keeping it from the police. I'd say that's a big, fat mess otherwise known as *withholding evidence*.'

'Matt denied the affair. He swore to me.'

'That's not enough against proof,' she says simply. 'Stone-cold proof.'

'Not of the murder,' I whisper. 'But maybe... of the rest.'

Jess perches on the arm of the sofa. Her eyes flick to the window, then the hallway, then back to me.

'Look, Mum, you're not the only one implicated by this.' Her voice softens slightly. 'Ed's been saying I should tell the police what I heard that night.'

I blink. 'What night?'

'A few weeks before Kendra disappeared. I overheard her on the phone to someone. She sounded upset and angry. She said, "You told me you were going to leave her. You said you loved me."' Jess swallows. 'I told Ed and that's when he said he thought he'd seen Matt with a woman who looked just like Kendra from the back.'

I look down at my hands. I don't want to hear this. It's so bloody painful.

'At the time I didn't want to believe it was true, but now... Ed thinks we should tell the police everything. He keeps saying he's worried Matt might show up here. When he's working late at the studio. When it's just me and the baby.'

'And what? How can you say that? You know Matt would never hurt you or Scarlet Mae!' It feels like an insult. A slur on me, too.

'The Matt *you* want to believe exists might not hurt anyone, but maybe he has another side to him! You've got to open your eyes, Mum. Look at the facts... the earring.'

I don't know what to say. My eyes are drawn again to the

painting. The darkness of it looks exactly like the inside of my head feels.

I take a breath. 'I want you and the baby to come back to mine. Just for a couple of nights. Just until we know more. Until—'

Jess laughs in disbelief. 'You want me to come back while Matt's living two doors away and popping in for coffee like nothing happened?'

Her words hang there and reality shifts into focus. Like a light bulb coming on, I suddenly realise the obvious: I can't protect him. And if he is the monster Jess and Ed obviously believe, if he ripped that earring from Kendra's ear to keep as a grisly trophy, I don't *want* to protect him.

'Mum, what are you going to do? About the earring?'

'I don't know.' I close my eyes. 'I don't know what to believe anymore.'

Inside, I do know. I'm going to the police. Of course I am.

But first, there's something I need to get cleared up.

FIFTY-TWO

SYLVIE

Margaret Ellis is already at the café table when I arrive, hands wrapped around a mug of tea as if it might warm more than just her fingers. She's late fifties, maybe early sixties, with tidy grey-blonde hair and a floral scarf tucked neatly into her jacket. *Sensible*. That's the word that comes to mind. Someone who irons absolutely everything and never leaves wet clothes in the washing machine overnight.

She gives an efficient smile as I approach. 'Margaret? Thank you for coming. I'm Sylvie Tyce.'

We shake hands and I slide into the chair opposite her. Her hands are lightly tanned from her recent holiday, I expect. 'I appreciate you agreeing to meet up. I know it must be awkward... talking about Brenda like this.'

I explain the situation: how Brenda came to live across the road, how she flagged Jess's urgent medical condition and looked after us all. Then I tell her how Brenda is kind of refusing to let go.

Margaret lets out a soft sigh, her eyes drifting for a second or two. 'I still think about her, you know. About how it all ended at the hospital. I'm still not sure I did enough to support her.'

That catches me off guard. 'Sorry... you feel responsible?'

She nods. 'You see, Brenda worked under me for nearly eight years. She was a good nurse. Thorough. Calm. She had all the necessary attributes, and she also had this way with the more difficult patients – especially the elderly. A kind of fierce gentleness, if that makes sense. It was like they understood each other when the younger staff would rub some patients up the wrong way. But I'm afraid Brenda didn't always manage boundaries well. And she didn't always respect them.'

I frown. 'Boundaries?'

Margaret leans in slightly, her voice lowering. 'When she moved to the children's ward with me, she started to get emotionally attached. Over-involved. It started off small. Bending rules about visiting hours, sneaking in extra snacks for her favourite young patients, that kind of thing. Fairly harmless. But later, Brenda started resisting input. Other nurses would suggest a change of care plan and Brenda would shut it down. She didn't like being questioned, even by me.'

I feel a bit queasy.

'There was a boy,' Margaret continues. 'Ten years old and a long-term case. He had this cheeky grin and everybody adored him. Especially Brenda. She used to bring him books, stories. Often sat with him long after her shift ended.'

She hesitates, looks down at her cup.

'When his observations changed, Brenda didn't escalate it as she should have done. It was like she had a mental block that anything could go wrong. Not on her shift. She thought he was just tired. She didn't want to "inconvenience him with fuss", I think were her words.' Margaret picks up her spoon and stirs her cappuccino. 'I remember that when I looked at his observation paperwork, her notes were vague when she was fully aware they needed to be the opposite.'

I go cold. 'What happened?'

'The child's condition deteriorated overnight. He arrested early the next morning and they were unable to stabilise him.'

'Oh no,' I whisper, my hand gripping the edge of the table.

'Brenda was suspended,' Margaret says gently. 'There was an inquiry and she was dismissed. We had a new management structure by then and they wanted things tidied up quickly. I didn't get a say in the matter.'

I swallow hard. My mouth's gone dry. 'You think Brenda... what, panicked? Or deliberately—'

'I think she cared too much in the wrong way. Brenda liked to be needed. I heard on the grapevine she'd been the same at her last hospital. Become very close to a patient, an elderly gentleman, who sadly died. Brenda had to take some time off to recover. She took control where she shouldn't have. Struggled with authority and limits.'

It rings true and my breath catches. I picture Scarlet Mae, wriggling in Brenda's arms that first time I left her with our new neighbour to take Jess to the emergency department. I did it because she'd been a nurse. I'd trusted her implicitly because of that.

'I didn't know,' I murmur. 'But it makes a lot of sense with everything that's been happening.'

Margaret reaches across the table, lays a hand on mine. 'You couldn't have known her history.'

'But I *should* have seen something. The way Brenda hovered. The way she neatly inserted herself into our lives, into *my* life.' I thought it was kindness. Or perhaps loneliness. But it was something more serious, more sinister.

And the thing that resonates the most, the thing I can't get out of my head, is that all this time... Matt has been right.

FIFTY-THREE

I'm a mess, driving home from the café. My thoughts are lost in a swirl of brain fog and keep slipping out of reach, spiralling away before I can grasp them. I take a wrong turn and almost jump a red light.

I get out of the car and glance across the road. Brenda's curtains are half-drawn. The lamp in her front window flickers like it's got a dodgy bulb – or maybe she's in front of it, moving and watching.

When I get inside, Matt is sitting at the kitchen table with his arms folded and his head bowed. There's a cup of tea in front of him, untouched.

He looks up slowly when I stand in the doorway.

'You've been gone for hours,' he says.

I don't answer. I take off my coat, hang it by the door with movements that feel stiff and almost robotic. My bag drops to the floor with a thud.

'I tried to call you,' he says from the kitchen. 'I texted and left a voicemail.'

'I've been with Jess.'

I walk back to the kitchen and stand with my arms folded,

back against the worktop.

'Is Jess OK?' he says, his voice flat. 'And the baby?'

I stay quiet and look at him. His face is pale and drawn, his hair unwashed and he's always been fussy about his hair. His eyes are bloodshot. He looks dreadful.

'I wouldn't say Jess is *fine*,' I say eventually. 'She's seen the police press conference. As I have.'

He exhales through his nose. 'Sylvie, you can't honestly think I killed Kendra?'

'I know you're lying to me about something.'

I expect him to come back with an instant denial as he has before. Instead, he stands, moves to the sink, rinses out the untouched tea. His hands are shaking.

'I'm not here to fight,' he says and for the first time I realise he's lost some weight. He looks thinner in the face and his collar gapes slightly.

'I didn't kill Kendra. And that's the God's honest truth.'

My throat tightens. 'Then explain to me how the earring missing from Kendra's body finds its way into your bedroom. An earring the police are actively searching for.' I can't believe I'm saying these words. It's sickening. Surreal.

'I think someone's setting me up, Sylvie.'

I stiffen. 'Setting you up in what way, exactly?'

'What if someone planted that earring, specifically so *you* found it?'

I make a sound of disbelief. 'Like who?'

'You tell me.'

I don't answer. I don't have to because I know who it is he's referring to.

I look out of the window and over the road. I can see Brenda's front room from here. The warm glow. Rose-printed curtains drawn halfway. I can see the edge of her armchair and the corner of her china cabinet.

Matt says, 'I don't know how Brenda would get her hands

on Kendra's earring, but I do know she'd do anything to split us up. To land me in trouble with the police.'

'I admit she's a meddler,' I say. 'But I can't imagine she'd go as far as to pervert the course of justice by planting evidence.'

'I don't know why, but she's always had a problem with me,' Matt says and he's right. But how would Brenda get the earring? I'd bet my house *she* didn't kill Kendra.

Matt turns and looks at me, his body sagging. My handsome, strong, dependable husband looks like a broken man, and I can hardly bear it. It's in my nature to jump up, wrap my arms around him and tell him everything is going to be alright. But I don't do that.

Instead, I meet his stare.

'I'm scared of losing you, Sylvie,' he whispers. 'I love you. I need you to believe in me. I need you to believe I've done nothing wrong.'

I look down at the table. I want to believe him so badly. God, I really want to.

But each time I close my eyes, I see Kendra's lovely face and that damned earring.

His voice breaks into my thoughts again. 'Let's sit down and talk it through. Can we do that?'

He doesn't wait for my answer. He opens the cupboard and gets out two wine glasses. Then he walks to the fridge and gets out half a bottle of Chablis that I opened a few days ago. He pours what's left into the glasses and offers me one. I hesitate.

He says, 'It's just a glass of wine, Sylvie, that's all. It's not a bribe. Not poison. Just a drink to help relax us. Please.'

I take it and we move into the living room. I snap on the lamps and the glow light on the fire. Then we sit. Me on the sofa, him in the chair.

I take a sip of the wine and wrinkle my nose slightly. It tastes a bit off. I open my mouth to say so when there's a knock at the door. Three sharp raps.

We look at each other and Matt, who'd usually be the first one up to answer the door, freezes.

With my heartbeat pounding in my throat, I walk out to the hallway and open the front door.

DI Helena Price stands on the step, her neat brown bob damp with rain. Beside her, DS Kane Brewster is all ill-fitting suit and narrowed eyes.

'Mrs Tyce,' Helena says, looking past me into the hallway, 'is your husband here? He's not answering at his address, but his car is outside. It's imperative we speak to him.'

The house is utterly silent behind me. Matt is staying where he is, keeping quiet and not giving any clues to the fact he's in here. It would the easiest thing in the world to tell them he isn't here. That I haven't seen him today. It would give us some time to talk honestly at last.

I glance down at my handbag containing the missing earring then I stand aside and say, 'You'd better come in. He's in the living room.'

Sylvie Tyce ushers them in and turns to close the door. Before she follows Brewster down the hallway, Helena catches a glimpse of her squeezing her eyes closed as if she's steeling herself for what's about to happen. She looks stricken.

It's fairly obvious she knows why they're here. And if that's the case then why hasn't she already been in contact? Helena knows there are a clutch of reasons why good people sometimes fail to do the right thing. Loyalty, fear, a sense of misplaced duty. Or maybe, Sylvie Tyce is more concerned with her life falling apart.

She glances around the neat hallway, notes the faint smell of wine on Sylvie's breath when she walks past her. The echoing silence in the house – no television, music or signs of movement from her husband – suggests to Helena the atmosphere here had already changed before they arrived.

In the living room, Matt Tyce sits stiffly on the sofa, his wine glass in hand. Sylvie's glass, almost full, sits on the coffee table. Matt's wine is almost gone. He glances up at them as they enter and then looks back at the wall.

Brewster makes their introductions. 'We have some ques-

tions to ask about an ongoing murder investigation.' He looks
pointedly at Matt. 'Mainly questions for you, Mr Tyce. Perhaps
you'd like to answer them in your own home, rather than—'

'Talking here is just fine.' Matt looks at Sylvie. 'I've nothing
to hide from my wife.'

Sylvie invites them to sit before Brewster begins. 'Mr Tyce,
I'll cut to the chase here. We have reason to believe you are in
possession of a piece of evidence that is crucial to our current
investigation of the murder of Kendra Marsh.'

'I don't know what you're talking about,' Tyce replies curtly,
taking a final gulp of wine before setting his empty glass down.

It's not lost on Helena that neither he, nor his wife, ask what
the piece of evidence is. It's possible they've seen the press
conference, of course. She glances at Sylvie, who looks frozen
solid, the only moving part of her being wild eyes, flicking alter-
nately from the detectives to her husband. Rising high colour in
her cheeks gives her a startled and anxious appearance.

'We're looking for an earring.' Brewster turns his phone
screen so it is visible to all. 'An earring that is identical to the
one you see here. We've recently appealed to the public for
information and that response has led us directly here to you
today.'

Matt frowns, looks at the phone then back at Brewster.
'How does that work, then? Why come for me?'

'We received some information as a result of the appeal,'
Helena says carefully. 'Information that led us to believe you
may know the whereabouts of this piece of jewellery.'

'You mean you've had a tip-off?' Sylvie's voice sounds faint
and fearful.

Brewster nods. 'If that's what you want to call it, yes.'

'From who, exactly?' Matt's expression darkens. 'If someone's sent you here to interrogate me then I have a right to know
who it is.'

'I'm sure you're well aware we are not at liberty to provide you with those details,' Brewster says easily. He taps the phone screen to bring their attention back to the photograph. 'Mr Tyce, are you in possession of this piece of evidence?'

'Nope. Never seen it before.'

Helena notices Sylvie's eyes flick on and off him in the space of a second.

She says, 'Mrs Tyce, is this earring familiar to you?'

'What?' Her eyes widen and gravitate to the photograph. Her cheeks turn crimson. 'No! I mean, it's not mine.'

'We're aware of that,' Brewster says grimly. 'This earring belongs to Kendra Marsh, a young woman who was murdered a few days ago. Your daughter Jess's best friend, as I'm sure you know. Had you ever seen Kendra wearing this earring?'

'No.' Sylvie looks away, still shaking her head.

Helena can smell fear lacing the air between the couple like incoming rain.

'Mr Tyce, when was the last time you personally saw Kendra Marsh?'

Helena watches as Matt shifts in his seat. Foot tapping, fingers scratching. His face set like stone.

'Mr Tyce?' Brewster presses him again.

'Ages ago! She was Jess's friend, so I only saw her in passing. Why are you bothering me with this crap?' His hand flies in the air, wafting Brewster away. 'It's nothing to do with me.'

'Define "ages ago",' Brewster continues calmly. 'When exactly did you last see Kendra Marsh?'

Matt looks over at Sylvie but she won't meet his eyes.

'I don't know, maybe a few weeks ago,' he snaps. 'She came over to see the baby. Right, Sylvie?'

Sylvie doesn't answer. As Matt tries to grow bigger in the chair, bracing his shoulders, sitting upright, knees splayed, Helena sees how Sylvie seems to be shrinking into her own seat. As if she's silently praying for the sofa cushions to swallow her up.

'Mrs Tyce?'

Sylvie jumps slightly when Brewster addresses her. Her hand flutters up to her throat.

'I know you spoke to us briefly at your daughter's flat. Can you recall when your husband visited your house at the same time as Kendra?'

Sylvie shakes her head almost instantly. 'Sorry, no.'

'That's interesting because we're in possession of some door cam footage.' Brewster places a small tablet on the coffee table and presses play. The footage has been speeded up but is very clear. It shows Kendra ringing the bell before entering this very house, greeted by Sylvie, who opens the door. Soon afterwards, Matt enters the house using his key. 'This was two weeks ago.'

'That answers my question,' Matt snarls, staring at the screen. 'No surprise it's that bitch, Brenda, who's put you up to this.'

'Matt!' Sylvie gasps. 'You can't say that!'

He points at the screen. 'It's obvious the vantage point from the footage is from her front door!'

Sylvie covers her face with her hands. 'You don't know for certain it's Brenda.'

Matt glares at Brewster. 'Anyway, you have your answer. That's when I last saw Kendra... and you knew all the time. So why play silly games by asking me in the first place?'

'I'll ask the questions, Mr Tyce.' Brewster swipes the screen and a similar video appears at a slightly different angle. This time the view is of Matt's house. 'Here we have a different day altogether. In fact, this was recorded just two days before Miss Marsh's body was found.'

The video starts to play, and Helena hears Sylvie's breathing growing louder, more laboured.

The room is hushed as all eyes gravitate to the screen. For a few seconds, it ticks along with no activity. The street is empty,

Matt's house quiet, front door closed. His car isn't parked outside.

A slight figure appears to the far left of the picture. A slim young woman, walking quickly, glances down at her phone and then up at the street. As she nears Matt's house, Helena sees the recognition on Sylvie's face that this is Kendra Marsh.

She enters the front gate and, at the door, immediately bends forward. She tilts the flowerpot and reaches down. Then, with a key now in hand, Kendra stands up, looks furtively around before opening Matt Tyce's front door and slipping into the house.

FIFTY-FIVE

Helena starts as Sylvie Tyce jumps up and out of her chair without warning and hurls herself towards Matt. He stands up and raises his hands in front of him as she balls her fists in readiness to attack him.

Helena jumps up, raising her voice. 'Sylvie, I understand this must be upsetting for you, but please sit down and let's discuss this like adults.'

Sylvie spins around to her. '*Upsetting*? Talk about an understatement. You've no idea how he's lied through his teeth to me!' She pivots back to her husband, leaning forward, fists still balled. 'You dirty liar. I asked you! *Begged* you to tell me if there was someone else and you swore...' She starts to sob. 'You swore that all this time, you've been...'

'Sylvie, no! It's not what you think.' Helena sees that Matt's previous confident stance has deflated. He looks pale and shaken. 'It's... it's not what you think.'

Brewster presses pause as the video beings to replay. 'Can you tell us exactly what this *is* then, Mr Tyce? Because it very much looks to me as if Kendra Marsh is letting herself into your property with a key you left there for that specific purpose. It's almost as if this might have been a regular arrangement that—'

'No! It wasn't a regular arrangement. It was...' Helena can virtually see the cogs turning in his head. 'It was because Kendra was worried. She was worried about Jess and said she wanted to talk.'

Sylvie lets out a sharp, mocking laugh. 'Why on earth would Kendra talk to *you* if she was worried about Jess? She'd have come to me. And how did she know there was a key under the flowerpot? You've never done that before.'

'I'd left it there... for my mate. I didn't know she was going to let herself in, did I?' Matt protests, warming to his angle of defence. 'I got home and asked her to leave. I told her she shouldn't be there and she had no right to—'

'Took you the best part of two hours, did it, Mr Tyce... to tell her all that?' Brewster leans forward and taps the tablet screen. A video of Kendra leaving the house starts to play. She kisses a very willing Matt at the door before walking quickly back the way she came. Matt leans out of the door, looks up to Sylvie's house and ducks back inside, closing the door.

Helena looks directly at Matt and speaks clearly. 'Mr Tyce, were you having an affair with Kendra Marsh?'

'No! I mean... look, it wasn't an affair. No way was it serious. It was... just a fling. She meant nothing to me.' He looks regretfully at his wife. 'It was just a mistake; it was nothing, Sylvie. I swear.'

'You liar. You dirty bloody liar,' Sylvie hisses, choking back a sob.

'I'm sorry. I—' Matt starts to get out of his chair, but Brewster raises a hand.

'Stay where you are, please. We need to clarify the facts here.'

'You just heard the facts. That's it!' Matt snaps. 'It was a one-off. I told you. It was a terrible mistake. I've been stressed, I've—'

'Save it, Mr Tyce,' Brewster interrupts, pointing to the tablet. 'I have another two videos on there I can play you if you like? It's fairly clear this was a regular arrangement between yourself and Miss Langley. She let herself in while you were at work and an hour later, you'd arrive back to spend a considerable amount of time with her.'

'Did Nige know about this... about what you were up to?' Sylvie spits out the words.

'Nige?' Helena frowns.

'His loser mate who's always round at his house.'

'I need to say at this point that we'd like to continue this conversation down at the station,' Helena says, nodding to Brewster, who picks up the tablet.

Matt shakes his head. 'Why do I need to come to the station? You've asked your questions, and a one-night stand wasn't a crime, the last I heard.'

'I'm heading a murder inquiry, Mr Tyce,' Helena says, her voice like ice. 'And as you have admitted having an affair with the victim, we have rather a lot more questions that need to be addressed immediately.'

Matt stands up. 'No, that's not right. I mean...' He looks at Sylvie, who turns away. 'Jeez, a quick shag doesn't make me a killer! This... this *fling* ended way before she died. I'm not going anywhere.'

Brewster sighs. 'You know, this can be a fairly straightforward process if you come with us now. Or we can have enough blue lights and uniforms to fill the entire street within minutes, if you force my hand. So what's it to be, Mr Tyce?'

Helena glances at Sylvie, who has fallen silent. She looks as if she's aged ten years in the last ten minutes.

'Listen,' Matt addresses Brewster, adjusting his tone to be more amenable, 'all you've got is a fling. No weapon, no motive because I've got absolutely nothing to do with Kendra's murder.' He smiles amiably at Brewster and then Helena. 'Someone's stirring up trouble for me, surely you can see that? It's probably that nosy old cow over the road. You've no idea how crazy she is.'

He looks from one stony-faced detective to the other. Helena thinks, *He's scrambling, but he's not stupid.* He's an accomplished liar and this is the first time she's realised it.

Then, just as Helena thinks he's about to have another go at talking his way out of the situation, Sylvie stands up. The raw emotion in her face is gone, and in its place is a look of steely determination.

'I'd like to disclose something,' she says quietly. 'I found Kendra's missing earring, the one in the photograph, on the floor of Matt's bedroom a few days ago.'

Matt starts. 'Sylvie, shut it!'

She turns away from him slightly and addresses the detectives. 'I didn't realise its significance until I saw the police press conference. I'm sorry, I know I should've—'

'Where is the earring now, Mrs Tyce?' Brewster cuts in.

'I wrapped it up and hid it. I didn't know what to think, you see. I couldn't believe that he would... I'm sorry.'

'Could you get it for me now, please?'

Sylvie nods and heads out into the hall.

Helena regards Matt Tyce with cool, watchful eyes. His face registers shock but also something closer to panic. 'It's a mistake,' he mutters, twisting his fingers together. 'It's all a terrible mistake. I'll come down to the station and explain everything, OK?'

Sylvie returns with a handkerchief, which she unfolds to reveal the missing earring. Helena inspects it without touching. Silver, with the distinctive knot design. She looks at Brewster, who nods grimly.

'I – I swear I've never seen it before,' Matt stammers. 'Sylvie, I was telling the truth, I—'

Sylvie doesn't respond. She's stopped crying now and sits very still, staring at the tabletop. Helena recognises the response as one she has employed herself in her own life. It's about bracing yourself and staying strong until you can let it all out. She has no doubt that the minute they leave with her husband in the back seat of the police car, Sylvie Tyce will dissolve into a quivering wreck.

While Brewster produces an evidence bag and begins to formally log the earring, Helena quietly asks Sylvie if she's alright.

'I thought I was,' she says in a hollow voice. 'Now I'm not so sure.'

Helena regards the broken-looking woman in front of her. Today, they have hopefully taken long, helpful strides towards solving the case. On the other hand, she feels like she just witnessed a marriage fracturing in real time.

Sometimes, Helena thinks, *this is truly, all at once, the best and worst job in the world.*

FIFTY-SIX

SYLVIE

I've checked my phone seven times in the last twenty minutes and there's still been nothing back from Jess. It drives me crazy that ever since Ed bought her a Galaxy phone last Christmas, I can no longer keep an eye on her with the Find Friends app.

The baby gurgles in her bouncy chair, blinking slowly at the ceiling like the soft glow from the light fitting is the most fascinating thing she's seen before. I kneel beside her and stroke her leg through the stripy sleep suit.

'Don't worry, Mummy will be back soon,' I murmur, though I'm starting not to believe it.

Jess brought her over and said she was popping out for an hour. She didn't say where she was going. That was four hours ago. I'm not sure she's left the baby with me for that long before, not for a simple errand or whatever it is she's doing.

I sent a simple text message first when I'd heard nothing from her after two hours. Then another. I tried to call. Then I left a light-hearted voicemail joking if she was coming back at all for Scarlet Mae or whether I should apply for official adoption.

All the stuff I'm worrying about is whizzing around my

head like a nonstop fairground ride. It feels like it's going to blow a hole through the top of my skull at any moment.

The footage on DS Brewster's tablet is on full technicolour replay at the front of my mind. *Kendra letting herself into his house, the two of them embracing at the door...* An ice-cold fist squeezes around my heart.

How could he do this? How could he look me in the eye and lie so easily? This man I adored, who made me avocado on toast a million times for breakfast and insisted I was the centre of his world?

The thought of him at the police station, being questioned in relation to a murder investigation... the killing of *Jess's best friend...* it's terrible, surreal and crazy all at the same time.

But I've got to shake it off. I can't afford to think about this now. Jess has got to be my focus. She never goes quiet. Not like this, anyway, and not when it concerns the baby. She's a lot of things but being careless about Scarlet Mae isn't one of them. A single point of clarity pierces the mush: *It's time to escalate my efforts.*

I scoop the baby up and carry her to the car seat. She's warm and sleepy, her blue eyes fluttering closed before I've even got the harness buckled. I move gently, try not to jostle her. I'm not even sure what I'm planning to do when I get to the flat. Just stand outside until she gets back? Knock on her neighbours' doors and ask if they've seen her?

Infuriatingly, I remember I no longer have a door key to the flat. Jess didn't return it after she borrowed my spare at the park. I suppose she's had enough on her mind. It's probably in the bottom of Jess's handbag, mixed up with baby wipes and lip balm and her emergency formula sachets.

If we're lucky there's a chance she'll be back home by the time we get there. But I can't just sit here worrying.

I drive over, park in one of the resident bays and punch in

the key code on the entrance pad. I carry Scarlet Mae up to the first floor in her car seat.

Breathless, I hammer on the flat door. Nothing. The mailboxes are in the foyer, so there's no letterbox to shout through. I knock again and loudly call, 'Jess?'

Scarlet Mae is sleeping, so I put down her car seat outside the door and pace back and forth on the landing outside the flat, glaring up at the cracked ceiling, willing someone – Ed or Jess – to come back.

Nobody does.

I curse under my breath, teeth clenched, and leave the building.

Back at the car, I strap the baby in again, her tiny head lolling to one side. I shut the door and get into the driver's seat, my heart hammering so loud I can barely think straight.

I get into the driver's seat and she makes a funny gurgling noise. It sounds wet and uncomfortable.

I'm about to start the car when she lets out a whimper and the sour smell hits me. She's been sick.

'Oh poor darling...'

I reach into the backseat and fish around for wipes. Her bib and chest are sticky. I clean her as gently as I can, whispering apologies. I change the bib, wipe down her vest. She's half-awake now, fussing, her eyes not quite focused but already half-closed again.

I'm leaning over, making sure she's OK when something catches my eye through the windscreen.

A familiar figure emerges from the building foyer. Moving quickly, furtively, like he doesn't want to be seen.

Ed! My heart lurches. *Why on earth didn't he answer the door?*

My hand flies to the car door handle to shout out to him, but the way he pauses at the gate, glancing furtively over his shoulder, stops me in my tracks. So I wait, and watch.

His head moves in short, jerky movements. He doesn't see me – I'm parked slightly further down the street, half-shadowed by a tree.

Then he starts to walk. Quite fast. Not jogging, but not casual saunter either.

I stay still, hunched low in the driver's seat, barely breathing.

He heads straight to a small van parked at the end of the road. I watch as he climbs into the driver's seat. A second later, the van pulls away.

My mind scrambles to catch up. Ed can drive but he doesn't have a car, and Jess hasn't yet passed her test. They've always been on foot or in cabs, unable to justify the money a car would take to run. I've picked them up myself numerous times – after nights out, from the hospital, when Jess was going back for follow-up appointments.

So, whose van is *that*?

As it joins a short queue at the junction at the end of the road, I check Scarlet Mae again – her eyes are closed, mouth slack. She's fast asleep.

I start the engine and follow.

FIFTY-SEVEN

SYLVIE

The white van winds south, out of the city, past the industrial outskirts and into more open lanes. I stay two or three cars behind, far enough not to draw attention.

My mind races. I try to remember the last time I saw Ed properly. He's been really good with Jess and the baby and I've been pleased he seems to encourage her to be more open and talk to me.

We merge onto a quieter road and the traffic starts to thin. I ease off, drop a little further back. I don't want him to see me following him. It could be something completely innocent in which case he'd think me a proper busybody. But if he is up to no good, then I'll not get a better chance than this to see what he's up to.

Seven or eight more minutes and I lose the cover of other cars. It's just me and him now, a stretch of road between us.

He turns right, down a narrow lane edged by few spindly trees and no road markings here. I can't follow him all the way down, not yet. If he checks his rear-view mirror, he'll see me. He knows my car well enough.

Instead, I pull over into a layby, hands gripping the wheel. I count to sixty, slowly, deliberately before I set off again.

The lane is long and mostly empty. At the bottom is a single brick-built building that looks neglected. A long, weathered sign hangs crookedly: *Beats Studio.*

I recognise it from Jess's description of the studio he works at as a session musician and sometimes records with his own band.

Jess's words – 'it's in the middle of nowhere' – echo in my head. Why did I never wonder how he got out here with no car? This might have once been a working studio, but I can see by the state of the sign and the building, it no longer is. Hasn't been for some time.

Scarlet Mae is still asleep.

A little further up, there's a barely visible turning. Overgrown, uneven, a gravel track that looks like it hasn't seen much use.

I slow, check my mirror, then swing the car around there and come back.

I take the turn close to where I saw the van disappear.

The track judders beneath the tyres. Scarlet Mae stirs but I'm grateful she doesn't wake.

I slow down and stop at the top of the track. There's a clearing beyond and in it is a small, weather-worn detached building.

Ed's van is parked right outside it.

The studio's door is boarded up. Paint peels from the exposed wood and unchecked ivy snakes around the guttering. The front windows are boarded up with rotting planks and if it wasn't for the van parked outside, I'd think the place had been abandoned altogether.

I get out of the car and close the door with a soft thud before I lock it. Scarlet Mae is still fast asleep in her car seat and I'm not going to be long. I just need to check what's happening here and find out why Ed ignored me when I came to the flat.

It's midday, but the sky is low, flat with grey cloud. The light is dim in the middle of the trees and the air feels too still here. I can't hear birdsong, or traffic. Nothing. Just the faint creak of branches in the trees surrounding me.

Slowly, carefully, I walk around the perimeter of the building. There are no fences or gates. It looks as if someone just dropped this place at the end of a random lane.

It seems to be just two rooms wide and another two deep. A squat roof, the chimney half crumbled. The back door, though, shielded from the lane, is oddly pristine. New wood and strong fittings. Incongruous to say the least on a place like this.

I step closer to the door and catch a flicker of movement behind one of the boarded windows. A crack between the slats. In the dim light, I think I see a figure. Still and watching.

'Hello?' I call out, trying to sound confident and failing.

Nothing at first and then I jump at a loud noise. The scrape of a bolt.

The door swings open and there he is. Ed. He looks pale and unnerved.

He's not holding the door open like someone who's pleased to see me. He's blocking it with his body like he doesn't want me looking inside.

'Sylvie?' he says finally with a nervous little laugh. 'What are you doing here?'

'I could ask you the same thing.' I glance up at the building. 'I never realised the studio was so run down.' I fix my eyes back on his. 'Or that you had a van.'

He swallows. 'I borrowed it.' Then he smiles and looks around him. 'But yeah, it could do with a refit, that's for sure.'

He looks all wrong. Too tight and twitchy for the Ed I know.

'Come in, Sylvie. There's some stuff I need to explain to you,' he says, standing aside.

That surprises me. If he was up to something here with someone, another woman, I thought he'd try and get rid of me.

'The baby's in the car, asleep,' I say.

'She'll be fine for a few minutes; there's nobody around here but us. Come on,' he says again, firmer this time. 'It won't take me long to explain. I've been really worried about Jess and there's stuff you need to know.'

A prickle races up the back of my neck. Has Jess got herself in some kind of trouble? I step inside and take in the chaotic scene.

Dust lies like a thick blanket over mixing desks with missing knobs, a cracked, torn fabric swivel chair, a tangle of old cable that trails like a dead vine across the floor. A faded soundproof panel sags off one wall, exposing the yellowing foam behind it.

In the corner, a drum kit stands half-collapsed, the cymbals dented and coated in grime. A microphone hangs limp from its stand, like a noose. It's crystal clear that no one has recorded in here for many years, least of all *worked* here, as Ed has claimed all this time.

'What's going on... this is not a working studio.'

The door shuts behind me and before I can say a word, he grabs me.

I gasp, lurch backwards with the shock, but he's faster. His hand clamps around my arm and he yanks me down the narrow hall. I shout, twist, try to dig my heels in.

'The baby! She's in the car! Ed, let go—'

He doesn't stop. Doesn't blink. I try to scream louder but it comes out hoarse and strangled.

He drags me through a door and into a room with a single light bulb hanging from the ceiling. He shuts the door behind us, locks it and slips the key into his pocket.

There's a bed in here and someone sitting on it. A girl I don't know.

And then I realise I've seen her face before. Plastered all over social media. 'Are you... Ellie Walker?'

She looks up at me, eyes flat and unreadable. She says nothing. She doesn't look afraid or injured. In fact, she looks strangely calm.

Her eyes flicker to the corner of the room and then I see her. *Jess.*

My Jess, bound and gagged. Curled up, her eyes wide with terror, her cheeks streaked with tears.

A sound tears from me – a half-sob, half-scream. 'What the hell—'

I start to rush over to my daughter and Jess whimpers through the gag, her whole body trembling.

'What have you done?' I cry.

Ed jumps in front of me, his pale face gleaming with sweat.

'She deserves it,' he spits. 'She always thought she was better than everyone. Better than me. Little princess, Jess. Spoilt and ruined by her mother. It's your fault she turned out to be an evil liar.'

'What?' I look from Ellie to Ed. 'It seems to me you're the liar.'

He's lost his mind. All the times I've seen him looking dishevelled and distracted... I'd put it down to the stress and upheaval of having a new baby. Then the disturbing painting at the flat jumps into my mind... maybe his creation of that was an indication of something far more serious.

I decide to appeal to his better nature. It must still be in there somewhere.

'Ed, let's just calm down,' I say carefully, never feeling more panicked inside. 'Jess doesn't deserve this. I know you've had your problems before, but you got over them and—'

He turns to me, his eyes wild. 'You – you made her like this.

You and your rules and your smiles and your tidy little house. You didn't see what a little cow she could be. You never taught her how to behave. She deserves her comeuppance just like that bitch Kendra did.'

Ellie lets out a small, strangled laugh. 'Did we teach *her* a lesson!'

Matt didn't kill Kendra...

I freeze, staring at him. He's shaking now. Grinning and shaking and suddenly 'little house mouse Ed' seems like the most sinister man I've ever met.

I look across at Jess, her eyes wide and terrified. 'It's OK,' I tell her. 'The police are on their way; I phoned them when I arrived.'

Ed laughs. 'I don't think so. There's no signal around here, not for miles.'

Panicked, I realise I still don't know what the hell is going on here. My eyes gravitate to Ellie. 'Why are you here, with him? You know half the country is searching for you and your parents are devastated?'

Again, that infuriating smile is all I get.

I glance at Jess, her eyes downcast now, looking wretched, and my chest heaves with a sudden fury. 'And you clearly know he's married, with a child?'

'Ellie is the only one who ever really saw me. She understands. Gets me. And the baby – Scarlet Mae – she needs a new mother.'

'The baby? I think you mean your *daughter*!' My voice cracks. 'You're sick. You need help—'

He steps forward then turns suddenly, lurching towards Jess.

Roughly, he pulls off the gag and she lets out a terrified yelp. Her eyes wide and shining with tears.

'I loved you once, you know,' he hisses, crouching beside her. His fingers stroke a lock of hair from her face. Jess recoils, but he pinches her chin, holds it tight. 'Even when you were at your worst. Even when you and your family humiliated me... remember the barbecue? I was willing to forgive all of it. You could have been part of something – something real. But no. You had to ruin everything.'

'How did *she* ruin everything? You can't do this to her because Matt upset you at a bloody family barbecue, Ed! Grow up.'

He turns on me, his eyes burning. 'It's a bit more than that, Sylvie. I'm not the only one she's lied to. Do you want to tell her, Jess... or shall I?'

'Jess?' I say faintly, but she squeezes her eyes closed.

'Looks like it's down to me to spill the beans then. The baby, your beloved granddaughter? She isn't mine,' he says simply, watching for my reaction. 'The little slut admitted it, didn't you, Jess?'

'That's utter rubbish! Why are you saying that? It's not true. Jess? Tell him it's not true.'

Jess begins to quietly sob, but she won't look at me.

They split up briefly about a year ago, but got back together and have been strong ever since. Or so I thought.

'It *is* true though. Even you can't argue with a paternity DNA test, Sylvie.'

'You did a *test*?'

'She admitted it right away,' Ed says triumphantly. 'Knew when she was beaten.'

'It's not true... tell him, Jess!'

Jess looks at me then, her eyes welling up with tears. 'I'm sorry, Mum. It is true.' She sniffs, looks pleadingly at Ed. 'I've tried to explain, tried to tell him it was... it was a terrible mistake.'

I shake my head, rejecting the idea of it. *Think... think! How can this be true?*

They hadn't been back together for long when Jess

announced she was pregnant. I remember the euphoria I felt the night she came over and told me over a cup of tea. We'd hugged and cried with happiness together. My daughter had seemed devoted to Ed, to a future spent with him and the baby.

'When she told me she was pregnant, I did the maths. We'd always been careful because we had both agreed we were too young for kids, but when we got back together, Jess seemed eager to try for a baby.' He breaks off to give her another withering look full of hatred. 'Said she'd come off the pill, didn't you, Jess?'

She whimpers, looks imploringly at me.

'I'm sorry, Mum. I... I thought Ed was the father. I felt sure of it.'

For a moment I can't speak. The shock takes my breath away. 'But... who is... I mean, how can you know that—'

He laughs when he sees my face. 'You didn't think she just came clean, did you? Oh no, she'd have been quite happy to pull the wool over my eyes for the rest of her life.'

'I'm sorry!' Jess sobs. 'I told you how sorry I am. A thousand times.'

'A trillion times wouldn't be enough, you slut!' He turns to me, his eyes blazing. 'I was suspicious from the off, but I bided my time, see. Lulled her into a false sense of security and then we had one "romantic" night when I suggested we commit to airing any hidden secrets.'

He leans in to press a slow, deliberate kiss to her cheek. Jess shudders, lets out a strangled sob. 'And that's when you told me, isn't it, princess?'

Jess lets out a sob. 'I'm sorry. I'm so, so sorry, I'm—'

Ed takes a handful of his own hair and pulls it hard. 'It was a shock, Sylvie, as you can imagine. Even though I suspected something, even I didn't quite realise what a treacherous lying bitch she really was. How she'd slept with another man in a moment of drunken madness when we split but then tried to pass his baby off as mine.'

Jess begins to sob. I hold out my hand towards her, silently trying to convey for her to stay calm.

'Don't get upset, Jess. You'll see it can all be put right,' Ed whispers. 'Ellie will raise her with love and care.'

'What?' I look at Ellie. 'This is madness. How are *you* involved in all this?'

'I was so fragile when I met Ed,' she says, looking lovingly at him. 'I was angry, directionless... I'd had enough of life.'

'I know that's a lie,' I snap. 'Your story is all over the newspapers and online. You were training to be a nurse. You were committed and organised. Wanted to help people.'

Ellie lets out a bitter laugh. 'You've got it the wrong way around. *They're* the ones who are lying.'

'She was a budding musician who was controlled and oppressed by her parents,' Ed says, regarding her tenderly. 'We met at a music studio but we really got to know each other online. And we shared our most intimate secrets from the very beginning. United in our difference to other people... and in our strange desires.'

This crazy situation has gone on long enough. I want answers and I've got to try and get some control back. 'Who is Scarlet Mae's father, Jess?'

My daughter shakes her head and lowers her gaze again. She doesn't reply.

'Cat got your tongue?' he snaps at her. 'When I confronted her with the DNA evidence, she admitted it was Nige, your husband's best friend.'

'No!' I stagger slightly before taking a step forward. 'Don't you dare touch her again.'

He looks up, something feral in his face. He rises slowly, fists clenched.

And then he unleashes a rain of vicious blows down on my daughter's head.

FIFTY-EIGHT

Everyone jumps as there's a sharp cracking sound, and in a beat of stunned silence, the door flies open. Brenda stands there, her hand pressed to her chest. She's pale and shaking but she looks determined.

'Oh, it's just the crazy woman.' Ed lets out a relieved laugh and looks at Ellie. 'It's Sylvie's rottweiler, come to save her.'

Brenda walks forward, calmly. 'Get away from Jess,' she hisses. 'You moron. You were never good enough for her.'

'Brenda...' I try to catch her eye to urge her to be cautious. Ed is clearly unstable and if it's true that he's the one who killed Kendra, he will be capable of doing anything.

But Brenda doesn't even glance my way. She lifts her chin, and a sort of 'nurse-on-nights' authority slides effortlessly into place.

'Ed, step back.' Her voice is low and clipped and, somehow, impossible to ignore.

Ed looks shocked for a moment and then smirks. 'Or what?'

'Or you'll find out.'

Brenda keeps walking, as calm and paced as a metronome. Close enough to make herself the target. Surprised, Ed scrabbles to stand, losing his balance. Before he can launch himself at her, Brenda's handbag snaps open. A cold arc of spray flicks straight into his eyes. He swears, flinches as he goes for her, but she gives another hard blast of the hairspray that makes him cough and claw at his face.

He stumbles, half-blind, his fists swinging wildly.

'Sylvie, move!' she barks, not looking back, and I rush over to Jess, taking her in my arms.

Ellie freezes, eyes huge. Then she skitters sideways as Ed blunders, coughing, hands out like a sleepwalker before his arm springs back. Brenda takes the punch he meant for me, a powerful shove that slams her into the door frame, but she squares herself, plants her feet and keeps the spray going, hitting him full in the face again.

That's when I see it: a small red fire extinguisher on the wall. I wrench it from its bracket and, putting my body weight behind it, swing with all my strength towards Ed. It glances off the side of his head and he staggers, drops to his knees, groaning and pressing his palm into his temple.

And then, outside, I hear sirens, like music to my ears. Blue lights flicker through the cracked boarding of the walls, and a loudspeaker crackles. Heavy, booted footsteps thunder on the gravel all around the studio.

Ed rouses, on high alert, his furious expression dissolving into panic.

The front door crashes open and police pile in. The room fills with shouting, with the thumping of boots and blinding torches.

Ed tries to bolt, almost makes it to the back of the room, but they're on him in seconds. I hear the sounds of a scuffle, more shouting, the clatter of a chair going over. Then the brutal sound of handcuffs ratcheting tight.

I fall to my knees.

Jess cries out as two officers move to her, gently lifting her upright, cutting her ties. She clings to me, sobbing.

I wrap my arms around her fiercely, as if I can somehow squeeze all the pain out of her body with my own. Her hair is damp, her skin is cold... but she's here. She's alive. *My girl.*

I fight back sobs as an officer places a steadying hand on my shoulder and I brush it away, not unkindly... I just need to feel Jess warm and real against me. To remind myself that I'm not too late and she's still alive.

Across the room, Ed is dragged upright, his face slack now, dazed. As if all the rage has drained out and left nothing but flaccid, pale skin. He doesn't fight. Doesn't speak. Just stares straight through us as if we have all betrayed him.

Good, I think. *Let it sting. Let it burn into your cold, callous heart.*

Jess trembles in my arms. I tuck her in tighter, close my eyes for a moment. 'I've got you,' I whisper. 'I've got you now.'

I hear Ellie sobbing. 'He forced me to do it... abducted me... I had no choice...'

As we hold each other and I thank God my daughter is safe, I catch a slow, fleeting movement in the doorway.

Brenda stands there watching us, her hand pressed to her chest. She's pale and shaking but she's here. Looking out for us as always.

FIFTY-NINE

NOTTINGHAMSHIRE POLICE

TUESDAY

DI Helena Price taps lightly before hearing the required order to enter and pushing open the door.

Superintendent Della Grey's office is warm and smells faintly of coffee and something else. A clinical tang – hand sanitiser, maybe. The combination feels oddly fitting for a woman who runs her team like a sergeant major, but fusses over her two tiny dogs like they're precious porcelain dolls.

Grey looks up from her paperwork, her fashionable cat's eye spectacles perched low on her nose. She's smiling. A rare enough occurrence that Helena is momentarily taken aback. It's a real smile, not the tight, lips-pressed line she reserves for press briefings or case updates when things aren't going well.

'Price!' Grey barks, her voice full of slightly sharp warmth that Helena is all too aware can flip to frost in a heartbeat. 'Get yourself in here, you star. You look like you finally slept in an actual bed rather than a pool car.'

Charming. Helena steps inside and closes the door softly

behind her. The hinges squeak faintly – a sound she's heard a thousand times but still makes her think of school head-mistresses and breaktime detentions.

'Morning, ma'am,' she says, perching on the edge of the chair opposite the super's desk.

Grey gestures to a tin on her desk. 'Biscuit? Not those fancy ones you lot always bring in – sensible, plain digestives. Only my dogs get the posh treats.'

Helena laughs and takes one, breaking a bit off. Her eyes flick to the ornate framed photograph beside a china coffee mug. Two small dogs stare out, hair beribboned, their entitled eyes glinting like spoiled princesses.

'Sounds like your girls have got you right under their paws, ma'am!'

'Guilty as charged!' Grey smiles, leaning back in her chair. 'When I leave home in the morning, I always tell my two terrors, "Sit, stay, wait for the doggy day care girl and don't chew the superintendent's new shoes." They're more obedient than half the officers on my team, I'll say that much.'

Helena grins, some of the tension draining from her shoulders. She glances around the office – the neat stacks of files, the smell of fresh coffee. Everything in its place. Unlike her own thoughts from the past few days.

'Alright,' Grey says, clapping her hands together once, brisk as a dog trainer. 'Give me the full lowdown. Where are we?'

Helena clears her throat, draws in a breath and swallows the last of her biscuit.

'Well, as you know, Matt Tyce was released as he's in the clear,' she begins. 'At least in terms of criminal charges. He'll have to answer to his wife, obviously, but no further police interest from our side.

Grey raises an eyebrow, her mouth twisting. 'Some might say he'd survive the murder charges easier than an angry wife.'

'Quite. But he's off the hook thanks to Brenda Howard taking matters into her own hands.'

'Hmm, the formidable Nurse Howard. Tell me about her role in all this.'

'Brenda had been observing Matt Tyce because she had this misplaced sense of duty and protection towards Sylvie.' Helena grimaces. 'It has to be said, she's admitted to employing some questionable methods using surveillance equipment she purchased from a dodgy website, but that's a problem for another day.'

'Indeed.' Grey frowns. 'You didn't hear me say this, but it sounds very much to me like she saved the day in doing so.'

'That's right. Brenda admitted to officers she'd attached a tracker to Sylvie's car when she realised she was being cut out of her neighbour's life. She had a burning need to know Sylvie's movements, you see. Ironically, when Matt alerted Brenda to the fact Sylvie, Jess and the baby were all missing, she was able to track them to the abandoned studio.'

'And Brenda Howard alerted our officers?'

Helena nods. 'Simply because of a gut feeling something bad was about to happen, apparently. She said years of working in emergency departments had honed this sort of heightened sense of crisis detection in her.'

Helena snorts softly, but her expression sobers quickly when Grey says sharply, 'So how did we get it so wrong?'

'It comes down to Ed Daunt's secret hatred and resentment of both Jess, his partner, and Matt Tyce. It started before Jess even gave birth,' Helena says, glancing at her notes. 'There was an incident – at some family barbecue or gathering, as I understand it. Matt made a snide comment in front of everyone. Called Ed "Jess's little house mouse", asked if he'd got a record deal yet and whether he needed her permission to grab another beer. Everyone laughed, worse for wear after a few hours' drinking. Sylvie too. Even Jess.'

She pauses, almost feeling a flicker of pity. But not quite.

'What nobody realised was that Jess and Ed still had big problems between them after they split up briefly a while ago, which I'll come back to later. Ed felt humiliated and something snapped. He decided he'd show them all and wipe the smile off their faces – prove he wasn't the joke they thought he was.'

Grey leans forward slightly, her fingers steepled. 'But at that stage, his intimidation wasn't enough to drive him to commit murder, I presume?'

Helena shakes her head. 'No. At least, that's what he claims. But the anger metastasised when he found out the baby – Scarlet Mae – wasn't his.'

'Through a DNA test, I presume?'

Helena nods. 'She admitted it when confronted and more than that, she told him it was Nige, Matt's friend.'

'Ahh, the feckless Nige.' Grey frowns knowingly. 'Bit of a loose cannon, by all accounts, what with that business about Tyce bailing him out.'

'You could say that. Jess admitted that one night when she and Ed had briefly split up, she had a one-night stand with Nige. She told us she genuinely thought it was over between her and Ed, but she regretted it immediately. Then they patched things up, and she found out she was pregnant very soon after.'

'Soon enough that either man could have fathered the child?'

'Exactly. Jess decided not to confirm it. She didn't breathe a word to anyone... except, she said, to Kendra. She chose to believe Ed was the father and just kept the lie going.'

Grey makes a small, incredulous sound. 'Good grief.'

'Then Nige started spending more time at Matt's house. Close to Jess, close to the baby. Ed became obsessed. He convinced himself that everyone knew, that they were all laughing behind his back just like at the barbecue. He wanted Jess home so he could watch her, control her. Maybe even force her into confessing publicly.'

Helena's fingers twitch in her lap. She looks down and forces them to still.

'And what about Ellie?' Grey says, her voice low. 'I read her parents' statement when she went missing. Their account of Ellie achieving her life's ambition of becoming a nurse is either an outright lie, or they're deluded.'

'I believe they truly believed Ellie wanted what they pushed her into. It's a fine line as a parent, pushing for what's best for your child or letting them choose their path. I think the Walkers had been pushing for so long, they no longer even noticed Ellie wasn't happy.'

'Helicopter parents,' Grey murmurs.

'She and Ed were like kindred spirits, I think, especially when he told her about Jess and framed it as a betrayal not just of him but of the baby, of everyone. Ellie latched on. They fed each other's rage and sense of being done wrong at the hands of others but something else developed... a twisted fascination with acting out a stalking-victim scenario. Ed offered her a way of getting away from her unhappy life and Ellie offered him validation and respect: a kinship founded on a depraved fantasy. Together, they transformed all that into a plan.'

'A rather outrageous and illegal plan that could never really work,' Grey adds.

'But they were both fantasists. They couldn't see it.'

Grey turns on a desk fan. It turns lazily on its base, stirring the warm office air.

'Kendra Marsh nearly escaped from Ed,' Helena continues. 'She apologised for taunting him about not being Scarlet Mae's father – Jess had confided in her, you see. He said she swore she had no memory of bullying Ellie at school aside from a general falling-out amongst girls. But he'd become so unstable, he decided she had to die as a sacrifice to Ellie. Ed wouldn't let her ruin his "final act", as he called it in the interview notes. He wanted control of the ending. They'd already decided the baby would be taken and raised elsewhere – by Ellie or someone else. A fresh start. Clean slate. Once Jess had been removed from the picture entirely.'

'They'd planned to kill her?'

'Yes, we found a stash of sleeping tablets prescribed to Jess that Ed had stolen. Ellie admitted they were planning to force Jess to overdose.'

Grey doesn't speak for a moment. Instead, she stares at the ceiling, tapping her pen on the desk.

Finally she exhales, long and sharp. 'So that's where we are. Matt Tyce is out, Ed Daunt is charged with murder, with Ellie Walker charged as an accomplice. Jess Langley is still recovering in hospital, but she's alive. And the baby is with her grandma, Sylvie Tyce. A patchwork of poor decisions and an example of the damage festering egos can do, if ever I saw one.'

Helena makes a noise of agreement.

'It's always about control in the end, isn't it? When you strip away the excuses and the warped actions. It basically comes down to people wanting to control other people. Controlling outcomes of who gets to live, who gets to love, who needs to die.'

Helena nods, giving Grey's sage observation its moment.

'It's easy to dismiss Ed Daunt as just a jealous loser who lost control,' she says after a moment. 'But there's nothing random about it. Every step was rehearsed in his head, every humiliation and slight replayed until he believed violence was the only resolution. And that went on for a long time before he acted on it.'

'Definitely pre-meditated.' Grey drums her fingers against the desk, thoughtful. 'And Matt Tyce... I wonder if he realises just how devastating his stupid comment was that day.'

'I doubt it. I'm not sure he's the reflective sort,' Helena replies. 'I imagine he's got other priorities, trying to get his life back on track.'

Grey sniffs. 'Hmm. Good luck to that.'

Helena's mind drifts to the derelict studio, the way Jess's hands had trembled as she clutched at the blanket. To Sylvie's grey, stricken face and the baby's small, plaintive cry as an officer lifted her out of her car seat.

'Anyway, good work to you and your team,' Grey says finally, breaking the stillness. Her voice is steady but softer now. 'Like I always tell my two precious pooches: some days you drag the slipper through the mud, some days you bring back the crown jewels. You brought them back today, Price.'

Helena feels the warmth creep up her throat, an almost embarrassing flush of pride she isn't used to letting show.

'Thank you, ma'am.'

'Take a few days. Sleep. Walk in nature. Whatever it is you do to stop thinking for five minutes.'

Helena laughs, a small, surprised sound. She turns to the door but pauses, hand on the knob. The corridor beyond is filled with low murmurs and the muted shuffle of feet. A place teeming with small, unfinished stories.

'I've been thinking,' she says, glancing back, 'I might get a dog.'

Grey's expression brightens and she raises her mug in approval. 'You won't regret it. We all need something else in our lives that's not this place.'

Helena steps into the corridor, door clicking softly shut behind her. She breathes in, the stale station air somehow comforting and familiar. The echo of her shoes on linoleum, the endless shadows of the cases that are to come.

Another case closed. Another life – several lives – left smouldering in the aftermath.

For a few brief moments, Helena allows herself to feel it:

the thin thread of satisfaction that winds its way through the wreckage.

She holds it close as she heads for the team office. Something to remind her she's still here and still fighting for the underdog.

For now, that's enough.

SIXTY

BRENDA

ONE WEEK LATER, MONDAY

Brenda sits on the wooden bench, her fingers curled into her lap like long, wilted petals. The bench was here in the garden when she moved in, its slats neat and freshly painted like everything Penny and Brian left behind. Everything had seemed so perfect and now, Brenda feels her presence has warped and spoilt most of what's here.

The early December air bites at her thin cardigan, slicing through to her shoulders, but she doesn't move to go inside or fetch her coat and gloves. She can see Ivor watching her from the kitchen window, his yellow eyes bright against the steam-fogged glass. His head tilts slightly, as though he's wondering why she's acting strangely today.

Her phone lies heavy in her pocket. Penny's reasonable but firm voice still echoes inside her skull from her phone call this morning.

'Brenda, I don't know what to say,' Penny had said earlier with what Brenda imagined to be the distant sound of the sea behind her. 'I've spoken to Sylvie, and... well, after everything, I just can't see how you can possibly stay in the house.'

'Please, Penny,' Brenda had croaked. 'Don't ask me to leave. I've made mistakes, yes... I'm the first one to admit it. I've been foolish and overstepped the mark... but I meant no harm. You have to believe me. Sylvie – she was such a good friend, my closest friend in years. I was only trying to help her see... I just wanted her to be happy. Is that so bad?'

There had been a long silence. Brenda imagined Penny shifting in her chair, looking at that Portuguese sun spilling over tiled roofs, a world away from this damp little street and all her current misery.

'We both know it's not as simple as that, Brenda,' Penny said sharply. 'You admitted planting that poor girl's earring in Matt's house and—'

'It was wrong and I know that. But I found Kendra's earring outside his door. I tried to tell Sylvie that. Matt might not be a murderer, but he's far from blameless, Penny.'

'That's as may be, but there were other things too and I have to think about it,' Penny finally said. 'I feel responsible. I brought you to that street, and now...'

'Please,' Brenda whispered again.

But Penny's voice hardened. 'It's a serious matter, Brenda. You can't continue to meddle in other people's lives like this... it's not right. I'll let you know. But after speaking to Sylvie, it doesn't look good, I'm sorry.'

The line went dead. Brenda had stood in her hallway, staring at the blank phone screen until her arm dropped to her side.

Now, in the garden, regret presses against her chest, heavy as wet laundry. She really believed this was going to be her fresh start. After the disaster at the hospital, after the endless tribunal meetings, after they took her job and her uniform and left her in that tiny flat with her mother's voice ringing in her ears – this street was meant to save her.

Instead, she ruined it. And she knows she ruined it herself.

The regret feels like a fever burning through her. She did think she was helping. She *always* thinks she's helping. She tried to be there for the boy at the hospital when he was put under her care. She tried to be there for Sylvie, for Jess and for that beautiful baby with her rosebud mouth and trusting eyes.

Yet somehow, she has managed to turn them all against her.

She can't even blame Matt this time. She tried to twist the pieces into place, make herself Sylvie's number one, and it blew up in her face. All her life, she's overstepped the mark. Again and again and again…

She thinks of her mother. The way she used to stand in the kitchen doorway, arms folded, lips pursed.

'You always try too hard, Brenda. Always sticking your nose in, always overdoing it. You're pathetic.'

Brenda would scrub the kitchen floor until her knees ached, would lay the table and make her mother's bed the way she liked it with those sharp hospital corners. She'd fetch and carry and relentlessly try to please and please and please.

And it was never, ever enough. *She* was never enough.

Brenda leans forward on the bench, her head dropping into her hands.

A sharp wind skates across the garden, making her shiver so violently her teeth start to chatter. A hot tear slides down her cheek and it shocks her to feel its warmth against her freezing skin.

Brenda straightens, wiping at her cheek with the back of her hand. She doesn't even have the energy to go inside. She feels hollow, like a vase tipped and smashed, the pieces too scattered and broken to ever glue back together.

A cough. The scrape of shoes on gravel.

She jumps to her feet so quickly her legs buckle. She grips the bench for balance, her heart skittering.

Sylvie stands near the back gate, hair pinned up, her coat buttoned high against her throat. Her expression is careful, set like clay.

Brenda opens her mouth, but nothing comes out. Sylvie takes a slow step forward.

'Sylvie... is that... is it really you?' Brenda stammers, her voice so small and weak, she hardly recognises it as her own. 'I – I didn't think you'd ever come here again.'

Sylvie stops a few feet away. 'That would never happen, Brenda. Despite everything, I owe you so much. I'm sorry I haven't got over here until now; it's been crazy with Jess being in hospital and the baby and she's only just been discharged... you can understand, I hope.'

Brenda nods, her mouth twitching, her eyes filling. When she's able to speak, she says, 'I didn't mean to hurt anyone. You have to believe me. I just wanted to help. I thought... I thought if I could make things right, you'd see I was on your side. You, Jess, the baby... I just wanted to look after you all. Make sure you were safe.'

'And you did. Jess and Scarlet Mae are safe because of you, and you'll never know how grateful I am for that.'

Brenda feels like her bones are softening. The relief is palpable. 'I had to do whatever I could to look after you both.'

'But we're not your responsibility, Brenda.' Sylvie sits on the bench beside her and lays a hand on Brenda's arm. 'I know about the young boy who died on your ward before you left the hospital, the old man at the other hospital you worked...'

Brenda opens her mouth to speak but can't. How does Sylvie know all this?

'You seemed to know so much about us all from the moment you moved in. You've got to understand people can find it inappropriate, Brenda. Even though you mean well.'

'I did know about you all in a way. Arthur told me, you see. We'd have long talks and—'

'Arthur?'

'Arthur Smallbone. He lived at number forty-one.'

Sylvie gasps. 'Matt's *grandfather*?'

Brenda looks down at her hands. 'I loved Arthur in my own way, you know. Not in that way, but as a friend, a companion. It felt like the first time someone understood me.'

'He was... Arthur was your patient?'

Brenda nods. 'He was lonely, like me, and we'd often chat over a cuppa on my night shifts. He told me all about this street and the people who lived here. He was very fond of you, Sylvie, and "Little Jess" as he called her. He said you were so kind and helpful and Jess would run errands for him.'

'Arthur... he died,' Sylvie says gently.

'Yes, and I felt so, so sad. He told me he was going to cause ructions by leaving his house to his grandson, Matt. He said he hoped it would help him settle down and grow up a bit.'

The look on Sylvie's face isn't what Brenda wanted to see. She looks rattled, as if Brenda is someone to be feared, not pitied.

'I confess after I lost my job and retired, I started thinking a lot about Arthur again. I was at a loose end, so I tried to find out a bit about the street and the people he'd told me about and... well, I found the newspaper article about you and Matt and your unusual living arrangements.'

'And then Penny's house came up for rent?'

'Exactly.' Brenda gives a little smile. 'I thought... I thought this could be a place I might fit in and find some peace of my own.'

Sylvie looks down, her breath fogging in the cold air. For a moment, she seems to vanish into her own thoughts. Then she raises her eyes, soft but steady.

'Penny called me this morning,' Sylvie continues. 'She said

she's spoken to you about what's happened and she asked what I thought about you staying on here.'

Brenda trembles. 'Please, Sylvie. Please don't let her send me away. I won't interfere again; I'll stay away from you and your family, I swear. I won't... I don't even know how to say sorry properly. But I am so, so sorry. More than you'll ever know.'

Sylvie looks at Brenda as if she's weighing up every conversation, every cup of tea, every moment on doorsteps and in gardens and Brenda's care when they needed her most.

Then a shadow passes over her face and Brenda knows she's considering the bad things she did. The way she ignored social cues and completely overstepped the mark on several occasions. How she had the advantage of knowing Arthur Smallbone and had never mentioned it.

'You went too far but thank goodness you did, Brenda. Your concern comes from a good place, but you have to promise me from now on you'll try to build a life for yourself. You don't have to look after everyone else anymore, just yourself.'

Brenda flinches, the tears rolling freely down her soft, pale cheeks now.

Sylvie pauses, her breath catching. 'I've told Penny I don't want you turned out onto the street. I don't want that for you, Brenda. Not even after everything you've been through and everything you've done for us.'

The words sink in like a slow dawn light after a long, cold darkness, spreading warmth through Brenda's frozen limbs.

'You – you really mean that?' she whispers.

Sylvie gives the smallest nod. 'It will take a while to let things settle and I'll be grateful for your help, of course. But it can't reach the proportions of what happened before.'

Brenda chokes on a sob, covering her mouth. Ivor presses his paw against the kitchen window as if he senses her relief.

'Thank you,' Brenda gasps. 'Oh, thank you, Sylvie. I – I'll

make it right with you, and with Jess. I promise. I'll help in any way I can but subtly. So you won't even know I'm here.'

Sylvie's eyes flick briefly toward the overcast sky, then back to Brenda. She doesn't smile, but something loosens around her mouth.

'Go inside before you catch your death,' she says, her voice cracking a little.

Brenda nods, her breath coming in shallow bursts. The two women stand and suddenly Sylvie embraces her. Brenda closes her eyes and melts into the warmth and affection she feels for her friend. Then she turns toward the back door but stops, glancing back once more.

Sylvie stands where she is, hands deep in her pockets, her face pale against the grey sky. Brenda steps inside, her body shivering uncontrollably now – but something else stirs beneath it. Something new and welcome. A flicker of warmth, small and delicate, like a lit match.

She presses her back against the kitchen door, slides down until she's sitting on the tiles. Ivor circles around her feet, head-butting her knee with affection.

She presses her palm to his fur, her eyes closing.

She's not so lost after all. In some tiny corner of this cold, messed-up world, there's still a place for her, people she cares about and who care about her, too.

And although it scares her, maybe – just maybe – she could go and see someone to talk it all through. Someone who might be able to help her.

She thinks Sylvie might like that.

SIXTY-ONE

SYLVIE

TUESDAY

The next day, I sit on a low stone wall outside the café, my fingers curled around a takeaway cup that's long since gone cold.

Christmas lights loop from the lampposts. Glowing garlands with little golden stars twinkling in the afternoon gloom. Children in knitted hats and padded coats run past, shrieking, their laughter trailing in a wake behind them. The air smells of roasted chestnuts and the sharp bite of frost that's been in the air for a good few days now.

My breath hangs in front of me in slow-moving clouds. I pull my scarf tighter around my neck, even though I know it's not going to help the chill sinking beneath my skin today.

Some days, I feel hopeful. I imagine a new rhythm arriving to life. Days with the baby, walks in the park with Jess, quiet evenings at home with books I always wanted to read but could never find the time. Other days when I'm outside, I feel like my bones are hollow. As if one harsh wind just might blow me clean away like a feather.

Today is somewhere in between.

I can't stop thinking about Ed. How we all thought he was so mild and daft he might drop the baby if you handed her too quickly. The man who'd offer to do a late-night bottle feed, who laughed too loudly at jokes and seemed shy about everything. When, in reality, he was a seething mess of fury, twisted up with grudges and betrayals. And my daughter... how she had a secret she felt she couldn't share with me. How she let me think Ed was Scarlet Mae's father, kept Kendra's secrets even though she suspected about her and Matt's affair.

It's funny what actually gets to you when you find yourself in a life-changing situation like this. If I'd had to guess, I would have said I'd be preoccupied with Matt and Kendra's affair that he carried on behind my back. But that's not the case. I can't stop thinking about Ed. How for so long he seethed with hatred of us all, particularly Jess. I think about how he met Ellie and how her own hatred for her parents stoked up another level in his company and the two of them feeding on each other's sick fantasies.

While the rest of us naively plodded through each day, believing everything Ed told us, they mirrored each other perfectly and started to build something monstrous out of their shared bitterness. It sickens me, fascinates me, terrifies me.

I glance up as a slight figure crosses the street. It's Jess, pushing Scarlet Mae in her pram, her head down against the cold. My heart flares with warmth, that mother's instinctive pulse of love so strong, it makes my throat tighten. I stand quickly and wave.

Jess lifts her head, gives a weary half-smile. As she gets closer, I see how her clothes hang off her like they belong to someone else. The dark circles that look like bruises under her eyes, and the lank hair hanging around her face.

'Hi, Mum,' she says, her voice thin.

I kiss her cheek, touch the baby's soft blanket, though she's fast asleep.

'Shall we walk a bit before our coffee?' I ask.

She nods and we start to wander down the pedestrianised street where a few Christmassy pop-up stalls have been erected. Festive music hums from hidden speakers, the scent of cinnamon and mulled wine drifting around us.

'I wanted to ask you something,' I say gently. Her head snaps towards me, wary. I've pussy-footed around her since her abduction. Since the shock of it all. I've tried to give her some space but... it just feels right today. To ask.

'OK...' she murmurs warily.

'It's about Nige.'

She freezes. One gloved hand tightens on the pram handle.

'I... don't know if I'm ready to talk about it yet, Mum.'

'I'd like to know, Jess. The truth of what happened. And you deserve to say it out loud without fear of reprisal now.'

She looks away, her shoulders hunching as if she's trying to disappear. Finally, she takes a ragged breath.

'I've lost count of how many hours I've spent beating myself up about what I did,' she says, her voice thin as paper.

I stay quiet.

'It was stupid. So, so stupid,' she goes on, keeping her eyes looking straight ahead. 'You know Ed and I had split up for what I thought was the last time. I was walking home from town one night, crying, and Nige pulled up on his motorbike. He was really nice, concerned. He asked if I was OK. He had this spare helmet and he just... he told me to hop on the back. It felt daring, silly, like something a different person would do. I wanted to feel different.'

Her words spill out in fits and starts. I see her throat moving as she swallows, see the pain in her eyes. I don't push, just wait for her to continue.

'He took me for a spin. We ended up at some bar for a

couple of drinks. I should have gone home then. But I didn't. We went back to his flat for more drinks and... I didn't stay the night, though. I woke up late, realised what I'd done, called a cab.'

Jess presses a hand to her forehead.

'Then Ed came back a few days later, saying he couldn't live without me. We got back together. Three weeks after that, I found out I was pregnant. I knew there was a chance it wasn't Ed's, but I pushed it out of my head. I told myself the odds were small. Really small. After all...' She lets out a small, broken laugh. 'During that time, Ed and I had... well, we'd made up for lost time.'

We stop walking and I lean against a railing.

'Does Nige know?' I ask, my voice tight. 'About Scarlet Mae?'

She nods. 'He does now. When everything came out I got in touch because I thought it was the right thing to do, and... he ran faster than ever. The last thing he said to me was that he's not ready to be a dad. Not now, not ever.'

My mouth goes dry.

'When Ed found out, told me he'd done the DNA test, I sobbed. I thought it was all over, begged him to forgive me. But he didn't shout. He just... went quiet. Pulled away. That was worse than ranting on in a way. But then he told me he wanted to work through it, that he loved me, that it had devastated him but he loved Scarlet Mae and he didn't want to ruin us. Ruin our little family.'

'And you believed him?' I ask.

She gives a small nod, tears brimming.

'I did. We talked for weeks. I swore it was just that one night, that I regretted it more than anything. I thought we could fix it... what an idiot.'

She wipes her cheek with her sleeve.

'I even confided in Kendra. Told her Nige was Scarlet

Mae's father. I didn't tell you because... because I knew how angry you'd be with me. With Nige. You wouldn't be able to keep it quiet. Then Matt would get involved, and it would all blow up and there'd be no way of controlling it.'

I flinch. The sting of being left out cuts deeper than I expected and Jess reads it in my face, looks down at her hands.

'When I went to the house, Maz said you'd gone round there before and had a big row with Kendra. It was some time after that she went missing, but you claimed you couldn't think why she hadn't been in touch for a while,' I say. 'Why wouldn't you mention the fall-out you'd had?'

'I was stupid, Mum. So stupid. I suspected she was seeing Matt and... I went round there to have it out with her. I didn't – *couldn't* – think straight. Couldn't keep my mouth shut, but couldn't destroy you by keeping you in the loop.'

She breaks down and covers her face with both hands. Her body hunches forward. People saunter past us, giving wide-eyed glances before moving quickly on.

I step forward, wrap my arms around my daughter. I feel the bones in her shoulders sharp against my palms.

'It was a massive burden to bear on your own,' I tell her. 'You shouldn't beat yourself up.'

'But don't you see... it was all my fault. What happened to Kendra.' She cries against my coat, her breath ragged and hot. 'One night a few weeks before, she got drunk. Started acting the fool like she was. Ed was grumpy. Told her to grow up and she turned on him. Made some comment about the baby not being his. Ed erupted. He shouted that I'd sworn not to tell anyone, that I'd humiliated him. It turned into World War Three and now... now Kendra is dead.'

Jess pulls away slightly, her eyes wild.

'I never thought he'd hurt her. Never. He played the perfect partner after that. Apologised, told me he loved me, said he didn't want anything to ruin us. And I believed him. But all the while, he was plotting with Ellie. Plotting to destroy me next. And he hated Matt too. He'd never forgotten Matt humiliated him at that barbecue you had, and he'd totally convinced himself that Matt brought Nige back into our lives to ruin everything.'

Her shoulders shudder.

'A nightmare,' she whispers, shaking her head. 'All of it. An utter nightmare.'

I stroke her hair, my own chest tightening.

'But you're here now,' I say softly. 'You're here, I'm here and Scarlet Mae is here. And that's all that matters now. Today. Right now.'

Jess lifts her head slowly. Her face is blotched and raw. But her eyes – there's something fighting there, something that's still alive.

We turn and begin to walk again, slowly. The Christmas lights above us glow brighter as the sky deepens to a dusky blue. Music drifts from a nearby shop: a cheerful song about sleigh bells and snow.

I glance at her, at the baby snoozing beneath her blanket, tiny fists curled by her face. My heart swells and aches in the same beat.

I think of Matt. His promises, his warmth, that easy laugh of his that always made me feel everything was going to turn out OK. Until it didn't. The betrayals slid in unnoticed. Those secrets I missed that still gnaw at me in the middle of the night.

He's repeatedly begged for my forgiveness. But I can never forgive him. Not truly. Not for the deception. Not for gambling away our future, or for the shadows he pulled into our home.

But looking at Jess and my granddaughter now, I feel stronger than I've ever felt.

I will not fall apart. I will not let this define me.

My life will be built on this love. This daughter. This grand-daughter.

We stop again at a small Christmas stall. Jess wipes her eyes and smiles at a row of gingerbread biscuits shaped like snowmen.

'Mum,' she says, voice hoarse but sure. 'Thank you. For everything.'

I squeeze her arm gently.

'Always,' I say. 'When are you two girls coming home? Just for a while until you get your strength back.'

Jess smiles. 'I'd love that, Mum.'

'And I think Brenda might pop round later if you want to come back with me. She's promised not to come on too strong like before, labelling cartons, labelling us.'

We look at each other and burst out laughing.

'I'd love to see Brenda,' she says. 'I'm going to ask her to be Scarlet Mae's godmother.'

'That's nice, love. She'll be over the moon.'

As we walk on, I let the cold air sting my face. My bruised heart feels weak and vulnerable, but its beat is steady. Reliable.

And in that moment, with Jess at my side and Scarlet Mae in her pram, I know we'll all be fine.

Life won't be perfect for a while. Maybe not ever. And what happened – it won't be easy or quick to get over. But we will be fine. We're strong enough to get through.

Stronger than I ever knew.

A LETTER FROM K.L. SLATER

Dear reader,

Thank you so much for reading *My Husband Next Door*. I really hope you enjoyed the book. If you did and would like to keep up to date with all my latest releases, just sign up at the following link. Your email address will never be shared and you can unsubscribe at any time.

www.bookouture.com/kl-slater

Readers often ask how I get my story ideas. As with the inspiring article I talked about at the end of my novel *The Marriage*, a powerful source for my new ideas continues to be the media. I read most of my daily news online, some of which is curated for my preferences. So I'm always getting notifications for lifestyle stories or quirky articles.

The idea for this book was two-pronged. Firstly, a few years ago, I read about a certain celebrity couple who were married but lived in separate houses on the same street in London. The idea stuck in my head and kept coming back; it was what I call a 'keeper'. Then my attention was drawn to another article that gave the domestic situation a name – LAT: Living Apart Together.

When my editor suggested it might be an interesting angle, the idea was born.

I've often talked about how each book begins with a seed of

an idea and for *My Husband Next Door*, I began to think about how living apart together might work in practice. Then, of course, I asked the author's magic question: 'What if...' and the story started to take shape.

This book is set in Nottinghamshire, the place I was born and have lived all my life. Local readers should be aware I sometimes take the liberty of changing street names or geographical details to suit the story.

I do hope you enjoyed reading *My Husband Next Door* and getting to know the characters. If so, I would be very grateful if you could take a few minutes to write a review. I'd love to hear what you think, and it makes such a difference helping new readers to discover one of my books for the first time.

I love hearing from my readers – you can get in touch with me on social media or through my website.

Thanks a million to all my wonderful readers... until next time,

Kim x

https://klslaterauthor.com

facebook.com/KimLSlaterAuthor

instagram.com/klslaterauthor

x.com/KLSlaterAuthor

ACKNOWLEDGEMENTS

Huge thanks to my incredible editor at Bookouture, Lydia Vassar-Smith, for her expert insight and editorial support.

Thanks to ALL the Bookouture team for everything they do – which is so much more than I can document here.

Thanks, as always, to my amazing literary agent, Camilla Bolton, who is always there with expert advice and unwavering support at the end of a text, an email, a phone call. Thanks also to the rest of the hardworking team at Darley Anderson Literary, TV and Film Agency.

Thanks as always to my writing buddy, Angela Marsons, who is a brilliant support and inspiration to me in my writing career.

Many thanks to Bookouture's editorial manager, Hannah Snetsinger, and to copy editor Donna Hillyer and proofreader Becca Allen for their expert skills and eagle eyes in making *My Husband Next Door* the best book it can be.

Massive thanks as always go to my family, especially to my husband and daughter, who are always so understanding and willing to put outings on hold and to rearrange to suit writing deadlines.

Special thanks to Henry Steadman, who has worked so hard to pull another amazing cover out of the bag.

Thank you to the bloggers and reviewers who do so much to support authors and thank you to everyone who has taken the time to post a positive review online or has taken part in my blog tour. It is always noticed and much appreciated.

Last but not least, thank you SO much to my wonderful readers. I love receiving all your wonderful comments and messages and I am truly grateful for each and every one of you.

PUBLISHING TEAM

Turning a manuscript into a book requires the efforts of many people. The publishing team at Bookouture would like to acknowledge everyone who contributed to this publication.

Commercial
Lauren Morrissette
Hannah Richmond
Imogen Allport

Contracts
Peta Nightingale

Cover design
Henry Steadman

Data and analysis
Mark Alder
Mohamed Bussuri

Editorial
Lydia Vassar-Smith
Imogen Allport

Copyeditor
Donna Hillyer

RAISING READERS
Books Build Bright Futures

Dear Reader,

We'd love your attention for one more page to tell you about the crisis in children's reading, and what we can all do.

Studies have shown that reading for fun is the **single biggest predictor of a child's future life chances** – more than family circumstance, parents' educational background or income. It improves academic results, mental health, wealth, communication skills, ambition and happiness.

The number of children reading for fun is in rapid decline. Young people have a lot of competition for their time, and a worryingly high number do not have a single book at home.

Hachette works extensively with schools, libraries and literacy charities, but here are some ways we can all raise more readers:

- Reading to children for just 10 minutes a day makes a difference
- Don't give up if children aren't regular readers – there will be books for them!

- Visit bookshops and libraries to get recommendations
- Encourage them to listen to audiobooks
- Support school libraries
- Give books as gifts

There's a lot more information about how to encourage children to read on our websites: **www.RaisingReaders.co.uk** and **www.JoinRaisingReaders.com**.

Thank you for reading.

Made in the USA
Las Vegas, NV
15 November 2025